Praise for *Wilderness Run*

"Maria Hummel's poetically rendered debut novel contain- ^e stuff of great fiction . . . vivid . . . intriguino "
—Lisa Robinson Bailey, *The In´*

"*Wilderness Run* has many pluses and some lovely writing . . . dram.
—Melissa MacKenzie, *Rutland H*

"A gripping debut, shot through with poetry and violence, *Wilderness Run* traces the demons that divide us, whether as a nation or in our hearts. At turns radiant and shocking, understated and unbearable, *Wilderness Run* proceeds with the force of a coming locomotive."
—Nick Flynn, author of *Some Ether*

"A gifted poet has immersed herself in the history of her home territory to write a mesmerizing first novel. Maria Hummel's *Wilderness Run* is the work of a prodigious new talent."
—David Huddle, author of *The Story of a Million Years*

"Hummel's debut . . . is gracefully and evocatively written. . . . Hummel creates solid characters while capturing the day-to-day reality of military life during the Civil War . . . well-paced, elegant prose . . . poignant."
—*Publishers Weekly*

"Imagine Cormac McCarthy meeting Alice Hoffman and you have Maria Hummel's graphic, blood-and-bone battle scenes woven through the softer focus narrative musings of her characters, sons and daughters growing up quickly under separation and fire. . . . Riveting and poignant, impossible to put down, painful and sweet, difficult to ignore. Ambitious in metaphor, *Wilderness Run* is anytime, the War is every war, the loss is always personal. Maria Hummel's debut novel is worthy and unforgettable."
—John Valentine, The Regulator Bookshop, Durham, North Carolina

Wilderness Run

Wilderness Run

A Novel

Maria Hummel

St. Martin's Griffin
New York

For the dear ones

www.stmartins.com

Library of Congress Cataloging-in-Publication Data

Hummel, Maria.
    Wilderness run : a novel / Maria Hummel.—1st ed.
      p. cm.
    ISBN 0-312-28757-7 (hc)
    ISBN 0-312-32047-7 (pbk)
      1. United States—History—Civil War, 1861–1865—Fiction. 2. Vermont—History—Civil War, 1861–1865—Fiction. 3. Triangles (Interpersonal relations)—Fiction. 4. Tutors and tutoring—Fiction. 5. Fugitive slaves—Fiction. 6. Soldiers—Fiction. 7. Cousins—Fiction. 8. Nurses—Fiction.
    I. Title

PS3608.U567 W55 2002
813'.6—dc21   2002068356

First St. Martin's Griffin Edition: November 2003

10 9 8 7 6 5 4 3 2 1

Acknowledgments

Many thanks go to the following people for inspiration, guidance, or other invaluable assistance: Louisa May Alcott, Wilbur Fisk, Jenn Habel, John Hartford, Chad Holley, David Huddle, Walt Whitman, and my wonderful mother, father, brothers, and aunts.

My utmost gratitude belongs to Esmond Harmsworth, Fred Chappell, George Witte, and finally to Kyle, my dear heart.

My soul is among lions, and I lie even among them that are set on fire, even the sons of men, whose teeth are spears and arrows, and their tongue a sharp sword.

—PSALM 57:4

June 1847

Isabel's father claimed she was born on the day the train came to Allenton, a city that had never known the smell of a coal engine, or the squeal of wheels across metal tracks, or the weight of tracks against dusty pasture grass. When the train appeared on the horizon, Allenton pressed inward, like all invaded places. But it was too late. The black arrow broke one field from another, parting neighbors and enemies in a blinding instant of noise and velocity. Isabel slid out, purple, choking, on a snow of sheets. The doctor beat breath into her body. Smoke rose, a banner trailing back to the hills.

Later, Daniel Lindsey would tell Isabel that her first wail sounded like the whistle of the locomotive as it arrived—a high song, heraldic and longing. This was not a lie, but the kind of exaggeration a father makes to explain significance to his daughter. He did not say that her mother's labor was difficult, and that the house grew cold around him with the soreness of Faustina's screams. He tried not to listen to them, straining instead for the rhythmic commotion of the first train, which bore the Lindsey name, to arrive down in the lumberyards.

He stayed until the doctor emerged, wiping his hands, to say that Daniel had a baby daughter, and invited him to see. He kissed the wet petal of Isabel's body lying on Faustina's breast, and held his wife, who wore the white, relieved expression of someone whom pain has just abandoned. And only when Faustina's eyelids fluttered toward sleep after her first nursing did Daniel creep from his house to get a look at the train he helped to bring, and to feel what it was, for once, to be a destination.

The small, taut Irishmen who laid the rails were drinking from flasks that had worn white crescents in their hip pockets.

"Just look at it, Mr. Lindsey. The Allenton has arrived!" a man called, shifting his weight from one leg to another.

Isabel's father nodded and appraised the dark skin of the engine. He was entranced by its intricate pieces, the red cowcatcher and silver whistle, and the brass star that joined the two rear wheels of the engine with an *L* inscribed in its center.

"You going to drive it now?"

Daniel shook his head, touching the star with his good right hand. The left, crushed by a childhood accident, hid in the folds of his coat.

"You going to take it straight on to Montreal? Or back to Boston? We'll put down the track for you, won't we, fellas?"

"I'm not planning on it until it's full of lumber," another voice said from the opposite side of the engine. Daniel stepped back and peered around the massive metal flank.

The owner of the voice was his elder brother, George, who wore a well-cut wool suit but was oddly hatless, his gray hair guarding his head like a helmet. Immersed in his examination of the engine, George Lindsey did not notice Daniel immediately.

"Full of lumber," he repeated to himself, as if pleased by the impending commerce. In contrast to Daniel's scholarly, elegant pallor and narrow limbs, George's body was as robust as a marker oak on the edge of pasture, and he moved with a vital confidence, stepping back smartly from the train and finally catching sight of his brother.

"Daniel," he cried out. "Boy or girl?"

"Girl," said Daniel. "Isabel Prinz."

"A girl," George proclaimed for the crowd. He was the one who had convinced Daniel that they should bring the railroad to their little Vermont city; he had thrown himself into the project with such enthusiasm that he knew the names of all the workers and their wives and children, many of whom were still in Ireland. "A Lindsey girl."

The flasks were lifted again, and a few cheers shouted, which Daniel hardly heard. A warm spring gust stole the last smoke curling from the smokestack.

"And Faustina?" George's voice tightened like a rope.

"Tired, but fine." In Daniel's mind flashed the blood-spattered sheets in Mary's arms as she descended the stairs, her face pinched in silent prayer. The Irish servant girl began washing them immediately. He could still hear the splashed well water soaking the sheets, poured from a pitcher on the sink to cleanse the doctor's red-crusted knuckles.

Before leaving, Dr. Cochran had advised Isabel's father that they should have no more children. Because of her fragile health, Faustina had already miscarried three babies, and the very fact that Isabel was born was a miracle they should not attempt to repeat, the doctor said. George, on the other hand, already had twin daughters and a young son, Laurence, who rode around town next to his father in princely fur robes, and who bore a miniature whip he cracked at the air in time with the coachman.

"Glad to hear it. Shall I send Pattie by to visit tonight?" George inquired. A white gull settled on one of the metal rails girding the boiler and began to preen.

"Not tonight. Faustina needs some rest."

The women were not friends. Pattie was the busy socialite, the rigorous churchgoer. Faustina preferred to stay home and dip her head over a book Daniel had brought her from Boston, with her feet nestled catlike beneath her.

George disappeared around the other side of the engine again, and Daniel stared with a certain propriety at the train. Although he had always been a water man, understanding the intricacies of reservoir and canal building better than anyone else in the city, Daniel rocked back on his heels in awe before the black musculature of the engine.

Allenton was no longer an island, but a peninsula, the crested hills around it finally blasted to make valleys. He crouched down to examine the wheels and saw George doing the same, his likeness, his opposite, brother and enemy. Their eyes met for the first time that day, each peering uncertainly into the shade, testing the other's gaze. George mouthed something and then looked away, and to the end of his life, Daniel did not know if it was *lower* or *love her* that his brother said, or why he answered *yes*.

December 1859

Chapter One

Isabel set one timid boot down on the creek, a white pastry of ice and fallen leaves, where her cousin Laurence was already running and halting to slide. Her thick honey-colored braid had loosened and a few wisps spoked about her face like the bristles of a much-used broom. She was at that age where girls are big-headed, her body a stickish protrusion of legs and arms.

"Hurry, Bel," Laurence said as he coasted away from her. He never called her Isabel. No one did but her father and mother, and consequently she associated the name with a dutiful and somewhat dull version of her twelve-year-old self, who would have stayed at home and practiced her stitches instead of sneaking outside with her cousin.

"Is it safe?" she asked.

" 'Is it safe?' " He mocked her in falsetto and nearly lost his balance. "You sound like Mary."

Mary worked for Isabel's parents and was always secreting Bel off to say the rosary, her cold black beads burnished by frequent use. Although she insisted she was still "in the neighborhood of twenty," Mary had the nervous disposition of an elderly spinster and her red hair already showed a few strands of gray.

Bel let the other boot down quickly and began walking stiff-kneed toward her cousin. Beneath her, the ice felt like a ballroom floor just cleared of dancers, hushed after a long waltz. The steep banks of the creek bed lifted the winter wind to the world above, and a cove of warmth rose between her coat and skin.

"Try sliding," Laurence instructed her, and demonstrated the quick sprint and splay of his feet as he let the ice take him. Bel followed his motion. The surface smoothed her steps away as she ran and then balanced herself to glide. On the second attempt, her boots hit a stick jutting from the white glass. She tripped and landed with an abrupt swoop, her ankle twisting.

"Try again," Laurence shouted. "You'll get it." He was far away now, skimming down the creek toward the nearby lake. The black coat, tailored to join at his hips, made her narrow cousin look even longer than he was, like a grasshopper dressed for a dinner party.

"We aren't supposed to—" Bel started, but she let the wind carry her voice away and eased herself back upright. Laurence was seldom home, and he was so much more fun than any of the playmates her mother tried to arrange for her. He and Bel had spent six blissful years together as children before her uncle George shipped his son off to school in Boston. Although they wrote frequent letters to each other, it was her seventeen-year-old cousin's holiday returns to Allenton that she looked forward to, for they meant all sorts of adventures and journeys, even in the dead of winter.

Laurence was always in search of a new secret place, a "wilderness," he called it, where the foundations of an abandoned house lay ruined in the weeds, or a belt of woods raised up birds, chittering, unseen. Every new discovery was given a name with *wilderness* in it: Lost Wilderness House, Wilderness Woods, Isle of the Wilderness (this last always unreachable, a knot of land in the middle of the bay where geese landed on their way south). Bel's favorite place in winter was the creek. Locally known as Potash Brook, their steep-banked Wilderness Run protected them from the harsh wind, and led to the open lake, an icy expanse that bordered Allenton to the west and smelled in December of clean, pure things, and vast distances.

Upon reaching his seventeenth year, Laurence had stretched himself tall and angular, more like her father than her uncle, although he had George Lindsey's determined brown eyes. His blond hair had darkened and his voice deepened, occasionally squealing like a new piece of furniture. From far off, she could still hear him clearly calling to her.

"Come on, Bel. I have something to show you."

Bel mustered up a limping dash and slid carefully toward her cousin. Even beneath the thick wall of ice, the water flowed, just a trickle maybe, but still she feared falling into that dark current. Once she had seen the shadow shapes of fish flitting deep below a clear patch on the lake. They looked like slivers of the moon, and the sight of them had made her feel impossibly cold.

When she glanced up from her mincing steps across the ice, Laurence was standing at the entrance to the lake, waiting for her. The white plain sharpened his figure to a silhouette. As she approached, he opened his arms with a gesture of ownership.

"Wilderness Lake. It's like the map of a new continent," he whispered. "See all the borders?" He pointed to the fissures and ridges running along the lake's surface.

"Is it frozen all the way across?" Bel asked.

"I don't know. You want to see?" Laurence jogged in place as a shrill wind bore down on them.

Bel answered her cousin by glancing back in the direction of Greenwood, the house her father built for her mother when she was born. Steep banks blocked her view of their part of the hill, the elm avenues lined with iron gates and brick houses. Greenwood would stand among them on the horizon of the city, watching over it in case invasion came. But nothing ever invaded Allenton but the seasons, and Bel was suddenly aware of how unnecessary the grandeur of her neighborhood was, when other people lived in plain clapboard homes.

"You didn't ask me what I wanted to show you," Laurence chided. "Look to your left."

On the bank beside her, the frozen architecture of a midwinter storm rose over red rocks, glistening like the domain of an absent ice queen, with giant thrones, glassy towers, and ramparts for her henchmen to defend her. Bel regarded the crested curls of wave and stone. There were easy footholds all the way up.

"How could you miss that?" Laurence shattered her awe. "How could you walk out here and not see that right away?"

"I was looking at you," Bel stammered. Her cousin's mercurial moods often confused her, much as she was used to them.

"You were looking back at Allenton. You missed the whole world for that stupid little city. You're going to end up like Lucia and Anne." Laurence kicked a leaf free from the ice as he pronounced his sisters' names. The twins, both in the perilous age between girlhood and wifehood, were excruciating in their daily routines of dances and dresses and calls from local young men.

Insulted, Bel turned away from her cousin to clamber up the stiff formation of ice. Finding herself a clear throne, she carefully plucked a downy feather from its seat and let the wind take it toward the lake before she sat down. The hard ice pinched her hips, and she squirmed to get comfortable.

"I'm sorry, Bel. It's just that you haven't really seen Boston, or these other places where—"

"I've been to Boston." Her breath clouded the frozen room around her.

"For two days! And with your father. But to watch the immigrants from Ireland and Italy hired at the docks in New York—"

"I've seen Irishmen, too."

With a snort of disgust, Laurence commenced climbing a tower of ice higher than her own. From her seat, Bel could hear his breath go ragged with the exertion. His cheeks were stained a deep raspberry.

"Are you tired?" she asked softly.

"No, of course I'm not tired. Just think about it, Bel. Think about all those grand cities in Europe that we've never been to, and ask if you're satisfied with stodgy little Allenton."

"If Europe is so wonderful, why are they all coming here?" She refused to meet his gaze.

"Oh, Bel. That's a thoughtless question. Because not everyone gets to live in a castle like us. You haven't grown up as much as I thought."

This was enough to goad Bel to utter silence, and she stared fiercely over the lake. It was Sunday afternoon, and on the nearby bay, the wooden fishing shanties of the lumberyard workers glowed like shells on a strip of sand. She could see men moving among them, arms crossed, chins tucked against the cold. Beyond them, the lake lay in a skirt of silver and blue, hemmed by the purple shadow of the Adirondacks looming on the opposite shore.

Laurence began to whistle and leaned out on a frozen prow, holding it with his arms. The sun sank a fraction below the mountains. Bel shivered discreetly. She would not be the first to mention going back.

"Be you the friend of a friend?" said a hoarse voice, and she looked down.

A dark-skinned man was standing on the ice, shivering. On top of his head perched a hat made from a burlap sack stuffed with newspaper, its unkempt and somewhat accidental appearance reminding Bel of a capsized bird's nest. Newspaper also patched large gaps in the man's homespun shirt and breeches: A headline announcing the funeral of John Brown crossed his chest; another, proclaiming the rise in tobacco prices, covered a hole above his knee.

The man took a step closer, his rag-bound feet whispering. Bel started and almost lost her balance. "Laurence," she said softly, watching the apparition.

"Be you the friend of a friend?" he repeated in exactly the same pitch and rhythm, as if they were the only words he knew. His teeth shone the sharp milky yellow of the ivory tusk Bel's father kept in his study. She shrank back.

"Yes, I am the friend of a friend." Laurence's voice rang out importantly as he slid down the ice. The man noticed him and bunched up to run. "Friend of a friend," Laurence repeated in a more soothing tone.

"Laurence!" She saw that her cousin wore the same frowning grin as on the day he had made Bel steal a horse with him and go riding to the edge of Allenton.

"Hush, Bel, I know what I'm doing."

As the boy clattered awkwardly to the lakeshore, Bel regarded the stranger from her safe height. Aside from the extraordinary outfit, his most prominent feature was a white scar curving like a fishhook below his left eye. The round cheek it marked made her remember a sketch of Hottentots in one of her mother's issues of *Frank Leslie's Fashion Gazette,* a thin volume that came every month with stories of Africa and Arabia, fairies and magicians, and the intricacies of fashion in Paris and New York. While the Hottentots had a certain comfortable roundness to them, this man was wiry and short, with a chest that bulged beneath his shirt like a laborer's. His eyes were the ugly gray of wet mud.

Everyone knew that some people in Allenton secretly helped the runaways get to Canada, where slavery was illegal, and Bel had heard her own mother proposing it to her father in hushed tones one evening when they thought she was already asleep. But the Lindsey brothers were public supporters of Stephen Douglas, the Vermont-born senator from Illinois, who was in favor of letting each state choose on the issue of slavery. They would never approve of Laurence trying to rescue a runaway.

"Canada." Laurence pointed up the lake, then took off his coat, offering it to the man.

The man snatched it with one quick hand. "Friend of a friend," he repeated, and patted his stomach with the other.

"He's hungry," Laurence said, his eyes shadowed with a strange triumph. "We'll have to take him home."

"What, just march him up the street?" Bel demanded, suddenly angry with her cousin. "He could be dangerous." She didn't like the way the man clutched the black coat hard to his hip, as if he thought Laurence might try to take it back.

"If he wanted to harm us, he could have done so already, Bel. We hardly noticed him creeping up."

"But what will your father say, or mine, for that matter?"

"They don't have to know. Unless you tell them," Laurence added with heavy emphasis.

"They don't have to know?"

"Your mother will help us."

Bel tried to envision her mother's response but could see only the color darkening across her father's high cheekbones and his blue eyes going to ice. Daniel's left hand would begin to shake, and she would feel instantly ashamed. His misshapen three fingers were only a slight disfigurement, but they made Bel love her father with a deep, pitying devotion. As a young girl, she had often asked him to tell her the story of the injury, relishing the details of the molasses barrel tipping slowly from a wagon, crushing his fingers as the sweet brown sludge spilled over his arm. He was standing in the wrong place, he always said. He didn't get out of the way in time.

This slowness to act still pervaded his decisions. Although Daniel favored abolition in theory, he didn't believe the system could change overnight, and Bel recalled his response to her mother's whispered request. He said that he could help the slaves the legal way, by voting and campaigning, but never by harboring runaways. *That is a job for other men, who have less to lose than myself*, he had said. *What good will it do for me to get arrested?*

Bel wielded the phrase on her cousin. "What good will it do if we get arrested?"

"Bel. We're young. We don't know any better." Without his coat, Laurence's shirt flapped like a sail, and his ruddy cheeks had begun to mottle with white patches. The runaway's eyes rolled toward the lumberyards. "Canada," he muttered, pulling his burlap hat lower.

Laurence shook his head. "If we don't help him, he's going to keep going and die. I think we should hide him up the creek a ways, and I can come back to get him after dark. Come on, sir." He motioned for the African to follow him and started back toward town.

Bel didn't move. Her legs ached from the coldness of the ice seat. The cry of a nearby gull sounded harsh in her ears. The man gazed up at her, and back at Laurence, then planted his feet.

"Please, Bel. He won't come if you don't," Laurence said. "You'll always regret this if you don't help him. Things aren't going to stay the way they are."

Still confused, Bel stood up from her throne. As she stepped onto the steep glassy bank, her right boot slipped and she lost her balance. The sky wagged above her, blue and gray. After a moment's hesitation, the runaway dropped Laurence's coat and reached out to lift her down the way a gentleman would help a lady from a horse. Against her ribs, his fingers felt hard as sticks stripped of their bark.

The odor of sweat and leaves and earth filled her nose, so unlike her father's clean lemon scent. Daniel had stopped lifting her in his arms years before, but now Bel remembered the delirious sensation of being swung, the power and the surrender. She squirmed in the runaway's hold. He gripped her tighter, his face so close, she thought his parted pink mouth would swallow her. Her toes met the flat ice. When she stood safely on the lake, the runaway let go, and the two of them backed away from each other warily, like boys who have decided not to fight.

"Are you all right?" Bel heard Laurence in the distance of the moment. But she was already running, her steps sliding away even as she took them, her leather boots making soft hammer taps on the ice of Wilderness Run, Potash Brook, the creek that swelled with rain from the farmers' fields and spilled it into the lake. Laurence called her name twice, three times before she turned around. Despite her exertion, she was hardly fifty feet away from them. The runaway had not moved at all. Laurence looked at her, at the man, and back at Bel again.

"He won't hurt you," her cousin said in a disappointed, accusing tone. His shoulders quivered with cold, but he rooted himself like a soldier facing an advancing army. "He didn't hurt you, did he?"

Bel shook her head. She did not lessen the distance between them, breathing in deeply to erase the smell of the runaway. It clung to the back of her throat, thick as chocolate or clay.

"I'm going to rescue him." Laurence folded his arms. "You go home if you want to. I know your mother will help me."

Bel swung around to face the brook as it wound up the hill and into Allenton. The white path stretched before her, pocked by summer stepping-stones. There was nothing alive, nothing moving in the frigid air but a tuft of dead blond grass rustled by wind. The breeze flattened her coat against the ribs the runaway had touched. A chill spiked up her spine.

"I'm going home," she announced to the emptiness before her. Laurence did not answer. She heard only the subdued trickle of water below her as she passed over the fragile roof of ice but did not fall through.

Chapter Two

By the time Bel reached her house, the sun was just a wedge of light behind the Adirondacks. Dusk made the city lonely and infinite. Snow-laden boughs dipped over hushed yards, the iron gates shaken of their whiteness into a stark and guarded black. Bel plowed two blue-shadowed furrows through the street with her boots, turning around often to see if Laurence followed her trail. He did not. Instead, a red sled coursed over the hill and past her, pulled by a lone black mare whose hooves alternately kicked up and vanished as she trotted through the drifts. The smaller of the two passengers called back over her shoulder.

"Hello, Bel Lindsey! Where are you going?" It was Mary Ruth Cross, one of the many Allenton girls Faustina tried to make Bel befriend. Mary Ruth's face shone like a misplaced moon beneath her fur hat. The way her wide nostrils aimed outward reminded Bel of a piglet, but Mary Ruth was generally accepted among the adults as the girl who would grow up to be the heartbreaker around town. Her fair hair and blue eyes were so admired that Mary Ruth had already begun to acquire a bewildered string of boys who tripped over themselves to do something sweet for her without knowing why.

"Home," Bel said.

"But where is your darling cousin?" Mary Ruth's question drifted faintly back as the sled picked up speed. Apparently, the driver had no interest in his charge's conversation.

Bel pretended she didn't hear Mary Ruth and stared instead at Laurence's house as she passed it. A French château-style with long awnings on the second story, it never looked more like a fortress than in that moment, when the crimson brick absorbed the day's last light. Only the awnings diminished this vision. Completely unsuited to Vermont's heavy snows, they sagged and dented each winter under the white weight, and each spring, Laurence's mother stubbornly tried to beat them back into shape.

In contrast to the ornate proportions of George's mansion, Daniel had designed Greenwood during his wife's pregnancy to be a stately but simple expanse of brick and wood. Greenwood had only one decoration in its two stories and gabled attic: the peculiar windows, set into the walls, each with a small arch above and a lip below for Faustina to plant boxes of flowers. These delicate decorations looked like lashes and every window a feminine eye that peered out on the elms in the front yard and the garden behind. Greenwood was always cool inside, summer and winter, and smelled faintly of the cedar doors from Lebanon that Faustina had installed in the upstairs closets to keep the moths out.

The sled swept over the crest of the hill as Bel scuffed through Greenwood's open gate. Johnny Mulcane, the tall, gruff hired man, was standing on the porch roof, sweeping the snow from it. His silhouette loomed across the lashed windows, the broom brushing wide arcs of white down onto the yard. Johnny acknowledged Bel with a tight little nod as she passed. Ever since she had evangelically tried to teach him to read a few summers before, he had grown silent and cold in her presence. She remembered pressing her small hand over his, trying to reveal the triangle of the letter *A,* the first of the alphabet, like a small pointed house, an Indian tepee—the way her tutor explained it. Before she got to *B,* Johnny Mulcane had retracted his hand and lurched off to the garden, his shoulders bowed. The half-finished *A,* spindly and large, had remained on the copybook, embarrassing Bel when her tutor checked her progress the next day. She stoically did not confess its author.

As she reached the kitchen door, the entrance that she and Laurence took out of lifelong habit, Bel looked back one last time, hoping to see her cousin. A snowy cascade swept across her sight, blurring the street beyond. She thought she glimpsed the two of them, boy and slave, creeping through the dusk, their backs bent together, heads propelled forward like dogs searching for a scent. But when the air cleared, this vision vanished, and the tip of Johnny Mulcane's worn boot appeared at the edge of the roof. She knew he must be watching her, but Bel did not look up at the beardless, balding man who always wore the same wrinkled gray trousers that bagged about his legs and smelled of something dark and foreign. She missed Laurence with the suddenness she felt after receiving one of his letters from Boston, when she realized it would be months before she saw him again.

The kitchen door opened just as she was about to twist the brass knob. Grete appeared in the threshold, ruddy, fair, and obstinate in posture, as if she were always being buffeted by a strong wind. If Mary's official domain was the linen closet, Grete's was the kitchen, and she ruled over it with wooden spoons and the heavy shields of bread dough she thumped on the counters.

"So," Grete said, deepening the vowel so that it bore both the sound of discovery and the grief that such discovery was not pleasing at all. "Where is the Laurence?"

"He's coming," Bel said quickly, wishing she had prepared some excuse. "One of his old friends wanted to have a snowball fight, and I was cold, so I came home." She peeked guiltily up at Johnny Mulcane's boot, as if he might somehow contradict her testimony, but the cracked black sole was gone and she heard the scraping sound of his broom resuming its arcs. Johnny was collectively shunned by Mary and Grete, who had determined long ago that he had some Indian blood, which made him unworthy of their Irish and German attention. *Not to mention the fact,* Mary hissed to Grete one day when she thought Bel wasn't listening, *that he ain't God-fearing like the rest of us. I tried to get him to go to church with me, and the man said no, outright no, like I had insulted him.*

Grete widened the door slightly to allow Isabel passage into the interior. A wave of warm rich air swept out, making Bel suddenly ravenous. Grete's mother was from Germany, and she had been brought to the United States by Faustina's own father, who had cultivated a taste for all things German, particularly his table. Isabel grew up with the pungent beef of sauerbraten, the pounded crispness of schnitzel, and clouds of cream cakes on Sundays, when her mother enforced *Kaffee* in the late afternoon. Grete was an excellent, if disgruntled, cook, whose burly shoulders and pinned blond hair were far more formidable than the lines of soldiers a local general commissioned every year to practice on the town green.

Grease crackled in the skittle on the claw-legged stove. Bel entered the dry heat of the room and paused, her cold cheeks stinging.

"You are too late for cakes," Grete announced dramatically. The cook used the word *cakes* indiscriminately for all sweets. She jostled past Bel and began to crack eggs into a bowl. Bel watched the yolks slide from their shells, top-heavy and bright. She did not want to leave the kitchen until Laurence came back. She wanted to tell him, wanted to say she was sorry, or wrong, or both. When was the last time she had opposed her cousin? She couldn't recall refusing him anything, especially now, when they saw each other so seldom.

Grete began whisking the eggs, muttering about the people who always invaded her kitchen at exactly the wrong time, people who had no respect for those who worked, day in and day out, to keep others comfortable.

"People," she concluded with a grunt, as if the very word were enough to disgust her. Her white apron shook as she swept past Bel, holding the whisked yolks, and began to pound pieces of pork flat with one of Johnny Mulcane's mallets.

"May I have some hot chocolate?" Bel asked, hoping to stall until Laurence arrived.

"If you fetch the milk." Grete brought the hammer down on a pink slab. Bel sighed. Grete always managed to persuade someone else to retrieve things from the cramped, unheated pantry, where she kept the perishables in winter.

Soon after Bel headed in the direction of the pantry, Laurence stormed in. "Where's Bel?" he asked, his voice like a plucked string. Bel ducked past the jars of canned peaches, cucumbers, and cabbage and into the yellow room. As she poured the milk from a metal pail into a pot for the stove, she heard Grete's rumbling retort. The liquid looks like melted bone, she thought, remembering the hard, fleshless fingers of the slave.

Laurence's reflection flared across the jars behind her, his head made long and spoon-shaped by the curve of the glass, his shirt still radiating cold air from outdoors. When she set the pail down and raised the pot in front of her chest, Bel's wrist shook and the milk sloshed against the sides. Her cousin stood just beyond the pot, wearing a tense, exultant expression. She could see the tiny hairs spoking between his eyebrows, and smell his sour, boyish breath.

"I'm sorry." The words swept out of her.

"Are you?" he said, almost in the same instant. "He came with me anyway. I've got him hidden under the last bridge. Behind the hemlock tree."

Bel imagined the green spray of branches, the runaway crouched behind them, his knees clutched against his chest. She couldn't remember his face, just the burlap hat, the newspaper sticking in his frizzy black curls.

"Will you help him?" Laurence pushed closer to her. The milk spilled against the coat she still had not taken off, making a stain. Laurence's eyes were deep brown, chipped with almond lights.

Grete's hammering increased, the *pound-pound-pound* shaking the floorboards beneath them. Bel swayed against the shelves, while Laurence remained still, unaffected by the mild vibrations, gazing at her. She nodded, finally, letting her chin dip toward the white liquid and then raising it. She shoved the milk pot at Laurence, making him step back. A splash of white fell with a smack against the floor.

"I will if my mother will," she added faintly, and the thought immediately reassured her. Her mother would tell them they were right to save him.

"Of course she'll help." Laurence said quickly, but he was staring at Bel as if he were seeing her for the first time. Bel stared back. A fleck of dirt was stuck to his lower lip, and she reached up to brush it away. His red mouth closed around her finger, gently holding it a moment before he let go.

The hammering stopped, and they both blushed and looked down. When Laurence still did not move, Bel pushed the pot ahead of her again, this time slowly, so nothing spilled.

Just after the two young Lindseys emerged from the pantry, Mary appeared in the doorway, her hands fisted on her hips.

"Laurence, were you out that whole time without a coat?" Mary had the near-translucent skin of a true redhead, and an entire constellation of freckles now darkened with worry at the sight of Laurence's blotched face.

"No, I forgot it at a friend's house." He tried to act nonchalant, but a shiver cracked his sentence in half.

"On a night like this? Oh, sar, your mother will be worried sick!"

"If you tell, I'll say I saw you go meet Nicky in the coach barn the other night," Laurence threatened. Nicky, Mary's longtime beau, was a blacksmith. He came to take her for walks on Sundays in the summer and fall but showed no signs of interest in marriage. At this threat, Grete emitted a hoarse, unfriendly chuckle and set Bel's pan of milk onto the stove.

"Laurence! You wouldn't. It's not true." Mary attempted to stare him down.

"I would. And it is."

"Well then, I suppose I'll just tell them that you're finally home," Mary snapped at Bel, who was an easier target than Laurence. Bel nodded, preoccupied, her finger still tingling from the light pressure of Laurence's lips. She rubbed it against her dress, trying to erase the sensation.

"Tell them also that I have made Mrs. Lindsey's favorite dish," commanded Grete, ushering Mary out the door with a wave of her wooden spoon. Laurence gave Bel a confident nod at the mention of her mother. The milk in the pan puckered and began to boil. Grete whisked it off the metal surface and stirred a dark syrup of sugar, water, and cocoa powder into it, staining the white liquid in quick swirls. The chill of the pantry had made Bel realize how fast the temperature was dropping outside, but Laurence seemed unperturbed, as if her allegiance in the matter was all that he had sought. After the cook handed a cup to each of them, brown and hot, Bel gulped hers too quickly and scalded the back of her throat without even tasting the sweetness.

Chapter Three

D o you know that when the Little Giant was an infant, his father was holding him in his arms, sitting by the fire with his friend James Conant?" began George Lindsey as he sawed into Grete's schnitzel. "And the good Dr. Douglas had a heart attack just then and nearly dropped his son into the hearth. Conant barely managed to save little Stephen from the flames, but his father was dead."

"Perhaps that is what stunted his growth," murmured Faustina, who had favored Abraham Lincoln, Stephen Douglas's taller challenger for the famous Senate race.

Laurence, at the other end of the table, laughed a short, humorless bark. In his restlessness, he had already spilled his water glass twice, and he fidgeted in a damp huddle, trying to catch Bel's eye while the adults droned on.

"That's quite a story, George," encouraged Pattie Lindsey, the dull, pretty socialite who had bestowed on Laurence his straight blond hair.

Instead of acknowledging her, George glanced sharply at his brother's wife but could not meet her lowered green eyes. "It does not seem in your good heart to jest about someone's height, Faustina," George said, finally mastering the schnitzel.

"I only jest about Stephen Douglas. There I draw the line," Faustina said.

Bel folded her hands into fists, making the nails bite hard into her palms. How long would her uncle talk before they could get her mother alone? Faustina and George always argued about everything: the railroad lines, politics, and especially the issue of slavery. George teased Bel's mother for her subscriptions to the abolitionist papers, and in turn she defiantly recited word for word Jefferson's Declaration of Independence, the Vermont constitution, and any other official document that talked of human freedom. They were like two spring robins, always chasing and pecking at each other.

"We saw the most cunning thing today in *Frank Leslie's*," Lucia interposed, talking mainly to her mother. "Tell them, Anne."

"It was a Druid's cape," pronounced Anne, touching her piles of dark blond hair. Bel didn't think either of them was especially pretty, but somehow their many attention-seeking mannerisms worked on the boys their age. Aunt Pattie was always bragging about their list of callers.

"It has a darling little hood, and it drapes down the back with a fringe," Lucia added.

"A green fringe, like the forest," said Anne solemnly. "That's what Frank Leslie said."

"Well, and would it enable you to make the trees do your bidding?" asked Daniel.

"Oh, Uncle Daniel." Lucia giggled, shooing him with a braceleted wrist. "We would have to own one to know that."

"I was thinking it might save us thousands of dollars if the trees could just cut themselves down," Daniel concluded, and Pattie and her daughters laughed enthusiastically. "Would you like one for Christmas, too, Isabel?"

Her father's well-intentioned inclusion of her made Bel blush. "Oh, no, I wouldn't want one, Papa. I don't need any new clothes."

"What would you like, then, Bel?" Faustina asked, noticing her daughter's discomfort.

"I should like . . ." Bel thought fast, wanting to impress Laurence. "I should like drawing lessons."

"Drawing lessons!" Pattie said. "My daughters never asked for those, although they can play a few tunes on the piano. Can't you, girls?"

"I think that's a wonderful idea," interrupted Faustina. "Perhaps she could paint all our portraits one day."

Hoping to avoid further notice, Bel shrank back in her seat, one of the eight oak and velvet thrones that rounded the table. These, too, had come from Germany, a wedding gift from Faustina's father. They possessed the curious power both to raise and diminish their occupants, so that down at the other end of the table, her twitching cousin looked as if he were trying to swim up from a dark sea of cloth.

Now the adults were talking about something else, which had to do with the price of paper and how it might affect the lumber trade, and George was saying that soon there would be no trees left in Vermont and it was best if they didn't rely on them. Her uncle's main passion in life was business, what would make his family and his city rich. Although both he and her father frequently traveled to Boston, they loved their native state, and remained devoutly loyal to all the generations that had come before them. Bel's grandfather Lindsey had made his fortune breeding the merino sheep given to him by the ambassador to Lisbon. And Faustina's father, the lumber baron Henry Gale, had worked in concert with Mr. Lindsey to tame the wild forests of Vermont to pastures and stone walls.

Bel saw Laurence jerk his head, signaling his impatience—but he had promised that they would include her mother, and Faustina seemed not at all inclined to leave the table. When Bel didn't respond, he pushed his chair back with a scrape.

"May we be excused?" Laurence said, interrupting his father's lecture on the superiority of the American train stations to those of Europe, the latter of which lay on the outskirts of town rather than in its center.

"In England, the passengers arrive at the dismal, swampy limits of the city. In New England, they disembark in the middle of it all," said George, glaring at his son as he concluded.

"I suppose you may," Daniel said mildly, looking at Laurence. He sat like a strung bow opposite his wife, his long spine arched toward the table.

"I want dessert," Bel said, obstinate. Her mother still showed no signs of getting up; Faustina had fixed two sad eyes on the window, as if some wintry creature out there were the cause of all suffering.

"As I was saying"—George searched the table for someone still interested in his tirade—"the centralized station just proves that the railroad has become the vibrant heart of our culture, every track an artery—"

"Your father would hate to hear it," Faustina broke in. "He adored his Morgans. He thought *they* were the heart of our culture."

"He adored horses because he didn't know any better," said George. His gray hair wagged in agreement to his words. "But who would want to trade the smooth ride of the railroad for the bumpy, ditch-ridden conveyance of a wagon?"

"What about the canals and steamships?" Daniel protested. Bel's father had once dreamed of being a ship captain. He could stand all day watching the boats move up and down the lake. In the summers, he often crept off at dawn to swim, something only the young boys did, daring one another in races across Lake Champlain's scattered coves. "You seem to have forgotten how our fathers sent the lumber south."

"Miasmal, winding little waterways." George drew a curve into the tablecloth with his knife, then crossed it with a straight line. The fabric furrowed around his knife. "Railroads can take a man right to the desert, to the mountains, and someday all the way across our country, Allenton to San Francisco. Why long for the soggy steamship or the lame horse when you can ride in a fast, dry, comfortable car?"

"Because a man had all the time in the world back then. Time wasn't a commodity the way it is now," Daniel said.

"You're always mooning about the past, Daniel," George said dismissively. "You don't even like horses. You've been afraid of them your whole life."

Daniel sighed at his empty plate. " 'Why beholdest thou the mote that is in thy brother's eye?' " he intoned, hiding his left hand in his pocket. A silence fell at this bitter recitation. Bel felt ashamed for him, and, for the first time, a little defiant. Her father would never dare to help a runaway slave, she realized. He would just talk about it. The realization set her firmly on Laurence's side.

"Your father," said Faustina, breaking the silence, "would say precisely the same thing as Daniel. Horses, unlike machines, have a motion familiar to our own—"

"Familiar enough to make my rump ache," George grumbled.

Faustina tossed up her hands and refused to continue. The last bit of meat Bel swallowed was still sticking in her throat. The runaway must be so hungry by now. Out on the ice, she'd had a bread crust in her pocket to feed the few winter birds. Why hadn't she remembered to give it to him?

"George, please don't use that kind of language at the table," said

Pattie. "Girls what were you telling me about Thomas Van Sicklin and the youngest Pomeroy daughter?"

Lucia and Anne, sensing discord once again, turned the conversation back to a gossipy river of reflections about the various young couples in Allenton. Bel watched as the windows around the table went indigo. Greenwood lay beneath a darkness deeper than the sea, and somewhere a man was freezing, waiting for them to rescue him. Mary brought out dessert, a flaky strudel made from the apples Grete kept in the root cellar beneath the house.

Letting the hum of voices wash over her, Bel examined her father's creased forehead, the way his eyes flicked to his wife now and then as if to measure something in Faustina. Always quiet and bookish, he rarely seemed passionate about anything but his own designs for the new train station, or a reservoir, or a canal that would branch down beside the lake. With his good right hand, he sketched for his family his dreams that one day Allenton would have a pavilion along the waterfront, where the lumberyards and warehouses now bustled, dirty and loud. A park where ladies could walk, and a few restaurants that served tea and sandwiches along the shore—this he imagined for his wife and daughter; this was his version of happiness.

About the approaching war, Daniel said little, refusing to believe in it. *How could brother fight against brother?* was his refrain. *Above all, we are brothers, under the same laws, the same flag.* To this, his wife would give an indulgent, if strained, smile and change the subject. Because Bel loved her father fiercely, she had tried to agree with him, and grew angry with her mother's cynicism. *How do you know?* she would begin when they were sitting together in the afternoon, Faustina teaching Bel how to stitch. *Maybe the people in Virginia are saying the same thing as Papa.* Faustina, in the midst of her embroidery, would pause, needle raised. *Your father has never been much of a prophet, because he is no good at predicting human ugliness. He does not believe in it.* And the needle would pierce the fabric again with a small tearing sound.

Her uncle stretched back from the table to smoke, offering a cigar first to his brother. Daniel refused with a frown. Soon, a bittersweet cloud ensconced George from his daughters, who continued with their own dimly pleasant talk. Laurence, thin and restive, swiped the crumbs back and forth across his plate, not even faking an interest in the conversation.

Just when Bel was about to invent some reason to get her mother alone, she felt the table shake. Her father stood up.

"If you'll all excuse me," he said. "I have some work to attend to."

"At this hour?" said Bel's uncle.

"Stay with us, Daniel," Faustina pleaded.

"Let him go." George shook his head. "It pleases my brother to build castles while the rest of Allenton dozes by their hearths."

"If they have a hearth," Laurence said, gazing straight at his cousin. But Bel was watching her father depart without answering her mother, the top of his shoulders bowed as if he carried a light but constant weight.

Chapter Four

"I wonder what they did with the swan after they were together forever," mused Bel after Faustina finished reading to them the "Lay of Milun," by Marie de France. In the story, two lovers, parted by the lady's marriage to another, communicated with each other for years via a white swan. They had a son together, who was raised by her sister, and when he grew up, he went off in search of his father. By then, the lady's husband had died and the reunited lovers lived together happily, with no further mention of the messenger bird. The book of lais was Bel's favorite; each story began with a plate that showed armored knights, damsels leaning from their towers, and even dragons, baring rows of blue razor teeth. Its pages were painted gold on the end, the color of treasure.

"I imagine they gave him his very own pond outside their window and threw him cake crumbs every morning," her mother said after a moment, her face yellowed by the candlelight. As she approached womanhood, Bel despaired that she would never be as pretty as her mother, whose lustrous brown hair still fell in curls around her smooth cheeks. At forty, Faustina seemed ten years younger than Aunt Pattie, although they had been born in the same year.

"Or they let him go free," Laurence said. His eyes had the hot dryness of an old man's. He and Bel had managed to steal Faustina away after dinner by asking her to read them a story in the library. This was a dated tradition in the Lindsey family, largely abandoned after the children learned to read themselves. Entering the room with its high bookcases and smell of mildew and age, Bel felt a wave of memory pass through her, of being small enough that she had to be lifted to her chair beside the thick oak table, of the seat's coolness seeping through the fabric of her dress as she waited for the story to begin.

"Mother, we have something to ask you," she said, her heart pounding.

"I thought so." Faustina shut the book.

"Aunt Faustina, what would you do if you found a man in trouble, with no one to help him?"

"I would help him," Faustina said promptly. "What kind of question is that?"

"Even if it was dangerous to do so?" Laurence ran his finger along the book's gold edge, not meeting his aunt's eyes.

"Even if it *were* dangerous, Laurence, not *was*. But perhaps you should just ask me what you want to know. You're a bit too young to succeed at Socratic questioning."

"We met a runaway on the lake today, Mother," Bel said, ignoring Laurence's glare. "A Negro."

"Are you certain he's a runaway?" asked Faustina.

"He asked us if we were the friend of a friend," Laurence whispered. "I want to help him."

"We have to help him," Bel said.

Faustina fixed her gaze on both of them in turn. The musty smell of the library deepened. Books towered like judges from their high shelves.

"Neither of your fathers would countenance this," she said finally.

"Do they have to know?" Laurence pleaded.

"He looked very cold, Mother."

"He has my coat, Bel," Laurence shot back.

"He could sleep in the coach barn, at least, with a blanket," Bel said.

"Hush. Both of you." Faustina held up her hand, and the three of them sat in silence for several anxious moments. Below them, Bel heard the distant tinkle of the twins playing the piano for her aunt and uncle.

"Help me take down my hair, Isabel," Faustina suddenly ordered, tilting her body sideways on the chair. Her mother's hair was so thick that, pinned for a day, it would grow kinks that had to be painfully unraveled. Faustina preferred her daughter's hands to Mary's savage fingers and often requested Bel's companionship at bedtime to undo the tangles.

Laurence propped his cheek with his palm, watching Bel pull out dozens of silver pins and let them drop to the table. After awhile, he sat up and began making towers with them, only the tense, bobbing motions of his shoulders revealing his restlessness. Could the runaway wait even through this? Perhaps they had already taken too long.

As the locks fell down her mother's neck, knotted by their captivity, Bel wondered if one day she would have the same problems with her own hair. It never bothered her now. Maybe she had her father's texture, her mother's color. She had never thought of being such a mix of them before—more that she owned one piece of her father, his eyes, another piece, his height, and two pieces of her mother, her hair and arched feet. It would be easier if she weren't such a combination, for she never knew which side to take when they fought. Finally, one of Laurence's towers clattered to the table, and her mother spoke in a low alto.

"Did anyone see you?"

"No," they answered in chorus. Laurence swiped down all his defenses with one blow.

"Where is this runaway?" The song below pounded to its finish and Bel heard the high, praising tones of her aunt.

"Behind the hemlock near the first bridge over Potash Brook," Laurence said.

"He's hungry, too," Bel added, knowing this persuasion had worked on her mother when peddlers came to the door.

"I need to send a man with you, Laurence," Faustina muttered. Her loose hair made her appear suddenly young, capable of being rash and innocent.

"Not Papa," Bel said, hating the haste in her voice.

"No, not your father." Faustina swept the silver pins into a pile with her hand. They looked like the bars to a bright little cage. "He would want to turn the man in. But I—we—couldn't, could we?" She stared at Laurence for confirmation.

"What about Johnny?" Laurence's question made Bel frown, remembering the way the hired man had watched her earlier that day. *Not your father.* But Johnny was always devoted and shy in Faustina's presence. Johnny would do anything for her mother.

"Johnny could take you. He's big enough to intimidate the Negro, too." Faustina began to nod.

"He won't try anything anyway," Bel insisted, remembering the gentle way he had set her on the frozen lake.

"Bel, have you ever not eaten for days on end?" Faustina shackled her daughter's wrist with her ringed left hand. The fierce grip frightened Bel. She shook her head and tried to pull her arm away. "Then don't presume to know what a desperate man will do," her mother said before releasing her.

"Can we go now?" Laurence asked, oblivious.

"Once we find you a coat." Faustina rose, smoothing the blue wool of her skirt. Bel looked back at the windows as they exited the library.

A frost had embroidered the edges with the silver shapes of fallen leaves.

Much as she tried to stay awake that night, the deep warmth of Bel's goose-down quilt stole her resolve, and the next thing she knew, her father's bass voice woke her. She opened her eyes to the filigreed sun the lace curtains drew across her bed.

"I can't understand you, Mary," Daniel Lindsey was saying impatiently. "Please slow down."

Bel dressed quickly and crept along the hallway, to see Mary and her father at the foot of the spiral oak staircase that wound through the center of Greenwood. She watched the top of her father's black hat bobbing, his shoulders already encased in his mink winter overcoat. He looked small and stiff, like a figure in a tableau.

"He—he's got fangs and a head of fire," Mary stammered, her brogue thick. The maid's usually tidy appearance was marred by a torn petticoat peeking from beneath her hem.

"Where?"

"In the c-c-coach barn, sar," she said, shifting out of Bel's vision.

"Cerberus in the coach barn? I didn't know we were so close to the gate of Hades," Daniel Lindsey mused aloud. "Perhaps this war . . ."

"Sar?"

"You say there's a dog in the coach barn?"

"Not a dog, a Negro!" Mary burst into ugly sobs.

Daniel's hat tipped back and he slapped his calfskin gloves against his wayward left hand. "We'll see about this. Tell Johnny to get my pistol right away and meet me out by the barn."

"Wait!" Bel called from behind a balustrade. "Papa, I don't feel well." She uttered this with her best impersonation of fever.

"Then find your mother, please, sweet girl. I have some business to attend to," he said without looking up, and put on his gloves, the left hand unsteady, yanked on finger by finger. He turned to Mary. "What were you doing in there anyway?"

"Oh, sar." Bel saw Mary's skirt spread over the floor in a deep curtsy, the petticoat a smile of white. "Sometimes Nicky will leave me a present there."

"Hmm," Bel's father grunted, and Bel heard him open the door to the quiet morning. December's silver light spilled around his feet. "Tell my wife and daughter to stay inside."

When he shut the door, Bel hesitated for a moment, considering. Her mother would not emerge from her room for hours, and then what could she do? Admit that she had tried to hide a runaway slave against her husband's wishes? It was better that it was Bel's deceit. She thundered down the stairs, flying to the coat closet to pull on her boots. "You can't go out there!" she heard Mary say in a waspish voice as she ran after her father.

"Traitor," Bel hissed over her shoulder, and fell into an unladylike sprint across the stiff crust of snow.

Her father was standing in the doorway of the coach barn, preaching to a congregation of family-owned carriages, tipped down from their high wheels. His thin legs spoked from beneath the long mink coat. "You had better come out, or I shall have to get the constable. I don't want to do you any harm, but I will not violate the laws of this country to save you." After each statement, he would pause and peer into the gloom, staring past the carriages toward the ladder to the hayloft.

"He can't understand you," Bel said, touching her father's cuff. The silky fur slipped through her fingers. *You can't understand him,* she added to herself, remembering with shame her own flight the day before.

"Bel! Get back in the house!" he ordered.

"He can't understand you, Papa, so he won't come out," she repeated, backing away from his hard blue stare, his gray beard burned metallic by the winter sun.

"How do you know?"

"I found him. By the lake. He was hungry and cold, so Laurence and I brought him home, and I told Mother that a peddler wanted to sleep in the coach barn," Bel said, lying. "She said that was all right, and asked Grete to fix him a plate of food."

"I will not harbor runaway slaves," Daniel said, as if repeating something he had memorized.

"But you will let someone die in the cold?" Bel thrust her chin at her father. As she did so, Johnny Mulcane appeared, humped in his coat, the pistol dangling from his fist. His red face belied nothing of his actions the night before.

"Johnny—" she pleaded, not wanting to reveal her mother's part in this. The man ignored her, looking instead at her father.

"Sir?"

"Isabel Prinz, you will go in the house right now," Daniel roared.

Instead of obeying him, Bel skirted past and into the interior of the coach barn. Beyond the carriages loomed the darker cages of the empty coaches. They smelled of leather and wood: the one with the red satin pillows that Faustina loved, the one with the buffalo robe that her father had bought when he was in the West, and the delicate white surrey that Lucia had already requested for her still-nonexistent wedding.

"Friend of a friend," Bel whispered softly, heading toward the ladder to the hayloft. The worn wooden rungs extended through an open trapdoor. Sun from the upper window illuminated a thousand dust motes drifting slowly down.

"Isabel!" she heard her father cry. She scampered up the splintered rungs, nearly tripping in her skirt. The wood was so cold, it burned her fingers.

"Friend of a friend," she called again, and the runaway's burlap hat appeared above the trapdoor, its shadow shrouding his eyes. "Please come down. I know I can get my father to let you go free," she promised in her gentlest tone. He didn't move. She repeated her request, staying as still as she could, remembering what her grandmother had taught her about feeding wild birds. *You must become a stone*, her grandmother had said. *You must become a tree, a reason for them to trust you.*

"Johnny, come here," her father barked. "I see him." There was a loud crack as Johnny crashed into the white surrey, snapping one of the thin wooden hitches.

At the noise, the runaway retreated. *What is a stone to a bird but a place to land?* her grandmother used to utter like a prayer, making Bel repeat it silently while she waited for the sparrows to find the food in her palm. *What is a tree but a home?* But it wasn't just her. It was what she stood for—it was the two men charging in behind her, and the leathery quiet of the carriages, and Greenwood beyond, a house too grand for its few occupants, and the gun in Johnny Mulcane's hand. The runaway would not look down at her again, like the sparrows who used to guess her deception and fly away with a throat-caught sound.

Her father moved closer, but she could only smell Johnny, rancid and musty at once. She heard the rustle of his boots across the frost-buckled earth. *Keep climbing*, she ordered herself. *He's coming.* Her body froze in place, stuck like a wheel in the snow. She wished desperately for Laurence's courage. If he were here, he would think of something, but she didn't know what to do.

"Don't," she said feebly, clinging to the rungs as her father reached up to peel her from them. The ladder swayed dangerously.

"Let go, Isbael," her father commanded, pulling her hands apart. One by one, her fingers tore from the wood. "Let go."

When she finally did, she sagged against her father's chest, allowing even the bones to melt inside her body. In her mind, she would see the rest of that morning like a story her mother read at night, narrated with all the bright details an author can muster when talking about tragedy and what shouldn't happen but always does: Mary's cold, scratchy sleeves dragging her inside Greenwood to watch behind the starched lace of the windows, which did not muffle but somehow compounded the single shot and the thump of a man falling to his knees, a man used to running when he could run, and perhaps killing if he had to, who knew there was no hope for him now, even on this white, frozen brink of freedom. He slumped in Johnny Mulcane's arms, dangling his shattered right foot, deprived of his last and only possessions, the will to flee and the means.

The story would go on for years in Bel's mind. She would be telling Laurence how it happened that they had lost the one thing they'd thought they could save, as the war came so quickly after that, and the end of all the young boys who raced their sleds, or stitched the fields to the headlands with their wooden plows, or battled for who would dance with the best girl. She would remember for both of them, because for eight days, Laurence would be ill with fever. Her father had Johnny carry the wounded man into Greenwood, stricken with what he had asked another man to do, and yet not quite asked; he would say this to himself and to Faustina, who, for almost a month, could not look at him with her full green gaze because that would mean forgiveness.

Bel would tell Laurence of things she should not have seen, the bloody rags and shattered foot beneath, Mary tossing the burlap hat into the fire, the hatred in the runaway's eyes when Bel touched his stiff fist. She would remember the blur of the doctor arriving, and that

41

Johnny Mulcane stole the bullet from the basin where it lay, then vanished for three days. He was not punished by the pudgy, myopic constable, who spoke to the runaway in a loud voice about how the kind Mr. Lindsey had offered to buy his freedom if no slave owner claimed him for a week, and that this was unusual generosity, but in Vermont they didn't believe that some men could not be free.

She moved through that week numbly, knowing that Dr. Cochran had said the runaway's foot would never heal entirely. She wished she could plot with her mother how to rescue him, but Faustina was like a stone underwater those days, moving only slightly with the current of life around her. Whenever Bel brought up the runaway, a shadow would cross Faustina's face and she would send her daughter to Mary, who made the girl thumb clumsily through the rosary and ask forgiveness for betraying her father's wishes.

Meanwhile, Laurence tossed listlessly, his brown eyes wide with delirium. When Bel went to sit with him, he alternately muttered and shouted about ice and darkness, and mentioned his coat several times. His mother brought it to him, washed clean of the smell of the runaway, but he refused it, saying, *This is not mine.* As soon as he recovered, his father booked him on the next train to Boston, and Laurence did not even enter Greenwood to say good-bye, hunched to his chin in a heavy coat, his eyes already distant.

Bel's father buried himself in business, spending all day at the lumberyards. He designed plans for a new building on the nonexistent waterfront, a floating hotel that newlyweds could reach by a narrow walkway, because he did not fully believe a war was coming to drain his city of all the young men who might marry. Yet it was he who bore the news to his family, telling them that a farmer from Georgia had claimed the runaway, that he seemed like a good man, that they had already headed back together on the train. *Why didn't you buy him?* asked Faustina. *I was too late*, replied Daniel, taking off his gloves and then putting them on again, over and over, as he spoke, his left hand sticking in the fingers.

And if the law changes, Daniel, will you finally be ashamed, if the law tells you that we were wrong?

We are prominent citizens of this city. If we break the law, who will abide?

You and I no longer live in the same city, Daniel.

In the story Bel told her cousin, this was one ending, her father and mother facing each other across the stairs, where Bel hid behind a balustrade on the second floor. The other ending was the continuing of time, her hope that the slave might have escaped again, more than a year passing, the first shots fired on Sumter, and her father going down to the green to watch the new Vermont regiments learning how to fight instead of hunt. The news came that Laurence had arrived from Boston to join the Second Vermont at the last minute. Bel's cousin would march alongside farmhands and blacksmiths in a gray uniform faced with green to honor their ancestors in battle, the Green Mountain Boys. Most of the recruits thought they would be back for harvest. They were negligent in their kisses good-bye, their nonchalant waves as they boarded one of the Lindsey trains. They jostled one another for a seat by the door, where they could swing out and feel the wind take them—and then swing back inside to smell the sweat of men, to hear their voices again, far away at first, approaching like rain.

June–July 1861

Chapter Five

L ikely to know your Bible by heart by the time you reach battle," the accordion player observed, slumped against the hard seat. He was constantly adjusting his cap to a jauntier angle and did so now, turning the brim so that it aimed out the window. "Hey," cried the accordion player, speaking louder to be heard above the commotion of the car. "You practicing to be a preacher or something?"

Laurence looked up, covering the book with his hand. The volume of poetry had been banned in Boston, and he had secretly procured a copy from the author's sister, whose husband ran a hardware shop in Allenton. "It's not a Bible," he said hastily.

"Whatever it is, then." The musician's blue eyes strayed over the pure silver buttons Laurence's mother had insisted on stitching on his uniform. "What's your name again, sir?"

"Laurence Lindsey."

"John Addison." They shook hands, the other soldier's grasp firm and lasting a little long, so that Laurence was the first to withdraw. They had been drilling together for two weeks in Allenton, but John Addison had always been flanked by a number of other recruits, who directed their jokes and comments toward his square red-blond head, searching for approval. This he doled out in barking laughs, making the whole company join in, as if all along the men had been waiting for the order to enjoy themselves.

Laurence quickly found his place as a loner and a bookworm, tolerated by the farm boys but largely ignored. His only friend was an awkward, blushing fellow named Lyman Woodard, who wished, of all things, to be an actor. A staunch abolitionist, Woodard pronounced views diluted straight from Greeley to anyone who would listen. All day, he trailed an eager half step behind Laurence, his blond hair sticking in the corners of his mouth.

"Lindsey's father owns the railroad," Woodard interjected. Laurence gave him a baleful glance.

"He and my uncle," he amended, shoving the book in his haversack and waiting for the onslaught of questions. He considered himself the only boy alive not fascinated by railroads, although he had been once, before he decided he did not admire his father. Now he preferred horses, pausing on avenues to admire their muscled lines and sweet, grassy smell, imagining a world without the loud rumble of wheels and tracks.

But the usual fury of railroad conversation—where the newest lines were being laid, what the best engines were, and who would win the race to cross the West—did not erupt, and Laurence realized from his comrades' awed expressions that this was the first trip many had made by locomotive.

"Can he get me a job driving them engines?" asked Pike Rhodes, one of John Addison's acolytes. He was sitting in a jumble of elbows and knees beside his brother Gilbert, and he scooted forward to the edge of his wooden seat. Redheaded, boy-faced, and adorned with freckled ears that tipped forward in an expression of constant curiosity, Pike Rhodes had already become the object of much good-hearted humor. Now he was staring at Laurence with his mouth agape, body perilously balanced over the aisle.

"Maybe." Laurence hesitated, hoping to prolong the boy's sudden interest. "I don't know."

Gilbert reached over and clapped his brother's mouth shut. "We have to whip the sec, first, Pike," he threatened, his black hair falling in his eyes.

"That won't take long." Pike slid back into his old slot beside his brother. "I told Pa I'd be back for harvest."

"Told mine I'd be back for supper," John Addison said, and grinned. His neighbors broke into obliging laughter.

Laurence, looking down at his hands, did not join in. He was thinking of his father's assessment of the rebellion. *War*, George Lindsey wrote to his son after the firing on Fort Sumter, *is just a peculiar kind of commerce, one where men's lives are spent for land or ideals. It will take a long time for the rebels to spend every penny they have. I had hoped my boy was going to make an intelligent business-man, and would not be seduced from duty by all those buncombe speeches. There are plenty of other lives less precious or ready to serve for the love of serving.*

"What's wrong, Lindsey?" asked Addison.

"I don't think they'll give up so easily." Laurence did not look up. A trickle of sweat ran down his temple, and he swabbed it with his sleeve.

"Why's that?" The question was not asked, but nailed on the air with a soft squeal of Addison's accordion. Laurence felt a hundred eyes on him. No one had ever talked of losing the war, of even losing a single battle.

"They're defending," he explained patiently. "It's always easier to defend. Look at us against the British. Look at Troy. It only fell when they took the horse inside its walls."

" 'S true." Addison lifted his cap and let it settle slightly more askew, as if a branch had knocked it in passing. The train rumbled and clacked. They were far away from their own hills now and the blue sky drowned the flattening land.

Noting the serious gazes of his companions, Laurence continued: "And you know what the horse is." In his mind, he saw the lake and the runaway slave he and his cousin had failed to save.

"What?"

"Negro regiments," he said triumphantly, but the soldiers' faces hardened and he had to look away, out the window to the green fringe of trees beyond the pastures. Only Woodard nodded vigorously, his long nose stirring circles in the air.

"If we listen to the schoolmarm, we might as well just toss our muskets into enemy territory and be done with it," said Gilbert Rhodes, whose most prominent feature was his nose, broken in so many places that it no longer had the look of a single organ, but a composite, several jigsaw pieces glued together.

"That's not what I'm saying," Laurence said to the trees.

"He means we should train them to fight alongside our regiments," Woodard said, interrupting for the second time. His high, reedy voice did little to persuade the others.

"What's to say they don't start firing at us, too?" Gilbert countered.

"Who?" Laurence turned to him.

"Your regiments of niggers."

Laurence shook his head and bent over to search his bag for the book of poems. Wrenching it out, he cracked it open, hoping the lines would swim through his mind and replace the ugly indifference of the men. *Lives less precious*, his father's voice intruded. *Ready to serve for the love of serving.* George Lindsey had begged his son to train with the officers, but Laurence had refused.

"They wouldn't fire," John Addison offered after a strained minute, "but they might not fight so good, either. I'm ready to try myself, though." This seemed to settle the matter, and the soldier began to play "Lorena," a ballad about a soldier and his lost love. Pike sang the verses, the muscles of his thin neck rippling, and the others joined in when they knew the words. At "What we might have been, Lorena, had our loving prospered well," Gilbert Rhodes cupped his crotch and everyone laughed.

The car's tiny windows were ringed by a scum of black mildew, making the outside world blur at the edges, as if a shadow were encroaching on all sides. As the men's voices filled his ears, Laurence looked to the endless south stretching before them. It was like peering through a dozen keyholes at once, each one holding its own version of the same hidden room beyond.

Chapter Six

"Watch this," said Gilbert. He was sitting at the mouth of the tent he shared with his brother, Laurence, and John Addison. The others were sleeping, except Laurence, who lay on the damp earth, writing in a crack of sunlight. Every few moments, he would have to shift the paper to change the place illumined by the ray, but he was too exhausted to go outside. After a week of marching, camp-raising, and drilling in the hot July sun, most of the recruits could barely move on their free afternoon. Gilbert was eternally awake, however, his undershirt tight around his ribs, the uniform his mother had sewn for him dripping from a tent line. He had already washed it twice. "Watch this," he said again, and Laurence turned on his aching side to see Gilbert thrust one foot out of the shadow of the tent.

With a soft grunt, Lyman Woodard fell facedown against the earth, his blond hair streaming over his cheeks. At the sound of the impact, John Addison cracked one blue eye, then let it fall slowly shut. Laurence sighed and stared at his letter. Every day since they had arrived in their camp outside Washington, Gilbert had managed to trip the clumsy soldier.

"When you going to learn to watch your feet, Woodard?" Gilbert grinned. "When the secesh start shooting at 'em?"

"That's unfair," Lyman Woodard said, pushing himself onto his knees. "You know that's unfair."

"Since when is drill unfair?" Gilbert said. "I just invented a new drill, that's all."

"Well, I don't like it." Woodard stood up and brushed himself off. He squinted into the shadows of the tent. "Who you writing to, Lindsey? You got a sweetheart?"

"My cousin," said Laurence, blushing. They wouldn't understand his friendship with little Bel.

"Girl cousin," Pike amended, although the only way he could have guessed this fact was if he had been reading over Laurence's shoulder.

"How do you know—" Laurence began.

"Keeping the money in the family, ain't you?" Gilbert interrupted, grinning. He fingered a limp dark curl. "Just wait till I start courting her."

"It's not like that." Laurence covered the letter with his arm, glaring at Pike, who scrabbled busily in his haversack and refused to return his gaze.

"Sure it ain't." Gilbert nodded.

"I'm going over to the contraband camp tonight to hear them sing, Lindsey. Wanna go?" asked Woodard. The former slaves who took refuge with the government army were given the nickname "contrabands" for their status as war bounty. They were treated terribly, given the worst jobs in camp and often made the subject of soldiers' pranks, but the evenings were their own, and they held rousing prayer meetings a short distance from camp.

"I can't," Laurence said. "I'm on picket."

"Well, some other Sunday, then," Woodard said hopefully. He continued to brush himself off. "I might not go tonight."

Gilbert snorted. "What a bully idea. Learn me some nigger songs, why don't you, Lindsey. When you go."

"I will," said Laurence coldly. He took out the poetry book and propped it over the letter. Silence fell over the tent again.

"Is it good?" Addison asked Laurence in a voice entirely awake, although he did not open his eyes.

Laurence nodded. "Listen to this: 'I know that the hand of God is the elderhand of my own. I know that the spirit of God is the eldest brother of my own, and that all men ever born are also my brothers. . . .' "

"Do you really believe that?" Addison's eyes remained closed.

"I do," Laurence said. "At least when I'm reading it, I do."

Woodard was still hovering at the mouth of the tent, blocking Laurence's single ray. "Get on," Gilbert said. "You don't have my permission to stay."

"So? You ain't captain."

"Then how can you shoot a secesh?" asked Addison, pursuing his line of questioning. "When the time comes."

"Get on!" Gilbert yelled this time, and swiped at Woodard with his fist. The other soldier backed up clumsily.

"You ain't captain," he repeated bitterly, but he turned and began to shuffle away.

"Let's play," said Pike, sitting up to pull out a deck of cards, arching them at the tips. "I want to play."

"When the time comes, I guess I might feel differently," Laurence said, turning to Addison, but his friend was snoring softly, his body quaking with the first spasms of sleep.

This kind of scenario happened so often in their tent, Laurence had learned to have conversations with the others in his mind, battling with their ignorance and unkindnesses as they sweat through drill and later when they rested together, their bodies stretched along the warm earth. It was easier this way, the quiet settling over the damp, ruined grass inside their quarters, the haversacks heaped beside him, a canteen passed from hand to hand. When the flare of whiskey touched his lips and tongue, he gave the appropriate gusty sigh.

After two weeks in sunny Virginia, he suspected that the others viewed him as a useful but somewhat odd accessory to their tribe, asking him to write their addresses in his neat cursive, to decipher their own missives from home. He knew Addison liked him, but he could not quite understand why and so accepted his friendship grudgingly, as if he were doling out a favor to the handsome soldier. Watching him sleep now, Laurence wondered what it would be like to wake in Addison's body, to open his eyes and see what Addison saw. It would be a light-filled world, he decided, like a spring day in Boston when the harbor gleamed like some lost treasure and, walking beside it, a young man could watch his own reflection lengthened and shattered and lengthened again.

At dusk, they stumbled out to picket, a sentry duty that spread men a half mile apart in the woods, guarding in shifts. Most soldiers, it was discovered, were more afraid of the dark than of any imminent secesh attack. False alarms sounded the first few nights, until Captain Davey, the company's weary-eyed leader, told them he'd shoot the next man who cried wolf.

Laurence liked the solitude after the close quarters of camp life, and he eagerly followed his comrades out to the Big Reserve, the prostrate woodlot where men waited to go on their shifts. Damp spiderwebs tore across his face and made him think of his mother, whose graying hair had dragged over his cheek as she kissed him good-bye, begging him not to forget his family. What this request really meant was that he should not lose his position in the world, son of the richest man in Allenton, that he must return after this youthful escapade and assume the mantle of his father's business. The spiderwebs stuck to his fingers after he tore them from his eyes. He could not imagine going home.

When he reached the Big Reserve, Laurence dismissed Allenton from his mind and sat down to watch the boxing match. The first night he had gone on picket, he had realized he had never before seen men fight in earnest, heard the hollow thud of fists on flesh, the crack of bone. Tonight, the often-victorious Gilbert had been challenged by a stocky drummer boy, and Pike scurried among the men, taking their bets of pennies, doughnuts, and dirty pictures.

Meanwhile, Gilbert launched into his elaborate prefight routine. First, he stripped off his shirt and hung it carefully over a branch. Then he uttered a brief prayer from the Psalms while he flexed his arms, popping his knuckles: " 'My soul is among lions: and I lie among them that are set on fire, even the sons of men, whose teeth are spears and arrows, and their tongue a sharp sword.' "

He had just finished pronouncing the last words when the drummer boy swaggered up, rocked back and forth on his heels a few times, and crashed to the ground like a felled tree. A disappointed murmur spread through the men, and the boy's companions confessed that he had been drinking all afternoon.

"Who else?" Gilbert shouted into the close, cloud-covered night. The fire flickered weakly and men averted their eyes one by one. None of them liked fighting the older Rhodes, who had a twisting punch that could leave a lingering bruise.

"I'll take on two of you, then." Gilbert tossed his head.

"Not tonight, Gilbert," someone called finally. A wind lifted through their wool uniforms, making the men scratch and shift their positions on the earth.

Gilbert toyed with his shirt but did not put it back on. "So you mean to tell me that I've got to go into battle with a bunch of goddamn cowards who won't even fight a body two to one."

Above the clearing, the branches of an oak speared the moon. A silvery light fell through the forest.

"I'll fight you," came Pike's small voice. "I ain't no coward."

The younger Rhodes walked toward his brother, his fists lifted. There was something both grand and defeated in his posture, something Laurence recognized but could not place until Pike crossed a strip of moonlight, and seeing him silhouetted there, Laurence saw his uncle Daniel seated across from his brother at the dinner table, losing every argument, accepting it.

Before he was fully aware of what he was doing, Laurence leapt to his feet, pushing Pike away. "You don't need to fight your own kin," he said, disgusted. "I'll do it."

Pike resisted his shove at first, and the three of them stood in the center of the ring, so close that Laurence could smell the sweat darkening Gilbert's hair and Pike's sour breath.

"I'll do it," Laurence repeated harshly, and Pike stepped away, his eyes as hollow and lightless as the interior of a walnut shell. A weak cheer rose from the men as Laurence stripped off his shirt clumsily, his arms snagging in the sleeves. The cool air pricked his skin. He could feel the workings of his muscles as he took a few swings at the empty air.

"Can I change my bet?" called a man, and a loud clamoring ensued, Pike dodging among them with his head lowered like a dog. The last soldier to fight Gilbert was still limping, and he threw a bet down on his former opponent with a flourish. There was the rushing sound as a flock of birds descended to a tree nearby, and then everything fell silent. Even the noise of Laurence's breath lifted away from him as he danced opposite Gilbert, waiting for the other man to swing.

It had been Gilbert's strategy to stare down his opponents until they threw their first wild punches. Then he would knock them off balance with a blizzard of tiny jabs. Laurence and Addison had discussed this tactic and how to oppose it. "Just wait him out," Addison had said. "That's what I'd do. Smoke him out like a nest of bees."

Under the pressure of Gilbert's gaze, his dodges and feints, Laurence found it hard to follow this advice. He wanted the fight to be over, to plunge headlong into it the way he had plunged through his father's rage when he told him he had enlisted, not as an officer, but as a foot soldier. They had stood opposite each other on the muddy spring earth outside the house, shouting as melted snow trickled down the brick walls and over the ludicrous green awnings his mother had ordered from Paris. At Laurence's news, his father had tried to box him on the ears, but Laurence had pushed him away clumsily and run off through the muddy streets so that his father would not see the tears on his face.

Shrugging off the memory, Laurence waited. Around him, the men sang out their complaints. The fire sank to a dull red coil.

Finally, Gilbert punched toward his gut. Instinctively, Laurence blocked him, and soon after that, the storm of fists descended, battering his mouth and neck. He closed his eyes and hit back, his fists opening. His skull rattled with pain. Somewhere on his face, the skin split, and when he could look again, Gilbert's fists were streaked with red.

Laurence danced away, an old defiance overtaking him. He remembered being five years old, rising in a midnight thunderstorm and running to the kitchen to beat a cast-iron pot with a wooden spoon while thunder boomed outside. Awakened by Laurence's loud response, his father had appeared in the threshold and told him to go back to bed. When Laurence kept clanging on the pot, he carried his son outside in the rain. Lighting flashed around them.

You're not loud enough to drown it out, are you? his father had said as rain spattered Laurence's nightshirt and made it hang heavy on his shoulders. *You never will be.*

"Smoke him out," he heard Addison call, and he stood his ground just beyond Gilbert's reach. He resisted the urge to touch his throbbing cheek or turn his head to see the others.

"C'mon," Gilbert snarled. "I ain't waiting all night to win."

Laurence shook the blood from his eyes and maintained his distance. His brogans carved small circles in the earth, the weeds unrooted, kicked aside. Gilbert pursued him all the way to one flank of the audience, and Laurence felt the men's breath on the backs of his knees as his opponent swung.

This time, Laurence waited for him to throw his whole weight into the punch, taking the blow but responding with one of his own. Laurence's ribs screamed, but he was rewarded by the sight of Gilbert staggering back, holding his cheek. The crowd murmured as Laurence struck again, this time against the father who had tried to stop him from fighting because he thought that this war was just another kind of storm. Then, blood-blinded, he only glimpsed pieces of the other soldier before he hit them: the arch of Gilbert's shoulder, the veins that branched above his temple, the ash of whiskers on his chin.

Gilbert wavered and fell to his knees under Laurence's fury. A howl rose from the crowd. The sky shifted colors, going red, then blue-black, then red again, and Laurence, lifting his fists, felt it wash over his body. It was like a lake, that sky, and when he lowered his hands, he was swimming up through it, able for one split second to look down on them all, standing together in a deep woods dotted with lonely sentries dreaming of home.

His cut lower lip made it impossible to speak when the recruits crowded around him. It was better this way. Silent, he could be one of them, and if he spoke, he would once again become a stranger, saying something they could not hear or understand, something about the way some men waited dully in a dark wood for their time to pass and others called out, frightened by the whispering trees and the certainty that somewhere, something was watching them.

Only Pike did not join the throng, going immediately to nurse his brother, who was still kneeling a few paces away. Out of the corner of his eye, Laurence saw the boy pull out an already-blood-spattered handkerchief and dab at his brother's wounds.

"Never thought there were a fighter in you," said the man who had lost to Gilbert three days before, thumping Laurence on the shoulder with his bruised hands. They both winced.

Addison came up close and his blue eyes met Laurence's. They were lit with a strange emotion, part envy, part satisfaction, the way a gull looks just after it gets tossed a fish. Laurence blinked. "Smoked him out." Addison grinned and shook his head, then turned swiftly toward Gilbert, who was now lying flat against the earth, his jaw working but no sound emerging.

"He said he's all right," came Pike's clarion voice. Laurence felt blood trail down from the gash on his cheek, curving until it touched the corner of his mouth. It tasted warm and salty. The men continued to gather around him, the few who had won the bet shoving in to thank him. As he accepted their praise, he thought he heard the hoarse whisper of Gilbert, who still lay splayed on the ground.

"He said he's all right," Pike said again to the unlistening crowd. "Just leave him alone for a while."

Chapter Seven

A yellow boy with a nose as flat as a plate stood in the center of a sagging tent of contrabands, singing. "I see the angels beck'nin, I hear them call me 'way; I see the golden city, and the everlastin' day!" It was a potent, magical voice, higher and richer than a white man's, with a timbre seasoned like Virginia, by warm weather, days of rain.

The other contrabands, with eyes shut and feet stamping, came in on the chorus. "Oh, I'm gwine home to glory; Won't you go along with me, Whar the angels beckon, an' the Lord my savior be?"

Crouched together behind a thicket of blackberries outside the tent, Laurence, Woodard, and Pike listened to the roar and pulse of the hymn. Soles slammed the earth, calves bunched, and spines twitched like trees in the wind. A woman Laurence had seen bowed over her daughter by day had her arms raised, mouth open, drinking the air. He wondered if he would ever see his runaway among them, dancing on his crippled foot.

"See, it ain't the devil's work," whispered Woodard. "They're good Christians." They watched together behind the veil of thorns and hard green berries, Laurence sucking at a scratch on his thumb, Pike swaying as the song sped up and the dancers began to spin and leap in tight, convulsive bounds.

At first, a lone woman with the waistless, oblong torso of a bathtub began to call out hoarsely. It sounded like she was being strangled, but she stood alone in the circle of dancers, her head flung skyward. Then a second woman joined in, her own garbled speech directed toward the earth. She moved in stiff, jerky steps and pointed her thin arm at the fire, as if she glimpsed in it a creature that would leap out and devour them all, and only she could keep it at bay. A man with a grizzled beard started hissing and popping like the fire itself, and then he fell to the ground and lay there, rigid, his eyes open, drinking the stars.

Laurence was afraid to look at his companions, afraid he would see in their faces his own dubious envy of the overtaken slaves, or, worse, that they would understand more than he. But when he heard beside him a soft echo of the contrabands' hymn, he turned, to find Pike singing, his hands cupped around the blisters on his heels where his too-large boots had worn the flesh away. Although the boy seemed unaware that he had joined them, his sweet, eerie soprano rose from the thorns and bloomed into the night above. The contrabands danced on, undisturbed, and Laurence heard something in the way Pike's voice echoed the sway and jerk of their bodies, something he knew he had not heard before, and he understood suddenly the fear at the root of his fascination. This war would change them all, the dancers and the watchers, the soldiers and the families that stayed at home. They would never be the same again.

Finally, the singer ran out of verses and the song came to a swelling close. The afflicted ones fell to the ground in a heap. Silence filled the air, and Pike slumped, exhausted, against Laurence's right side.

"Gaw," he whispered. "Their hands look like the dark got rubbed off from holding things." Laurence could feel Pike's heartbeat thumping through his bony ribs, and he shifted to let a small channel of air flow between them.

"Cotton," Woodard affirmed. "It will tear a man's hands to shreds. I read that somewhere."

"It isn't cotton," Laurence hissed, irritated. "They're born that way. The babies have it, too."

"Shh," Woodard said, and pointed. Another man stood in the center of the circle now. Narrow-hipped and with a regal lift of head, he petitioned the Lord to remember the days when they had nothing to eat, and no time to sleep from working all day in the tobacco fields, when they had been kept out in the frost and snow, and suffered in every way imaginable. The Lord would smother his enemies, said the petitioner; the Lord could help Mr. Linkum win.

"Mr. Linkum," said Pike. Disgust flooded his voice. "He can't even say the name of the president right. Gilbert says they ain't human, really."

After all they had seen and heard, this comment angered Laurence, and he cuffed the boy on the neck. "Think for yourself," he hissed.

But Pike had been precariously balanced to avoid any contact with his blistered heels, and the light blow knocked him into the thorns. He gave a sharp cry. The contrabands turned in its direction, the hum of agreement dying out on their lips. In a matter of moments, the men and women vanished one by one into the mouth of dark beyond the fire. Laurence blinked and yanked Pike back by the collar. He had been gazing so long in the direction of the blaze, his eyes were blind in the near blackness.

"Goddamn it, Pike," Woodard said. He could never effectively pull off cursing, and he sounded like a schoolboy practicing the language of men. "You had to scare 'em off, didn't you?"

"He didn't meant to—" Laurence began, attempting to explain his own action.

"I didn't mean to," said Pike, interrupting him. "I just fell." He was less than a foot away, but still Laurence could not see him. He stared until the boy came in focus. Blood welled into a long scratch winding down Pike's cheek, and he wiped it with the heel of his hand, refusing to meet Laurence's eyes.

Never before had anyone been afraid of him, and the thought made Laurence feel sick and triumphant at once. He watched a moth take off from a leaf, its ugly gray body aiming for the light of the contrabands' fire.

"Well, that's all we get, 'cause of you." Woodard punched Pike lightly in the shoulder. "The show's over."

"I didn't mean to," Pike repeated. The blood had left black streaks up his wrist. He did not rub them away, even after they all stood up and began to walk back toward the tents, stumbling over roots and fallen branches, not knowing which was which until the branches snapped and the roots held fast.

Chapter Eight

Addison's heel plowed up and down a small area in the dirt, leaving the headlands, a curve of untouched earth at the edge of each row.

"I told Betsey if she waited for me, I'd come home and buy a nice piece up the Onion River and we'd settle there," he said over the groan of the stump he sat on. "But if she ain't waiting, I ain't buying."

The lounging soldiers looked at their own feet, uncomfortable with Addison's confession about his negligent sweetheart. He had painstakingly written Betsey several letters already but had received nothing in reply. Only Addison's mother had written him, and with unfortunate news: Her cough had worsened, their larder was nearly bare, and his little sister was running around wild. Addison's allotment in the correspondence department seemed particularly unfair to Laurence, who got the most letters of anyone in the company. His mother, aunt, and cousin competed for his attention with almost daily frequency, and his haversack rustled with their written greetings every time he lifted it.

"Maybe the post is slow," Laurence offered, shuffling a deck of cards.

"My mother said her mother was fast and Betsey would turn out fast, too," Pike blurted out.

"Bully for your ma." Addison placed his hands on his knees and hauled himself up. He stared out over the jaw of pointy teeth the tents made across the field. "Did it ever occur to you she was jealous?"

Pike pursed his lips together to say something else, but Gilbert slapped him on his bony thigh and spoke instead. "Ain't we gonna play cards?"

"You can. I've got to go see about a horse they can't break over in the paddock," Addison said. He walked off into the bright afternoon.

Laurence let the deck splay over Addison's future hay field. "Can I come, Addison? You said I could see you break this one."

"Don't see why not."

"Can I go, too?" Pike sprang to his feet.

"You said you'd play cards," protested his brother.

"Nope. Too many of you will scare the horses," Addison said, his voice carrying through the sunny air. Pike continued to stand, swaying on his blistered feet. The scratch on his face had healed to a thin line, and he cupped it gently with his fingers.

"Let's go," called Addison. Laurence paused for moment, pitying the boy. Noticing Laurence's eyes on him, Pike plopped down beside his brother, hissing at the pain of the blisters.

"If the schoolmarm already shuffled them, then we can start, can't we?" he said in his determined little voice. He leaned over and scooped the deck from the dirt.

"I ain't playing with just you." Gilbert fished Laurence's mirror from the tent and eyed the growth of his black beard. Since their fight, Gilbert had gone back to being a frequent victor, and he was always trying halfheartedly to bait Laurence into a rematch. Laurence refused to consider it. His ribs still bothered him when he breathed.

"I'll play," Laurence heard Lyman Woodard offer as he jogged after Addison, skirting the white flags of undershirts hung out to dry.

"I wasn't thinking straight when I asked about Betsey," he apologized when he caught up.

Addison wagged his hand in the air. "I'm touchy about it," he said.

"Perhaps she's just a bad letter writer?" A wet sleeve hanging from one of the tent ropes dragged a chill across Laurence's arm.

"Perhaps I ain't the one she wants to write to," Addison said.

They reached the rise where the officers kept their horses. The rolling Virginia pasture was already grazed down to the root. Bales of hay sprawled at its edges, ignored by the mares, who preferred the sweet taste of new clover to the dry dust of last year's fields. At the end of it, a pond, deep with spring rains, wavered and held the noon heat. The few lone trees were nipped of their lower leaves, and they provided only the faintest shade for the horses.

"Private Addison." Captain Davey strode up with a rope slung over his shoulder, a hunting knife in his hand. On the ground, Davey looked awkward and shambling, his body bulging at the gut and filling the square shirt he wore half-tucked. His eyes were fixed in a perpetual squint, as if he were gazing into an unpleasant distance the rest of them could not yet see. Only in the saddle did the captain acquire the grandeur appropriate for an officer, his bowlegs fitting perfectly to the contours of the horse, his hands graceful as a conductor's with the reins.

"He won't tell us how he's going to break him," Davey informed Laurence, his lower lip bulging around a plug of tobacco. "Just a pond, a tree, a knife, and a rope, he says."

"Where's the horse?"

The captain pointed to a corner where a well-muscled bay stallion was eyeing the fence as if considering jumping it.

"Furlough's a reb stallion escaped from their camps," Davey explained, and spat. "He went crazy after a bullet almost hit him in the eye, and he won't let a man near now. You won't get close enough to ride him," he warned Addison.

Addison grinned and took the rope from the captain, motioning for him to keep the knife. "I'm not gonna ride him. But I may need your help heading him off, Cap."

"Sartainly, sar." The captain made an exaggerated salute.

"Lindsey, you should stay clear," warned Addison. "Furlough's liable to kick."

Nodding, Laurence stood his ground while the other two men approached the stallion cautiously, their legs bent at the knees, arms flung back. As soon as the horse smelled them coming, he wheeled and began charging toward the corner above the pond. Addison tied a lasso while Davey slid to the east, blocking Furlough's exit.

Out of the corner of his eye, Laurence saw Pike come up to the rail fence to view the proceedings, his intent face propped up by the highest rail, arms looped over and dangling like a criminal in the stocks. Laurence was used to the boy following him now, and he ignored him, knowing Pike would prefer it that way.

A light wind riffled the manes of the horses, carrying with it the percussion of clicks and whistles Addison was making to soothe the stallion, and, softer, below that sound, Furlough's breath wheezing in and out of his lungs. He was a gigantic beauty of a stallion, the kind the poet described in Laurence's book: "limbs glossy and supple, tail dusting the ground, eyes well apart and full of sparkling wickedness." Addison's noises had little effect on him at first, but after a minute, Furlough dipped his head to nip at an invisible tuft of timothy. When he raised it again, a graceful, looping lasso fell about his neck.

The pasture exploded. Furlough reared up with an angry scream. Sod flew from his muddy hooves, falling to the earth. Addison began edging toward one of the trees near the pond, nearly pulled off his feet by Furlough with each step he took. The horseman's mouth opened and, after a moment, his cry emerged, a high *hyah, hyah, hyah.*

At every call, the horse's hooves kicked up, narrowly missing Addison's head, and every time they came down, he ducked at precisely the right moment to avoid being crushed. The horse seemed irritated by this and rose higher, descending with greater force. But Addison stayed calm, and when Furlough was finally between him and the water, he swiftly knotted the rope around a tree trunk and took the flashing knife from Captain Davey. Furlough reared again. His dark body heaved high as the doorway of a barn, and at the moment it reached its zenith, Addison stepped forward and cut the rope.

Loosed suddenly from the cord that held him earthward, the horse flopped backward and into the water, flinging up a white wall that showered Addison from head to foot. He tossed the knife to the grass and waited as the pond closed over the stallion. Sunlight bled across the surface, and then the water parted, streaming over the horse's head. After a moment, Furlough emerged with a loud whinny and stood, struggling like a newborn colt on legs rickety with shock. When Addison waded in and grabbed the rope, the horse shied slightly from his approach, but he did not rear up.

As Addison led Furlough out of the water, his soaked wool trousers sagged against his legs, but his jaunty cap was dry and intact. The soldier finally allowed a sliver of a grin to spread across his face.

"He needs to be fussed over and given some oats, if you got 'em," he said to Davey. He reached out slowly and combed the stallion's wet shoulder with his hand. Furlough's muscles flickered, but the horse did not pull away.

"Oats," said Davey admiringly. The two of them faded into horse talk, appraising Furlough's still-shaking body, and Laurence jogged up the pasture to greet Pike. The boy's face was tipped skyward, his cap nearly sliding off. His nostrils flared as he breathed.

"Did you see that?" Laurence shouted needlessly, thrilled that he had witnessed something worth recounting to the others. He was already formulating the story in his mind. "A pond, a rope, a knife, and a tree, he promised Davey. I heard him."

"Don't look up," Pike said without lowering his chin a fraction. His arms were still dangling over the high rail.

Ignoring this advice, Laurence cranked his head skyward, saw a trio of buzzards circling above the pond, their wings extended, motionless.

"I told you not to look up," Pike said reprovingly. "Now you're stuck like me. It's bad luck to look away before they flap."

"It's just a bunch of birds, Pike," said Laurence, disgusted. But he kept his eyes on the dark shapes as they spiraled higher and higher, climbing an invisible stair. The wings did not move.

"Superstition," he added, still watching. The buzzards spun so high, he could barely make them out. His neck began to ache. The sun was a hot white hole, and it pulled a trickle of sweat down his temple. He blinked. He could no longer see the buzzards and was about to say so, when Pike spoke.

"We have an uncle on my ma's side who works for the Lindseys." He said the name as if it didn't belong to Laurence, but to some distant people he had never met. "Uncle Johnny used to come over some nights and tell us stories about people who lived rich like that, in great big houses with a hunnerd windows—"

"Hardly a hundred." Laurence was glad they could not look at each other. His sweat-soaked collar clung to his neck.

"And Gilbert, he used to say he was gonna have a big house with a cook and servants to do the washing and—"

"Why didn't you tell me before?" asked Laurence, interrupting him. "About Johnny."

"Gilbert asked me not to," said Pike. "He doesn't want Uncle Johnny to know a Lindsey whipped him in a fight."

Laurence snorted. The black specks descended, taking shape again.

"What kind of stories did Johnny tell?" he demanded. "Did he say he shot an innocent man?"

"He said he once had to fire at a runaway nigger because Daniel Lindsey asked him and then later he was punished for it."

"That's a lie," Laurence said to the sky.

"He was punished," Pike insisted. "He said it was all the same—no matter what he did that day, it would have been the wrong thing, and they would have punished him for it because they couldn't blame themselves."

"He's a liar," retorted Laurence. "He's a drunk and a thief and a liar. Everybody knows that about Johnny Mulcane."

Pike did not answer this time, although Laurence heard the rail fence creak and Pike's feet thump the ground. The birds were dropping down fast, as if the spiral of air that lifted them had reversed course. Their wings were still rigid. Laurence tried to imagine Johnny Mulcane, but he couldn't see his face, only the edge of his boot as he stood on the roof, sweeping snow down on the yard.

"Anyways, I think I seen one flap." The boy's voice was coppery and final, like a penny falling to a table.

Laurence lowered his head. "I saw it, too," he said, although he knew they both were lying.

Chapter Nine

By the sloped light of midmorning, the regiment reached a stream with a hill swelling behind it, dotted with sweet gum and sycamore. The trees cast a serene, speckled shadow down on the rail fence that crossed the hill. Only the loud racket coming from the other side made it possible for Laurence to believe that this was the entrance to his first battle.

All day, the companies had heard fighting, but it remained in the distance, someone else's story, and while the men told jokes and poked one another with their muskets, Pike and Laurence drifted out of line to gather blackberries, cursing as thorns scraped their wrists. Laurence was gnawing on his last sweet handful when the soldiers' chatter was silenced by Davey's shout to march *quick,* and then *double quick.*

In a chaos of yelling and splashing, the troops crossed a shallow ford. When he reached the soft grass beyond, Laurence looked at the faces of the captains, guessing by their desperate glares that the soldiers had taken more time than the battle plans had allotted them. He wondered where the generals were, with their field glasses and maps. Could they see the outcome already? *Double quick, double quick.* Laurence tossed down his knapsack and bedroll with the others and charged up the hill. His canteen tolled against his chest.

"We'll hang Jeff Davis from a sour apple tree," sang Pike, speeding ahead of Laurence, the soles of his brogans already worn and flopping off.

"'My soul is among lions,'" Gilbert muttered before hurrying after his brother.

Up the hill, the scene changed abruptly, as if a storm had swept across the land but reached no farther than the green summit, the white church rising above it. Everywhere, there were bodies, some scattered, some lined up in rows, and ladies who had come to worship that day in their pastel Sunday dresses were bent over men they had never seen before, trying to keep them from death.

When he reached his first casualty, Laurence halted for a moment, transfixed by the red shell hole gouged in the man's belly and the soft squelching noise that rose out when he tried to breathe. A woman walked by the dying soldier with a pail of water, her stride unbroken by his cries. The man continued to call out after she passed, but when he saw Laurence's eyes on him, he averted his face, ashamed. Behind his ear, a bullet had carved a pathway to his glistening gray brain. Shards of skull lay matted in his hair.

Addison sprinted by, cuffing Laurence on the shoulder, and he started forward again to reach the crest of the hill. Across from him, the white smoke of the rebels' guns puffed up just after the crack of fire. Minié balls whistled past his ears. Suddenly, Laurence was thrown to the ground. Pasture grass ripped at his cheek, cutting the skin.

"I'm shot," he said. He could not feel any pain, but he had read that some fatally injured men went into shock and did not suffer before they died.

"No, you ain't shot yet, you goddamn fool," Addison yelled in his ear. He was lying beside Laurence. "I knocked you down so you wouldn't be. Now load. Davey's about to call the order to fire."

Laurence thought he heard the woman with the water pail scream

73

as he rammed a ball down the barrel of his gun, but when he looked back, he could not see her. Ahead of him, a white house stood on the hill between the armies. Its walls lay in pieces on the ground, boards showing their mottle and knots, bits of glass blinking among them. He finished loading the gun and aimed just to the south of it, toward the Confederate army.

"Fire!" Captain Davey yelled from a few yards away. Addison felled a man on the other side. Laurence's shot went too high, above the heads of the rebels. Fumbling for another bullet, he loaded again, the musket burning his fingers.

"Fire!" Davey's voice rang out.

When his second shot spun into the clouds. Laurence turned to Addison, embarrassed, but his friend was dodging back and forth along the line, rallying the others. He heard a woman shriek once more and realized the sound was coming from the house on the hill.

"There's a woman in there!" he yelled, sitting up, casting about for someone to listen.

Captain Davey did not look at him, absorbed in loading his gun. His squat body pillowed up from the earth. A few rods away, Lyman Woodard turned and blinked, uncomprehending. He lay on his stomach, his hands folded over his head, his gun beside him.

"There's a woman in there!" Laurence yelled again. A blast of grape sailed over the hill and crashed down between him and Woodard, who whimpered and scooted backward on his elbows, leaving the gun behind in the grass.

Davey lifted his gun. "Fire!" he ordered.

A long swath of shingles slid from the roof. Laurence watched it sway on the air, tossed like a maple leaf in autumn. Halfway to the ground, it got caught in the crossfire and split into shards that stabbed the grass below. The woman wailed again, her voice ancient, his mother weeping on winter nights when his father was away, his sisters crying in the next room as they woke from nightmares, a startled lament, one that cannot believe its own origin in sadness and terror, one that will not be comforted. Smoke stung his eyes as he loaded again, tearing the packet of cartridge powder with his teeth, tasting its peppery ash.

He raised his gun, aiming this time at a stocky, wide-hipped secesh with sandy hair and two canteens slung over his shoulder.

"Fire!" Davey sounded distant now.

When Laurence's bullet hit the secesher in the shoulder, the man staggered back, flapping, spinning on his toes as if he thought he might take flight before he fell, face-first, into the torn green pasture.

Later, by the river, Laurence stumbled alone, searching for a place to cross. The captain had yelled to retreat and he had obeyed, moving clumsily back from the firing line and down the hill to the water. His breath came in ragged gasps. He could see his shadow flicker over a body before he registered the body itself, tossed like driftwood onto the shore of weeds.

The boy's legs were splayed, and one arm lay across the barely breathing chest, the other pointing north. Laurence recognized the streaks of berry juice on the small white hands before he recognized the face. He fell to his knees, the impact making his teeth clack together.

Pike's throat had been gashed open by a shell and the long red wing of exposed flesh fluttered lightly when he breathed. Beneath him, the grass was blood black and matted. It reeked of metal, vinegar, and ash. Laurence began to retch, hearing his own voice reciting poetry to the boy in the days before: *I guess it must be the flag of my disposition, out of hopeful green stuff woven.*

When he could sit upright again, Laurence stared at the body, hoping someone else would arrive and tell him what to do. Pike had the half-shut eyes of a man playing the piano or singing alone, transfixed by some inner music. The last time Laurence had seen him, he'd been lying a few feet back from Gilbert, loading and firing. How he had gotten here alone, Laurence could not guess, unless Pike had followed him as he retreated, leaving his brother behind to fight. Laurence would not have seen him. Soon after he began to run, the seceshers had opened up with every last chunk of their artillery, and there was no looking back.

Daylight shuddered on the nearby river. The sounds of the battle receded to a dull thrum. Pike was still breathing, his breath a soft, intermittent rattle. Out of the corner of his eye, Laurence saw a sparrow dive deep into the hedgerow, vanishing. Its wings were flecked with blood.

Soon after, a retreating soldier vaulted right through the bushes and splashed clumsily into the water. The soldier's momentum took him to midstream, where he floundered, batting his hands against the current. So few fellows had ever learned to swim, but Laurence knew how, because his uncle Daniel had taught him in the summers on Lake Champlain. Uncle Daniel entered the water the same slow way each time, walking deeper and deeper, a little smile on his face, as if he enjoyed his own disappearance, limb by limb.

"Help me, goddamn it," the soldier shouted from midriver, waking Laurence from his reverie. He realized he had been waiting for orders and that none would come. It was up to him to save Pike and this stranger, too. His lungs swelled with air. Grasping Pike's skinny ankles, he pulled him gently toward the bank, then leapt into the river. The bridge downstream echoed with the high-pitched screams of horses. Another tug and Pike rolled into the river beside him, his eyes fluttering as his body hit the cool water. Laurence towed the boy by his coat as he swam for the other side. The water sucked at his uniform. His boot-weighted feet felt like hooves, but he had never before felt so sure of his own strength. He kicked hard, and they caught up with the other man, whose arms windmilled wildly but did not propel him forward.

"Stay there. I'll come back and get you," Laurence shouted to the soldier, cupping Pike's skull to keep his nose above water. The gashed neck gurgled as Pike tried to breathe. He hadn't expected the boy to be so heavy. "I just have to get him across, and then I'll come back."

But as the pair began to pass him, the man's wet eyes bulged, and he launched up from the water. Laurence swerved too late. The other soldier managed to wrap his arms around Laurence's neck, plunging him down. He felt the water ride over his head, green-brown and flecked with slow light, and he hung suspended there a moment opposite Pike, too surprised to fight back. He could not hear the battle anymore except for the far-off crash of feet pounding through a crowded ford upstream.

Before him, Pike frowned and twisted his face toward the sky, and for a minute it seemed like the boy might save himself. Pike's arms beat feebly once and his ankles twitched, but the effort failed and he began to sink again. Bits of moss and river silt drifted into his open mouth. A necklace of bubbles spiraled from his throat.

"Goddamn you," Laurence shouted, wasting his last breath, and punched upward at the panicked soldier with his free hand. But the current slowed his fist. Pike's collar tore from his grasp. The boy's body went down, casting a boat-shaped shadow into the river. Laurence punched again, this time kicking with his own frenzied strength. He thrust the man off him and gagged on the wet air. The river tasted like sweat.

"Goddamn you," he screamed again, thrashing around for Pike, but the boy had sunk, irretrievable, to the bottom. When the man lunged again, Laurence bunched his knees and pushed off from the soldier's ribs, cracking them to power himself swiftly toward the bank from which he had come. He closed his eyes to the water streaming over his face. The distance seemed endless as he darted, fishlike, freed of weight. When at last he lifted his waterlogged body onto the muddy earth, he heard the man give a last shout, but he did not look back. Thundering in him was the urge to fight again, even though his weapon was lost, and he started running blindly uphill against a tide of fleeing men.

"There's a black horse cavalry coming," a retreating soldier yelled, his legs tumbling fast down the bank. He wore the tight government-issue coat of New York and his lips were smeared black with cartridge powder. Laurence thought he could hear the rumble of horses, and he turned for a moment to watch the speeding trajectory of the soldier. From his new height, he saw the stone bridge they had used to cross the river the night before. Most of what remained of the Army of the Potomac swirled around it. Another retreating soldier slammed into his back, knocking his breath loose. It was no use. He stumbled down the hill, coughing, holding his bruised neck. The battle was already over and they had lost.

Everywhere, two-wheeled limbers tipped sideways, caissons of minié balls spilling onto the dust. Horses still attached to them screamed and kicked, trying to break free. Dodging past them, Laurence slipped on the canteens and haversacks and bedrolls abandoned by others as they ran. A wagon had overturned on the bridge, blocking the way across, and Laurence had to halt behind it to avoid being kicked by a rearing horse. It was then he first noticed the spectators, picnickers who had flung down their bottles of wine and sandwiches to flee to Washington. A lady in dancing slippers tore out her petticoats and ran like man through the chaos, her hands fisted in her raised skirt. The undergarments swept over the side of the bridge and mushroomed down to the stream.

Beyond her, Laurence saw Addison threading among the horses, cutting them free with his bayonet.

"Don't. You might get hurt," Addison yelled as Laurence fell in behind him. "Stay here and I'll come back and get you."

"Where's Gilbert?"

"Behind us. He lost Pike somehow when Davey called the order to retreat." Addison's eyes swept over him. "What happened to your uniform?" he asked.

The overturned wagon groaned as two soldiers tried to tip it upright.

"We can't wait," Laurence pleaded, unable to answer the question. Drips from his wet clothes splashed on the dust, making dark pocks. He saw Pike drifting down through the water, his arms raised. "There's a black horse cavalry behind us."

"Think I wouldn't know the sound of horses coming? Just set tight right here. I got two more." Addison gestured to a stallion staggering against the side of the bridge, one hind leg dragging. His dusty yellow mane, clotted with mud and ash and blood, stood as erect as the manes on the helmets of ancient knights. It was the only quiet thing in the whole noisy scene, that horse stumbling and righting himself. Laurence watched Addison load his gun and dodge through the crowd. When he reached the animal, the private fired through the yellow temple and danced out of the way. The stallion slumped against the stone rail and nearly fell into the water, but some force kept him suspended, the dead eye aimed toward the center of the earth.

Without further deliberation, Addison jumped on the last mare still attached to a limber and cut her free with two sweeps of his bayonet. He steered the horse toward Laurence and helped him clamber up behind, yanking him forward as he slipped on the wet steam of her hindquarters. They rode bareback into the water, past a parasol embroidered with tiny violets and several drowning havelocks, useless white cloths stitched by industrious mothers and sisters to keep the sun off the necks of their soldiers.

Wading nearby in the shallows of the river was Spider, a high-waisted and balding man from their company. The oldest soldier in the regiment, Spider was the camp's usurer and resident sutler, making loans to the needy soldiers, selling flasks of black-market whiskey. Now he sifted through the wreckage of the picnics and stuffed the waterlogged items in a knapsack that sat like a hump on his spine.

"There's a black horse cavalry coming!" Laurence yelled. He could hear them now, their pounding hoofbeats just over the rim of the hill, and the terrified screams of the men leaping out of their way, the steam rising from the dust, the dust turning to smoke at their hooves. But Spider merely waved gaily back, holding a newly filched pocket watch in his hand. Sunstruck, the round face shone like an eye without a pupil. Laurence shuddered and turned away as the mare charged up the steep bank on the other side. For a moment, it looked as if they were riding straight for the bone-colored clouds.

Chapter Ten

"Did you see him?"

"No. I'm sorry, Rhodes."

"Sorry, fella. He's gone."

"He ain't gone! I heard his voice behind me during the retreat, only I dint retreat yet because there were so many rebs to kill first."

"There was a shell that fell among us as we ran." As we ran. Where had they come to? A place halfway between the battle and the capital. Soldiers from other companies said they would not stop until they got to Washington, but Davey made them halt in the storm beneath a stand of sweet gum and wait while he found Sergeant Hamilton, who had been asking other companies about Pike Rhodes, the only one missing among them. It was getting dark. The trees arched over the gathered men, spilling small handfuls of rain.

"Lindsey, you see him?"

"There was smoke and fire in the air."

"If you seen him wounded, I'm going back."

"He's not wounded, Gilbert." The roots of the sweet gum were ugly, exposed. He wished they were buried.

"Then you seen him. I know it! You seen him and you kept running."

"He was dead." His mouth tasted of metal. "He was dead because he followed me."

"He didn't follow you," said Gilbert, his fists rising.

Laurence lowered his head, waiting for the blows. They had been marching for an hour, but it had not brought him any farther from the grassy bank where he first found the dying boy.

"He did," Laurence muttered at the ground.

"What are you saying, Lindsey?" Gilbert demanded.

A tense silence fell over the crowd, and the rain came down harder, splashing the back of Laurence's skull. What was he saying? That he blamed Pike for losing his life because he followed him? He kicked at the wet roots of the sweet gum.

Addison's voice rang out after a moment. "He must have been lost. You know Pike couldn't find his way out of a round barn, much less a battlefield."

Laurence raised his head, seeing Gilbert consider this.

"The confused little fellow," said a tall, bearded soldier named Alfred Loomis, nodding at Addison as if some unspoken dialogue was passing between them, "he was probably looking for some sugar."

Gilbert's fists stayed high, but the anger in his face began to slip away and he gave Laurence a pitying glance. "He didn't follow you," he repeated.

"Where did you find him, Lindsey?" asked Addison. The white crust of dried horse sweat marked his thighs.

"By the river. His neck was split by a shell," Laurence said haltingly. "He couldn't even breathe through it. . . ." He paused, unwilling to continue.

"Davey can send someone back to fetch him, then," declared Gilbert, touching his own throat. "It won't be hard to find him by the river."

Laurence swallowed and did not answer. He saw his own skepticism reflected in the expressions of others. Davey would not be sending anyone back soon.

Addison opened his mouth as if about to ask something else, but then he shook his head and said quietly, "I should have looked for him after retreat was called."

"I heard him run past me," added Alfred Loomis, tugging at his beard. "I should have stopped him and made him stay by my side."

"I always thought he was hardly old enough to be a drummer boy," Woodard said mournfully, "much less a soldier."

One by one, the men spoke up while Laurence and Gilbert stood close in the center of them, not fighting, breathing each other's breath. Gilbert's coat was torn across the shoulder. Rain fell on the long scrape beneath and made his blood run in pink streaks down his shirt. Behind him, Alfred Loomis began binding another soldier's arm with strips of a picnic cloth the spectators had left behind. And there were more injuries—Woodard limping on a twisted ankle, Addison's wrist bruised from where a panicked horse had bitten him—but none that would stop their whole company from going into the next battle, because there would be a next one, and a next. To redeem Pike's lost life, they would have to fight until every last picnic blanket in Washington was torn up for bandages and the rivers filled with the dead. That was the way it would be in every company, Union or secesh, now that this day was over.

"Did he say anything?" Gilbert whispered finally.

Laurence was about to explain that Pike had been past speech, but then he looked Gilbert straight in the eye and answered loudly, for all of the men to hear. "He asked me if we won," he said. "I told him yes."

July 26, 1861

Chapter Eleven

Heat changed the color of the world outside the party, bleaching the land and trees to a dull gold. It looked like the coat of a lion, Bel decided. She stood at the rim of the gathered adults in her yellow party dress with the frilled sleeves, lace neckline, and green ivy her mother had painstakingly embroidered around the hem. She longed to taste a cake from the laden table, but no one was eating yet except for the flies that wagged back and forth over the piles of food, shooed by servants' hands.

It was strange that Aunt Pattie had chosen not to cancel her recitation party when they first heard news of the fighting in Virginia, but she claimed she wanted to distract herself from worry over Laurence, and to honor her good daughters. Lucia and Anne were graduating from Mrs. Laurel Ellsley's School for Young Women, a place Faustina insisted Bel would never attend, as she didn't approve of the way Mrs. Ellsley taught girls to be subservient and meek. A thin blond woman with big teeth, a refined Boston accent, and the lidded gaze of a lizard, Mrs. Ellsley once had a husband, but he had died in a train wreck, leaving her childless. To pay her way, she started a finishing school at her house, which quickly became popular with the wealthy mothers around town.

Bel was afraid of Mrs. Ellsley, and she suspected that the girls who went to be "finished" felt the same way. Even sanguine Lucia and Anne spoke their schoolmistress's name with the lengthened syllables of weariness and obligation. But Faustina outright disliked the teacher, and, to challenge her methods of instruction, she had forced Bel to learn the longest recitation of all: King Henry V's speech to his men at Harfleur, Shakespeare's famous rallying cry to stir the British soldiers to victory. Bel would precede Lucia and Anne's verses from Tennyson with her bold and patriotic call to arms, and she resented it completely.

The gathered crowd was composed of mostly women, along with a few fathers and even fewer suitors. The majority of the affluent young men were waiting by the post office, eschewing the delicate speeches of ladies for the real news—who had won, who had lost, who had died. She imagined their upright male bodies as they jostled one another, kicking up dust on the dry ground, pipe smoke curling from their mouths. Even the boys who opposed the war had taken to talking about it as if they knew all about drilling and marching and battle strategies.

"First and foremost," Mrs. Ellsley began her introductory remarks, "I would like to thank the mothers of these talented and excellently trained girls, for they lead by example, while I can only instruct."

Faustina bent down to whisper into her daughter's ear. "Are you ready?"

Bel nodded, inhaling her mother's clean scent. She was proud that Faustina was the prettiest woman in the room, prettier even than Lucia and Anne, whom everyone called the "golden Lindsey girls"— a reference Bel's mother said was crass, and not entirely related to their blond hair. She was ready, but she would have to wait through several of the graduates first. At the front of the room, Mrs. Ellsley was introducing Mary Ruth Cross, who would recite a portion of *The Song of Hiawatha.*

It was a very short portion indeed, and delivered in a blushing stammer that made the gathered mothers wave their fans faster, as if to speed up time itself. The fathers loaded their pipes and settled in for a long wait through Hannah Fithian's tolerable version of Milton's "When I Consider How My Light Is Spent," and several attempts at Psalm 23 by the girls who so succeeded at Mrs. Ellsley's schooling that they could not decide anything for themselves and had gratefully accepted an assignment. Upon the last half-whispered "and I will dwell in the house of the Lord for ever," Mrs. Ellsley cleared her throat viciously and announced that they had a "special guest" in Miss Isabel Lindsey, who had not attended her school but who had undertaken the task of memorizing Shakespeare. The audience clapped dutifully. Swaying slightly in the new heaviness of her petticoats, Bel walked to the front and faced them all.

In the back, by the tall windows that looked out on the road, Lucia and Anne stood with Morey Aldridge, the son of a shipbuilder. His severe features had been transformed lately into awkward grins and guffaws by the twins' attentions. Aldridge was rumored to be coming into a large inheritance, and the twins fought over him with gentle savagery, each employing her best wiles. Lucia was winning, for she had a prettier voice than Anne, and her low, indulgent laugh was contagious. She had worn her sallow blond hair loose for the occasion, and it hung limply in the heat, but Anne's was worse, knotted in numerous braids that wound around her head like snakes. Bel saw Morey Aldridge whisper something in Lucia's ear, his black eyebrows knitting together. When Lucia smothered a giggle with her hand, Bel was suddenly struck by the fear that soon they might all be laughing at her.

Although she had uttered the speech a thousand times, now the dull, expectant eyes of two dozen adults and children blended into one giant gaze. Opening her mouth, Bel waited for the sound to rise as it always did, but nothing came. The wind blowing through the propped door smelled like sawdust from the lumberyards. Her neck itched. Then, looking out the window behind Lucia's head, way in the distance, Bel glimpsed a boy running up the lane toward her uncle's house. He must be coming from the post office, she thought, and the wonder at the news he would bring jarred her into speech. She had to say it now, or she might never again get the chance.

> *"Once more unto the breach, dear friends, once more,*
> *Or close up the wall with our English dead!*
> *In peace there's nothing so becomes a man*
> *As modest stillness and humility . . ."*

The boy stumbled and fell to his knees, ripping a hole in his trousers. He rose and ran on, the torn piece flapping. His blond hair slapped against wide red ears. Bel recognized him, the son of the liveryman in town. His hair was always too long and his pants too short, and he often delivered messages because he was the fastest runner among all the boys, even barefoot. The speech came easily now, but the messenger was so close, she could see the spurs of dust lifting from his heels. She went on, watching him come, his face tight with excitement. What would he say? Would the war be over? Would Laurence come home?

" 'On, on, you noble New Englanders,' " she commanded, changing the speech, as the fathers and mothers began to turn to the sound of the boy's feet on the stairs, in the hallway, at the door. " 'Whose blood is fet from fathers of war-proof! Fathers that like so many Alexanders, have in these parts from morn to even fought, and sheathed their swords for lack of argument.' "

But the boy was shouting over her now, and the men were rising to surround him. He was saying McDowell had lost, that it was a great rout—"the great skedaddle," the boys at the post office were calling it. And the wounded? (For they could not say *dead.*)

"There's a list," the boy said. The men began throwing on their coats, the women folding their fans, lifting bonnets from the backs of chairs. "I have it memorized," he boasted, and the commotion came to a halt. The men nodded proudly, staring at his sunburned cheeks.

"Tell us," shouted Uncle George. He was one of the few men in the room with sons fighting in Virginia.

"No, come to the front and tell us," Mrs. Ellsley said encouragingly, and led him right up beside Bel in her yellow summer dress with the green ivy stitched along the hem. For the first time in her life, she became fully aware of how others must see her, standing there in that frilly gown with her budding breasts pressed up by the bodice, her hands fisted like a boy's. She saw how she refused to move aside at first, the speech still in her mouth, the dream of the war's glory ending as she was dragged away by her mother, who sat her down on a chair, hard, so a pain jolted up her spine.

The boy began to recite his litany of names, those who had fallen at a place called Bull Run, the wounded first, then the dead. It was shorter than they anticipated, the numbers of Allenton's sons who had enlisted fewer than they thought. Laurence's name was not among them. Neither were the poorer cousins of the Pomeroys, two boys who had gone off on the same train in April, nor the husbands of their servant girls. In fact, the crowd had to strain to recognize the dead, who were the faceless lumber workers' sons and brothers, and the farmers scratching a living from the soil outside town. For a moment, Bel had the feeling that it wasn't their war at all, but someone else's, to which they listened with voyeuristic intensity in order to find out what it was like to suffer.

But then her uncle called out that he knew three of the men. They were his sawyers and lumberjacks, and Daniel should know them, as well. Bel saw her father nod and turn to a window as if to witness the dead soldiers departing right then into the clear blue sky.

"Shall we have a prayer?" Mrs. Ellsley put her hands on the boy's shoulder, directing him to heaps of cakes and sandwiches, on which he began obligingly to gorge. His scraped knee was bleeding, but everyone ignored it. "Girls—Hannah, Jane, Clara—I'd like you to come up again and lead us in Psalm Twenty-three," commanded the schoolmistress.

Bel thought the adults would protest at this, but they leaned forward in their seats, eager, fans snapping open again, new pipefuls lighted. And the three girls, with obedient, downcast eyes, stumbled through their verses once more, only to have the adults join in this time, murmuring at first, then speaking louder and louder. Bel sank low in her seat, hearing the lost words of King Henry V in her mind: "And you, good yeomen, Whose limbs were made in England, show us here the mettle of your pasture." Didn't anyone care that they had lost? King Henry would have cared. King Henry would have told them to keep their eyes on the final goal, which was, in Bel's mind, and, she was sure, in Laurence's, to end slavery. At least he was alive.

Aunt Pattie began to pass out the tea cakes, then called for Mary, on loan from Greenwood, to start pouring the punch. The neat rows broke into untidy groups, the adults' voices hoarse, as if they had all been talking for a long time. Bel's mother turned to her, her face strangely vibrant. "Aren't you glad?" she said. "Laurence is fine. We would have heard otherwise by now, don't you think?"

But Bel was staring out at the lawn, where the young boys circled around the son of the liveryman, listening to him recite the names over and over, dying mock deaths as he did so. Their bodies collapsed on the grass, then leapt up again. They held invisible bayonets and fought against one another with their mouths open, limbs as fluid as animals. Bel struggled to stand in her heavy dress, conscious of the rim of sweat beneath her lace neckline, and of the drooping ivy-laden hem.

"You looked beautiful up there," her mother said quietly. "I wish you could have finished."

"Yes," Bel said, and walked toward her cousins, Lucia and Anne, who had burst into happy tears and were being comforted by Morey Aldridge. Lucia smiled and took his handkerchief to dry her eyes, her fist hardening around it as if she might never let go of the snowy cloth. "We're so lucky," she said to Bel when she approached, and Bel nodded solemnly, knowing it was true, that they might have found out that very afternoon that they had lost Laurence.

"We're so lucky," Anne echoed. "I was dreading having to go up there, and now I think Mrs. Ellsley has entirely forgotten."

"We're done with all that," Lucia said with her beautiful laugh. She looked defiantly at Morey Aldridge, who responded by giving her a grim smile and taking the opportunity to touch her arm. "We're 'finished,'" she added. "We're women now."

July 1861–September 1862

Chapter Twelve

After a few days of marching and waiting for orders from a soon-to-be replaced General McDowell, Davey set the company to building a new camp outside Washington. As they dug latrines and square holes for their quarters, news came from Sergeant Hamilton, who had been sent back as part of a large detail to gather the dead from the battlefield. Pike's body had not been found. He was officially counted as missing, assumed dead.

Hearing this, Gilbert hounded Laurence for more details, but Laurence would reveal nothing else. He couldn't explain about the other soldier now because it would sound like an excuse. "I found him by the river," he said over and over, "and then he died." Gilbert finally gave up, but in the meantime, Laurence discovered that his companions had grown clumsy around him with their shovels, sometimes casting dirt toward his lowered face, or jabbing his feet with the blade itself, never apologizing before they turned away. Red ants appeared in his bedroll, and his canteen was often emptied surreptitiously.

One night after the building of the camp was nearly done, a high, razoring sound filled the air. The soldiers looked up from their fires, to see Laurence prop his book against his ribs and begin to tear. White leaves fell to the ground around him. They were ankle-deep when Gilbert, hard-faced, grabbed a page and began to read aloud. " 'Has any one supposed it lucky to be born? I hasten to inform him or her it is just as lucky to die, and I know it.' " He threw the page into the fire. A flame speared up the middle of the paper, ghosting it black.

Laurence paused in his tearing and peered at the others. His blond hair had lightened to a feathery gold and it hung in his eyes as he crouched down among the torn pages and began to collate small piles, doling them out to different members in the regiment. The men who could not read handed the pages to their friends, who whispered over the text, cruelly at first, as if they thought Laurence was trying to make amends. He went back to ripping, but he heard the verses rising from their awkward mouths.

" 'Loaf with me on the grass . . . loose the stop from your throat.' "

" 'Urge and urge and urge, always the procreant urge of the world'—whatever the hell that means. What the hell do you think it means, Loomis?"

" 'What do you think has become of the young and old men? What do you think has become of the women and children?' "

Laurence tore until there was nothing left except the empty covers and the frontispiece, where the author lounged, his undershirt showing. These he shoved in his haversack, next to the letters from home.

"Say, this ain't half-bad," said Alfred Loomis, the tall soldier who had spoken up first about Pike after Bull Run. He stroked his heavy black beard. "Listen to this: 'I mind how we lay in June, such a transparent summer morning. You settled your head athwart my hips and gently turned over upon me—' "

"No wonder you couldn't put it down at night, Lindsey," said Woodard, his tone nasal, judging, although Laurence had never told of his comrade's cowardice at Bull Run. "It was a dirty book."

"It wasn't a dirty book," Laurence said in a low voice.

Gilbert grunted and inched closer to the fire, poking the last of his verse to ash.

"What is it, then?" Addison's voice rang out. He was watching Laurence curiously, his pages propped on his knees, unread.

Instead of answering him, Laurence swept the remaining paper into his arms and rose to walk toward the creek that ran near their camp. The pages looked like a white bird mashed against his chest.

"Read some more, Loomis," urged Woodard as Laurence crossed out of the firelight.

"All right." Loomis gave his audience a twinkling glance. "We had the head on the hips part, and now we get: 'And parted the shirt from my bosom-bone, and plunged your tongue to my barestript heart.' " He stopped and tugged at his whiskers.

"Read the rest," said Gilbert, his eyes flicking to Addison, who stood up and followed Laurence.

"It ain't so great after that," mused Loomis. " 'And reached until you felt my beard, and reached until you held my heart,' " he finished lamely. "It goes on, but the good part's over."

"I don't care," raged Gilbert. He lurched up and stood over the other man. A light wind flattened his shirt over his ribs. "I said, read the rest."

"All right," Loomis said. "It's long, though:

"Swiftly arose and spread around me the peace and joy and
    knowledge that pass all the art and argument of the earth;
And I know that the hand of God is the elderhand of my own,
And I know that the spirit of God is the eldest brother of my own,
And that all men ever born are also my brothers . . .
    and the women my sisters and lovers,
And that a kelson of the creation is love;

And limitless are leaves stiff and drooping in the fields,
And brown ants in the little wells beneath them,
And mossy scabs of the wormfence, and heaped stones,
*   and elder and mullen and pokeweed."*

"All right," said Gilbert, echoing Loomis's pet phrase. "Now burn it."

"No."

Laurence heard the refusal as he strode toward the creek. He stared at the stars leaking through the sieve of night.

"Who does he think he is, saying things like that? It ain't Christian, talking about ants and people like they're worth the same." Gilbert's rant pierced the air, making Laurence smile a little to himself. The pages rustled as he pressed them closer to his chest, and he did not hear Addison following him until the other man called his name.

"Lindsey. Where you going?"

"To the creek," Laurence said.

"Why?"

"I can't read it anymore—" He stopped, his throat closing.

"What really happened by the river that day?" Addison was a blue shape in the dark behind him. "If you just told, they'd stop." He paused. "You were soaked to the skin. I remember."

Laurence reached the cluster of bushes that guarded the creek and pushed through. The pages glowed in the moonlight as he knelt down and scattered them on the water. Some sank right away, dragged down by their corners. Others floated on the black current like shavings of starlight. Somewhere, in the rivers of Virginia, a boy's body tossed against the silt, crossed by fish and rain. Every day, another piece of him drifted away.

"Pike was almost dead when I found him," Laurence said wearily. "He would have died no matter what I did."

"What did you do?" Addison was above him now, his face framed by thorns. Laurence shook his head and began to tell about wanting to save Pike and the other soldier and how he had almost lost his own life. When he finished, all the pages had sunk or drifted past the oxbow's curve and out of sight. His fingers felt chapped, and he stuck them in the warm water, feeling it slide through his fingers.

"If you had only told me then," said Addison in a voice thick with grief.

"Then what?" said Laurence. "He'd still be dead. That's what they don't understand."

As he stood up, Laurence slipped on the mud and had to grab Addison's sleeve. The new blue uniform was coarse and stiff. "No matter what I said, they'd both be dead," he added.

"You're right," Addison admitted after a moment. He turned his back on Laurence and pushed out of the brush, holding the branches so they did not slap his companion.

"Sometimes you can't be the hero and live," said Laurence bitterly. He took the branches from Addison's hands, waiting for the other man to answer. But Addison said nothing as they walked past the tents to the fire where the soldiers were swapping pages with one another, trading for ones they liked better. Only Gilbert sat alone, fiercely polishing his brogans with grease.

"Sunday morning, we're going pig hunting," Addison whispered before they rejoined the others.

"Who, you and Gilbert?" Laurence asked. "I thought he was going on picket."

"No, you and me," Addison said. "In honor of Pike Rhodes."

Chapter Thirteen

"You've never hunted before, have you?" Addison said after they had crept past the dewy tents and into the brush beyond. The air was cool and still and every sound they made intruded on the quiet, bruise-colored world. But Laurence dutifully scoured the dim forest with his eyes, looking left and right for pigs.

"One time, my father tried to organize a fox hunt, like they have in England, but he couldn't get the right hounds," he said.

"I reckoned." Addison sighed. "You go about it wrong."

"What do you mean?"

"Don't look. Listen. You can't stare down a pig."

Laurence closed his eyes obediently. He heard a spring trickling nearby, and the ticking sound of leaves.

"What are you doing?" Addison hissed, already ten paces ahead of him. "Keep walking, but keep your ears open, too."

The veil of dark lifted shade by shade as Laurence followed his friend deeper into the woods. Soon it would be dawn and reveille would call them back to camp, but for now there were only the trees sharpening their branches on the faint light and a few birds that scuttled through the canopy.

The dimness reminded him of his house on winter Sundays, when the drapes would stay shut against the chilly dark and everyone spoke in muted voices. On such mornings, his mother would read to him and his sisters from the Bible while they squirmed and longed for the noon meal, usually ham and stewed cabbage that would grow translucent and cold before Laurence could finish eating it. His father always presided at mealtime, quizzing them on the stories of the Old Testament.

"Who was David's downfall?" he once asked, sipping from a heavy pewter cup.

"Absalom," Laurence answered, remembering the unfaithful son.

"Bath-sheba," his father corrected him, thumping the cup for emphasis. His mother sighed and rubbed her temples.

"His own pride," she said to her plate.

"By golly!" A great crashing sound followed Addison's cry, and a sow appeared, her skin the color of milk after strawberries have rested in it. She plowed through Addison's bowlegs and started huffing right toward Laurence. Falling on her with a heavy *ooof*, he buckled his arms around her belly as she kicked and dragged him across the roots of an oak tree. Her back hooves dug into his chest, and she began making the ugliest noise Laurence had ever heard. He roared to cover it.

"Hold her now," Addison said. He loaded his musket and aimed at the sow. Laurence shied from the dark hollow of the gun, and the pig would have escaped had one hoof not tangled in the buttons of his uniform. Moss and dirt flew everywhere, landing on Laurence's open mouth.

"Hold her," Addison commanded again, and this time Laurence obeyed, his fingers digging in the furrowed throat. The bullet entered the sow's face, splitting the forehead between her small eyes. She shuddered and her violent squalling halted abruptly in a slow sigh, like air escaping a tin can. As the heat left the slumped body, Laurence continued to hold the sow until a dark, reeking puddle leaked from her hindquarters and then he flung himself away.

"I forgot to warn you about that," Addison said, smirking at the fresh brown stain on Laurence's coat.

Laurence stood, scrubbing at the stain with a handful of leaves, his palms stinging from the sow's coarse hair. The pig twitched a little, and Addison gave her head a final whack with the butt end of his musket.

"You caught her." He punched Laurence's arm. "You're the bulliest pig catcher I ever seen. You can quote me on that to your pa when he tries to pull strings for your promotion."

"I don't want to be promoted," Laurence said as Addison handed him his haversack and musket and knelt down by the pig. "I don't want to be an officer."

Addison sliced the sow's throat. Blood spurted out, pattering the leaf-strewn forest floor like a sudden rain.

"It'll be best to gut her now," he muttered as the stream of blood slowed, "even though Loomis won't like it. We have a far piece to haul her."

He shifted on his haunches and cut a line down the sow's belly.

"Why won't Loomis like it?" asked Laurence. The tall, genial Alfred Loomis was now a denizen of their tent and had become their default cook, disguising their meager rations with fresh herbs he found in the forests and fields around camp.

"Never slaughtered a hog before?" Addison looked up, his knife pausing. "Generally you boil them first to get the bristles off and then you work on the innards. Keeps the flavor rich. But I ain't dragging this thing two miles with the guts still in it. Now hold the skin open, if you will, sir."

Laurence crouched beside the maw of sow intestines, his hand slipping on a bloodied nipple as he pried the skin aside. The ribs creaked apart with the slow complaint of long-shut doors. Inside, the steaming guts were black and red, and Addison was doing his best to saw them out in their entirety, but the loops of intestine kept slipping off and battering his wrist. Laurence gave one bark of laughter before he saw deep in the cavity beneath the sow's flank the sleep-eyed bodies of half a dozen piglets curled against one another. Addison's knife cut the veiny sack around them and a bluish water spilled out.

Laurence gagged, unable to tear his gaze away. The fetuses each had perfect, unhardened hooves and blank pink skin.

"Don't breathe through your nose," Addison advised, still carving. Just then, guts came out, sliding across Laurence's knees, their weight slippery and hard at once. He swore and shoved them off.

"Why not be an officer, Lindsey?" Addison demanded, his voice ugly. "Can't watch 'em die?" He was cutting the fetal pigs away from their mother now, and they tumbled to the earth, still curled and breathing. Unwilling to answer, Laurence let the sow's ribs fall shut and wiped his hands against the pine needles. Red crescents curved under his fingernails. Nearby, a crow scraped its throat into call.

Standing up, Addison took his musket and gently began to crush the heads of the fetal pigs, one by one, letting the wet brains spill out. After a moment, Laurence joined him, pressing down until the small unfinished skulls popped and the trembling life exited the bodies. Above the quiet of their work, a metallic chorus of crickets commenced singing.

When the soldiers were finished, the fetuses no longer curled around one another, but splayed apart, like petals torn from a flower.

"We can toast these up for a first course," Addison said, tossing them back inside the carcass. Laurence nodded dully. An intense weariness had replaced his nausea. He picked up his end of the sow and they began dragging her toward camp. Behind him, he heard the crow flap down to the steaming pile.

"You never answered my question," Addison commented after a few minutes. Laurence regarded his friend's blood-spattered profile.

"Who'd want to be in charge of that bunch of fools?" he said with false levity.

"Those fools are going to be the best goddamn soldiers in the Army of the Potomac." Addison turned on him, his face serious. "I didn't see one of them shirk at Bull Run. Not a one."

Laurence thought of Woodard and Spider but said nothing. They dragged the pig in silence for a while. "It's not just that," Laurence added hoarsely. "I'd be above the rest of you."

"So? You always have been. Even with what happened to Pike. You're probably the only man in the company who can swim, and it was your knowing too much that got you in trouble. But as an officer, being different wouldn't hinder you like that," Addison said, readjusting his hold on the hooves. "I told Davey so."

"I'm not that different," Laurence said, thinking of the ants in his bedroll, the dirt chucked in his face.

"What I mean is, you're just not our kind. We don't understand you so much as we understand each other. Gilbert, I would have known what he would do every day of his life, even if I just met him here in Virginia." Addison looked up at the trees, giving a soft chuckle. "You're like a gentleman stranger."

"Is that what I am?" Laurence tried to laugh, but the noise that emerged from his throat was more like a ragged sigh.

Reaching the rim of the forest just as the bugler began reveille, they scanned the camp. Gilbert was out on picket and Alfred Loomis sat alone in front of their fire, darning his socks, in what had become an almost-daily ritual. His feet were too big for the standard army footwear, and he refused to learn a proper stitch, making clumsy black loops that tore almost immediately.

Addison and Laurence pulled the sow toward their tent. The dusty ground flattened behind them, two furrows pushed up on either side. A slow parade of half-dressed soldiers rose from their fires and began to follow.

"Damn if it ain't a real porker," said one of the drummer boys.

"Shot right through the forehead," another soldier added admiringly.

Addison and Laurence ignored them both, their heads high.

"How'd you catch it?" Loomis asked as they reached the Sibley.

"Lindsey here just stared her down. I've never seen a hunter like him. The way he caught her was a caution. All eyes," Addison finally pronounced for the soldiers pulling on their coats and boots. Laurence lowered his head, noticing a splash of brain on the butt end of his musket. He wiped it clean on the grass.

"That so," Loomis said calmly, placing a few stones in the hollows of the campfire. "I don't suppose it was your idea to gut her, though, was it?"

Laurence shook his head.

"It wasn't your idea to destroy the tender flavor of this fine game by asking me to boil it hacked open like this?" Loomis went on, and then instructed two of the camp's drummer boys to fetch more water from the stream.

"I'll bet there's not a man here who would refuse this fine game, no matter how you ruin it with your cooking, Loomis," said Addison, casting a proud glance around. The gathered soldiers cheered and laughed, and a few of them thumped Laurence on the back and congratulated him before they hurried off to roll call. In return for a good piece of meat, Woodard would make their excuse known to Davey.

"There's a surprise inside for you, Loomis," said Laurence, getting into his role. He stood with one hand on his hip and grinned as Loomis pulled open the sow and found the fetal pigs inside.

"That almost makes up for it," Loomis said with a twist of his lips, and tossed them on one side of the fire.

When the boys came back with the water, Loomis sent them off again to borrow another company's massive cooking pot. The morning grew hotter, and Laurence could hear the other soldiers answering at roll call. He had never missed it before, and he wondered what Captain Davey would say when he saw the hog, if he would believe Laurence was the one who had caught her.

The boys returned, dragging the black iron pot, which Loomis filled halfway with water. Then he took a pair of tongs and lifted the hot stones, dropping them in until a great steam billowed out. Somehow, the sow seemed lighter as Laurence helped Loomis carry her to the pot and ease her in. Watching the water rise, he asked Loomis if he thought the meat would be enough for the whole company.

"Enough," Loomis repeated, looking hard at Laurence. "How much do you think they need?"

Laurence blushed and looked down. In the boiling water, the sow flesh whitened, and Loomis moved it slowly around with his tongs.

"Just catching it was enough," Loomis said in his gentle bass. "Although, you know, Addison's been tracking that sow for weeks by himself."

Surprised, Laurence turned to Addison, but the other man was halfway down the path to the stream, his shadow lengthening like a sail behind him.

"Don't tell him I said so," Loomis added.

"No," Laurence said, both grateful for the gift Addison had given him and relieved that he had passed his test. He breathed in as Loomis let another hot stone fall, hissing, into the water. The steam smelled like the dense air that filled the kitchen at Greenwood when Grete cooked up bones for soup. Laurence felt his empty stomach twinge with hunger and something deeper releasing itself with the white clouds rising.

"Smells like home," he said, and breathed in again.

Chapter Fourteen

Emerging from his bedroll to the cold yellow air of the tent, Laurence coughed and rubbed his temples. Winter sickness had swept through the camp since November, leaving no one untouched except Addison, who remained singularly robust while the rest of the soldiers became as thin and rheumy as old men. Laurence counted himself lucky to be suffering from a mild cough. Measles had struck the Third Vermont, and today he was going to visit a recently recovered soldier, Morey Aldridge, an Allenton boy, the son of a shipbuilder, and the man his sister Lucia was engaged to marry.

Morey Aldridge. Laurence imagined him a male version of Lucia, bright and empty-headed, a dandy who polished his boots daily. Morey Aldridge would find Laurence too serious, no doubt, and write to his sister about how he intended to cheer her brother up. It would become a weekly ordeal, Sunday afternoons with Morey, so that they could get to know each other better, and become like real brothers.

Laurence glanced down at his mother's letter. *Please go meet Mr. Aldridge when you have the time,* she wrote. *He is so looking forward to making your acquaintance.* The letter was a month old, and Laurence had found one reason or another to put off the visit until today. He wondered why he dreaded meeting someone from his own society. Beside him, Addison and Gilbert snored loudly, and Loomis was curled into an awkward ball, only his beard poking from the blanket. These were his brothers, men who rarely read books or parted their hair in the latest fashion, but who understood him better than anyone.

Over the winter, their routine together had changed. Drills were shorter; nights in the tent stretched to a huddled eternity. They were always cold, always hungry, and they became domestic, bickering over the placement of their few possessions, developing an ever greater fixation with the intricacies of mealtime. Nights when rations were poor, they talked about catching another pig and building a smokehouse to make bacon and ham. This fantasy lasted through entire sodden meals of hardtack stew. Loomis and Gilbert could haggle for hours about the best wood for smoking or the correct temperature for the fire, then resume the conversation the next night as if nothing had been decided.

Laurence had a difficult time explaining such humble camaraderie to his family, so he stopped writing as many letters home. Even Bel's little sketches of frost, flowers, and other familiar household items seemed to belong to another time. But he collected them dutifully in the flaps of his torn-up book and carried them everywhere.

The bleating notes of reveille filled the air, and Addison bolted awake, his blue eyes landing on Laurence.

"Sunday, ain't it?" he asked.

Laurence nodded.

"Praise the Lord for this half day of drill," said Addison. He threw off his covers and rose.

"I'm going to see my future brother-in-law today," Laurence said. "Want to come?" Addison's easy way with people would make it more bearable.

"Can't," Addison said, and lifted the flap of the tent, revealing a dull gray day. "Davey promised he'd let me take Furlough for a ride."

When they woke, his other tent mates also declined the offer, so after drill, Laurence set out alone for the Third Vermont's quarters. A muddy path led him through pitted pastures and bare, silvery woods, ending at a small sea of Sibley tents, sunk into the ground like their own. He couldn't help thinking that the Third Vermont's camp looked shabbier than his regiment's, but the men were just as lively, and when he asked how to find Morey Aldridge, a young recruit immediately offered complicated and colorful directions, which sent him to the latrines first, then to the officers' quarters, and finally to the tent Morey Aldridge shared with two other soldiers.

The trio sat outside it around a low fire, playing a silent game of cards. Uncertain which was Aldridge, Laurence called out the name and waited. At first, there was no response; then the largest among them raised his head. His mountainous shoulders took a long time to twist in Laurence's direction.

"Looks like you got a visitor, Aldridge," said one of his companions.

Morey Aldridge's gray eyes widened at the sight of Laurence, but he nodded slowly. "You must be Lucia's brother," he said. "I can see the resemblance."

His face was full of crags and shadows, his mouth a straight, severe line of red, as if someone had drawn it with a ruler. Measle scars dotted his neck and chin. Laurence hovered for a moment, staring, before he realized his rudeness. He introduced himself and was about to sit down among them, when Aldridge held up his hand.

"Let's take a walk together," he suggested. "I've been sitting at this fire too long."

Nodding again at men whose names he would never remember, Laurence allowed Aldridge to lead him silently out of the camp and into the woods beyond. As soon as they had entered the trees, the other soldier slowed and turned.

"You must think I'm impolite," he said, the cold air making ghosts of his words. "But I wanted to speak with you alone, and I'm never alone in camp."

"I'm glad to meet you finally," Laurence said truthfully, relieved that Aldridge was nothing like the dandy he had expected.

"Likewise." Aldridge inclined his head. "Although your sister told me so many stories about her dear Laurence, I felt like I already had." He swiveled back around and strode deeper into the winter woods. Dead leaves crunched beneath their feet. "In fact, I wouldn't be here if it weren't for you."

There was no accusation in this statement, but still it surprised Laurence. "What do you mean?"

"Your sister wants to marry a hero like her brother," said Aldridge, veering from the path they had been following, his gait heavy and purposeful.

"I'm hardly a hero," said Laurence. "And anyway, my father would probably approve if you refused to fight. He never wanted me to enlist."

"He's proud of you, too."

"He must put up a good show, then," Laurence said.

"Times have changed since you left," said Aldridge. "With so many fellows gone off to war, it's all anyone talks about anymore. And that gives your father a lot to say."

"You understand him well." Laurence laughed, but Aldridge did not join in, guiding them toward a bower of pines, the green needles luminous in the dull light.

"I was planning to join the navy eventually, but Lucia begged me to go to Virginia and take down General Lee with my bare hands," he said, raising one massive fist as they pushed through the soft wall of needles. "Anyway, there's something in here I wanted to show you."

The smell of pitch filled Laurence's nostrils and made him miss his aunt's annual Twelfth Night party, when all of Greenwood was festooned in hemlock and spruce. He could imagine his father there, holding forth on the war, a respected authority because his son was at the front.

"Your father was a navy man, wasn't he?" he said, emerging from the pines into a small clearing.

If Aldridge responded, Laurence didn't hear, stopped in his tracks by the sight in front of him. Rising from the dead leaves was an immaculate waist-high ship constructed from whittled branches, complete with a slender mast, birch-bark sails, and an anchor of twigs trussed together with grass. All the wood had been carved past the bark, and it had a muted white hue, resembling old snow. If it were ever set on the sea, it would look like a ghost ship, but it seemed at home on the wavy russet floor of the Virginia woods. Laurence walked around the vessel slowly, taking in the portholes and the tiny helm, the name etched on the stern, *Lucia*.

"How on earth did you make this?"

"While I was sick, I worked on one piece at a time," said Aldridge. "After I got well, I came out here and put it together."

"You should take it into camp," Laurence said. "This would be the bulliest thing they've ever seen."

"I can't. My captain would accuse me of idleness," said Aldridge. "Besides, I don't want word getting back to Lucia that I'd rather be a shipbuilder than a soldier."

"You should be a shipbuilder." Laurence watched Aldridge straighten a sail with his large hands.

"The sparrows like to play on it," he said. "Maybe they dream of being gulls on the sea."

"Are you just going to leave it here?" asked Laurence

Aldridge regarded him for a long moment, his dark brows sinking.

"It kept me alive, putting her together. And now that she's finished . . ." He shrugged, trailing off.

"But you're well now," Laurence protested. "You don't need it anymore."

"I love your sister." Aldridge sounded ashamed. He went back to looking at the ship.

"She loves you," Laurence said, although he couldn't imagine his frivolous sister saying the words in seriousness.

"If you bend down here," said Aldridge, "you can see below-decks." He motioned for Laurence to see, and then, circling the ship, he pointed out all its features with grave pride. Laurence followed, stooping, praising, watching his future brother-in-law out of the corner of his eye. Morey Aldridge reminded him of his uncle Daniel, a man who tired of people easily and preferred to work alone with inanimate things, making them come alive. Laurence liked Aldridge immensely, but he also had the feeling that they could never be friends. There was too much between them and too little time to understand it in their soldiering lives.

Aldridge seemed to sense this as well, and when they finished examining the ship, he and Laurence walked back toward his camp without speaking. The woods were brighter now, and Aldridge's face glowed like white granite, his measle scars fading. When they reached the rim of the forest, he halted and held out his hand.

"I'll see you again," he said, and Laurence had the curious impression that Aldridge was looking right through him to something beyond.

"Of course." He tried to sound casual. "You should visit me next, although I have nothing so astounding to show you."

"Please don't speak of my ship to anyone," Aldridge said. "I'm going to destroy it before we move again."

"I won't," Laurence assured him. "I'm not sure they'd believe me anyway." Then he took his leave of Aldridge, almost running back to his own camp, eager to get home.

Soon after, both regiments were transported by ship to Fort Monroe, where, on a low peninsula, McClellan would assemble them to attack the enemy unawares. Laurence caught sight of Aldridge on another deck, staring out to sea, his thighs pressed against the rail. Gulls wheeled between them, crying, coasting on the warm spring wind. Laurence waved, but when Aldridge did not respond, he let his arm fall and watched the other man open his mouth to the salty air, taking great, needy gulps, as if he hoped it would drown him.

Chapter Fifteen

In a month, the icy mirror of April rains would narrow to a crooked stream, but now it claimed the whole field, shimmering with reflected clouds. It was the kind of place Laurence remembered geese landing on their way north, their beaky cries and dense, perfect bodies heralding spring. One day, they would depart, the wide pool would vanish, and summer would begin, the grass burning green where the water had once lain. This flooded river crossing was called Lee's Mills by the generals. Beyond it, the Confederates waited. The onslaught of rebel artillery had stopped soon after Laurence's regiment arrived to support the Third and the Sixth Vermont, and the smoke was starting to clear over the water.

Laurence jostled for a spot behind the pines. His regiment would cover the Third and Sixth as they crossed the sunken field, bracing for a counterattack, hoping it would come. They had been trading fire with the rebels since picket the night before.

"Before the day is over, you'll see your share," Davey told his company as he squinted into the lifting haze.

When the Third and Sixth regiments set foot in the water, their blue legs vanished first in the silver-plated surface, and then their whole bodies were wiped out by drifting gray clouds. Laurence looked for Morey Aldridge among them but could not find him for the chaos that ensued almost as soon as the first men disappeared—the crack of fire from Confederate rifle pits, and Vermonters screaming as they fell beyond the wall of smoke.

Panicked by their calls for help, he started to load his own rifle, the crook of his shoulder pressed against a sticky tree.

Davey huffed up beside him. "You can't fire from here," he said. "So what are you doing, Lindsey?"

Laurence did not respond, his hands fast but clumsy as they handled the gun. So many bullets were hitting the stream, it sounded like it was boiling.

"It's not our time yet," said Davey, grabbing Laurence's arm.

Laurence shook him off. "I'm not afraid," he said. Beyond them the last of the Third had vanished and the water looked darker now.

Davey's next words were drowned out by Union cannons firing. The ground quivered and caused the captain's heavy face to shake as if he were riding a hay wagon on a bumpy road. As the bombardment went on, Laurence was transfixed by the sight of his superior's trembling cheeks and loose, flapping mouth. Davey's ridiculous appearance made him think incongruously of an argument his father had made long ago about offering all his countrymen the smoothness of a railroad ride in place of the old, bouncing cart. Then the artillery stopped and Davey's face resumed its usual shape. Looking away again to the white-gray void before them, Laurence suddenly understood that his father had been trying to make a point about human dignity and how it could be achieved by anyone, but also lost so easily.

"You'll see your share," said Davey, louder than he needed to. The rifle fire continued from the Confederate side, but it sounded weaker now.

Laurence nodded, relaxing his hands on the gun. He wanted to explain that he had been afraid, not of dying but of waiting to die and watching others go in his place, and that this could undo a man more than death itself—but Davey was already turning away.

A bugle bleated, and a few minutes after, the survivors from the Third and Sixth reappeared, carrying the wounded on their backs, on stretchers, helping them hobble up the swampy bank. Morey Aldridge was not among them. The soldiers' wool uniforms were dyed purple with water and blood, and cartridge boxes hung uselessly from their waists, the powder soaked to a wet, ashy mud. They said they had made it to the rebel earthworks beyond. They had been struggling hand-to-hand with the enemy, and they didn't understand why the generals had called them back.

Meanwhile the Fourth had made their way to the other side. By the Third's accounts, the rebs numbered in the hundreds, and Laurence imagined them like a line of ants, stretching back through the marsh.

"Stand ready!" Davey shouted. If the Fourth succeeded, their turn was next. Laurence gripped his gun, ready to enter the smoke. He looked left and right at his companions, Gilbert adjusting his cartridge box, Addison propped calmly against a pine. The artillery had petered out and the silence was sharp in Laurence's ears.

A bugle called again, a ridiculous, cowardly bleat.

"Stand ready!" Davey repeated the order, but his voice was less certain now.

Laurence heard Gilbert clicking his teeth.

"What the hell kind of battle is this?" Gilbert muttered.

"What the hell is right," Lyman Woodard echoed from his tree a few yards back.

Laurence unknitted his fingers from their cramped clutch on his rifle. As he shook them loose, he heard Addison's angry, questioning murmur and Sergeant Hamilton's clipped reply, something about General McClellan "not wanting a general engagement at this time."

When the smoke began to clear, Laurence could see the Fourth retreat, running three steps at a time and tripping, then standing to run again, trying to dodge the bullets. A bugle sounded once more.

"The day's over," Davey announced, but he was looking at the pines and not his men.

Laurence slumped forward against the tree trunk, letting his arms dangle, holding nothing. The Fourth rose and fell through the last stretch of water. They had learned this tactic from the mistakes of the regiment before them, and therefore they had fewer to mourn when, three mornings later, a truce finally allowed the Vermonters to gather their dead.

Like books left out in the rain, bodies curled everywhere in the shallow water. Vultures had scarred most of them blind, and many looked heavenward from their sightless sockets, knocked back by bullets, their blue mouths open. Above them, the air was greased soft with the smell of rot, making the approaching soldiers gag. They paused to tie handkerchiefs and rags over their faces.

The first body Laurence came to was kneeling like a man in prayer, head bent and hooded by his own bloodied yellow hair. Laurence lifted at the man's shoulders, but the fabric of his uniform tore immediately and the soldier tipped backward into the water, the hair fanning out, the chest gouged with blackened holes.

"This hair won't get off of me," Gilbert said behind him, stooping to rinse his fingers in the water. They had orders to search the soldiers for personal effects before burying them, and he tossed a lock of someone's sweetheart's hair on the shore before wading deeper, his back stooped. The men turned to stare at him behind their masks. "It won't get off," he nearly shouted.

"Not in this water," Addison pronounced, standing knee-deep in it. "This place ain't ever going to be the same again."

"That's where you're wrong," said Captain Davey, splashing after

Gilbert and pulling him upright. "These places don't change. They'll turn lovely as soon as we leave. Even before."

A silence fell over the company. Laurence paused in his attempt to move the dead man. His hands were filmed up to the elbows in water and blood, and he suspended them away from his sides like a boxer about to fight. Davey was the only captain to apologize to his company for the botched attempt at taking Lee's Mills, and this had made him less popular with the men. Addison looked annoyed to be corrected and stood with his weight on one leg, the other thrust out to the side.

"Spring comes and the land erases us. It doesn't need our wars and our glory to go on. That's what we can't stand," Captain Davey added lamely.

"Come on, Lindsey. Help me with this one," said Addison, interrupting the captain and wrenching another body from the stream. His hands extended beneath the soldier's burly arms, and it took Laurence a moment to recognize the rough-hewn features, the huge dangling hands. It was Morey Aldridge.

"That's my sister's fiancé," Laurence muttered, feeling more disgust than grief. Aldridge's gray eyes were wide, his mouth slack, his unified expression silly, astonished.

"He don't look erased to me," Addison added with a grim glance at Davey. He let the corpse slump to the ground. "You take his haversack. I'll do his pockets."

Laurence accepted the limp bag and started leafing through it. Morey Aldridge's extra pair of socks was starred with sodden bits of hardtack. Cold ammunition dribbled through Laurence's hands.

"Nothing," he said, and tossed it with a thump against the dead soldier's thigh. Nothing that belonged to the ship in the clearing, or the artist who made it.

"Wait." Addison pulled a small metal plate from one of Aldridge's pockets. "There's a picture here. I think it's your sister."

He held out a wet, blurred daguerreotype of Morey and Lucia. Aldridge looked pleased, seated with his big pale hands lying in his lap like a blossom. Beside him stood Lucia, shy and elegant in a print dress buttoned high up her neck. She had one hand on her fiancé's broad shoulder, and Laurence could see by the tension in her fingers that she was squeezing it hard.

Crouched beside the corpse, Laurence tried to imagine his sisters and mother in the brick house in Allenton, waiting for news. They would perch about the room, embroidering dainty handkerchiefs, or practicing elocution. Lucia might go to the piano and plink through her scales, restless, acting different from the way her sister did to emphasize the new distance between them. She would have a deep, syrupy laugh now, and adopt a mock indulgence for her sister's travails with the dwindling body of suitors.

Hoping to prompt her niece's emergence into ladyhood, his mother would invite Bel to sit with them in the long afternoons, giving her sewing projects to occupy her idle fingers. And Anne would treat Bel as her twin treated her, exerting small superiorities, setting her handkerchief of tight, perfect rosebuds beside Bel's loose daisies and giving her cousin a sighing smile.

But beneath all the old routines, they would watch through the bee-loud lilacs for messengers and read the papers with greater interest than ever before. What would the journalists say about Lee's Mills—a brave engagement, a gallant attack? Lucia would never know that her future husband had been killed crossing a flat field of water and crossing back, the awkward death of a grounded sailor, a shipbuilder in an inland sea. But she had wanted a hero, and now she had one.

"Addison, Lindsey, get on up here," shouted a gruff voice.

Addison took the portrait gently from his fingers and pushed it into Laurence's chest pocket until the hard plate slid in above his heart.

"Come on," said Addison, rising. "Davey wants us to bury 'em now."

Laurence stood and followed Addison up the hill. When he reached the crest, where men were digging graves, he saw a soldier's worn cap flung against the roots of a sycamore. Violets bloomed beside it, and already a spider was spinning a silver sail between the brim and the ground. He kicked it just to see it torn.

Chapter Sixteen

The flies were so thick that the men who could still walk after the vicious battle at Savage's Station did so incessantly to keep the soft black insects away from their faces. Sweating in the July heat, Laurence and Addison strolled first together, then alone. After days of fighting, there was nothing they could say to each other, and it was difficult for two to pick a path through the bodies and the exhausted contrabands, who were digging graves right beside the soldiers as they died. The earth was damp with rain and their shovels sank easily. It's a small mercy, Laurence thought as he paused to watch a Negro burying a heap of sawed-off ankles and legs.

Short but wiry in the chest and arms, the contraband had a careless strength, allowing him to lift the limbs without strain and toss them into the pit, occasionally overshooting it. A hairy red-flecked ankle smacked against Laurence's trousers and he kicked it toward the hole.

"You need to be more careful," he said to the contraband, his voice almost drowned out by a man screaming in the doctor's sagging tent. They had run out of ether at noon. A nurse had announced it to the waiting line of wounded, blinking in the glare as he wiped his hands on a bloodstained apron. Then he gave the soldiers a single canteen of whiskey and told them to share.

The contraband glanced up, and Laurence suddenly noticed the fishhook scar beneath his left eye. His eyes traveled down the man's shirt, his string-hitched trousers, and finally to the right foot, wrapped in rags and swollen slightly, tipped to one side like a boat on a high wave.

Another scream ricocheted from the tent. The few trees in the field shuddered and darkened.

"Do you know me?" Laurence asked, breathless.

"Suh?" The voice was low, resonant as a drum.

"Have you seen me before?" Laurence asked, pressing him.

"No, suh. I ain't never done nothing to you, suh." Waving one hand to scatter the flies from his eyes, the contraband went back to digging.

"That's not what I mean. Do you remember asking if I was the friend of a friend?"

The hole hummed with the black music of insects.

"I ain't got no friends, suh." He lifted another pile of limbs, pitching them high, so that Laurence had to retreat a step or stay in the path of their reeking trajectory.

"What's your name?" Laurence asked, thinking of the starless night when he and Johnny Mulcane had gone back to collect the shivering slave. The three of them had stumbled into one another as they walked back, their bodies touching, pulling away.

"My name Nathan, suh." But the man shook his head as he said it, as if he did not believe his own words. Laurence felt his throat tighten. The most recent amputee was carried from the doctor's tent and laid on the grass. His right leg was missing below the knee, and, for the lack of bandages, the doctor had tied the stump with corn husks, which crackled now as they touched the earth.

"I thought I remembered you," Laurence said, bending over to set on the ground the only thing he could think of to offer the former runaway—a small sketch of lilacs that Bel had sent him. The delicate, feminine lines of the flower seemed to stretch beyond the paper and touch the dirt beyond. "I apologize."

The contraband shook his head again and went back to widening his grave. A sheet of flies shifted over the sawed-off stumps, and for a minute, the dark, humming cut in the earth was the only thing moving in the entire field. After watching it a few more moments, Laurence walked away into the silent expanse of dead and wounded men. When he looked back, the sketch was gone and Nathan's dark arms drew purple stripes in the air as he threw shovels of soil down over the bloody limbs, faster and faster, as if there were not enough dirt in the world to cover them.

Chapter Seventeen

The smell of fresh blood was like rain. It lingered in the cool autumn air, thickening with every breath. Laurence kept staring up at the sky beyond the orchard, trying to see if the night clouds themselves had reddened, would loose the spilled blood back down to the ground. But the smell did not come from the sky; it crept earthward, through the cornfield, over ditches and the beetled turf to the cove where they lay under the crack of shells.

Loomis stretched out on one side of him, Gilbert and Addison on the other, their foursome separated by a brier patch from the rest of the company. Davey would not object—there was nothing they could do now but wait for the shelling to stop and morning to arrive, and then rejoin the brigade.

It had been Loomis's idea to come this far, inching on his elbows and stomach. He was a consummate frontiersman and disliked crowds, continually promising that when the war ended, he would take his wife, Sallie, and their two boys out west to California. Or to Texas, where they could build a sprawling ranch. No more Vermont winters, he said. No more waiting for a brief four months of summer, when everything had to be sown and reaped in rapid succession. He had been talking about it for hours in a steady drone.

"It's getting worse," commented John Addison. The shadows of the apple trees drew jagged streaks down his face, like a watery ink. Laurence looked at him without recognition, and Addison punched him hard in the arm. "Wake up," he commanded. Laurence managed a ghastly smile.

"I think we're winning." Gilbert always thought they were winning, even though the secesh had defeated them in nearly every battle.

"Put the paddock right behind the ranch house, and five or six horses," Loomis was saying when a shell hit close and made leaves lift up and slap their faces.

"Will you just shut up?" Gilbert brushed the leaves away. "It's bad luck to—"

"It ain't—" Loomis began, when a shower of grape skimmed just past his ear, so close that if he hadn't turned his head to retort to Gilbert's accusation, it would have been knocked off. As it was, Loomis howled and gripped the affected ear. The briers behind them broke with a crash and a shocked rabbit sped out. With catlike swiftness, Gilbert caught the animal, holding it just below the neck.

"Are you all right?" Addison yelled as Loomis ducked away from them, opening a locket to kiss his wife's stern profile. He nodded, unable to speak.

The rabbit strained in Gilbert's scarred hands, its walnut-colored eyes so large, they held the reflection of the distant moon. The long feet thumped the earth.

"Should let it run," said Laurence, wanting to hold it himself. He reached out to touch the warm ridge of skull between the rabbit's ears.

"Why? It's mine," Gilbert snarled, and tightened his fingers around the squirming animal, making the soft eyes bulge.

"You're hurting it," Laurence protested just as another shell came down, this time so close, he was sure he was killed, until he felt

Gilbert's body jerk beside him, saw the hands flex and the rabbit's furry neck snap and go limp.

The animal slumped to one side, its fat, leaf-fed body making a small hill. Gilbert was screaming, pinned by the cannonball that had landed on his right heel. The moon died out in the rabbit's eyes, the cannonball rolled and settled on the flesh it had crushed, and somewhere Gilbert's call echoed off the trees and fell among them again. Or maybe it was the sound of other men in pain. Laurence could not tell by that point. The sky was so full of thundering artillery, and the hissing and splintering destruction of the trees, and the fallen apples and the rising groans of the dying, it could have been any sound or all of them put together that made Gilbert's anguish reverberate like a wave crashing against the rocks, once, twice, before it was pulled away.

Bile in his throat, Laurence sat up to help Addison shift the hot projectile off their friend's leg, then rolled Gilbert on his back as he continued howling. Loomis shook his big bearded head. "What happened?" he asked, as if he were half-blind and not half-deaf.

The smell of fresh blood was like a wet wind, and Laurence tried not to breathe it. Gilbert's ankle had shattered, the jutting bone glistening like a cracked egg. Biting his lip so hard that a trickle of blood ran through his teeth, the wounded man held back a scream until it emerged as a harsh, repeating gasp. Out of the corner of his eye, Laurence watched Addison lift the rabbit and toss it back into the brier patch, watched the thorns snag the body and hold it aloft.

When the rain came, it made the men stir again, the dead and the living. The cornfield sang in whispers and groans.

This was after a long stillness. After Laurence looked away from his friend and back to the apple trees, seeing the moon sink into a grail of branches. After the briers bowed under the weight of the rabbit until it touched the dirt.

Gilbert's lashes fluttered but did not open. Far off, a man was pleading to be released from beneath the dead soldier on top of him. When the rain came, he stopped calling for help.

Hours later, Laurence reached out to touch Gilbert's face, pale, sprinkled with soil, the eyes sunken. His cheek was as cold as a door handle in morning. Laurence shouted to Addison for help, although the other man was only two feet away. The rabbit hung upside down now, ears pointing into the dirt. The veins in its ears drew a branching map of rivers. Addison crept off in search of the captain. When he came back, his face was sharp with anger. "Nothing we can do," he said, shrugging, " 'cept keep him alive till dawn."

"I ain't gonna die."

The eyes opened. They held the moon for a moment. Then the clouds masked it away.

"My ranch won't have a single flake of snow fall on it," said Loomis.

Addison rooted through the haversacks. The rustle reminded Laurence suddenly of the runaway slave settling down in the hayloft, clutching his burlap hat. The slave had eyed them until they retreated down the steps, Johnny first, then Laurence, the rank, unwashed smell of the hired man drifting up behind him. Every man in the Army of the Potomac stank like Johnny Mulcane now.

The accordion looked dull in the rain-polished world, like a stone pulled from the lake water, allowed to dry on the high beach. Addison jabbed Gilbert in the ankle, making the wounded man howl.

"Tell a song you love or a song you hate."

No answer but the ticking leaves, Loomis whispering about his ranch.

"Tell me."

"'Annie Laurie.' That was Pike's favorite," Gilbert said, his voice eggshell-thin.

"I ain't playing Pike's song."

Shadows fingered their faces. A wind rose up, scattering the leaf-gathered rain. Laurence was cold, colder than he had ever been in his life, even in winter on Lake Champlain, when the bitter breeze tightened his ribs.

Once, when Johnny Mulcane found Laurence rooting through his bag of tools, he had slapped the boy with the flat of his hand. Laurence had never told, because he thought if he did not speak of it, he might not remember himself. And he had forgotten, for years.

"Tell me a song." Addison jabbed the ankle again.

A smile ghosted the ugly, bitten lips. "'The Vacant Chair,' I never could stand that one."

In Johnny's bag of tools, Laurence had found a rabbit's foot, the white fur burnished by touch. "What is it for?" he'd asked the hired man, still curious even as he held his stinging cheek, as tears squeezed from his eyes.

"For luck," Johnny had answered, striking the boy a second time.

Music rose, maudlin at first, then fading to a sweet, mournful loveliness. The briers released the rabbit and sprang skyward, thorns tufted with fur. Gilbert's face relaxed, the lines of pain and outrage erased. A sparrow coasted into the thicket and huddled there. Johnny Mulcane loved strawberries. He stole them from the gardens of the neighborhood, staining his fingers a deep, embarrassing pink. He couldn't help it, even after Bel's father caught him and punished him by withholding a week's salary. He couldn't help it; they would find him crouching in the ice shed, pressing the red fruit to his lips, kissing his theft before he swallowed it, the leafy stems littering the sawdust.

Another song and another, and far off they heard men singing from where they lay in the filth of the spent battle. The rebels had their own words, and they clashed and mingled in the night sky, and some voices died out almost as soon as they began. Laurence's uniform welded to him, a wool skin reeking of the sheep it had come from. He couldn't remember the last time he had bathed, or washed his hands, or tasted fresh meat. He tried to eat an apple, but it was wormy, the center mottled with holes.

After awhile, the land lifted the sun back over the east and the spreading light revealed the outlines of things—a leaf-stripped orchard, a pocked cannonball, and Gilbert still alive, his chin streaked with blood. Addison stopped playing, lifting his cramped fingers to his mouth and blowing on them with short, harsh gusts.

Davey's order came to move from Sharpsburg to another location. Loud and stumbling, as if they had not lived through the same bitter night as the rest of the men, Spider and Woodard appeared, sipping from their canteens. As the stretcher dropped with a rattle against the rooty earth, Davey came up behind them and stood with his stomach thrust out, uniform buttons caked with mud. His cap was yanked low over his eyes.

"I heard you the whole night. Did he stay awake?"

"Yes," said Addison, carefully stowing the accordion away.

"Then he won't die, for he has already passed through the valley," predicted their captain. Burrs had knotted in his beard and he tugged at them, wincing. "Go on now, and let the others take him."

"Sir," said Addison. "You would put him in the hands of drunkards now?"

Spider giggled. Woodard gave a snort of protest, swaying unsteadily, knocking a laden apple bough so that its fruit hammered the ground. He and Spider had been given the office of stretcher-bearers because they were the worst shots in the regiment, but Woodard refused to admit it.

"I ain't got a choice," said Davey. "We have to move." One of the apples rolled toward Gilbert's head and Addison stopped it with his foot.

"Let Lindsey and me take him, at least to the field hospital," he offered, toying with the apple. "We'll catch up."

"I can't spare you. Which means you ain't got a choice, either," Davey said quietly. "Move."

"Captain," Addison said. His hands balled into fists.

"We can't leave him—" Laurence began.

"Move," Davey ordered again, interrupting Laurence, although he only looked at Addison. Time slowed, Addison's knuckles going white, Laurence holding his haversack, Woodard about to speak, his thin mouth opening, then clapping shut. Then Loomis broke the silence with a grunt.

"He'll be all right," he muttered, and fell in behind the others, shouldering his musket.

Davey nodded and put his hand slowly down on the butt end of his pistol. "Lindsey, Addison, move."

A fly descended to Gilbert's smashed ankle, filling its soft black bottle. Laurence stared at Addison, but he wouldn't return his gaze. His hair was full of sun, his eyes washed the color of old stone. Daylight drifted through the trees, bringing their brightness back to them. The fly careened off toward the brier patch, where the dead rabbit lay, already covered in ants. As the insect flew with slow, dizzy gluttony through the tufted thorns, something in Addison seemed to shrink. He lowered his head and spat on the grass. Another moment passed.

"Go," whispered Gilbert, and he let slip away the stiff mask that he had been using for a face since he was shot. Laurence saw death lurking beneath the curling hairs of his eyebrows and beard, and he watched as Addison, seeing it, too, and repulsed by it, sprang toward the others and fell in behind them.

"Laurence." Davey used the name of the boy who had led the run-away through the dark, feverish and impossibly cold, who in the act of trying to save the freedom of another had succeeded only in taking it away. A string of gunfire ratcheted beyond the orchard. Laurence's chin sank to his chest and he stepped carefully over the cannonball and into line, lifting the long weight of his musket. Ahead of him, Addison stood so still, he could not have been breathing.

Davey gestured to the stretcher-bearers to commence their work and ordered the rest of them forward. Gilbert cried out as Woodard hauled him onto the narrow board with clumsy arms. But if the others heard it, they did not turn, skirting the blond remains of the cornfield without speaking or looking back.

January–February 1863

Chapter Eighteen

Winter had bent the garden into valley and drift. Snow filled the bright air between branches until the whole understory of flower and bush became root, and Bel could see all the way to the farthest hedge of her father's acres. She named it Wilderness Plain in honor of her cousin Laurence, whom she imagined would see a vast untouched desert in the covered garden and would set off like an explorer to find whatever secrets were hidden in its soft dunes.

Bel often went out alone into the garden. It was the only place she was allowed to go unchaperoned, and she could hear the tramplings and winter-loud voices of Allenton beyond, a society that became at once closer and more isolated during the long cold months. It started with spontaneous skating and sleighing parties, and then came the official rigors of Christmas and New Year's calling. Painted sleighs coasted down Main Street and Pearl with the breakneck speed of young men and the dignified slide of the elders, all coming to a crunching halt outside the Pomeroys', or the Mays', or the Lindseys'. The morning after one of the great houses had a party, the drive in front would be flat and stained with the manure of the waiting horses. A lady always lost her hat or glove, and a drunk young man always misplaced a sunken pile of the contents of his stomach, and everywhere there fluttered the unidentifiable remains of a party—colored bits of paper, threads of an unraveling coat, even a page of Christmas hymns abandoned. It took a full day for the red-faced coachman to restore it to order.

Today, Greenwood was all preparation for the first social event in Allenton after the exhausting New Year's calls, which sent the men all over town partaking from the wine and sweet-laden tables of waiting lairs of women. Twelfth Night was Faustina's yearly tradition, complete with an enormous fruitcake made from Martha Washington's recipe for "Great Cake," and a king and queen who would order the evening. Despite the disapproval of Allenton's most puritan residents, who would rather Christmas revelry be abolished altogether in favor of a simple church service, the event's popularity grew each year, and each year Bel was allowed to stay up a little later.

Sprigs of evergreen hung from the windows of Greenwood, affixed with scarlet bows that sagged under the previous night's snow. Bel spotted her father circling the house now, knocking the powder free with the pole he used to hang their flag in summer. He could have asked a servant to do it for him, but Bel suspected he was also escaping the indignant tirades of her mother as she prepared for the evening.

For all her gaiety once her Twelfth Night was in motion, Faustina hated throwing parties. Days of baking, cleaning, and decorating generated in her a unique form of rage. She would mutter to herself as she arranged towering piles of pears and apples, as she tied up the mistletoe into a kissing ball (which, of course, no one else could tie properly), as she shook the curtains Mary had already washed, hunting for spots or tears. Faustina's voice would tighten and thin like pulled taffy and she moved with the jerky, overdetermined steps of a marionette. She alternately chastised her family and servants for being in the way and for not helping enough, so Bel and her father often left the house together on guilty errands, seeking the peace of the frozen country, the raw, uncomplicated wind that in winter had no smell but its own clarity.

Bel was just about to investigate a new set of bird tracks when she heard her father calling her. "Isabel." His tone of reprimand summoned her back to the brick walls of Greenwood. Daniel Lindsey was facing one of his windows, the wooden pole thumped in the ground like the staff of a shepherd. As she approached the glass, Bel saw her reflection spring up across it—a tall blue-eyed girl with an abundance of honey brown hair sticking from beneath her winter bonnet. Bel was already more buxom than her mother, her arms stronger and the bones of her face heavy and wide as the tiger skull her father kept in the library. She often heard the adults murmur that she was "handsome," a description that seemed to contain within it a note of disappointment.

On the other side of the glass, her mother hovered, a shadow behind Bel's apparition. Even in anger, Faustina looked fragile, like the German porcelain figures on the mantel, treasures she insisted on dusting herself so she would be the only one to blame if they broke. Her mother's mouth was shaping words Bel could not make out.

"Your new French tutor is here," Daniel translated for his daughter before crunching off to the next dispirited bow.

Bel nodded and made her way around the tramped path of fallen icicles to the kitchen entrance to the house. A wave of air stung her cheeks as she entered the warm, busy cove where Grete was basting the roast goose. The bird's body lay like a hill in the deep pan, sown with a bright field of potatoes and carrots. Bel paused by the stove, thawing her face and hands while she watched the whirlwind of the German cook.

"Excuse me," Grete said in an accusing voice as she bustled past

Bel with a tray of gingerbread cookies. Their raisin eyes stared up unblinking as they were thrust into the fire of the oven.

"I'm sorry," Bel said, and moved toward the other side of the kitchen. Her boots felt damp and clammy, and the snow dragged in gritty pools behind her.

Faustina waited in the threshold of the dining room, arms folded across a green woolen bodice. On her face, an aggrieved and angry look that appeared only at holiday time had worn grooves below her eyes.

"Late," she said. The day of the party, Faustina's sentences were clipped to the bare essentials, as if only the slightest amount of her energy could be spent communicating with her unhelpful family.

"I'm sorry," Bel repeated, this time allowing mutiny to creep into her apology. She couldn't help wanting to avoid the new French tutor. The former one had been an aging widow who smelled of sardines and always forgot what she had taught Bel the week before. Consequently, Bel had a precise knowledge of colors, numbers, and fruits, but the rest of the French language loomed like an impenetrable forest she had no desire to explore.

She began to unbutton her lamb's wool coat and unlace the wet boots, still safely on the stone floor of the kitchen, where it was permissible to be wet and dirty. Her stockings sticky with snowmelt, she stepped onto the wooden slats of the dining room floor and took the slippers her mother held out.

"Where is she?" Bel asked.

"*He* is in the library," Faustina informed her. "His name is Louis Pacquette and he comes highly recommended from Mrs. M.J. Pomeroy. For the son of a St. Albans hill farmer, he has done quite well educating himself, and his French is impeccable." St. Albans was a northerly settlement, where Allentonians rarely traveled.

"He's not Canadian?"

"His mother is. She moved her family back there after his father was killed in a haying accident."

"Oh," Bel said. She had never had a male tutor, and the very fact that one existed threw her whole expectation of the coming hour into confusion.

"I suppose I have to go make sure Mary has indeed ironed Daniel's suit for this evening." Faustina once again assumed her mantle of martyrdom as she climbed the spiral stairs behind her daughter. Their right hands skimmed up the banister, one after another. The elegant white spread of Faustina's fingers contrasted sharply with her daughter's sturdy, nail-bitten digits.

"I suppose so," Bel echoed wearily.

"And if you have any time in your busy day, I'd like some help arranging the fruit."

"Of course, Mother." Bel took her hand from the railing and continued the rest of the way up the steps without touching it.

When Laurence was younger, he had bet her he could slide all the way down the very same railing—and he did, although he bumped his head at the end and a tender egg swelled up. Bel wished he was coming to the party, for then they could plot ways to make the adults meet under the kissing ball and crow with delight as their matchmaking succeeded.

It amazed Bel that she would not think about her cousin for days, and then miss him with sudden intensity. Three years had passed since they found the runaway together and almost two since she had seen Laurence for the last time, climbing into the train with the rest of his regiment. Since October, he and his comrade Lyman Woodard had been so sick with dysentery that they had to leave their regiment and were recovering in a Virginia hospital called Mt. Pleasant. In his last letter, he had written that they were being moved to another camp, and that he'd miss the daily soup and fresh bread, but beds at

Mt. Pleasant were dear, and his condition was improved enough to give his up to another fellow. "Not dear enough for my son," Aunt Pattie had muttered when she read this missive aloud to them.

"Let me introduce you to Monsieur Pacquette," her mother said as she and Bel walked down the hall together, their shadows lengthened by the window behind them. Faustina's dark silhouette flickered over Bel's when she pushed past Henry Gale's portrait to beat her to the library. The patriarch's disapproving gaze did not alter.

"I can introduce myself, Mother," said Bel.

Faustina looked shocked. "Of course you can't," she said simply, and entered the vaulty room. Now that Bel was almost sixteen, a hundred inexplicable rules of etiquette had settled around her like the bars of a cage. Corsets made their way into her daily dressing; constant bonnets and stiff, starched petticoats promised to hinder her for the rest of her life.

"Monsieur Pacquette, this is my daughter, Isabel."

The tutor rose to greet them. Lanky and tall, he had the narrow, intent face of a horse leaning through the paddock rails to reach a better crop of clover.

"Bel," Bel said stubbornly, for the nickname Laurence had given her was the only shred of childhood she could still claim.

"Mademoiselle," Louis said tactfully, and bowed toward her offered hand. The fingers that held hers were cool and dry.

"Well," Faustina said. "I have much more pressing things to do than to stand around listening to the lovely language of your people." She dipped her own head gracefully in an echo of Louis's bow, then turned and rustled out of the room.

"A beautiful woman, your mother," Louis said, striding back toward the table. His accent was present but faint, like the start of a sunset on the winter sky. Bel followed without comment and sprawled into a chair with an unladylike sigh.

"You prefer Bel to Isabel?" he asked, taking a seat opposite Bel and pulling out his books. He looked at least twenty-five by the calloused wear of his hands, but his cheeks were lightly freckled and smooth as a boy's.

"I hate Isabel. It sounds like something itchy," Bel said.

"Isabel is a woman's name," reflected Louis. "Bel is like the name of a pretty little girl."

Bel frowned and picked up the white sleeve she had left in the chair earlier that day. Every morning, she made progress on a shirt cut from a pattern her aunt Pattie had commandeered from the Sanitary Commission. Bel was in competition with her friend Mary Ruth Cross to see who could finish one first. Mary Ruth had a brother in the war, about whom she talked constantly, her almost-white eyebrows arching up as she listed his many accomplishments. Laurence had yet to win any commendations for bravery, and Bel rather hoped he would hurry up and get some, just so Mary Ruth wouldn't shake her blond head in sympathy at the lesser courage of others.

"I'm making a shirt for my cousin Laurence. He's in the Army of the Potomac," Bel announced.

"Il est dans la guerre?"

"Yes."

"Oui."

"Oh, sorry. *Oui.*" Bel did not look up from her stitching. The needle was cool and slippery against her thumb, and suddenly the row of thread seemed to be straightening. The tutor waited in silence.

"Mademoiselle." Louis finally thrust his face into her peripheral vision. He smelled like tobacco and lemons. "I will answer any question you ask as long as you ask me in French."

The temptation was too great, and Bel laid down her stitching to meet his brown eyes. *"Est-ce que—"* she began, and then faltered. "I don't know how to say it."

"What do you want to ask?"

"Why aren't you fighting, too?" She was thinking of Laurence's twin sisters; Lucia and Anne were both marrying men who had decided to profit from the rebellion rather than enlist. She couldn't stand either of the copperhead fiancés, because she had heard them poking fun at the stiff, patriotic letters Laurence sent to his mother and father. She knew that beneath his brave lines her cousin must be burying a separate, more painful truth about the war.

"Fighting for what?" Louis opened one of his books.

"Fighting to end slavery," Bel said, her cheeks hot.

"My country does not have slavery," he answered, scanning a page. "I don't need to fight."

"You don't live in Canada. You live here."

"For a time." He shrugged.

"I would if I could. I would die for it."

"That's because you have never been close to death, I think," he said to the text in front of him.

"I've never been in love, either, and I would die for that, too," she said, half-frightened by her own words.

Louis raised his head from his book. This time, Bel stared back, defiant, clutching the white sleeve in her lap. The light in the library faded as a cloud crossed the sun. Nodding and biting his lip, her tutor closed the book with a soft thump, and in that moment Bel felt something inexplicable pass between them, like an unseen wind parting the summer leaves.

Just then, Faustina rustled past the threshold with an armload of hemlock. "How is the lesson going?" she asked. A few needles fell soundlessly to the floor.

"*Très bien, Mama,*" Bel said, avoiding the tutor's eyes.

"Louis, you know as one of the few single young men left in Allenton, you are a necessity to the festivities this evening. The girls will mob you the minute you walk in." In the company of strangers, Faustina was all graciousness, reserving her ire for her household.

"I am honored, madame," Louis bowed his head. Bel looked out the window, to see the sun reappear above the maple branches.

"Wonderful. We'll see you at eight o'clock, then," Faustina said. Her armload began to slide and she scurried off, clutching it to her chest. "Mary!" she called, her tone of indignation returning.

Louis resumed flipping through one of his books and opened to a page, smoothing it with his palm before sending it across the table to Bel. "Please read," he commanded.

"You never really answered my question," she said, taking the book.

"You never asked me in French," he countered. *"Lisez ce passage, s'il vous plaît."*

Chapter Nineteen

Oh no, every year I refuse to put my name in," said Faustina, declining her sister-in-law's offer with a wave of her hand. "Daniel and I are our guest's servants and we couldn't possibly claim the throne."

Daniel compressed his lips in agreement as Pattie Lindsey moved on, shaking the hat of names. Although his black suit and trimmed silver beard easily made him the most elegant man in the room, Daniel didn't like parties and wore the air of a man burdened by his own success.

"Let it be known that I gave you a chance," Aunt Pattie said over her shoulder, already smiling at the next victim with practiced cheer.

Faustina was wisely making use of her sister-in-law's managerial enthusiasm by putting her in charge of the name-drawing for king and queen of the evening. After her only son had enlisted in the Second Vermont, Aunt Pattie had finally found her calling as an organizer in the women-run Sanitary Commission. If Mrs. M.J. Pomeroy, the matron leading the Allenton chapter, was the general, Aunt Pattie was her faithful colonel, carrying out all commands with an alacrity for which others could not help commending her, although their praise often sounded like complaint.

She was always bustling somewhere with her fist in a ball of lint for bandages or whisking through a mess of lists she had made with Mrs. M.J. of all the things that needed to be manufactured, counted, and shipped to keep her brave boys safe and well fed. Since the war began, Aunt Pattie had gained an enormous amount of weight, as if her own necessity to "our boys" had swelled her past her previous shape and into one of greater consequence. Tonight, she coursed through the waltzing couples like the ironsides the Union had built to destroy the *Merrimack,* thick and unstoppable, her gray-blond hair shining.

From Bel's vantage point at the top of the staircase, Allenton offered an even sadder showing at the party than it had the year before. The lack of young men gave the dance floor a spiritless air, although many young girls obligingly waltzed with each other to fill out the numbers. Bel had already refused to dance with Mary Ruth Cross and Hannah Fithian, both of whom were fascinated with boys and hoping to practice their skills in preparation for the war's end. The partnerless young wives and fiancées faked a desperate sort of merriment, while their elders sat around the rim with fans raised, nodding as if they expected the world to fall apart just this way and there was nothing to do but to enjoy complaining about it.

Bel's bird's-eye view allowed her to see the real circulation of the party: Lucia and Anne with their copperhead beaus, Aunt Pattie raising the hat of names that would determine who would be king and queen of the evening, her mother leaving Daniel's side to check on the kitchen. Soon after, Uncle George extracted himself from a conversation with the minister to follow Faustina, and Louis Pacquette arrived, his eyes blinking rapidly, as if he had just walked into the sunlight. Momentarily distracted by the tutor's entrance, Bel forgot to monitor her mother and uncle. She suspected them of sneaking off to talk about Laurence. Everyone was worried about him being moved from the hospital.

Just as Faustina had predicted, Louis's name was entered into the hat and he was signed up for several reels before the butler even took his coat. Dragged onto the dance floor by Mary Ruth in the next instant, Louis looked both pleased and terrified. Bel thumped down the stairs and drifted to the kitchen, ignoring the gaze of the tutor, who followed her with his eyes as soon as he spotted her. Still, she straightened her spine and was inwardly glad for the first time that her mother had insisted she wear a blue silk that matched her complexion perfectly.

As Bel entered the dining room, she saw two figures silhouetted behind the Oriental screen, her father's Christmas gift to her mother. She ducked into another of her favored hiding places, a nook in back of the piano. The space was almost too small for her now and her spine scraped the wall. Although she knew her elders would be scandalized if they caught her eavesdropping, to watch the private conversation play across the exotic screen was far more interesting than waltzing with Hannah Fithian.

In the past year, Faustina had acquired an obsession with the Orient: She devoured books about Arab empires and Chinese dynasties, and lectured Bel one day on silk making, telling her daughter about the rooms of tiny caterpillars that would spin a thread so fine, it felt like water in your hands. The screen had come from a Chinese junk docked in New York, where Daniel had bargained for it, from sunup to sundown, he said. He'd brought it home on Christmas Eve and triumphantly unfolded it for his wife. While Faustina gave a sharp cry of delight and exchanged modest kisses with her husband, Bel studied the gift. It was decorated with sprays of pink flowers, a village of small thatched huts, and a distant, fantastic mountain range that curled up in green spirals, as if it were made of taffy instead of earth. A dragon lounged in one panel, breathing fire. Bel longed for it. She had never seen anything so beautiful and strange, and she sulked a little over her own gift, an ornate jade teapot with a frog for a handle. She didn't even drink tea.

Mary, on the other hand, viewed the screen with utter and unfounded superstition, calling it "a pagan abomination." She had howled with dismay when Faustina insisted on placing the canvas in the evergreen-bedecked dining room for Twelfth Night. But there it stayed on its bamboo legs, smelling faintly of ginger. The two people on the other side of it now seemed unaware that their shadows drew over the curling mountain range an exaggerated dance of their low conversation. Bel recognized her uncle from his jutting stomach and the way his hands jabbed the air when he talked. The woman was her mother.

Although she was unable to hear a word they were saying, Bel watched, transfixed by the sword of his raised arm, her mother's arched neck. They were fighting about something, and then her uncle reached for her mother's elbow, cradling it briefly in his palm. Her mother backed away and a stretch of white canvas made a channel between their shadows. He was pleading now, both arms out in a peacemaking gesture, and she was refusing, her head flicking back and forth.

After another moment, Faustina burst out from behind the screen and marched quickly toward the kitchen. Her eyes looked swollen. Cramped and dusty, Bel saw her uncle emerge and stride into the ballroom, smoothing his waistcoat with his right hand. He threw his head back before he entered the light, and Bel hated him in that instant for upsetting her mother, whatever he had said. She pushed out the other side of the hole behind the piano, only to find her exit blocked by a pair of legs.

"Move," she hissed, and batted one of the calves, suspecting Ernest Pomeroy, a tubby thirty-year-old bachelor who often hid in the dining room at parties to consume whole plates of sweets.

"Excuse me?" came the polite voice of the tutor. His dark hair caught the candlelight as he bent down to investigate.

"What are you doing here?" she demanded, brushing dust from her dress.

"I could ask the same of you," Louis retorted. He offered her his hand and she took it, straightening up to stand beside him.

"Did you hear any of that?"

"Any of what?"

"What they were saying."

"I don't know whom you're talking about," he said honestly. "I just came in. I was trying get away from all those girls." He gave a tragic shrug.

Bel laughed in spite of herself. "I know a good place to hide," she said, suddenly daring. The blue silk and all the starched petticoats beneath felt like a cloud around her legs.

"You are not waiting to be queen?" Louis picked at invisible lint on his coat. It was too short in the sleeves and the bones of his wrists protruded from the cuffs.

"I never put my name in. My mother says I have to wait until I'm sixteen." Bel felt stupid for admitting it.

"And when is that?" Louis said without looking at her.

"In a few months." She shrugged to show him she didn't care. Mary bustled past with a tray of oysters, managing to simper in Louis's direction.

"Anyway, meet me outside the front door in five minutes," Bel commanded suddenly, irritated by the maid. "I'll go around another way."

"Outside? Can't we hide in a warm place?" He regarded the dim dining room.

"It's the only place that's safe from dancing girls." Bel nodded to Mary Ruth Cross, who was fast approaching, her yellow hair yanked up in a tight crown.

"Five minutes, then." Louis grimaced and stalked deliberately past Mary Ruth on his way to the cloakroom. The girl paused after he passed and addressed Bel. Her white-blond eyebrows arched to a new zenith.

"If I get to be queen, I'm going to make him waltz with me the rest of the night. He's a divine dancer," she oozed.

Nodding, Bel watched as her mother returned to the ballroom. Not a hair was out of place and her green eyes were large and serene. Bel turned back to the screen. She saw feathers sometimes on the dark, inky body of the dragon, and sometimes fur. It had no wings, but still she believed it must be able to fly, for how could a creature have the power to destroy if it could not save itself, too? After his wide nostrils breathed fire down on the village, she imagined that the dragon would just rise up and fly over the mountain range, to live on the untouched other side.

Chapter Twenty

Bel's candle threw a yellow glare on the dusty glass of the coaches, making her reflection flare across the panes, Louis a tall gray shadow behind her. The interior of the barn was bitter cold, the air so still, they instinctively blinked and rustled their feet to imbue it with movement.

"We hid a runaway slave up there," Bel said, pointing to the ladder that led to the hayloft. Her breath clouded around her finger.

"Are you the friend of a friend?" Louis looked at her with surprise.

"No. It was an accident." She shook her head, feeling the old shame return. "Everything was an accident."

Louis's only response was to stare at the coaches, carriages, and the white surrey Lucia had insisted she would be married in, before Morey Aldridge was killed at Lee's Mills.

"How did you know that, by the way?" Bel asked. She inhaled the dull leathery smell of the vehicles.

"What?"

"Friend of a friend."

"My mother assists the slaves across the border," Louis answered, still riveted by the coaches. He spoke with the overly correct English of one who has learned his vocabulary from books. "We have had so many inhabit our house over the years, I can't recall their names. They all look the same, though, so dirty and hungry and fearful; they cannot believe they're free."

Bel nodded, about to speak, but Louis continued, strolling between the carriages, touching their wheels.

"Last summer, one woman would not take off the chain on her ankle. My mother made her file it off one link a day, until finally she believed it was true." He paused. "Did he reach the border?"

"Who?"

"Your runaway."

"I think he did," Bel replied hastily. "Here." She handed him the candle and started climbing the ladder. The cold rungs made her fingers ache even through her gloves, and she could feel the heavy drag of her skirt. Suddenly aware that Louis would have a clear view up her petticoats, she stared down accusingly, only to find him gazing again, enamored, at the coaches.

"Are you coming?" she said. She entered the black cave of the hayloft. Loose straw whispered along the boards as she set her palms down to pull herself up.

"Why are we going to climb there?" Louis asked, still at the bottom of the ladder. He had the low, reedy voice of a bassoon.

"Do you want to go back to dancing with Mary Ruth?" Bel threatened, half-hoping he would say yes. The January chill began to seep through her cloak and needle her skin with goose bumps. Winter always made her feel thin and alone.

"No," he said.

The scant starlight revealed the shaggy heaps of the extra bales they had stored in the hayloft. "Then you better bring the candle up, so I'm not sitting here in the dark." Bel scrambled backward, trying to find a comfortable position. Down below, the light wavered as Louis began to climb.

Bel wondered for a second what she was doing in the dark with a man she had met only that afternoon, then banished her shock to the corner of her mind. As she inched back to make room for Louis, her thumb touched something thin and metal lying in the straw. She pulled it into the small glow cast by the candle.

"I liked it better down there," he announced, his feet still on the lower rungs. His elbows leaned on either side of the hole. The yellow light softened his sharp features into handsomeness.

"Shh," Bel said, as if the sound of his voice could somehow block her view of the silver chain in her hands. A bird-shaped locket hung on the end of it, the kind of keepsake a boy would give his first girl, the kind that would gleam in the jeweler's window—just cheap enough that she could allow herself to covet it, just expensive enough for him to feel he had made a sacrifice worth making. Bel let it swing back and forth like a pendulum.

"Did you lose it?" Louis asked.

"It's not mine," Bel said, unsnapping the locket with trembling fingers. A wisp of paper drifted up, then fell past the tutor's shoulder, through the hole to the floor below. Bel lurched after it, knocking Louis off balance. The tutor swayed from the ladder, the candle wagging in his hand and lighting Bel's long hair. He thumped her shoulder enthusiastically. The singed ends curled like wire. Bel cried out and clutched him by the neck, caught in the acrid scent of her burned hair, his lemon cologne, and the damp spice of her own skin meeting his. It was a long moment before they were able to disentangle themselves safely, arm by arm. When she was free, Bel withdrew to the farthest rim of the light, feeling strange and warm.

"So this is your substitute for dancing," Louis said with an indignant air, and attempted to smooth his ruffled person. This succeeded in making his black curls more comical than ever, and Bel began to giggle, forgetting about the locket until she felt the chain tighten across her fist.

"Whose is it?" asked Louis as she once again brought it into the light.

"I don't know. Maybe Mary's," said Bel. "Laurence said she used to come up here with the blacksmith. But he wouldn't marry her." She blushed immediately after this confession, realizing her own situation was not so different from the servant's.

Louis finally hoisted himself into the hayloft and sat beside her as they examined the necklace. "It's too fine for Mary," he said. "It looks like it would belong to a girl like you."

With a dark indent for an eye, and a downcast beak, the bird looked sleepy, its wings tucked neatly back, as if flight were only their secondary purpose, after beauty. The locket's clasp lay where the tail ended in a tip of metal, the loose hinge opposite, at the outer perimeter of the breast.

"In the old French fairy tales, the swan is a messenger bird for lovers who are married to others," Louis added after a moment.

"I read that story," Bel said, not remembering where or when.

"The swan comes to the woman with a letter folded beneath his neck. She starves him for a week while she writes a letter to send to her love, then sends him home. And so they go, back and forth." Louis touched the bird as he said this, his finger brushing across Bel's knuckles.

"The swan must always be hungry," said Bel.

"The swan is the sacrifice for them," Louis said solemnly, withdrawing his hand. "In the story, they don't get punished for their adultery, but the swan starves all those years."

"That's not fair." Bel kicked a piece of straw over the edge.

"No," Louis said simply.

The hay bales that surrounded them smelled of a long-lost summer, faintly green and sweet.

"Why did you come to the party if you didn't want to dance?" she asked.

"I came . . ." He paused, and stared down into the hole as if he were waiting to greet someone climbing up. "I came because I was interested."

"Interested?"

"Interested in what would make a girl like you tell me she would die for love. I thought there might be a man here who could make you say that, and if so, I wanted to meet him." He uttered his speech to the darkness below them. Bel stared down at the film of dust on her dress and shivered.

"I'm cold," she said, unwilling to acknowledge the seriousness of his statement. "And I don't love any man, except for my father, and my cousin Laurence."

"I'll give you my coat," he said automatically, and pressed his thumbs against the silver buttons, undoing them one by one.

"You don't want to go back inside?" Bel watched his shoulders flex back as he shrugged off the coat. He's a man, she thought, without knowing why. Behind his dress shirt, his collarbones jutted like branches.

"Will you marry your cousin?" Louis asked, instead of answering her. He spread the warm shell of wool over her shoulders and whisked his palms together to bring the heat back into them.

"Oh no," Bel said. Her love for her cousin had nothing to do with the romantic scenes she pored over in books, trying to dislodge her heart from its firm mooring in her chest. "He's like a brother to me. I know him too well."

Louis gave a satisfied nod. He seemed fascinated by the still room below them and would not look at her. Bel huddled deep in his coat and waited for another question. She liked the way the wide wool shoulders made her feel small and protected.

"Sometimes the slaves were too sick to live, even if they reached freedom," he said after a minute. "We have ten graves in the woods behind our house. Mostly babies. If they were about to die, the priest would come late at night and baptize them. My mother had me dig the holes for the small ones," he said, then paused. Bel was about to interrupt, when he cleared his throat. "Today when you asked me if I would fight to end slavery, just then I saw myself at fifteen years old, digging a grave at midnight in half-frozen ground. I always thought that was enough, that I was Canadian and it wasn't an issue for my country."

He tossed a gold length of straw into the void below them and continued. "I went and enlisted today after I met you. I came tonight to tell you that."

Chapter Twenty-one

The party had settled into its middle age by the time Bel and Louis returned to the house. All the guests had arrived, the less temperate men had tarnished their chins with the nutmeg of their fourth eggnogs, and the eldest elders were beginning to succumb to the long, slow blinks of approaching sleep. Uncle George was chosen king, and Mary Ruth Cross his lady queen. Together, they made a gangly monarchy of commands and giggles in the center of the room.

The cold air had colored Bel's cheeks, and she longed to creep to her former position at the top of the stair, where she could observe the party unnoticed. She and the tutor came in through separate entrances, the weight of their conversation having made them both awkward and eager to leave the silent confines of the coach barn. Bel hadn't known what to say about his decision to fight with the Army of the Potomac on her account, but she admired his sense of purpose anyway. Louis was just entering the other door, his hair still upended from their collision in the hayloft, when Bel heard her uncle, the king.

"Why, there is a girl who hasn't waltzed all night. Isabel Lindsey, I order you to dance with the last man who walked through the door."

"That would be me. I was the last arrival." Ernest Pomeroy stepped forward. The balding eldest son of her parents' friends had tried to kiss Bel in the dining room the year before, but she had run away from him, wiping her sleeve across her lips.

"That's not true!" exclaimed Mary Ruth Cross, placing her hands on her small and perfect hips, her paper crown slipping down over her forehead. "It was Monsieur Pacquette who just came back in."

As string players in the alcove by the staircase struck up a lively, light-footed waltz, Bel met Louis in the center of the room. He looked annoyed by the king's decision and placed his hand on her shoulder with a distracted air. Bel turned her cheek toward the cool fabric of his shirtfront. A clumsy, timid dancer, she generally avoided it at all costs and longed to escape now.

Louis, strong and assured, steered them in tight circles. Bel, seeing her mother watching from her seat beside Mary Ruth's parents, tried to appear happy.

"Relax," the tutor ordered after a few other couples began to pivot around the room. "Your body is too stiff for me to lead."

"Oh, so it's my fault," Bel retorted, defensive.

"Think of yourself as water pouring down a hill," he advised. "Let the hill take you where it wants to go."

"And I suppose you're the hill that gets to make all the decisions."

"The hill is the music, Isabel." He clicked his teeth in reprimand.

"Bel," she reminded him, although in her mind she was already trying to let the music decide her movements.

"I prefer Isabel," he said.

"Well, then I prefer Miss Lindsey, if you wish to be formal." Bel trampled the toe of his right foot.

Instead of answering, Louis suddenly picked up his pace, so that she was spinning, the whole room spinning, and the focal point his face, dark, intent, his mouth pursed into a line that balanced somewhere between concentration and disapproval. Bel surrendered to the steps, her feet flying up and down, back and forth as they never had before, her heels always in the air. Couples parted for them—blurred to a spectrum of muted winter colors, their figures fixed in their own small circles. And then the music loomed where the rest of the world had vanished, a high sawing that reached all the way to the creamy candles of the chandelier. When it stopped, Louis slowed his steps and released her with a contained bow.

"Mademoiselle, it was a pleasure."

Bel sank into a breathless curtsy. Her uncle approached them.

"Well, Monsieur Pacquette, I have heard from my queen that you are such a splendid dancer, I wondered if you would take a turn with the lady of the house."

Behind her uncle's shoulder, Bel saw Mary Ruth bite her lip in disappointment, evidently expecting that she would be the one appointed to the role.

"Monsieur," replied Louis, "I can't refuse to dance with the lady of the house, but after that, I must take my leave. I have had a very long day at the recruiting office."

"Are you trying to find a particular soldier?" Uncle George asked. "My son—"

"No, I'm a soldier myself. I enlisted today." This was said with forthright certainty, as if the young man had known of his decision for a long time.

Mary Ruth clapped her hands over her face with a small cry. Still dizzy from the dance, Bel stared at him, unable to believe he was really going.

"Well, because of your imminent departure into the company of men, perhaps you would like to dance again with a young woman," mused the king, straightening his lopsided crown.

Mary Ruth nodded with ill-concealed eagerness, but Louis shook his head and gestured to the approaching Faustina. "The young woman she was must have broken many hearts," he said.

The king flushed and tugged vigorously at his beard. Bel watched them with hard, dry eyes, irritated with her mother for stealing all the attention. The emotion surprised her, for she was accustomed to her mother's superiority when it came to men.

"Well, monsieur, you are just a sensation among the ladies," Faustina said, although she glanced at Bel when she spoke. "They haven't danced with anyone so skilled since Thomas Van Sicklin left with the Third Vermont regiment."

"I beg your pardon," said Ernest Pomeroy, crowding into the small circle. He was the kind of fellow who would make any comment just to insert himself and his round stomach into a conversation. Having conquered his position, he would stand there for as long as the talk lasted, just breathing. "I'm still here," he added.

"Yes, you are, Ernest. But I simply will not allow you to take up any more of Monsieur Pacquette's valuable time by trying to waltz with him," Faustina interjected. "I hear you have only one dance left." She held out her hand.

Louis accepted with a bow. "If it will please the king," he murmured.

The king looked as if he were trying to think of something both witty and merciless to say, all the while regarding Bel's mother. Finally, he waved his hand. "The king decrees it," he said. "Would you turn a reel with me, Bel?"

Bel nodded, swallowing hard. She was still angry at him for upsetting her mother, and she didn't want to spoil the pleasant memory of the dance with Louis. When her uncle placed his palm against her upper back, she couldn't prevent an involuntary shudder. In the past year, she had often found his eyes resting on her, and something about his touch disturbed her now. She wanted to avoid it, the same way she had avoided Johnny Mulcane after she had tried to teach him to write.

"That leaves us," said Ernest, turning to Mary Ruth as Bel waltzed off in the king's arms.

"I suppose you've heard that Laurence is leaving Mt. Pleasant," announced her uncle. They moved together toward the alcove, where the string players' bows moved like small jags of lightning. "And he's going to a place called Camp Convalescence, which your aunt says has a bad reputation with the Sanitary Commission."

"When will he get well, Uncle?" Bel's voice trembled. She wanted to think of her cousin as a soldier, not a sick man.

"When the winter is over, I suppose," Uncle George said as he tightened his grip on her hand. Bel shrank back in her clothing so as to have as little contact as possible between them. "If I were really king, I would order him home."

"Even if he wanted to stay and fight?"

"How can a man want to live in a dirty, vermin-infested tent when he could have one of our fine bedrooms?" the king said, trying to make it sound like he was joking. They swished passed her mother and Louis, who were talking and laughing like old confidants. Bel was momentarily distracted by them and didn't answer her uncle right away.

"How can he choose that life?" he added with a shrug.

"Because conviction is the one thing you couldn't buy for him, Uncle," she moralized. "Laurence doesn't want a fine bedroom, or even a rich house. He wants a world he can believe in."

Her uncle stopped waltzing but did not release her, his eyes flashing as they had in the old days when he and Faustina used to fight over Douglas and Lincoln at family dinners.

"The world isn't made of ideals, Isabel," he said. "It's made of men."

Unable to meet his gaze, she stared at his collar. The starched fabric pinched his neck and made the skin swell over it, but its stiff lines were beginning to strain, and by the end of the night, they would wear away, taking the same curve as his flesh.

"Let me go," Bel shouted, stepping back. She bumped into her father, who had come up behind her, obligingly dancing with the relentless Hannah Fithian. His damaged hand hooked around Hannah's, the three misshapen fingers splayed above her own delicate palm as if she held a knot of branches. Bel stood for a minute, paralyzed between the two brothers, and then twisted away under her father's raised arm to sprint up the spiral staircase to the second floor.

"She doesn't mean what she says these days," she heard her father say, apologizing to the king. "She's at that age where everything is difficult."

Faustina's voice rose above the din. "Let's have the cake, so Monsieur Pacquette can be fortified for his long journey south."

Bel looked back, to see Louis smiling at her mother, taking her in, as if he had forgotten there were any other women in the world.

Chapter Twenty-two

Mary was trying to wrestle the kissing ball down with a long pole when Louis knocked on the door for Bel's second French lesson. From her mother, who seemed to have become an expert on the tutor in one reel, Bel had learned that Louis would not be starting his training until the beginning of February, which left three more weeks in Allenton. Faustina insisted that the lessons to improve her daughter's impoverished French continue in the meantime.

The mistletoe splintered and fell in small sharp leaves as Mary jousted it with her pole, muttering in untranslatable Gaelic.

"The door," called Bel, sitting in precisely the same curve of the stairs where she had watched the Twelfth Night festivities the week before.

The broken leaves dusted across Mary's white cap and stuck in her hair. She let the pole fall with an aggrieved clatter and went to answer the door. Bel watched as the servant yanked the knob back, revealing Louis, silhouetted against the high banks of snow outside. He nodded to Mary, who gave a low, smitten curtsy and followed him inside. The servant's response made Bel study her tutor curiously as she descended the stairs. She hadn't thought of Louis as especially handsome, just pleasing to look at. Maybe he was more dashing than she thought.

"Monsieur," she said in the best accent she could muster. With her father away and her mother retired for an afternoon nap, Bel had safely put on her second-best dress and pinched her lips and cheeks to rosiness. The swan necklace made a small lump beneath her dress, but she did not dare wear it in the open with Mary around.

"Miss Lindsey," Louis said, setting down his strap of books to pull off his gloves. Bel blushed, remembering her irrational plea for formality.

"Shall we go to the library?" She turned to lead the way up the stairs. Mary began to follow, ignoring the mess of mistletoe. "I hear you are leaving us at the end of the month, Mr. Pacquette," Bel said, trying to assume her mother's gracious, teasing air on Twelfth Night. "Mary, would you please continue working on that mistletoe? I think we can find the library ourselves."

Mary glowered at Bel's sudden superiority, but she stomped obediently back down the stairs.

"Perhaps sooner," reflected Louis. "I must return to Canada to take leave of my mother."

They reached the top of the stairs and walked in silence down the portrait hall to the library. Henry and Isabel Gale regarded them with their usual cool distaste as Bel and Louis brushed against each other crossing the threshold. Bel had asked Mary to light a fire in the grate an hour before, and now it burned a lustrous orange.

"You mustn't mind Mary," Bel advised. "She gets so taken with young men, you know."

"I don't mind Mary." Sitting down at the table by the fireplace, Louis unhooked the leather strap and began flipping through his books. Bel hovered uncertainly between the chair right next to him and the one opposite. Finally, in a fit of shyness, she chose the one opposite. She watched Louis's dark bent head for a moment, expectant. He did not look up for some time, and when he did, he shoved a book across the table at her.

"I think this will be easy enough for you," he said. "Please read it aloud and we will work on that terrible Yankee pronunciation of yours."

Smarting from the insult, Bel took the book and began to read, her voice wooden and echoing against the walls of shelves. Every few seconds, Louis would stop her and have her repeat a word, his eyes boring into her. When they completed the passage, nothing of which Bel had the time or ability to comprehend, he had her read it aloud again, without interruption.

After she finished, Bel glared dully at the table, refusing to raise her head.

"Do you know what you just read?" His tone was gentle now. Against the polished oak, his hands looked like boats on a distant pond.

"No."

"You just read the first page of the 'Lay of Milun,' about the messenger swan," Louis said triumphantly.

"Oh." Bel touched the place where the bird locket lay against her skin. She met his eyes and a flash of heat washed over her. The walls of the room moved closer, the fire crackling loudly in the grate.

"I thought you would like it." He sounded disappointed by her reaction.

"Oh, Monsieur Pacquette, I'm flattered that you would remember our conversation," Bel answered, trying once again to adopt her mother's wiles.

"I wish you wouldn't speak to me that way. It's not becoming," he said quietly, and then resumed his teacherly manner. "Today, I think we should work on verbs."

"Why? I mean, why can't I speak the way I want?" Bel demanded.

"That's it precisely. Speak the way you want, not the way you think you should," Louis said, leaning forward on his elbows. "Now, most French verbs follow the same pattern, but some are irregular—for example, the infinitive *to be*."

"I thought men liked that sort of thing," Bel muttered. "My mother is rather successful at it."

"Because she believes she has to be," said Louis. "I have noticed that it doesn't come easily to her, either. She wasn't raised to be a hostess. I'm certain she was a lot like you."

This comparison both pleased and irritated Bel. "She used to live in the country," Bel admitted. "On a big sheep farm. I remember her telling me stories about going out at night to roll down the highest hill they could find."

"They?"

"She and my father. And my uncle, I suppose. They all grew up together." Bel bit her lip and stared hard at one of the books. "You said we were going to study verbs? I hate verbs."

"How can your sentence go anywhere without a verb? Verbs are like the horse pulling the wagon, or the coal in the train engine," Louis said, following the new direction of the conversation.

"Oh, please don't talk about trains. That's all my father and uncle go on about. The best new engine and the latest type of rail and who has a line going where. It's frightfully dull," she added, regurgitating an opinion that had originated with her cousin Laurence.

"Very well, then. Since trains are forbidden by the lady, we shall go back to verbs." Louis rapped the book with a pair of spectacles he had just pulled from his pocket.

"Before we do, may I ask you one more thing?" Bel pleaded, wanting to postpone the lesson.

"I am your servant, mademoiselle." Louis inclined his head. In the hallway outside the library, Mary drifted by with the deliberately absent expression of someone pretending not to listen. She was carrying a tall pile of white linen.

"Do you regret your choice to enlist?" Bel asked.

Louis sighed and put on his spectacles before answering. "I regret I must leave so soon." His eyes were the color of caramels.

Just then, Mary marched in with a feather duster. "Mrs. Lindsey, she wanted me to give the library a good going-over," she said in a loud voice. "But don't you mind me one bit. I like Franch, and one of my great-aunts in Ireland went to Paris and married a visscount there."

"So, let's start with the infinitive *to name*," said Louis, smiling at Bel across the table. Bel nodded, watching Mary's freckled arms stretch for the highest books, the dust raining down over her determined pear-shaped face. *"Comment vous appelez-vous?"*

"Je m'appelle Isabel," she answered.

Chapter Twenty-three

In the blue light of her bedroom, Bel pressed her lips against her arm to feel what it was like to be kissed by her mouth. Unmoved, and a little spit-speckled from the process, the arm fell to her lap. She kissed again, with greater fury this time, sucking at the skin below the elbow. The arm grew hot with her breath. Only when a stray hair tangled in her teeth did she halt her passionate advance and draw back to examine the arched red mark on her skin.

Today, Louis would leave for Virginia. Bel had been practicing for his departure for a long time, examining an array of her own reactions in mirrors and windowpanes: the soft pout, the trembling "I'm trying to be brave" look, the hard and studied carelessness of someone pretending her heart isn't broken. Her suppressed romance with Louis had made Bel's life seem much larger than before, made her remember with scorn the girl who hated dancing and giggled nervously when characters claimed their undying love in books.

Her mother called her name. It was time. Bel gave one more practiced smile at the silver mirror and stuffed the swan locket beneath her dress. She wanted Louis to see it, but she was afraid Mary's sharp eyes would notice the swan and claim it. She rose unsteadily, laden with voluminous petticoats, pinched her cheeks, and made her way to the stairs.

"Isabel," her mother called again. "Your tutor has come to bid us farewell."

"I'm coming," Bel said, wondering if she should sound surprised. For weeks, she had dreaded the day Louis would board the train for Brattleboro, where his training would commence. Their last two French lessons had passed under the supervision of Bel's mother, who must have surmised the budding romance between the tutor and his charge. Bel resented this intrusion fiercely and had treated her mother with more than the usual adolescent belligerence. Imperturbable, Faustina had attended the sessions, knitting quietly in the corner while a flushed Louis had pressed her daughter on proper grammar and punctuation.

She reached the stairs and looked down on her parents and tutor standing by the door. Louis had already donned his blue wool uniform, which, in contrast to his former clothes, fit him perfectly. In the gray February light, his face looked remote and thoughtful, as if he were considering a matter of politics or religion. There was the slight air of a clergyman about Louis, Bel realized, someone whom people would trust enough to tell their secrets but who would never relay his own in return. Her father and mother were clustered beside him, watching as she descended the steps. Daniel said something low, which made Louis give his pained smile and bow slightly. Bel blushed.

"I was saying that you are too lovely to be made to frown over grammar," Daniel told her in his awkward way.

Bel did frown then and they laughed, although Louis's eyes remained serious, even a little apologetic. "You're leaving us," she said simply. How much more she wanted to say, but her parents hovered like giant marble statues, immobile but listening.

"Yes," said Louis. "The train departs at two o'clock."

"And you'll look for Laurence when you get there," Bel said, her lips trembling.

"I have at least a month of training first. But when I get to Virginia, yes," he added stiffly. "Or wherever they send us."

"God forbid you end up in some malarial swamp in Mississippi." Daniel shook his head. Bel's father had been engrossed in his drawings before the tutor's arrival, and his thin hair spoked out in all directions.

"Hush, Daniel," Faustina said. "With luck, the war will be over before Mr. Pacquette even has to fight."

A silence fell over them. Bel had the urge to laugh. The scene was so ridiculous: her parents chaperoning her good-bye to her tutor. All the code she and Louis had developed to communicate during their supervised lessons was lost and they stared at each other helplessly.

"Well, good-bye." Bel extended her hand. He flashed her a single look of grave devotion as he bent over it, his lips lightly brushing her fingers. Bel's heart pounded.

"Yes, good-bye, Louis," Faustina said, offering her own hand. "And by the time you return, no doubt our daughter will have forgotten everything you've taught her."

"That would be a shame," the tutor said as he bent again. Not to be outdone, Daniel Lindsey thrust out his right fist as soon as Louis straightened.

"I admire the men and women of your generation," Daniel said, as if he had just made up his mind about some great, important thing. "You act, whereas mine waited. And you are stronger for that." Bel watched her mother glance at him with surprise.

"Yes. But they suffer for it, too," Faustina lectured, picking up on the usual tack of her husband. Suddenly, the two were reversing roles in an argument that had lasted for years. She pressed her hand over her collarbone and continued. "Our nephew will never be the same bright boy who left us, even if he comes back with all his limbs."

Why are they telling him this? Bel wondered, and then realized her parents weren't speaking to Louis at all, but to each other. "Maybe Laurence didn't want to be the same bright boy who left you," Bel commented, surprising herself. "Maybe he's a better man now."

"Don't speak that way to your mother," Daniel said, and Bel lowered her head, wishing the whole departure were over.

"I must take my leave," Louis said, as if sensing her thought, then turned to look out the window at the February landscape. Icicles made a sharp, jagged line across the top of the pane, descending from Greenwood's peculiar ledges like the teeth of a dragon. "I shall miss the ice," he said. "I fear there will be nothing so clear in all of Virginia."

There was a pause, and then Faustina spoke up. "We mustn't keep you," she said to Louis, but she was scrutinizing her daughter. Suddenly, all of Bel's practiced emotions fell away and she had to bite her lip hard to keep tears from flooding her eyes. Then her mother was thanking Louis for his courtesy, her voice polite but loud, as if she were ordering a roast from the butcher's. Daniel's left hand wagged in his pocket. Louis listened gravely, nodding already like a private receiving orders.

Finally, the taste of blood on her tongue woke Bel from her grief. She bid the tutor a calm good-bye and then watched him from the window, waiting for his figure to reach the lane.

Water dripped from the end of the icicles, framing the tutor's exit. After Louis turned the corner, a sleigh crossed his tracks, obliterating them. Bel's mother and father swiveled to look at her, and she gave them a fragile yet forbidding smile. "I suppose I'll forget everything," she said lightly. "In six months, he'd despair over my accent."

"It takes a long time to learn a language." Faustina tipped her lovely face toward her husband. "Doesn't it, Daniel?"

His crooked left hand emerged and settled on Faustina's shoulder, steering her away. "And a short time to forget it," he answered, sounding a little penitent. "Up in the study, I have a new draft for the reservoir," he added. "May I show it to you? I need your advice."

"Certainly." Faustina curtsied. "Bel?"

"I want to go outside," Bel said stubbornly. How excited she had once felt to be shown her father's plans, inked in his tiny, exact handwriting over sheaves of curling paper. He had even let her choose the metal spires for the new railroad station down in the lumberyards. But now his notes and sketches were like bird tracks to her, just another ordinary passage spelled across the yard.

"Don't go far," her mother warned.

"I won't." Bel allowed a note of bitterness to creep into her promise. The red mark on her arm had remained, a thin crescent the size of a fingernail, but the soft kiss Louis had given her fingers left no impression, as if it had not happened at all.

Her parents exchanged looks, then drifted off together, arm in arm. After they were gone, Bel went out into the garden alone. She broke off the largest icicle she could find and held it, burning her hands with the cold, until it melted.

January–December 1863

Chapter Twenty-four

When dark fell, Laurence found himself trying to sleep in a cramped, unstable tent with three other men. They were all drenched and hungry, but food and dry ground already seemed impossible to come by at Camp Convalescence. He and Woodard had arrived there that afternoon and then had had to stand in several long lines in the rain before they were allowed to enter the miserable campground, which was situated on an old plantation. All the majestic trees had been chopped down for firewood long ago, and the giant stumps glowed between tents as Laurence and Woodard sloshed down the muddy rows, searching for a place to sleep.

By dusk, they managed to team up with two New Hampshire men, who had commandeered a cast-off tent from a guard. After a grim hour of erecting the faulty apparatus in a downpour, there had been nothing to do but lie down in it. Laurence had drawn the shortest match and was stuck with the drafty position by the entrance. He heard his ribs creak as he huddled against the chilly earth, trying to remember the kind faces of the nurses at Mt. Pleasant and the rich soups he had tasted every day when he was there. The tent snapped and he burrowed deeper beneath his blanket, expecting a cold gust to follow.

Instead, he heard a small voice begging, "Make room, please." Laurence sat up and opened the flap. Outside it stood a young man, shivering. He had the rickety, unraveling build of a wicker chair, one shoulder jutting higher than the other, and his face was charcoaled by the shadows of hunger. Laurence pushed back to make some room for him, jostling his neighbors, who were still faking sleep.

"Hold on, now. 'M afraid we're full up," said the burlier of the New Hampshire men in a voice that indicated he was fully awake. His knuckles pressed into Laurence's spine.

"Keep on trying down the line. Sommun'll let you in," his partner added.

"I been trying," the young man insisted. The words ghosted from his mouth in delicate clouds. "You're the last tent."

"We could make room," Laurence said hopefully, although the hard-earned stability of their cast-off tent might truly be destroyed by another body.

"We ain't got any room to make. Sorry," said the first New Hampshire man.

"Sorry, son," the other one echoed, contrite. Laurence glanced to Woodard for help, but his friend feigned sleep, his face damp and serene.

"But I'm a Vermonter. Please, in the name of being a Vermonter." The boy would not give up. He crossed his arms over his chest and bent down to look inside the dim cavern. "There's room," he said eagerly. "I don't take up much."

"Let's make room for him." Laurence kicked Lyman Woodard, who shifted slightly but did not come to his defense. "He said he won't take up much," he added, as if the men could not hear the boy.

"In this democrissy, you air outvoted, sir, three to one." The burly New Hampshire man sat up. "Either give up your own spot or shut that flap. We ain't got room."

Laurence met the boy's eyes for the first time. His pupils were so large, the irises so thin, the center of his gaze was like the darkness just before dawn, when the faint sliver of light at the rim of the hills looks too weak to prevail. Laurence recoiled when the boy tried to smile.

"Naw, that ain't right," the boy said softly. "You keep your place," he added, as if Laurence had already offered to rise and trade with him.

"You said you walked the whole line," protested Laurence. Very slowly, his arm was letting the flap fall shut.

"I'll walk it again." The boy straightened and faced back up the row of tents. "There's someone'll let me in."

"If you say so," Laurence said doubtfully, but the arm had finished its work; the flap was almost closed, except for a thin crack through which he watched the boy drift out of sight. And although Laurence listened to the sloshing of his boots all the way up the lane, he never heard the boy's voice again.

Chapter Twenty-five

His small load of branches was hardly enough to last their miserable second night at Camp Convalescence, but they were all Laurence could find after three hours of gathering wood. The forests around the camp had been picked down to the bare earth, and many soldiers had taken to stripping the lowest green branches as well, making the trees look like they stood on stilts. Laurence hadn't walked so long in months, and the effort had exhausted his weakened body, his legs trembling as they climbed the last short slope.

He wondered if Woodard had fared any better with his chore, which was to find a tent for the two of them. Their domicile from the night before had leaked so badly, they parted ways with the New Hampshire men at dawn, eager to make a fresh start on their own. Laurence was glad to take firewood duty. He didn't like the look of the longtime residents of Camp Convalescence, a surly, obdurate bunch who crowded around their morning fires as if to hoard for themselves the very sight of the warmth and light. The wholesome air of Mt. Pleasant was entirely absent here, and he wondered at the effectiveness of a recovery camp that made its soldiers sicker.

Skirting past the garden wall of the old plantation, he saw a man limping ahead of him with a similarly small armload of sticks under one arm, a crutch under the other. If it had taken Laurence all afternoon to find his own stash, it must have occupied his neighbor's entire day. His bandaged right leg wagged out to the side, while the left hopped along with grudging speed. Laurence was about to offer to help, when a handsome blond guard accosted the soldier.

"Well, Davis," said the guard with a toss of his head.

"Well, Captain," Davis grunted, maintaining his slow pace forward.

"It's a small price to pay, but it will do," said the guard. "Give it here now."

Davis halted but kept his eyes aimed at the ground.

"Give it here now and I'll get you that little something you need to help you sleep at night," said the guard. Davis still did not move, but he allowed the guard to ease the load from under his arm. "Give it here," he said soothingly.

"When, sir?" said Davis in a low voice.

"Soon." The guard was already striding away, carrying his prize. Laurence waited until he had turned down another row, and then he caught up with Davis.

"Here," he said. "Take a couple of mine. You can have a small fire."

Davis looked at him. He had a dull, indifferent gaze and the flabby mouth of a drinker.

"Please," said Laurence, handing him a few branches.

"You must be new here," said Davis.

Laurence nodded and introduced himself. "Who was that?"

"Captain Ellroy. Captain of the guards," said Davis, limping forward again. "Don't cross him. He'll eat you alive."

He turned abruptly and hopped off in the opposite direction, the branches clutched tightly beneath his arm.

Woodard had already set up the tent by the time Laurence arrived, and he sat in front of it now, grinning. His hands were looped over his knees and shins, both so bony from loss of weight that they gave him a childlike air.

"I'm going to be part of an opera," he burst out, his usually eager expression honed to one of fervent joy.

Laurence shifted his pile of wood to one arm and pointed to the tent. "Where did you get it?"

"Captain Ellroy," said Woodard. "I went around asking this morning, and nobody would even look me in the eye until I met him. But he said he knew when he saw me that I might have acting talent, and he promised to help me out."

"A good-looking blond fellow?" Laurence crouched down and began to dig a pit for the fire.

"That's him," said Woodard. "He's organizing an opera."

"I wouldn't trust him too much if I were you," said Laurence. "I saw him take firewood from a cripple."

"You're just jealous," Woodard said. "You spent all day gathering firewood and that's all you found?"

"Firewood's impossible to come by," Laurence retorted. "That's probably why some people steal it."

"Some people also told me a bit of information you might like to know." Woodard folded his arms. Overshadowed by his giant nose, his chin looked like it was in desperate retreat from the upper half of his face.

"What's that?" Laurence began to arrange the sticks. "Did you get anything to eat?"

Woodard pulled out a small sack of hardtack and salt pork. "I got coffee, too," he said. "And a pot."

They hadn't consumed anything that solid for weeks, but Laurence supposed it was time to start trying. His strength was coming back to him.

"What was the information?"

Woodard bit into a piece of hardtack. "He's here," he said. Crumbs scattered over his lips.

"Who?"

"Gilbert Rhodes."

Laurence sat back, staring at his companion. "Gilbert Rhodes? Why don't we go invite him to eat with us?"

"We can't," Woodard said smugly. "He's praying."

The more interested Laurence looked, the longer it would take to pry the full story from Woodard, so he lowered his head and went back to the sticks.

"They call him 'the Preacher,' and he gives two sermons a day, one at noon and one after dusk," Woodard blurted out after a moment. "The rest of the time, he prays for our souls."

"How do you know it's Gilbert?"

"Ellroy took me to see him today. He used to like the Preacher, but now he's getting tired of him. That's why he wants to start an opera."

"Did Gilbert recognize you?"

Woodard shrugged, his lips pressed together. "I don't care if he did or not. I never liked him anyway."

Laurence looked to the west. Another hour until sunset. He sparked a few leaves with flint and watched the fire rise, thinking of the last time he had seen his comrade in the apple orchard near Antietam Creek. Gilbert had never written them, and Laurence had assumed he had either died or gone home to Vermont. To meet him again would mean reliving the horror of that night, but he had to go.

"What kind of opera?" he asked, shaking off the memory.

"A tragedy," Woodard said. "Ellroy wants it to be a tragedy."

Sitting in the mud outside the Preacher's tent that night was the sorriest bunch of soldiers Laurence had ever seen. A third were lame, their crutches rattling beside them as they sat down; a third were clearly ill, with gummy eyes and pale complexions; and the remaining men each displayed his own particular combination of unkempt hair, fuzzy teeth, and body odor.

"There he is," said Woodard as they arrived.

"Where?" Laurence looked around for Gilbert.

"There." Woodard pointed and waved. Amid the motley crowd, Captain Ellroy shone like a lantern on a dark night, his uniform and hair immaculate, his hands clasped behind his back. He gave them a nod and looked toward the lamp-lit tent before them.

The men fell silent as a flap opened and a man wearing two sewn-together officer's cloaks stepped out. It took Laurence a moment to recognize Gilbert Rhodes behind the long dark beard. In the tent behind him glowed heaps of ambrotypes, letters, and ribbons, the small keepsakes that soldiers carried with them as reminders of home.

" 'And I saw when the Lamb opened one of the seals, and I heard, as it were the noise of thunder, one of the four beasts saying, "Come and see," ' " said Gilbert in a low voice. " 'And I saw, and behold, a white horse. And he that sat on him had a bow and a crown, and went forth conquering.' "

After he uttered these lines, Gilbert looked at Ellroy, who gave a tiny nod, and seemed pleased when the Preacher proceeded through the ensuing passage from Revelations, which Laurence remembered vaguely from childhood Sundays. As far as he could remember, it was about the horsemen of the apocalypse, the false Christ on a white horse, and then War, Famine, Pestilence, and Death following him. Was Gilbert predicting the end of the world? A wind swept up and made the flap of the Preacher's tent fall shut behind him.

"What the hell is he talking about?" whispered Woodard. Laurence didn't answer. Listening to Gilbert's voice ring through the foul-smelling camp, it suddenly seemed possible that the earth had fallen into ruin, that all men were wicked, and a judging God was sitting in that yellow tent, waiting to be unleashed on the world.

"'And I looked, and behold, a pale horse: and his name that sat on him was Death, and Hell followed him,'" Gilbert suddenly roared in Ellroy's direction, making the men turn and stare at the guard. Ellroy's hands unclasped from behind his back and Laurence could see they had curled into fists.

"Death," Gilbert went on. "After my first battle in this war, I hated and feared death, like he was an old friend who had turned on me"—he nodded at Ellroy—"who said he was going to take away everything I had if I didn't pray enough, or fight enough, or give him his due. So I prayed in every battle not to die, and I had my own little lucky tricks, like the rest of you. I almost died at Antietam, where I lost my foot." He thrust the bandaged stump out from beneath his cloak. "But instead of asking death not to come, I just waited. And the Lord found it fit to save me, but only after he gave me a vision."

As if on cue, the wind coursed in again, opening the tent flap and revealing the lamp-lit possessions inside.

"A vision of my friend Death riding a pale horse through a fire," said Gilbert. "The Lord told me not to fear him anymore, but the fire he rode through. The fire that will burn men who do not live virtuous lives."

This argument went on for some time, building in fury. The men were so riveted that most missed Ellroy stalking away, but Laurence saw it, and he turned to Woodard.

"What did the captain tell you about Gilbert?" he whispered.

"He told Gilbert right to his face that he was getting bored with his preaching." Woodard seemed impressed by this. "And Gilbert, he promised to give him a good story tonight. One about a hero like him."

. . .

When he finished, Gilbert retreated immediately to his tent again, and the men filed off in twos and threes, their heads low. The crutches left little crescents in the mud, as if they had been made by tiny horses.

Woodard and Laurence hesitated a moment in the emptied arena, looking up at the star-filled sky. Laurence had thought Gilbert would recognize them in the crowd, and he didn't know how to approach him now.

Woodard cleared his throat. "He ain't going to come out," he said.

Anything was better than listening to Woodard complain. Laurence bent down and tapped on the tent flap.

"Go away," said the voice inside.

"Gilbert, it's Laurence Lindsey and Lyman Woodard," said Laurence. His voice sounded weak and thin.

The flap swept back and Gilbert peered out.

"Why are you here?" he said, examining them with a quick, irritable glance.

"Stomach fever." Woodard touched a spot below his ribs. "We had it terrible, but we're getting well again."

"Don't expect to get better here," warned Gilbert. He did not move back to let them inside.

"I'm glad to see you alive, Gilbert," said Laurence. Now his voice sounded too loud. "I'm going to write Addison tomorrow and let him know."

Gilbert grunted and toyed with his beard.

"What are all those, Gilbert?" Woodard peered into the tent.

"The fellows give 'em to me to pray over," said Gilbert. " 'Pray for me to get home alive,' they beg me. Nobody cares about winning the war anymore." He lifted a heap of letters and let them sift through his hands. "Except probably you and your nigger regiments, Lindsey."

Laurence flushed, remembering how much Gilbert used to irk him. "When are they sending you home? You obviously can't fight anymore."

Gilbert gazed at the sky behind him, not answering.

"You better get back to your tents. It's going to rain, and I ain't getting rained on." He started to close the flap.

"We'll come see you again tomorrow," Laurence promised weakly. "For old times."

"I'm a busy man," the Preacher said, scowling.

"Come on, Lindsey. He don't care about us," said Woodard. "He's a big preacher now."

"Soon then." Laurence pulled his coat closer against the wind, which seemed sharper and colder now, as if it had come across a frozen lake. "Right, Woodard?"

Woodard gave a sullen nod, but the second they both turned away, he fell facedown on the ground with a thump. Laurence twisted to see Gilbert's good foot retreating quickly back into the tent.

"What'd you do that for?" Woodard said, pushing himself up on his elbows. A splotch of mud had landed on his left eye and he rubbed it angrily.

Gilbert grinned. "For old times."

Chapter Twenty-six

Chilly gusts made the canvas tents snap and groan as Laurence stalked, head down, toward the corner of the camp where Ellroy had erected his theater. He was late. Woodard had left him earlier to go rehearse, and Laurence had dozed off after eating a solitary supper of hardtack. Sleep came and left him easily now, pushing and receding like a wave, sometimes stealing an afternoon but never lingering long enough to last the whole night.

It was a symptom, he had decided, of winter on the Potomac, which was neither fully cold nor fully warm, but a damp gray season that was somehow more dispiriting than its frigid, snowy counterpart in the north. The season had a vacuity that allowed the past to fill Laurence's mind, sensory and strange—reviving the lavender smell of his grandmother, the green park where they fed the birds together, the light prick of a chickadee's feet landing on his thumb. He would fall asleep comfortable and wake freezing, with rivulets of fallen rain flooding past his cheek, his hands stiff, aching when he flexed them.

They were numb now and he beat them against his thighs as he skirted the muddy pools that gathered in the rows between tents. Several of them were filled with piss and excrement. He looked up only when he heard a voice in the neighboring row call out, " 'And the fifth angel sounded, and I saw a star fall from heaven unto the earth: and to him was given the key to the bottomless pit.'" The voice paused. "'And he opened the bottomless pit; and there arose a smoke out of the pit.' And do you know what was in the smoke?"

There was no answer, where before there had been the murmur of a reply, from three dozen men, then two, then one, then a handful of stragglers who no longer sat obediently on the ground, but stood askance, their hands in their pockets, as if they might depart at any time. Tonight, there was no one outside Gilbert's tent but the Preacher himself, casting a long shadow over the mud. Laurence hid behind a flap of canvas and watched as Gilbert spoke to the emptiness, nodding and stroking his black beard.

He had hardly seen the Preacher since their first day in camp. Gilbert clearly had no interest in reviving their old camaraderie, and he kept to the little tent except when he came out to preach to his dwindling audience. It had been so long since their fight on picket, but now Laurence found himself measuring his former opponent like a boxer, seeing how his shoulder muscles had thinned, how his good leg was strong but the other as useless and weak as an old man's. His face, too, looked breakable, as if his newfound passion had scoured off the old violent weight, leaving behind only the emptiness he spoke to and the emptiness that listened back.

"Locusts," he was saying as Laurence turned away, splashing in a puddle and cursing softly as the scummy water soaked his calf. Locusts were the size and shape of bullets, Gilbert would go on to explain, making disastrous leaps of logic that always ended in a final question, shouted to the night: "'For the wrath of the Lord is come, and who shall be able to stand?'"

As he reached the edge of camp, Laurence thought he heard that same cry echoing across the rainy wind. In front of him, three tents formed an enclosed triangle that someone had labeled with the crude sign THE THETER OF WAR. The missing *A* was scrawled in above, but its author had made no attempt to join the letter to the word from which it was missing, and the *A* floated like a star above the others. Now in its fourth night of production, the opera had quickly become the most popular thing in camp, and Laurence's curiosity had finally gotten the better of him when he saw men carrying their invalid friends to it on stretchers. He jostled his way into the tents, which were already packed with blue uniforms.

A curtain made of gray blankets covered the back of the theater and hid the actors, although the cloth occasionally wagged and emitted loud curses, spoiling its mystery. In front of it, the crude stage was only deep enough to hold one low table, over which was draped a moth-eaten green curtain. Trying to look supremely disinterested in the proceedings, Laurence shoved through the crowd. As soon as he found a square of space behind his old New Hampshire tent mates, the lamps were snuffed. He stood in a blackness as dense as the hold of a ship.

Finally, one candle flickered and he heard the whisper of a skirt crossing the rough wood. The sound made a few men sigh audibly, until a lifted flame traveled up the moth-eaten blue taffeta gown, sunken at the hips and strained at the waist, past a conspicuous rib cage and over two lopsided but nonetheless prominent breasts to reveal Lyman Woodard's painted cheeks. The sighs turned to groans and then expectant silence. While the gown drooped from his narrow shoulders, Woodard's blond hair curled perfectly from beneath a crepe bonnet. He paced and wrung his hands for a dramatic minute before he settled on the single piece of furniture, making Laurence realize it was supposed to be a bed.

"THE CRIME OF AMNON," boomed a voice from behind the curtain. It belonged to Ellroy. Woodard blinked his sooty lashes and began to sing "When This Cruel War Is Over" in a grating falsetto.

When he reached the chorus of "weeping sad and lonely," the spectators started to shift and hiss. One spat a mouthful of tobacco at the green curtain.

The audience reaction appeared to Laurence to be part of the art of Ellroy's opera, for Woodard kept sawing away at the song until another fellow threw an empty canteen at his head and everyone laughed. This was the signal for the next thespian to appear, Ellroy himself, garbed in a butternut Confederate soldier's uniform and Union cap. His ensemble produced a second round of hisses, and many of the drinkers raised their canteens, taking long swallows and licking their lips in anticipation.

"Hello, sister," said Ellroy, toying with the saber at his hip.

"Hello, Amnon," squeaked Woodard, bounding up from the bed and adjusting his slipping right breast. Ellroy took Woodard's place on the wooden table.

"I am sick, Tamar." He lounged and coughed. "Make me some cake."

"Yes, brother." Woodard nodded vigorously, as if the crowd might doubt the affirmation in his words. After Tamar rustled back behind the curtain, Laurence heard a clanking, like a stove door opened to stoke a fire. He wondered at the choice of the story, and supposed it was a prelude to the political plot of Absalom, for the shaming of Tamar was really a lesser tale than the one of David's favorite son.

"Get on with it," a man in the crowd urged the prostrate Ellroy. The captain grinned. Rain pattered against the tent walls.

"Bring me the nourishment in the bedroom, so that I may have it from your hand," Ellroy said to the curtain behind him. At this, the clanking ceased and Woodard's Tamar appeared, bearing a tray of hardtack. She proceeded to the bed and held out the tray.

"From your hand," growled Ellroy. The men around Laurence

tensed, then leaned forward. Watching Woodard lift one square of hardtack from the tray and offer it to Ellroy, he felt his own heart quicken.

A raucous moan rose from the audience when Ellroy grabbed Woodard's wrist and pulled him on the table. Woodard's petticoats flashed, revealing his thin, bare calves. The tray fell with a clang. Crackers shattered everywhere as they hit the stage.

"Show more leg," said the burly New Hampshire man.

"Come, lie with me, sister," said Ellroy, pinning the petticoats with his butternut thigh.

"No, my brother. Do not shame me," whispered Woodard. The candle near the curtain was snuffed by a hand and then they heard only the noises of the men straining against each other. Beneath them, the table moaned, threatening to break.

Repulsed, Laurence was about to push his way out of the crowd, when the right wall of the tent tore in half. In the gap stood Gilbert Rhodes, ghosted by moonlight. He was clutching with his free arm the letters, ambrotypes, and good-luck tokens that had rested inside his quarters to be prayed over and blessed. His black eyes were dulled by the lack of light, but his voice rang out over the hushed men.

" 'Babylon the great is fallen, is fallen, and is become the habitation of devils, and the hold of every foul spirit, and a cage of every unclean and hateful bird.' " Rain threaded silver down his face. Dropping his cane and the keepsakes, he raised his arms in the most ancient of gestures—arms straight, palms flat—both the surrender and the embrace of the world. The cane clattered on the dirt, followed by letters, cameos, and portraits of wives and sweethearts cascading down.

Woodard and Ellroy untangled themselves just as the table shuddered and broke beneath them, and for a moment Laurence thought that Gilbert had won, that they would all file out, penitent, from the filthy tent. They would go on to live as brave soldiers and good brothers and husbands, never again looking in the direction that the stage had taken them. But then a canteen was lobbed from the crowd, hitting Gilbert on the shoulder. Although he flinched, he did not lower his arms.

"Get out!" someone shouted, and his cry was taken up by the others.

When the canteen bounced back into the crowd, the crippled Davis plucked it up and threw it harder against the Preacher's chest.

"Get out!" It became a chorus.

Gilbert coughed but did not move from the gap in the canvas. Another canteen caught him across the cheek, making it bleed. Then a piece of the shattered table cracked against his temple. He staggered, his eyes rolling back.

"Leave him alone!" Laurence yelled, but his words were swallowed by the crowd's angry chant. "Leave him alone," he repeated, seeing Pike's face falling down through the stream, hearing the boy's sweet voice rising above those of the contrabands. He pushed through the men toward Gilbert and took his own share of the flung canteens, slipping on the spilled letters. Catching the Preacher's tumbling body, he hauled him from the tent. Gilbert's once thickly muscled torso felt like a bag of sticks now, light and easy to lift. A fight broke out behind them as the men started scrambling for their fallen keepsakes.

After staggering down two rows of tents, Laurence paused to breathe. Gilbert blinked, moaning. " 'Babylon is fallen.' "

Laurence hushed him. "They might come after us," he whispered, pulling the Preacher upright. Gilbert hopped on his good leg.

"My cane," he said. "I carved it myself."

"We can't go back. It's too late, Gilbert."

"It's always too late, ain't it?" He stared at Laurence with the old accusing eyes before swiveling and trying to hop back in the direction of the theater.

"I would have saved Pike if I could," said Laurence, refusing to let go of the other man. "Why could you never believe that?"

It started to rain again.

"My uncle Johnny"—Gilbert slumped forward, his surge of strength gone—"he taught me to carve. He could whittle a stick into anything God made."

"I never knew," Laurence said softly. He had tried to forget about his uncle's hired man.

"He said your father once asked him to carve a swan and give it to Mrs. Faustina Lindsey, secret like. . . ." Gilbert paused.

The clouds completely masked the stars. No reflection shone in the puddles of mud and filth. They stumbled through them, Laurence holding Gilbert to keep him from falling.

"And when he did, she threw it in the fire. She let it burn while he watched. The bird he had taken a month to carve and had made so pretty because he loved her—he watched it burn until it was ash." The last words dribbled from the corner of Gilbert's mouth and he began sliding down, losing consciousness again.

Laurence let him crash to the earth, seeing the fire and his aunt's perfect hands, seeing the triumph in Johnny Mulcane's ugly face after he slapped Laurence across the cheek for prying into his things. Gilbert splayed against the mud, his uniform filthy, mouth agape. *Because he loved her*—Laurence could see the phrase falling with the rain, letter by letter.

Bending down, Laurence gathered Gilbert roughly in his arms and lifted him, cradling the Preacher's flopping head against his chest. There's nowhere to escape to, he thought, looking up at the ceiling of clouds, their soft shapes pushed north by unseen currents. The Theater of War. A cold, wet gust swept over the camp. The men behind him were still bickering with one another over the lost possessions, but their words splintered against the walls of rain, and he could not understand what they meant.

Chapter Twenty-seven

A square of light fell across Laurence's bed every morning, drifted to the floor in the afternoon, then ascended up the musty side of Lyman Woodard's cot, resting on the soldier's face until it died with the advance of evening. For the first three days in the southern Vermont hospital, Laurence had not been aware of the path of the light, only that in the morning he felt calm and serene, by afternoon jittery, and, by nightfall, gripped with the certainty he would die. He wept in his sleep and when he woke in the dark room, where other men sighed and sobbed their lovers' names, he was sure death had already taken him away.

The Vermont winter was thick with snow. It ghosted up the side of the window, rounding off the lower corners. On the fourth day, Gilbert, who lay across the row, knocked the pane free of the white weight, and Laurence suddenly noticed the outlines of the square of light. There it was, lying like a capsized sail over his body; there, it slipped to the floor. After years of living outside, he had forgotten that the sun could be broken like this.

Then it snowed again, and Gilbert no longer tried to knock the drifts away. Ever since the night in Ellroy's tent, the Preacher had gone silent. Even after they had been moved from Camp Convalescence to the tidy Brattleboro hospital their governor had established for ailing Vermont soldiers, his lips still moved in prayer, but he uttered nothing aloud, and he let his hair and beard grow long and shaggy. Laurence took to watching him, guessing what he was praying, and Gilbert didn't appear to mind, as if all along he had expected their old enmity toward each other would one day fade to simple curiosity.

Laurence himself was content with the slow, quiet days in the hospital, and he looked forward to seeing his mother and cousin, who had set out from Allenton as soon as the railroad tracks were cleared. Woodard, on the other hand, grew more restless by the day. He missed his brief theatrical glory and wrote copious letters to Ellroy, which were never returned. He talked loudly about starting his own dramatic company when he got back to the regiment, but no one listened. Both he and Laurence had suffered a second, worse bout of stomach fever, and Woodard, shrunken and yellow, was more like a scarecrow than ever. Just as he was relating his ideas for a Cain and Abel opera, Laurence's mother and cousin arrived at the threshold to the ward to visit him.

Pattie Lindsey hitched herself up like a general and peered down the long gap between beds. Raising his head to be recognized, Laurence was suddenly aware of his shoulders protruding sharply beneath his shirt, the dark scribble of beard on his chin. His mother's eyes swept past him and he sank back.

"Laurence Lindsey," she boomed.

"She's looking for you," Woodard hissed. "Why don't you wave?"

"They're not looking for me," Laurence muttered as he struggled to sit up again. "They're looking for who I was."

But on a second search, they spied him, his mother and his cousin, who walked lightly behind, and he saw how they, too, had been changed by distance and time. His mother had swelled to twice her former weight and she thrust her ample chest ahead of her like a battering ram. Her face had the military glow of a well-oiled cannon, but her eyes were somehow smaller, as if she had to peer through the wall of her own lavish flesh.

Bel's transformation was more pleasing. The childhood symmetry of her features was gone: A larger, adult nose carved a wide gap between her eyes, but the eyes were bigger, too, and the pale blue of cornflowers. Her red mouth had become sensual and expressive, twitching uncertainly as she absorbed the soldiers' hungry glances.

"Laurence," she said, a half step behind her aunt, and they assaulted him with kisses, Bel's shy and retreating, his mother's possessive, slightly wet. And so began a brief interlude of bliss, where he forgot his suffering and enjoyed the pleasantries and Grete's sauerbraten, his favorite dinner. For three days, it was like a dream—they showed up each morning with a new hamper full of food, the first day cooked by Grete, then, afterward, purchased from the inn where they were staying, and they talked long into the afternoon about Allenton, about his days at Camp Convalescence (greatly abridged), about the war still raging while they reunited in that brief cove of peace.

Their visit made Laurence remember the old days at Greenwood, the wilderness-seeking missions he and Bel would make through the garden and down to the lake, where the whining saws of the lumberyards mixed with gull cries and the lapping waves. Virginia, rich and overgrown, had none of the clarity of the winter lake on which they had skated and played, and he realized how much he missed it, and his cousin, too.

He began to think that Bel was sweet on him, and he basked in her attention, giving her fond looks when his mother was not watching, touching her sleeve. She never pulled away, and she laughed eagerly at his feeble jokes. When Mrs. Woodard came that Sunday to visit her son, Bel held Laurence's hand while they listened to her long-winded, embarrassing stories about Woodard's youth. Every time Mrs. Woodard said something especially outrageous, they squeezed hands, all their bottled mirth going out through their fingers. It was like the old days—only Laurence felt an undercurrent of desire surging beneath their affection. He let his eyes linger on her pale winter forehead, on the sweep of hair pinned at the base of her neck. Once lighted from within like summer wheat, it had darkened to a deep honey blond.

"You have your mother's hair," he told her when Pattie Lindsey excused herself to visit the outhouse. It was their last day together, and they were leaning close so they could speak without the whole ward hearing. "It's lovely."

"Thank you," said Bel, patting it. "Since I started putting it up, it gets full of knots by the end of the day, just like hers."

"Bel—" he said urgently. "Would you let me take it down?"

His cousin's mouth twisted. "It takes me forever to pin it again," she protested.

"Please." He tried to grip her hand, but she pulled it away crossly.

"Stop it, silly. I don't want the bother of putting it back up."

They moved apart. Bel fussed with her pins, as if Laurence's request alone had managed to undo them, and he realized she did not comprehend what he was asking, that one does not discover innocence until one has lost it, and that Bel was innocent, while he was not.

"Anyway," she said, returning to her previous topic. Her raised arms made her breasts strain against her bodice. She had no idea she was a woman now. "My father has just finished the railway station down by the waterfront. When you come home—"

"When I come home," he echoed, laughing.

Lying on the next bed, Lyman Woodard made a noise in his throat.

"Hush, dear. You're shouting," his mother said as she returned.

Bel looked confused and fisted her hands in her skirt. "You'll come

199

home," she said finally, breaking the silence. "And when you do, Grete has promised to cook such a feast, you won't be able to eat for three days after. She speaks of it all the time."

"Does she," grunted Laurence, suddenly sick of her patter. "What about Johnny? Where is he now?" he asked, his voice harsh as the image of the hired man rose in his mind. Johnny with strawberry stains on his wrist. Johnny watching his swan burn to ash. Across the ward, he saw Gilbert's praying lips go still.

"Johnny was fired last fall," said Pattie in a tight voice. Did she know about the swan? Laurence wondered. "He couldn't leave off the spirits, and your uncle had to let him go."

"He was ashamed," Laurence said to himself, although his mother and cousin bent closer to hear. "I understand him now."

"Do you?" Bel asked anxiously, but his answer was cut off by his mother.

"I think you need some good rest." Pattie Lindsey's cure-all, whether it was for grief or illness or pain, was to shut her children in their rooms and make them wait it out alone. Laurence had so many memories of his ceiling, days that stretched into weeks, the games he would play across his sheets.

"I brought you a book as a going-away present," Bel said. She unearthed a faded gilt-edged tome from the hamper. It was the *Lais* of Marie de France. "My tutor," she added, reddening, "taught me how to read them in French. He's enlisted in a Vermont regiment— perhaps you'll meet him."

"That was thoughtful of you," said Laurence. "But it's a book for children, and anyway, I can't carry it back with me."

"You could give it away." Bel's disappointed advice made Laurence's mother scowl. A full-blooded New Englander, Pattie Lindsey disapproved of waste of any sort.

Laurence accepted the book with reluctance, letting it lie like a weight on his lap, unopened. He refused to meet his cousin's eyes, knowing that she had planned to give this message to him, a reminder of their old lives, that she was trying to convey to him that she was on his side, no matter what. He could feel his eyes prickle with tears, and in order not to weep in front of them, he glared stonily at the dusty rafters.

"I think you need some good rest," his mother repeated. "We're going to leave you now, dear," she said loudly.

"Good-bye," he whispered to the room, and did not turn his head to acknowledge the kisses planted on his cheek by his mother first, then Isabel, then his mother again, who said with a rush of all the tenderness she had kept inside, "My dear, dear boy." Laurence almost wept then, but he saw Gilbert staring straight at him and he only sighed.

"Good-bye," said Bel one last time. She spoke to the direction in which he gazed and not to Laurence himself. He watched as they retreated in a blue-and-white parade down the row of beds, not looking to the left or the right, and he knew that they would have come again if he had asked, but he had not asked because their part in his life was over. Home was no longer the sound of their voices, of doors shutting and opening in the big house, or the jays lifting their cornered wings above the yard. Instead, it had become an abstraction he carried to keep himself whole, a sheaf of letters going brittle as the ice that shatters during the first spring storm.

The square of light had fallen between the two beds when Gilbert's kin descended to take him back to their small farm outside Allenton. His mother, a crow-haired, stringy woman with savage hands, sat down immediately beside her son and began to knit. If the occasion arose, she spoke in quick outbursts, her strongly accented English erupting from a mouth so similar to Gilbert's own, it surprised Laurence when he heard it.

His pa, silent and stern, was the kind of man who wore so many layers of underclothes, his wrists poked from their cuffs like chicken bones. He had Pike's freckles and tipped ears, although he had long since lost the boy's incredulous look, eyeing the world instead with the grim gaze of someone who sees in spring not the promise of the earth but the threat of floods. Two boys not older than eight completed the Rhodes clan. They played out obscure adventures in the dust beside Gilbert's bed, speaking with the hushed and coded confidentiality of children.

Gilbert stood up as soon as his mother sat down. He hopped furiously around the room to show them how he could power his own locomotion. Swish, stamp, tap, first one leg, then the other, then the cane.

"But cain he walk?" Gilbert's pa asked in his sonorous voice. The mother did not reply, for he spoke to some invisible confidant over his left shoulder. Gilbert hopped a few more steps. The boys did not look up from their playing.

"Don't seem worth thirty dollars a month to lose his limb," his pa continued, giving a curt nod, as if the invisible confidant had confirmed his opinion.

"Pa," said Gilbert's mother. Her needles paused in their knitting, poking through the thick yarn at right angles.

"It don't," insisted the older man.

Gilbert spun on his single foot, facing his father. He spoke for the first time in weeks, the Preacher's heraldic violence receding behind the old protesting tone of the angry son.

"I didn't do it for no thirty dollars. I did it first because of my brother, and then because of my God, and then because some men are free and some ain't." His voice was rusty from lack of use.

"What'd they turn you into, one of them fool ablishinists?" His father folded his arms across his narrow chest.

"No. That's just what I believe." Gilbert rubbed the scar at his temple, where the board had struck on the night of the play. His beard was matted and thick. "There ain't a man alive who deserves to belong to other men. Nigger or no, they belong to the Lord."

The long ward had fallen silent and the patients propped themselves on pillows and elbows to hear better. Ashamed, Laurence tried not to listen. He practiced making his button vanish behind his ear, up his cuff, beneath his cap. It was the last of the expensive silver ones his mother had insisted on sewing on his first gray coat.

"Have you all your things, Gilbert? It's a long ride up to home." Gilbert's mother set down her knitting and stood up between her husband and her son. She perched an ugly bonnet atop her head and began to tie the wilted ribbons.

"You gave up your leg for a passel a niggers." His pa spat on the wooden floor.

"Sir, we don't allow spitting in here," said a plump gray-haired nurse from the far end of the ward.

"He looks like a wild man, my son," Gilbert's mother murmured to herself.

Lyman Woodard broke in, blushing as he spoke. "He's right. He's absolutely right. As long as slavery exists, no man is truly free. It is worth fighting for—not for us, but for our children."

The two young boys glanced up as if their names had been called. They had drawn two armies in the dust.

"This is *my* child," Gilbert's mother said. "He cannot even walk no more."

But Gilbert was staring Woodard down, and Laurence suddenly realized that he had not once looked at Woodard since the night of the opera, even though they had lain ten feet apart all this time. He knew then, although he had not seen it, that Woodard had thrown the board that knocked Gilbert down, and Gilbert knew it, too.

"Thank you," he said in a surprisingly humble voice. "But my pa don't understand that kind of talk. I got all my stuff right here, Ma," he added. "Let's go."

"You can walk home." Gilbert's pa turned his back. The boys glanced up again, their faces made tear-shaped by shocks of black hair. "See if you can walk."

"No! He is my son. He is my first son," Gilbert's mother whispered at her husband, jabbing her knitting into his chest. His father stepped back and shook his head, letting his large hands curl into fists. The younger brothers' eyes swiveled from their father to Gilbert and then back again.

"I never stopped being a God-fearing man," Gilbert said in the direction of his brothers. "I never stopped."

The square of light had climbed to Woodard's bed. He was bathed in gold rays, and he sat straight up, like a boy who has just been wakened. Gilbert's pa watched him and not his son, and Woodard, for once, stayed quiet and resolute.

"All right," the older man said to the room with an air of finality. "Let him come."

They left in a grand and painful silence, first the father stalking out, then the mother, carrying all of Gilbert's possessions except the musket, which was willingly borne by his two young brothers. Gilbert followed, stumping and swishing along without waving good-bye to Laurence or any of his pards, his pant leg pinned at the calf, the cane knocking in hollow rhythm to his exit. Just as his friend crossed the threshold, Laurence dropped the button. It went skittering across the floor and into the corner where the boys had been playing. He did not retrieve it.

Down the long ward, no one spoke for a long time, except for the single busy nurse, a dove-shaped woman who had been sorry for Gilbert and now began trying to talk it out in her mournful coo, declaring how awful his pa was for saying that. Most of the men didn't answer her, turning their heads to the windows or to books they pretended to read. Still angry at Bel, Laurence had given the *Lais* of Marie de France to the whole ward. Now the patients made up their own fairy tales, mixing their war in with the old French stories, and one of them said to the nurse, "Even the kings have a hard time of it."

Miffed by their apparent lack of compassion, the dove wrenched the sheets from Gilbert's bed, revealing the old stained straw tick beneath.

"I shouldn't have said anything," commented Woodard as she bustled away.

"No," Laurence answered. "We all should have." He should have told Gilbert good-bye; he should have told Bel he was falling for her—because the moment would pass whether he spoke or not, and it would be too late.

Woodard sighed a long gust like a horse about to be saddled. The square of light was dying around him and he resumed his old pallor.

"It's not your fault, Woodard," Laurence said, annoyed. He could still see the button glinting in the dust. "You did the right thing."

"It's just another time I didn't," his comrade continued.

"Of course not. You—" Laurence was about to speak of the night in Ellroy's tent, but Woodard stopped him.

"One time in Allenton, I was supposed to help a runaway slave, and I found him too late."

"Too late?" Laurence asked.

"A fellow from Georgia claimed him," explained Woodard. He turned to Laurence with his hopeless, empty eyes. "I couldn't try it again. I couldn't lose another one."

"We all have fellows from Georgia," Laurence said, not allowing himself to wonder if it were the same runaway they all had let slip through their hands. "Anyway, stop suffering about it. You look like you're enjoying yourself too much."

Woodard made a noise in his throat and turned his bony back on Laurence. "You think you're fighting for the same reason you enlisted," he accused his pillow. "But I bet you ain't sure you believe in it anymore. Do you?"

"I believe in freedom more than ever," Laurence said coolly.

"And if there was a chance you could run away, go out west, find a girl, instead of sitting sick on a bed or waiting to die on a battlefield, you wouldn't do it?" Woodard's voice rasped like a razor down a stubbled cheek. "Ain't that freedom?"

"It is," Laurence admitted, letting the vision enter his mind. His own dream would take him to London or Paris, some dense European city that smelled of bread and ash. And the girl? He tried to imagine a foreign beauty, but her features would not coalesce. The nurse returned to Gilbert's bed with fresh linens clasped tightly to her chest. "That's one freedom," he added. "The other is the chance to die for what you believe in. . . ." But his voice trailed off as he said it, and he watched the woman spread new sheets over the tick, erasing his comrade's presence.

"Like Gilbert Rhodes," Woodard said bitterly. The nurse tucked the ends under and hurried off, singing in her low, unpleasant alto, "We are coming, Father Abraham, three hundred thousand more."

Chapter Twenty-eight

Take it back," Addison was saying when Laurence rounded the corner and strode down the lane of tents. The April day was soft and fine, and now that he was back in Virginia, his health was fully restored. Returning to his regiment had felt like a homecoming, even though many things had changed in his absence, most significantly the loss of Sergeant Hamilton to chicken pox. The day after he was buried, Captain Davey had promoted Addison in his place. Since then, his friend had adopted the pained but earnest glare of a boy given jurisdiction over his schoolmates, and he policed the camp with aggravating vigor.

"I made you all promise not to forage," Addison ordered the slump-shouldered Spider, who had a chicken slung beneath his arm. "And I aim to make you keep that promise."

"I swear it was running wild in the woods," Spider pleaded. "You caught a pig that way, and you can't let me have a little bird?"

"A bird that fat and that stupid ain't running wild." Addison jerked his head at Laurence. "Now you take us to the place you stole it from and we'll help you give it back."

"Let me keep it." A blade of sunlight illuminated one of Spider's green eyes. "I said I wouldn't do it again."

"That's not good enough," answered Addison. "Come on, Lindsey. Spider's going to show us the countryside."

He plucked a burr from his wool coat and let his thumb stray to the wooden handle of his new weapon, a government-issue revolver. Laurence sighed, wishing he hadn't turned the corner just then. He had been studiously avoiding Addison ever since he'd returned, because he couldn't bear to watch the new strict and moral self replace the one he remembered. Addison hadn't even been interested in what had happened to Gilbert. He had tightened his jaw and stared at the sloping Virginia horizon as Laurence recounted the tale of the Preacher, the Theater of War, and Gilbert's awkward homecoming. When Laurence was finished his story, Addison had grunted and said "Just as well. He'd have lost his life soon enough."

"Is that all you have to say?" Laurence had demanded then. "You're not the same anymore."

"Are you?" Addison had countered furiously, then stalked off, his once-jaunty gait replaced by a new, stiff-kneed stride. Since then, they had hardly spoken to each other, except through Loomis, who conveniently retained his deaf ear to all things, particularly dissent among his friends.

"Shall we?" Addison asked with his old lazy smile, although his eyes were hard.

Laurence nodded reluctantly.

"Lead on," the sergeant said to Spider, who hissed angrily through his teeth and started off toward the nearby pinewoods.

In Addison's defense, Loomis had told Laurence that the conditions in camp had been terrible before their friend was promoted. The remains of men's rations had littered the ground between the tents, the latrines had been overfull, and, because many of the contrabands had died from the epidemics of pox and typhoid, there'd been no one to shovel or haul in their place.

Loomis said that when reveille had sounded every morning, the drumbeat had been drowned out by hundreds of fellows waking and coughing as if their lungs would bust. When Addison had joined Captain Davey in running the camp, it was he who had worked hours on end while Davey grieved, unaware that Addison had suffered his own loss. Loomis said he wouldn't even have known, but he was there the moment Addison got the news, a little yellow letter that couldn't have had more than twenty words scrawled on it.

"My sister was alone in the house for two days after Ma died," he had said quietly, refolding the letter. "She didn't tell anyone for two days." And then he'd explained that after his father the blacksmith passed on and he left for war, his mother could no longer keep the shop and had moved to a small farm outside Allenton. There, she and his sister could grow enough vegetables to get through the winter, but their nearest neighbor was two miles away, and his mother, a city dweller by birth, had never learned to make country friends.

"My sister's only eight years old," he'd added, and then the matter was closed, Loomis said. No matter how he tried to bring it up again, Addison had refused to listen, trotting off to search for violations of his strict rules. Lately, most of the infractions had been Spider's and Woodard's; they smuggled whiskey into the camp, making a tidy profit, and often drinking a large portion themselves. Addison hadn't figured out how to catch them yet, and Laurence supposed this was why he was being so severe about the stolen poultry.

As they walked softly now on the carpet of orange needles, Laurence pulled up the rear, watching his sergeant's straight shoulders rise and fall. The air was sweet with the smell of pitch.

"This path looks worn," commented Addison.

"Maybe it's an old Indian route," said Spider.

"Or an old smuggler's route." Addison scuffed the needles with his boot.

"Or a rebel spy route," offered Laurence. "They could be spying on us." He wondered why he came to the defense of Spider, whom he generally despised.

"Or a counterspy," Addison said mildly. "You been telling the rebs some secrets, Lindsey?"

"Everything I know," said Laurence. "Which isn't much. Although I heard a rumor that we were going to march soon."

"From who?" Addison's voice rang out in the hushed woods.

"Loomis. Is it true?"

"Davey says Lee's moving north," admitted Addison. "How far is this house, anyway?" He jabbed Spider in the back. The older man stumbled forward, nearly losing his hold on the brown bird.

"A short piece," said Spider indignantly. "If you'll let me get there." After a few more minutes, the thick woods ended abruptly in a clearing. A rail fence bordered a rocky slope that tumbled toward the run-down farmhouse. The odor of a wood smoke rose to meet them. It had been a long time since Laurence had seen a house like this, weather-beaten, the roof in need of repair, a tilted woodpile flanking one side. A droop-waisted woman with bony, jutting elbows was sitting on the porch, sewing. They climbed over the fence and loped down the pasture, the incline lengthening their strides. At their approach, the woman disappeared into the house with her stitching and came out again with a rifle, shouldering it with an awkward shrug.

"Ma'am," said Addison, holding up his hands with fingers spread. "We surrender. You done caught three soldiers in the Union army."

The woman did not smile or let the gun waver.

"Ma'am." Addison halted. "This sorry soldier on my right wants to return something that is yours and apologize."

Laurence looked over the dilapidated house. The glass panes in the two front windows were spotless, but the shutters sagged at odd angles. In one of the windows, a girl sucked on a blond braid, gazing sorrowfully at Laurence.

"I see you have a daughter," Addison said uneasily. "How old is she?"

The woman's shallow, dish-shaped face furrowed around the mouth and eyes. She would have been pretty as a young girl, delicate about the waist and hands, but an exhausting life had thickened her features and worn them slowly downward, like a candle under the persistent heat of flame.

"Give it back, Private," Addison ordered, slapping Spider hard on the shoulder, for the older soldier was half-deaf. Spider staggered toward the leaning porch.

"Four years old," said the woman, lowering her gun and pointing it at the thief.

"She'll be a pretty choice of it one day." Addison nodded, but the compliment caused no further reaction except a quivering of the gun.

"Apologize," the sergeant roared as Spider dropped the bird on the soft earth. The chicken's feet stuck up in the air, the claws the texture of onion skin.

"I'm sorry," Spider mumbled in the direction of his lost prize.

"That was Minnie's fav'rite." The woman spoke to the blue sky above the clearing. "That was her pet."

"We do apologize," said Addison. He was slowly backing away now, his eyes glistening.

"I told her a fox took it." She continued to address the clouds and let the gun slump into her neck. "Now she knows it weren't no fox."

As they climbed back up the slope to the rail fence, Laurence heard a loud but almost immediately muffled wail. He stopped and turned. The porch was empty, the chicken lying in the same position on the ground, its legs spoking up.

"Did you hear that, Addison?" he asked.

"No," Addison said, and kept striding up the hill, his shoulders bowed. "I didn't."

By the misery in his denial, Laurence wondered if Addison had heard the wail but could not listen to it, if behind them was a house just like Addison's, owned by a woman who could have been Addison's mother, retreating back into the gloom to bend over her daughter and stifle her cries so they would not reach the men. Had the other soldier turned around at that moment, he would have seen the emptiness of his own yard, the saplings encroaching on its edges, as if the clearing no longer had the strength to hold back time and season. Had he turned around, he could not have turned back again to the cause of the Union. So he straddled the fence ahead of Laurence, swinging one leg over the rotting wood, then the other, careful not to touch a single rail, and stalked into the forest, its shadows swallowing him.

Chapter Twenty-nine

At the top of the hill outside Fredericksburg, the captured Mississippians sat in a huddle by their old fire pit, whittling pine twigs. It had been a long time since Laurence had seen the enemy up close, and he stared, knowing the others were doing it, too, watching the men who had become abstractions become men again, with yellow teeth and bony, muscle-hard shoulders, strong legs and ordinary feet mashed in boots that were too small and split at the seams. There was scarcely a uniform among them—one wore a gray coat, another the trousers, another the Confederate cap with a tarnished front buckle. The rest of their outfits were recognizably Yankee, stolen from living and dead Union soldiers, and yet Laurence knew they looked nothing like him and never would.

One of the Mississippians glanced up. He had a scraggly blond beard and long-lashed eyes, the right one slightly askew, as if it could not agree with its partner which world to watch.

"What are you staring at?" he asked. "We ain't gonna try anything. We figure we'll be fed more as Yankee prisoners than as Lee's soldiers."

It had been the hardest charge in the war, straight up a slope through burning brush to conquer the summit. Men had died trying to win the same hill the year before, and twice as he'd ascended, Laurence felt a chill pass through his body. When they took the heights, Davey had announced proudly that the victory was key to crippling nearby Fredericksburg, and it bothered Laurence to hear the Mississippian dismiss their surrender as a matter of better rations.

"What were you fighting for, then?" he countered.

"Shoot. What kind of question is that?" The man looked around at his companions for reassurance, but they were whittling or trying to sleep or writing letters to loved ones about their capture. He shrugged. "Because you're here," he said.

Laurence recognized Addison's forceful new gait coming up behind him.

"We need to take their knives from them," said the sergeant.

They wouldn't have won without Addison spurring them on, fighting enough for two men, but Laurence refused.

"They're pocketknives, Addison."

"Throw down your knives," ordered the cockeyed secesher lazily, as if he were telling them a story. There was a silence and then a series of soft thumps as the men obeyed, some digging in their pockets, others making one last carve before letting go of their weapons. The blades shone on the orange pine needles. Far off in the valley, Laurence heard a high scream. It was not the sound of any living creature. He glanced down through the trees, seeing nothing but the black shapes of branches.

"If you got me captured, you've got them all, Sergeant," the Confederate continued. "We already gave you our lives, our land." He gestured to the valley, but his wayward eye was watching the sky behind them. "And it ain't enough, is it?"

There was another scream, and a few of the prisoners looked up this time, brushing the soot from their hands, but Addison and the blond Confederate faced each other with the intensity of lovers. The trees drew dark bars across the space between them.

"I take you on your word," Addison said finally in a quiet voice. "I don't know what 'enough' is anymore," he added, spinning on his heel.

The knives disappeared again, one by one, into pockets and fists, and the prisoners went back to their letters and daydreams. Laurence felt their leader watching him with his wayward eye, so he, too, walked away into the pines, his legs so tired, they stumbled on every root they crossed. It was only later, when they had marched back down the hill, grabbed their haversacks and gear, and set off toward the next battle that he realized the source of the screams.

Beside the rail line that led to Fredericksburg, someone had spent the afternoon with a few horses and a giant fire, melting rails, twining them up trunks. Thinking of his father's railroad tracks in Allenton, weed-thick, shifted only by winter frost, Laurence felt a flicker of rage at such easy, useless loss.

"It ain't enough, is it?" He heard the secesher's voice, and turned, but only Addison was behind him, marching with his head down, his hand on his revolver. They had let another company lead their prisoners away.

"They won't survive the winter," Addison said to his boots, and Laurence decided he must be talking about the trees, their bark scored and black, some still smoldering. He wondered briefly why the screams had come from the metal as it was twisted from straightness, and not the destroyed trees, which would die as silently as they lived, dropping their leaves, going hollow in their cages.

Chapter Thirty

I hope I can remember my manners," Laurence confessed as he sat down opposite his father in the spacious hotel dining room. The last time they had had a full conversation was the spring day Laurence told him he would not train to be an officer and his father had struck him, and he had run away. It seemed amazing to Laurence that they would meet again in New York, a place to which he had never been until the city's violent draft riots so overwhelmed the local police that Union soldiers had to be called in to keep the peace. Since the late summer, his regiment had been encamped in Washington Square Park, and a steady stream of families and sweethearts came to visit them.

By some persuasive miracle, Laurence's father had managed to convince Davey to let him take his son away from camp for the evening. Now Laurence sat in a grand dining room for the first time in years. He hardly knew where to look first—at the chandeliers dripping their glass rain, at the waiters drifting back and forth, their trays raised, or, strangest of all, at his own father, who was sitting across from him.

Age and worry had gentled the abruptness of George Lindsey. It surprised Laurence to see how carefully his father took his own seat, placing both hands on the table before he lowered his body. He never thought two years would make such a difference, but white strands now wove through his father's beard, and around his eyes he had grown the extra folds of skin that make an old man's gaze look far away.

"Your mother would be greatly disappointed if you forgot them," said his father.

"It's just that we don't have enough amenities in camp to sponsor a great deal of etiquette. One spoon suffices for several fellows." Laurence eyed the array of silverware in front of him.

"What do they feed you?" His father wagged a snowy napkin before setting it on his lap.

"Hardtack and salt hoss, as the boys call it," Laurence said. "Everything fried in bacon grease, if possible, although when we're on the march, it's just confounded hardtack, hardtack, hardtack."

"What about all those baked goods and cured meats your mother sits tallying at night for the Sanitary Commission?" His father shook his head, chiding. They were both trying so hard.

"I suspect they rot on the wharves in Alexandria, Papa." Laurence said. "Or the sutlers steal them and try to sell 'em back to us."

Just then, a waiter came, and Laurence allowed his father to order for them both, for George dined there often when he came to New York on business. The waiter, a turnip-headed fellow with a resoundingly artificial British accent, appeared relieved that he didn't have to speak with Laurence, whose hands were so tan and calloused, they looked like pottery instead of flesh.

"They don't understand it here, do they?" Laurence asked his father after the waiter had strutted off in a haze of cologne. George Lindsey sat back in his chair and began digging in his breast pocket.

"What do you mean, son?"

"What we're fighting for." Laurence felt the back of his neck go hot.

"There's not many men left in New York who are willing to fight, no," his father answered mildly, and offered him a cigar before lighting his own. Laurence took two and thrust them quickly into his coat. The cigars would be a valuable commodity when he got back to camp.

"Would you like another?" His father raised a shaggy eyebrow. "I have more."

Laurence blushed and took one from his pocket. "Bad habit," he said, lighting it. The smoke was sweet and thick. "We soldiers like to barter."

"I'll send you a box," his father promised.

"No, don't," said Laurence. "The others don't like it when a fellow's got more than they do."

"Like a promotion?"

"Exactly," Laurence matched his father's ironic tone. "Anyway, what about you? Do you understand why I'm a soldier?"

"Laurence. You're my son. I think the hardest thing my father ever faced was understanding his two sons." Behind the smoke, George's face had a silvery cast, like the bark of beech trees.

"Why? He wanted you to be rich, and you got rich, didn't you?" Laurence's voice rose with challenge.

His father puffed on the brown thumb of tobacco. "My father deeply loved horses, Morgans especially. He never wanted anything to replace them. He thought change would come with the railroad—things we wouldn't be able to stop," he said, and Laurence saw his chin quiver. "You're too young to remember, but he died angry with me. I was the one who altered Allenton. And, according to him, I was the one who made the sheep farms fail."

"That's what you said to me about the war, too," Laurence countered. His father's residual guilt suddenly sounded like his own. "You said we wouldn't be able to halt what we started."

"You haven't yet." George Lindsey stabbed out his cigar.

"Isn't slavery the same thing?" Laurence demanded. His father looked around the dining room before leaning across the table, so close that Laurence could feel the heat emanating from his skin.

"No," he said softly. "Slavery is worse than war. Slavery has no cause but greed, which the men involved call 'business.' I would never countenance it in my house."

"But in your country?" Laurence punched his own cigar into the ashtray.

"Laurence," his father said thoughtfully, as if reconsidering the name of his only son. "You cannot save another person from suffering. But all my life, I have wanted to save you from it. And now you've rushed headlong into the worst suffering yet in our history, with thousands of sons lying on battlefields, unburied, while their fathers wait at home to hear the news."

"They are buried." He thought of Morey Aldridge's grave near Lee's Mills.

"Let me finish," George Lindsey commanded. "Not a day went by that I wasn't certain I had lost you. And now I see that I have."

"You haven't lost me." Laurence shook his head, scowling. "I'm still here, with all my limbs, which is more than I can say for a lot of fellows."

"But you're not the boy that left us. Your eyes"—he paused, peering at Laurence—"your eyes have measured everything in this room since we entered it, including the fact that I am older, and perhaps not worth fighting with anymore. You've started to read men, which you never did before." He grunted. "A fine quality for a businessman to have, I might add."

The waiter arrived with soup and set it neatly in front of Laurence. "And if I don't want to be a businessman?" he retorted, but his anger was fading.

"You may change your mind." George lifted a spoonful of soup delicately to his lips. Perplexed by his father's new, agreeable nature,

Laurence turned to his own bowl. The delicate flavors of cream, mushroom, and potato soon absorbed him so greatly, he forgot his confusion and concentrated on savoring each spoonful. When he glanced up again, he saw his father watching him with a bemused expression.

"You're beginning to look so much like your uncle Daniel," the older man said, running his spoon along the inside of his bowl. Threads of soup clung to it.

"You think so?"

"You have his bearing, even his hair, I think, although yours is a little lighter."

"But your eyes," Laurence said.

"That's right, my eyes, and my father's eyes before me. The color of chocolate, your aunt Faustina used to say." George Lindsey's spoon clattered into the empty bowl. Laurence watched him carefully, wanting to ask his father a thousand questions. Did he really approve of Lucia's and Anne's copperhead suitors? Was Bel all grown up now? Why had he had Johnny Mulcane carve a swan for Aunt Faustina, and why had she thrown it into the fire?

"What about Bel? Do you think she favors your uncle?" George said suddenly.

"I think she favors her mother more," Laurence answered, his ears burning. Did his father suspect his feelings for his cousin? They sat back in silence as the waiter brought their second course, two round lamb chops for each of them and crusty white rolls that puffed from a basket in the center of the table.

"How is she?" Laurence said casually. He would act differently around her now, cool and distant. She was his cousin, after all. He tore open a roll and covered it with vigorous sweeps of butter.

"She's an odd girl, Laurence, always in the garden or reading in some secret corner of Greenwood," his father said. "Truth is, I think your aunt and uncle keep her shut in too much. Your sisters were always out calling at Isabel's age." He plucked his own roll from the basket, ripping it to expose the steaming white interior.

"She's never been like Lucia and Anne," Laurence said. "She's probably not ready to let her happiness depend on what color bow will match her dress, or how she can convince her father to buy her the latest silk from Paris."

"Don't you think I know that?" George Lindsey half-shouted, his mild exterior falling away, revealing the paterfamilias Laurence remembered from his youth, the man who would not be corrected. "I knew that the day your uncle told me she tried to save that unfortunate slave. I knew she was more like you."

His confession startled Laurence. They had never spoken about the runaway. After he had recovered from the fever, his parents had wanted to protect him from the truth, from the story of Johnny Mulcane and the bullet he fired in the dim hayloft, and Uncle Daniel's reluctance to intercede after the act. It had become, he realized, a story they remembered about Isabel rather than himself, and he felt a surge of jealousy.

"I told her to do it," he said. The stale, grassy smell of the runaway returned to him. He saw the man swinging Bel down to the ice. "She wasn't going to do it on her own. She was afraid of him."

"I know," said George, and Laurence thought he saw a spark of admiration in his father's eyes. It burned out as he continued. "But the trouble with raising girls to be like boys is that they don't grow up to be men. They grow up to be women. Your aunt and uncle think she's safe if they keep her at Greenwood, but it's not safe. She needs to be around other young people, or she'll end up—" He stopped and threw up his hands. "It doesn't matter," he muttered.

"She'll end up what? An old maid? If that's her future, so be it," Laurence said, for he didn't like the idea of his young cousin simpering to attract the attention of some ridiculous suitor. She was to find a husband late in life, if she found one at all. "There are worse fates. If she were a man, she could end up in the infantry like me," he added bitterly.

George tugged at his beard. "There are worse fates."

Laurence sat back and observed his father, deciding then that he was the kind who would be killed within a few hours of action. George Lindsey would fly out of the cover of woods, or over a rough earthwork with a roar, trying to end the war in a single charge.

"Anyway, she's only—what, sixteen?" Laurence said, pursuing the topic as he chewed his last bite of meat. The rich taste of animal blood made it difficult to speak. "It's hardly too late for her to find a beau." Although for Bel, he decided, it would always be too early. He couldn't stand the thought of another man pawing her. "Aunt Faustina will help her," he added.

"Will she?" George replied, sounding suddenly weary of the conversation. He glanced at Laurence's empty plate. "Are you still hungry?"

Laurence nodded, surprised. George Lindsey had never cared so deeply about matchmaking, and he used to scoff at the tribulations of his daughters. As if to deflect Laurence's impending inquiry, his father resumed talking about the latest development in the railroad industry—luxury transport that would carry passengers across the prairie and all the way to California.

Laurence could sense by his father's enthusiasm that the truth of the war had not really reached him, for how could velvet curtains, manicurists, and full baths on private cars excite him if he knew how easily his rails could be ruined forever, twisted up the trunks of trees? But he let his father cast the spell of a Pullman car around him; he let him explain the ornate tile above the sinks, the hand-carved compartments for ladies' shoes.

They left the hotel after his father had ordered a second plate of lamb chops for Laurence, coffee from a silver pitcher, and cherry pie for dessert, then walked back to Washington Square, lingering over the carved doorways and window casings, for George Lindsey had always envied his brother's easy knowledge of architecture. Their voices rose above the haze of streetlamps, mingling with the conversations of others on their balconies and in their upstairs rooms. Laurence had never noticed before the labyrinthine sound of the city, and he enjoyed how anonymous they were suddenly, not Union or secesh, not one regiment or another, members only of the company of humanity. Were he not still in his ragged uniform, he would have forgotten he was a soldier, just the son of a rich man, or even just a son.

Chapter Thirty-one

When Betsey Knox strolled into the Washington Square camp, the heads of every idle soldier twisted in her direction as if pushed by the same strong breeze. Smiling to herself with knowing amusement, she asked the closest blue-uniformed soldier for Sgt. John Addison. The request had hardly left her mouth before the young man scrambled off obediently in search of him.

Slouched against a nearby oak, Laurence knew Addison was at their tent, but he did not alter his position when he heard Betsey's high voice say his friend's name. He was taking in her doll-like perfection, every inch arranged to be noticed: the straw bonnet arched over her blond hair, the curl of lace at her throat, the useless fan she clasped in her right hand. Betsey caught his eye and he lifted his cap, a gesture to which she replied with a barely discernible nod.

When Addison arrived, Betsey hung back coyly and held out her gloved fingers to be kissed. With an air of utter devotion, Addison bent his head to her hand—and then pulled it sharply so that her arm wound around his back and they stood close.

"Why, you devil." Betsey squirmed, raising one blue sleeve to adjust her hat back to its jaunty position.

"Ladies should never cuss," Addison said, releasing her slowly.

"*Devil* ain't a cussword," she said, making a moue.

"Isn't. Ladies should also never use improper grammar."

"Aw, what do you know about ladies?" She chucked him on the chest with her fan.

"Not much, ma'am," Addison confessed, taking her by the elbow and towing her away from the ring of onlookers. He stopped as he passed Laurence, who was still posed by the oak tree. "But my friend Laurence Lindsey, he's an expert."

Betsey fixed her round brown gaze on Laurence, making his cheeks go hot. "Are you?" she asked, tilting her head to the angle of her hat.

"I suppose," he mumbled.

"Well, in just about everything else, then," said Addison, grinning. He hadn't looked so happy in months. "His pa got him educated in a Boston private school. He's the schoolmarm of us all."

"You must be terribly smart," Betsey said, not absorbing Addison's delicate insult.

"Not smart enough to find a lady like you," Laurence answered with his courtliest bow. He still did not smile, but his eyes remained on hers.

"What do they teach you, then?" she teased. Her lips were the color of ripe apples.

"How to be an upright, self-reliant man—"

"Who don't have to work for a living," said Addison. Ignoring Laurence's glare, he tugged Betsey's elbow. "Shall I show you the camp?" he asked, and she turned away reluctantly.

Laurence watched as the two of them began their promenade, and then he left the oak to return to his tent. September had covered the ground with orange leaves and he sat down to sketch them on the back of one of his mother's letters. He wanted to remember them when the army returned to Virginia; he wanted to memorize their outlines and dry, waxy smell, as they reminded him of home. So absorbed was he in the task of drawing the curl of a stem that he didn't notice when Addison and Betsey ended their stroll in front of him.

"Well, I didn't come to see you to be marched in circles like one of your colts, Mr. Addison," Betsey said. Laurence looked up. Her face was red and seamed across the forehead with a light layer of sweat, and he suddenly saw that in her prettiness, Betsey was more like his mother than his aunt Faustina, possessing something in the flesh that would fade, rather than in the architecture of the bones, which stayed.

"Please," Addison pleaded with an uncharacteristic whine. "I never get to talk to you alone."

"We can talk right here." Betsey deposited herself on a crude camp stool opposite Laurence. He withdrew his outstretched legs but did not stand or offer Addison the other seat. "I ain't ruining my new dress sweeping it through another layer of dust and spiderwebs. Mr. Lindsey, with all your fine upbringing, I don't understand how you can live with all this *dirt.*"

"You shouldn't understand it," Laurence said. He couldn't help noticing the curved outline of her breasts as she tipped slightly forward. "War isn't for ladies."

Addison snorted at this platitude, hovering like an angry bee.

"Your father is the most divine-looking older gentleman," Betsey claimed, changing the subject. "I see him riding his carriage down to the lumberyards every morning."

Laurence had never thought of his father as handsome before, and he considered this statement. "Do you think I've inherited any of his charm?" he asked seriously. Addison's boot ground into the earth beside him.

"All of it! And I suppose you'll inherit his whole legacy," Betsey answered.

"I suppose I may." Laurence frowned at this comment and returned to his sketching. He couldn't decide if he should approve of this girl, pretty as she was.

"Ready for another round, Betsey?" Addison asked in a tight voice.

"Why don't you sit beside me, instead of trying to trot me over all them stumps," she ordered, lifting her chin. "I told you I've had enough promenading, and I am so enjoying the company of your friend."

"He's a bully friend all right," Addison mumbled as he settled on a patch of ground beside Betsey. He fixed an insolent stare on Laurence.

"Addison saved my life," Laurence offered, hoping to appease him.

"Did he?" Betsey tilted her hat toward her sweetheart. Addison did not peel his eyes from Laurence's face.

"He saves lives all the time. I've never once seen him afraid—in battle," Laurence added, thinking of the house in the clearing, Spider's stolen chicken lying in the yard. "And he rescued at least two dozen horses at Bull Run."

"See now? He writes the dullest letters and never tells me these things," she said in an injured tone. " 'I saved the lives of two dozen horses' would be a bully way to start a letter. But I get them ones that begin 'Dear Betsey, it snowed today and yesterday, too.' "

Laurence laughed and she joined in. Addison's face twisted. "I was just doing my duty," he said.

The misery in his voice finally attracted the attention he sought. Betsey let her gloved hand run lightly through his hair. None of them spoke for a few moments, and against the tableau of their young love, Laurence felt the whole city of New York go quiet. A cool breeze swept over them, filled with the scent of cooked meat and horse manure, of wet dirt, and even the faint salt breath of the sea.

He rose and took his leave of them, suddenly ashamed for staying so long, then went on his own promenade around camp, listening to the hushed tones of lovers. Maple seeds spun earthward and squirrels rustled through the fallen detritus of autumn, looking for acorns. Around him, Laurence felt the summer dying by slow degrees, and he began to dread another winter in the camps. He was tired of the company of men.

On his return to the tent, he was surprised to see Betsey standing alone near a loud, involved argument between Addison, Lyman Woodard, and Spider. Her expression of demure knowing had vanished, replaced by a wide-eyed uncertainty. Clapping the fan into her gloved palm, she gave Laurence a tremulous smile as he approached.

Addison was reprimanding the two drunks for escaping camp to visit a house of ill repute. They had been warned three times not to leave the park, but they had disobeyed, despite the punishment of latrine duty that awaited them each morning when they returned. A few days before, Woodard had whispered to Laurence to come along and find a cyprian of his own. He himself was nightly enamored of a Negress whose tongue had been cut out by an overseer in South Carolina, and he told Laurence that one day he would return from the war and buy her freedom from the madam. In the meantime, he promised that there were women of every shape and description just longing to be bedded by a soldier. Although Laurence refused to go— for such excursions made disease rampant in the army—he envied his two comrades, especially when the other men's sweethearts and wives began to visit, rustling and jangling their feminine way through the camp.

Woodard's sneer vanished as Addison grabbed his collar and threw him to his knees. Spider looked on, myopic, swaying slightly.

"Mr. Lindsey," Betsey said just as Addison loosed Woodard's collar with a final shake.

"One more time and Davey will have you lashed," growled Addison. He appeared more handsome than ever, his red-blond hair a helmet of autumn light. In contrast, Woodard had come to resemble his cohort Spider, eyes bloodshot as an old man's, his complexion tinged with purple.

"Mr. Lindsey, if you would escort me to the gate," Betsey said with trembling firmness, tucking her arm into his. Clearly, Addison's heroism was lost on her. "I'd like to go."

"One more time," said Woodard, and licked his lips, which were thinner now than they used to be. "That would make eight in eight days." Even his voice had changed since the beginning of the war, the high nasal pitch permanently lowered by smoke and a lingering cough.

"To the gate?" Laurence repeated dumbly as Betsey tugged on his coat.

"If you please." The dimples around her mouth had completely vanished.

Obediently, Laurence led her away from the scene, his head down. He did not raise it when Addison called to them.

"Betsey," the sergeant pleaded. "Wait."

"Keep right on walking," she ordered Laurence, a bright spot of color appearing on each cheek. Her fingers clutched the muscle above his elbow and he flexed it, wondering if she found his arm weaker than Addison's, or if she noticed at all.

"Don't you think you should say good-bye?"

"I come all this way," Betsey replied as she stumbled on a tree root and righted herself. "I come all this way to see him, but I ain't going to stay to watch him pick on a couple of fellows just to impress me."

"It's a little more complicated than that," said Laurence. They were nearing the iron gate to the park. He looked back, but Addison was nowhere in sight. "They were shirking, Miss Knox. They aren't supposed to leave camp."

"The old one said they went out sight-seeing," she protested. "Why does he have to punish them for that?"

"There's more than one kind of sight-seeing," Laurence said, still hoping Addison would appear. The girl's carefully tended hair had sagged a little during the afternoon and her round, uncomplicated face was marred by a frown. It was as if the glamorous Betsey Knox who had entered the camp that morning had been replaced by her plain younger sister. Laurence liked the replacement better.

"But he's changed all over, Mr. Lindsey. He's not the same," she explained slowly, as if speaking to a child.

"You can't expect a man to go to war and come back exactly like he was," Laurence said.

"He's changed," she repeated. "I don't know him anymore, and I don't think I have the strength to try." She let go of his arm and gave him a stiff curtsy. "I thank you for the escort, Mr. Lindsey. Perhaps we will see each other again some day in Allenton."

Laurence responded with his own jerky bow. "I still think—" he began, but his advice was interrupted by Addison's jogging approach.

"Betsey," Addison said, breathless. Laurence backed away. "I didn't mean to scare you. Did I scare you?"

"Good-bye, John Addison." The young woman raised her chin, making her bonnet's blue ribbons tighten. Her skirt swayed about her ankles as she turned toward the gate.

"It wasn't supposed to be like this," he said to her, retreating form. The camp grew still, and the soldiers guarding the entrance blinked in the sunlight. "I was doing my duty. Can't you see that?" he asked accusingly, but Betsey Knox did not slow her stride out into the busy New York lane. She raised her gloved hand and hailed the next passing hack, waiting with a set mouth as the driver dismounted and helped her onto the worn red cushion.

After the hack jiggled away on high wheels, Addison spun on Laurence. "What did you say to her?" he demanded.

"I was trying to tell her to stay," Laurence insisted, folding his arms across his chest. "To wait for you." He did not budge as his friend moved closer, assuming the old posture of the angry Gilbert, neck thrust out, hands flexing to fists.

"I don't believe you."

One of the soldiers at the gate sneezed and the other blessed him in a polite voice. They were new recruits from another company and they each had sweethearts who visited them daily. Veterans like Laurence and Addison were a mysterious tribe to the novices, full of their own language and custom.

"You would have once," said Laurence. Less than a foot remained between him and Addison now. Laurence could see where the sergeant had nicked himself shaving that morning, and hard beads of blood dotted his chin.

"Funny thing is," Addison said softly as he halted, "I can't understand why they don't run off for good. That what gets me so riled."

He turned back to the ornate iron gate. The wind once again filled the camp, lifting up the pale undersides of the last remaining leaves. A long spray of dried mud ran down the back of the sergeant's coat, like a road between two invisible destinations. "Once they go, why don't they stay gone?" he demanded.

Chapter Thirty-two

Because they could not light a fire, they invented a game to keep warm while they waited for battle, and played it in a small clearing beside the heap of knapsacks the Fifth Corps had left behind when they'd stripped for the charge. The two companies, Davey's and the one filled mostly with new recruits, faced each other across some Virginia farmer's abandoned woodlot. The opposing team had a balled sock they would try to advance across the clearing by tossing it to one another. Davey's crowd could intercept, or could knock a man down after he caught it—but never before—and thereby gain possession. Then they could drive in the opposite direction. To reach the far oak on either side was to gain a point.

No one knew who had invented the game, or its simple rules, of which one was tantamount: It had to be played in absolute silence. The Johnnies, who camped nearby beside a comfortable haze of fires, could not know of their presence. The Vermonters' running steps, their waving arms, the grunts of one man tackling another—all had to be utterly quiet. Standing at the edge of the glen, the captains and sergeants watched, their arms folded across their chests. The men knew they would stop the game if a single noise were made, and so they played with silent, lunging desperation, their muscles screaming while their mouths knit shut over bloodied teeth.

Alfred Loomis turned out to be the best player on Laurence's side, for his height enabled him to reach above the others' heads and his slowness melted away as it did in battle, replaced by a swift dexterity. The new recruits, in turn, had a quick Canadian with a knack for anticipating the movements of his opponents. His black hair beat against his cheeks as he sprinted for the far oak. Point for point, he and Loomis matched each other.

Clouds arched over their game, whiting out the sun. Although they heard the fighting start and stop again about a mile away, its seriousness did not reach them, and they threw themselves into their play, staring alertly over the grass, thinking up strategies to foil the other team.

After awhile, they stopped for a brief lunch of hardtack. Laurence learned from the whispered voices of the other team that the Canadian's name was Louis Pacquette, that he had been tutoring a girl from a rich family in Allenton before he enlisted and was sent to Virginia.

Laurence recognized the name with a start. Louis Pacquette was his cousin's tutor, the one who had taught her to read the *Lais* in French. She had mentioned him several times in her letters. "I am pleased to finally—" he started, but was interrupted.

"Why the devil did you give that up?" hissed one of the men sitting nearby. He was the oldest of the new recruits and had the sun-stained, leathery skin of a lumberjack.

"To fight for the freedom of men," said the Canadian. From anyone else's lips, it would have sounded like a mockery, but Pacquette's grave face showed no signs of humor. He bit a piece of hardtack and chewed with slow precision.

The lumberjack guffawed soundlessly, revealing a dark set of gums, few teeth. "Must not a been pretty, that one."

With a quick flick of one arm, Pacquette clapped the man under the chin and knocked him on his back. From that single, definitive gesture, Laurence knew that there must be some secret affair between Bel and this serious-eyed Canadian. He lowered his head, too outraged to continue with his introduction.

The lumberjack sat up and rubbed his chin. Breath steamed from his mouth in silvery clouds, but he said nothing more and the companies lapsed into an uneasy silence. Trying to look anywhere but at Pacquette, Laurence saw Woodard rise and creep away through the trees. Addison followed soon after. When it came to Woodard and Spider, the sergeant behaved like a jilted lover, always trailing after them with a strained expression on his face, as if he wanted to ignore their trespasses against his rules but couldn't allow himself to. A few minutes later, Woodard returned alone with a sullen frown, patting his pockets as if they had recently been emptied of something precious.

There was a sudden crack of gunfire. With a common mind, the soldiers rose from their slouches against tree roots and stones to line up opposite one another, shivering.

By the late afternoon, the teams were tied. They had stripped their coats, warmed by the exertion, and the heat and unwashed reek of their bodies filled the clearing. Their blue legs rustled through the cold grass in zigzagging, root-tearing strides. Whistling softly through his teeth, Pacquette streaked for the back quarter of the glen, then spun and held his arms up high. The sock sailed in his direction. At the last minute, it bumped into the branches of the oak and ricocheted off to the side, where a stand of pines sprayed a green wall against the latent light of winter.

Laurence was close behind him. His feet lifted and sank through the rotting leaves. He wanted Pacquette to drop it. He willed the balled sock to roll off the branch and tumble beyond the tutor's hand, and when he saw the man cup it in his palm, casually, as if he did not have to reach at all, Laurence hurtled forward. The point won, it was too late to tackle, but he threw himself around the waist of the unsuspecting tutor, driving him into the sycamore. The impact pleased Laurence, for he felt the man's body lift and give way as his own heels kicked skyward. For a moment, the sweetness of momentum overtook him and he heard the tutor's head thud against the peeling tree trunk.

The collision jarred his shoulder. Then, with blinding speed, the tutor's knee rose and cracked him in the mouth. Laurence fell to the damp skin of leaves. One tooth was loose and he hacked a red spray onto the earth, his tongue throbbing. When he had finished coughing, his anger about Bel was gone, replaced by a dull regret. Nothing in this world would ever be truly his, Laurence realized, staring at the dirt. It didn't matter what he wished for.

As he rolled over, he saw Pacquette standing over him, touching the base of his skull. "We won," the Canadian said softly to the low pink light dying in the west. "Not that anyone cares."

Laurence sat up on his elbow to look back at the two teams, scattered now, for the order must have come from Davey to break up and retreat back to their camp. The men were hitching on their haversacks, slinging their muskets over their shoulders, as if the game had never happened. Pacquette extended his arm.

"Lindsey, isn't it?" he asked, his voice calm. "I think I know your aunt and uncle." But the hand that helped Laurence to his feet was bloody and shaking.

Chapter Thirty-three

So many nights on winter picket had passed without incident, Laurence had taken to propping himself against a smooth beech tree and falling into a state of half sleep. His ears remained alert in case Addison rode by on his nightly patrol, but he shut his eyes and slipped into daydreams of stealing away in the dark and walking west until he reached the Rocky Mountains. There, he would change his name and embark on a new life, sailing a ship down to South America, or setting off to explore the Arctic. He had just hitched up a sled of dogs to explore some bare, frozen lake, when he heard a loud cry from the next post.

"Friend or foe?" Laurence yelled, and lifted the muzzle of his gun.

"Desert-ers!" came a shout, the word pronounced as if it were a band of Saharan inhabitants. It had to be Louis Pacquette. "Deserters!" he cried again.

"I'm coming," Laurence called back, and began to run through the woods beside the corduroy road that led to Richmond.

It was so quiet, the whisper of his footsteps surprised him as he passed across the leaves. Desertion was serious. Every man thought about it, toying with the idea of hiding in the woods until the army moved and there was a safe chance to run. They all knew the rebs shirked, but the rebs had a different code of honor and a lot fewer men to spare, making Laurence doubt if their officers carried out its consequence, which in either army was public execution. As he reached the clearing, he wondered what company would drive men to try to escape, when the whole regiment was promised a furlough in January, now less than a month away.

Pacquette was lying behind a grassy hummock, his gun leveled toward a barn's yawning doors. The building leaned in a quiet confusion of weeds, dirty and untended, the owner long absent. Inside it, Laurence could hear two men whispering and the heavy footfalls of a horse dancing in place. He lowered himself to the ground next to the Canadian, feeling the cold, snowy grass press his hips and stomach. They had not spoken to each other since the game between companies.

"We could fire on them until they come out," Pacquette said seriously.

"That's too easy. They'll expect it."

"Then I could wait here and you could get more soldiers."

"It's not safe for you to stay here alone," Laurence said, rankled at the suggestion. "You've never even been in battle before."

"I found them." The Canadian did not budge from his position.

They stared at the barn doors. A cold wind blew silvery scarves of snow over their faces.

"Wait." Laurence suddenly recognized the two voices. "I know them both." He rose, then swaggered toward the entrance. He would show the tutor what it meant to be a soldier, sharp-witted and daring.

"Are you going to let them get away?" Pacquette challenged him. Laurence looked back at the Canadian, taking in his meticulously flat collar, the way his black hair swept back from a high, intelligent forehead. He could not see the other man's eyes, and Pacquette's neutral tone betrayed no emotion.

"Of course not," Laurence retorted. "Keep your gun aimed. And fire if you think they're going to escape."

He approached the barn silently, his own rifle held loosely in one fist. The air smelled faintly of hay and animals. A heavy gray wasp's nest hung from one corner of the threshold.

"It's Laurence Lindsey," Woodard hissed from within the barn. "Just block us a minute, Lindsey, and let us run. You know they're going to kill us if they find out."

"Let us go. For old times," Spider pleaded. His eyes were like large silver coins.

Laurence hesitated, staring at the horse Spider held by the reins. It was Furlough, the bay stallion Addison had tamed so long ago by the pond. The stallion gave a loud, contemptuous sigh, as if to signify that his impression of humanity had only worsened since Laurence had last seen him.

"Why go now?" Laurence did not lift his rifle. He would show Pacquette how desertion could be averted without bloodshed. He understood these men. "We've got furlough next month. You can go home then."

"When did you get so stupid, Lindsey?" asked Woodard. The old eagerness was utterly gone, and his face looked peeled and sharp, like a stick stripped of its bark. "I'm not going home. And I'm not waiting around for McClellan or Hooker or Sherman or Grant or even goddamn Lincoln to win this war. We saw fellows in New York living bully lives, didn't we, Spider?"

The other soldier nodded, owlish.

"We watched them getting rich, while we're treated worse than slaves, Lindsey," Woodard added. Although Woodard was bowed under a swollen knapsack, Spider carried nothing but his old bent hat. "All along, I didn't see it, but now . . ." He shrugged.

"What about what you said to Gilbert's father?" Laurence retorted. "I thought you—of all people—understood we weren't fighting for ourselves."

Woodard shook his head solemnly and hitched the knapsack higher up his shoulders, fixing his eyes on the nest in the doorway. In summer, the holes would hold the slick brown bodies of the stinging insects, but now they were damp and empty. Husks of wasps curled on the earthen floor.

"I can't do it anymore," he said. "I can't face another winter in camp, another battle, another march. I just don't give a damn about anyone else." His voice was dead. "Not even you, Lindsey."

"Are you having trouble with them?" Pacquette shouted from the golden field beyond.

"Please let me shoot that French loon, Lyman," said Spider, and started walking forward with Furlough, pulling a pistol from his coat.

"Fire, Pacquette!" Laurence yelled. A shot rang through the air above their heads and thudded into the far wall of the barn. Furlough screamed and started to rear. Spider managed to hold him down by the reins, his white fist tightening in the leather straps.

"Come out," ordered Pacquette. But in the time it would take the novice to reload, Spider and Woodard would have their chance. Just as Laurence began to lift his own rifle, Woodard ripped it away and smacked him across his cheek, sending him reeling back against the wooden stall. The rifle clattered on the dirt. Furlough reared again and hay dust filled Laurence's nostrils. He staggered toward the weapon, his head thudding with pain. It took him a moment to feel the cold metal of Spider's pistol against his temple.

"Tell the idiot you've got us captured," Woodard said. "Tell him now."

"I've got them, Pacquette," Laurence said, tasting blood. "Stop firing."

"Sir?" came Pacquette's voice, followed by the clatter of a ramrod tamping the lead ball into the powder.

"Louder."

"Pacquette. Hold your fire. I've got them." It was hard to shout over the noise of Furlough's restless hooves. The pistol withdrew. Laurence kicked on the ground for his musket, but Woodard had already taken it.

"Get on, Spider," Woodard said, mounting the horse. "He's not going to run. I've got his gun aimed right at him."

The other deserter climbed up behind Woodard, cradling the knapsack with his long white hands. "And now you're going to lead us away from here like a good hostage," Woodard explained. "Then we're going to slip by you and ride out of this godforsaken camp. That way, you don't get in trouble, and we don't, either."

"What about Pacquette?" Laurence said. He took a step, his legs shaky and loose at the knees. He wouldn't let the tutor die.

"If he doesn't shoot us, we don't shoot you." Woodard assured him with a dignified frown. His spine was as straight as General McClellan's.

"Hands up," said Spider, jabbing Laurence with his boot. Laurence lifted his elbows to his ears and started walking ahead of them toward the entrance. "Tell him to hold his fire."

"Hold your fire, Private." Laurence tried not to let the desperation ring in his voice. Why had he tried to change their minds? The hard tip of his own rifle pushed into the back of his head. Emerging into the moonlight, he saw the Canadian stranded in the middle of the clearing, his gun still aimed at them. The ground reeked of the slow rot that spread across fields in early spring.

"You don't fire at us, we don't fire at him," Woodard proclaimed. Furlough strode with magnificent ease into the dead grass, as if he were bearing a king. The tutor did not shoot or lower his gun. His expression was that of a man facing his own death.

"Take care of her—" Laurence began, but his captor jabbed him in the head with the rifle. Pacquette nodded as if he understood.

"West," Woodard commanded. Laurence started walking toward the shadowed woods just beyond the old farmhouse. The trees were stiff as statues, their shapes tortuous and gnarled beneath a thin skein of snow. Laurence felt their shade pass over him like a sheet. He turned and saw Pacquette still keeping them within his sights, and he took a breath, conscious of the capacity of his lungs to empty and fill, of his whispering footfall and the slow, flooded thump of his heart. He faced the trees again.

The next moment passed with the blur of a century, as if a whole continent were settled, rivers breached by ships, and forests cut for pasture. Stars shattered and the earth rose up. The oaks ignited and went out with the sudden blaze of rifles, and Laurence recognized the roar of gunfire before he understood its consequence: a bullet flying through the air from the other side of the horse, Furlough staggering forward with a scream, the two deserters falling in a jumble to the ground.

When it was over, Pacquette was still standing in the same place, his rifle unfired, but Addison had burst into the clearing on a gray mare. Pulling his revolver from his belt, he dismounted near the roiling mass of horse and men. The mare bolted sideways, her mane flapping against a sweaty neck. Furlough lifted like a shipwreck before it sinks into the sea. Grass tore beneath him. Addison kicked the fallen musket in Laurence's direction and then, unflinching, aimed a single bullet into the temple of the dying stallion. The moon blazed.

"I arrest you in the name of the United States government for the crime of desertion," he said when he turned to Woodard and Spider, who were squirming to unearth themselves from beneath Furlough's spine. The back leg of the horse had been broken by the fall and Laurence could see the cracked line of bone beneath the reddish hair. The stallion's face had frozen in a loose, toothy snarl.

"Now, Johnny Addison, we were just going out for some good times," said Spider, slipping free of the horse. "You know the kind, and you know we can't find it in camp."

"What's in the knapsack?" said Addison. He wrenched Woodard out from beneath Furlough and tore the bag from the soldier's back, tossing it aside. It landed with a thump by Laurence's feet.

"Open it, Lindsey," Addison commanded, and Laurence found loose heaps of bills inside, their green gone gray in the half-light.

"Enough good times to last fifty years," he commented, inhaling the dense papery scent. He no longer cared to save them. Addison told the still-stunned Pacquette to guard the guns. Taking a rope from the gray mare's saddle, he began to tie the two deserters.

"Shame to waste the best damn horse in the Army of the Potomac on yellow cowards like you," Addison growled as he strung them together. His cap slipped on his head, and he righted it carefully before he yanked on the knots of the two prisoners, testing their hold. Spider fell forward with a jerk, but Woodard remained upright. With a sudden grunt, Addison whacked the deserter across the back of his head, making him slump forward into the stallion's red mane.

"And what was your plan, Lindsey?" Addison turned on his friend an instant later. His eyes were lightless.

"I was trying to persuade them not to run," Laurence said thoughtfully, as if the idea were no longer reasonable. He stepped back from the open knapsack, his snowy trousers clinging to his shins.

Addison snorted. "I ought to arrest you, too," he said in the direction of the barn. A bullet had shattered the wasp nest, making a ragged crepe flower.

"You ought to," Laurence agreed.

"He was brave, Sergeant." Pacquette's expression was sorrowful, and Laurence felt a strange triumph, for he realized that the Canadian truly admired what he had done. "He wasn't afraid of them at all."

"Brave or stupid." Addison's lip curled. "'It is just as lucky to die and I know it,'" he quoted. "Ain't that right, Lindsey?"

"That's right."

Having Laurence agree with him twice disarmed the sergeant. Addison shifted his weight back and forth. There was a dark ring around the horse where the snow had been kicked off. Furlough's fawn-colored eyes were filming over. At the far edge of the clearing, a tree filled with the shrill commotion of birds, but Laurence couldn't make out a single one.

"If you want to let them go, then let them go," Addison roared finally, stepping out of the ring. "If you think you know what's right, then do it, Lindsey."

"Let us go," said Spider, but at the same time, Lyman Woodard began to sing softly into the mane of the horse, drowning out his companion. He sang the last words of the last verse of "Lorena," the melody Addison had played on the train as they left Allenton on their way to war. The mournful strain rose above the ribs of the dead stallion and into the clearing. "I'll say to those lost years 'sleep on.' Sleep on, nor heed life's pelting storms."

They all paused to hear the end of the phrase melt on the air, the words where the soldier surrenders everything, even his own memories. There was no hope of return for any of them. Dawn drew thin cracks of light in the east and Laurence finally met Addison's searching gaze. "You can't unarrest them," he said, taking in the vein throbbing at the sergeant's temple, the sweat-limp hair that fell over his brow.

"You can't let them go now and you know it," Laurence continued softly. "And I'm not going to fight for their lives, because they had a choice and made it, and you had one and you made yours, and now—" He gestured to the dead horse. "They can't go back in time and ride away, and you can't pretend you weren't waiting in the woods for the one chance you had to stop them and save my life, too."

Looking over the top of the barn, he saw an owl make its humped and vestigial flight across the clearing to alight on a leafless tree on the other side. It was followed by a flock of loud, angry sparrows, their black shadows diving and crying until they drove the owl to another tree, and another. Addison did not answer, except to check the knots holding his captives.

"It don't matter, Lindsey," Woodard said in a weary voice. His cheek lay against Furlough's flank as if he were listening for a heartbeat.

They left the horse unburied in the clearing. Addison drove the two prisoners in front of him. Laurence went next and Pacquette took up the rear, his face furrowed with a deep frown. It was colder in the woods and it smelled of ice melting down bark. Next to the suddenly stoic Woodard, Spider walked with his head tipped earthward and stumbled over every branch he could.

"The winter is different here," Pacquette commented aloud. "It already feels like it's almost over."

The others did not respond, except Spider, who laughed in a high, unkind way as they walked the narrow path. Then there was nothing but breath and footfall, the snow going black with their steps.

Chapter Thirty-four

Addison laid white targets across the chests of the deserters and stepped back to see if they were crooked, then bent forward again to straighten them. His face was blue and slick with rain. When he was satisfied, he nodded to Captain Davey and left the deserters kneeling in their coffins. Spider bobbed and whimpered, but Woodard fixed his eyes down the metal barrels of the muskets.

"I am not ashamed," he began, and then his voice was drowned out by the "Rogue's March," an exact and simple dirge summoned by the fife and drum players clustered at the edge of the hollow. The guards loaded their guns.

When the captain shouted, *"Fire,"* it was over before the echo of his cry cleared the shallow gully. Woodard fell face-forward, reminding Laurence of the days when Gilbert used to trip him just for walking by. His light hair spilled to the ground like a fountain. Spider went less easily, twitching against the earth, his long fingers clawing in the dirt. Then he sighed three words, *Oh dear me,* and his eyes fluttered shut. The rain disturbed the silence of the scene, blustering over the men in small drops, making every one bow his head and blink as if he were weeping, although none of them would admit to grief.

Laurence saw Pacquette among them, but the other man's face was distant and expressionless as a winter pasture. He recognized in the tutor his own old refusal to accept the cruelty of war, and he understood how Bel could love Pacquette, for even hawk-nosed and wearing a filthy uniform, he possessed the inner handsomeness of a man who acts on what he believes. Addison stepped over to the dead men, wrestled the white targets from their chests, and pushed each deserter into his own coffin.

Woodard's pine box was too short and his knees jutted up, but this did not deter the sergeant from laying the lid over them and nailing it down with his blacksmith arms. The thud of splitting flesh and bone made Laurence's whole body ache. He stared out over the lowered clouds and, for one moment, he hated the whole world, horizon to horizon, and then he grieved for it, thinking of Lyman Woodard's knees and how they refused to be buried.

When Laurence left the hollow with the other soldiers, Addison was still nailing the lid down over Lyman Woodard, his arm rising and falling, but the thudding was gone, and Laurence knew that the wood had cracked across the middle, where it could not hold, and that Addison did not see it, so focused was he on keeping the seams together. The falling rain tasted fresh and sweet on Laurence's lips and he drank it thirstily, a silvered drop at a time. Walking past him, the drummer boy thrummed his fingers on the stretched skin that swayed from his chest like a second belly. Every once in awhile, the boy's hands would sweep the rainwater off the tight leather surface, turning the streaks into stains.

January–April 1864

❧

Chapter Thirty-five

On the third day after Laurence arrived home on furlough, he walked down the icy drive to Greenwood alone, shunning horse and sled to tromp in a soldierly fashion through the streets. Bel saw him coming. She hadn't intended to look out the window just then, but the passing shadow of a crow had distracted her from a sketch she was making of two wrinkled apples that sat before her on a plate.

After watching her cousin for a few moments, she bent back over the sketch. The apples were wizened like the heads of old men and she could not get them right. But the still life—her tutor Miss Omira Bottum had insisted—was essential to improving an artist's hand. In a fit of frustration, Bel had been drawing Miss Bottum's face on one of the fruits, but she scribbled the whole thing out when she heard the crunch of Laurence's feet on the steps to the door.

Homecoming had not been what any of them expected. Aunt Pattie had been certain Laurence would be haggard and weak, in need of "a good rest." She was partially right; Laurence had gained back little of the weight he had lost the year before, and purple hollows curved beneath his eyes. Uncle George had anticipated a brave and somewhat embittered soldier, remembering his own visit with Laurence in New York City. He was also right, for Laurence braced his shoulders like a young Atlas and watched out every available window as if he expected rebel troops to be arriving at any time. Bel's father had hoped for some good information on southern architecture, as he was sure the "bright boy" would have noticed such a thing, and her mother had said simply that she guessed Laurence would be happy to sleep in a house again.

Bel had refused to join in the predictions about the soldier who had walked in the door on Twelfth Night and barely spoke to any of them. Long after the trip to Brattleboro, she had guessed, with great embarrassment, that Laurence's request to take down her hair had been something more than a nostalgic gesture, and her memories of that afternoon made her blush. Bel's only hope was that the old Laurence would come back, bossy, intent, and furious with knowledge, the Laurence of her childhood summers, of tree-climbing dares and creek-bed adventures. She couldn't bear to think he had grown as dull and sappy as the rest of Allenton society.

When Laurence had appeared, a day early, on Greenwood's grand oak threshold, Bel was in her hiding place on the stairwell, feeling cramped and resigned. She had already deemed it useless even to enter the dance floor this year. Men were so scarce, even Ernest Pomeroy was in high demand, and Hannah Fithian had already secured him for three waltzes in exchange for a box of chocolates her uncle had sent her from France.

As soon as people realized just who had arrived, Faustina's party careened to a halt. The lilting waltz faded beneath sighs and murmurs of recognition, and the steadily circling bodies suddenly bumbled against one another like bees in a hive. Tanner and taller than when he had left almost three years before, Laurence remained on the threshold, letting the cold air stab through the open door.

Bel had felt the chill, even from her distant perch. She pressed her cheek against the wooden rungs and waited as Aunt Pattie fainted in a sodden heap, as Uncle George rushed forward to claim him with a loud, confident roar. Laurence looked bruised and wary, like an animal that had been beaten. His uniform was dusted with snow, which melted and dripped on the floor. Bel cringed as the assembled crowd issued their greetings, starting with her mother and father and declining in order of relation and importance. It didn't take long for the throng to become frightened by the returning soldier, for he hardly said anything at each new introduction, and by the time the line got to Mary Ruth Cross, he had stopped speaking altogether. The crowd around him dwindled and the music struck up again. Dancers craned their necks to watch him as they twirled around the room.

When Bel heard her mother saying her name, she finally stood from her hiding place and waved. She saw Laurence follow the angle of her mother's finger up the long stair to the balustrade, where she waited in the same blue dress she had worn the year before, insisting on it in a secret devotion to Louis. She saw how he lifted his arm ever so slightly, returning her wave, then turned and stamped out the door, his back crooked like an old man's. A flurry of Lindseys followed him, but she stayed. Her pride was hurt. After all this time, they were strangers.

News came the next day that Laurence was ill with a fever. "Every time his life overwhelms him here, he simply goes to bed," she told her mother when she heard.

"You don't know what he's been through," Faustina scolded her. "That you of all people should say that about your cousin."

"Well, then, what is it?" Bel demanded. "Mary Ruth's brother is home and he's just fine. He took her out sledding and bought her a new mink muff."

Faustina paced the living room, her skirt swishing over the Ottoman carpet that was this year's Christmas gift. Red leaves and circles and fans bloomed deep in it. "Sledding and a muff. I shall have to tell your cousin how easy it is to impress these days."

"Yes. Tell him," said Bel. "Tell him we require nothing but the most basic pleasantries. For instance, a simple greeting would do."

"You are angry with him, aren't you?" Faustina sat down beside her daughter and tried to touch her hair. Bel no longer allowed her mother to braid the long brown tresses, insisting on putting her hair up herself. Faustina's thin fingers scratched her scalp. Bel twisted her head away.

"I miss him," she had said simply. The three words echoed in her mind now as the door opened without a knock and Laurence stepped in, blinking. Bel appraised him, and knew he was doing the same. Her cousin's face fell from its bones in steep angles, and there was a hollow of shadow in the center of each cheek. He wore the scars of sunlight now, a cracking around the mouth and eyes, and a deep residual color across his skin.

Laurence even smelled different, the sweaty boyishness replaced by a dry odor, like that of an October garden, yellowed and bare. Clothes three years old slumped from his skinny frame. Except for the faded Union cap left over from his uniform, they looked like they belonged to someone else.

"I missed you." She spoke first. It was not what she had meant to say. A glade of light from the window divided them and Laurence blinked again as he stepped into it.

"Shall we go to the lake?" he barked, and she was relieved that he did not watch her eagerly, the way he had in Brattleboro. Instead, his eyes scraped right past her figure and out the window to the snowy yard. "I thought you might like to see it today," he added more gently.

"I would love to." She marched to the coat closet and pulled on her boots. "We should escape now, before anyone else sees you and tries . . ." She faltered.

"What?" A ragged, self-pitying grin spread over his face. "And tries to speak with me?"

From upstairs came the sound of a chair scraping across the floor-boards. Bel threw her coat over her shoulders and rushed to the door, cranking the iron knob. When she looked back, Laurence was still standing in the sunlight, watching the dust drift down.

"You forget that interiors have their own weather," he said in a wondering voice. "All that time in a tent."

"Come on," Bel pleaded. "It's cold, and I want to go before one of them notices."

He stepped out of the light obediently and hunched his shoulders against the January air. "You haven't changed," he muttered.

"Neither have you," she retorted as she felt the snow soften and steal her steps, each one slipping away.

There was no ice castle on the lake this year. The freeze had come slowly, without wind or storm, and the rocks leveled evenly down to the white expanse of water. The two cousins did not speak to each other. Bel tried once or twice to make conversation, or to point out some familiar place, Wilderness Run, Wilderness Isle, but Laurence only nodded and hissed through his teeth like a child too cold to be interested in conversation.

Turning from the mouth of Potash Brook, they picked their way along the shore to the vacant Sunday lumberyards and her father's railroad station. It was a fanciful building, even from behind. Towers jutted from the four corners of the brick and stone edifice, each topped with sloping, pointy roofs and metal spires that mimicked the onion domes of the churches in far-off Russia. These roofs repeated down the middle of the station like the spine of some exotic beast. A couple of them functioned as chimneys, but their use was so disguised by ornament that it was strange to see smoke rising from them.

Bel and Laurence stopped at one of the three arches cut for the trains and looked in. Cavelike and draughty, the station's interior was lighted by tall, narrow windows in the walls. An engine waiting for repair sat humped on the far-right track. Letting her eyes rest on the locomotive, Bel inhaled the smell of oil and coal ash. The short, grizzled stationmaster wandered across her line of sight with a bucket of tools.

"Wait here," Laurence whispered, pulling Bel back from the entrance. His finger pressed her collarbone. "I want to see the whole thing, all the way around."

While her cousin clambered off through the snowdrifts, Bel stood alone beneath a fang of ice that dripped from her father's cambering eaves. Everything about the station told of Daniel Lindsey's wistful admiration of the exotic. Rising beside the squat, plain lumber buildings, it had all the curves and contradictions of a wedding cake or a French horn, something that should not hold together but did. Her mother loved it. Uncle George thought it extravagant, especially since they were losing money on the train. Mending the tracks was proving costly in a state covered by snow six months of the year. And yet they could not give up on the enterprise. The station was two years old now and needing paint, but her father refused to sell it.

After what seemed like an eternity of listening to the stationmaster grunt and clang at the lifeless engine, Laurence appeared around the other side of the building, his chin tilting up from the collar of his coat.

"'I think I will do nothing for a long time but listen,'" he announced as he approached. His expression was downy and warm, like a young child's. "'And accrue what I hear into myself . . . and let sounds contribute toward me.'" He paused, and Bel, eager to reply, to have any sort of conversation with her cousin, began to speak. Laurence held up his hand.

"'I hear the bravuras of birds.'" He gestured to the puffed gray pigeons parading below the eaves. "'The bustle of growing wheat, gossip of flames.'" He raised his head to the wires of smoke gliding from one of the station's strange chimneys. "Let's go somewhere, Bel," he said. "I have somewhere I want to go."

"Wait," she began again, because she had to say something. "Did you like it?"

"Of course." He laughed, his boyhood self peeking out for instant. "Your father is a genius. He made me remember there are always reasons to live."

Then he set off in a rigorous march up the hill. It was the old jaunty stride, which always surpassed hers and necessitated his frequent halting and breathing impatient gusts into the air. Hurrying behind him, she felt her body start to warm up as they ascended to Church Street. They passed a bakery with its golden wands leaning in the window, and she breathed the buttery odor of bread, suddenly hungry. A thin layer of sweat grew on the back of her neck and beneath her arms.

When they reached the corner, Laurence swiveled abruptly by a snowbank and charged north, in the direction of the brick Unitarian church at the head of the street. Bel tried to take the turn with the same quick pace, and her right foot slipped on a patch of ice. She toppled over, landing on her hip. Tears flooded her eyes. As the earth's chill crept through her coat, she realized how it would have been to fall on the lake so long ago, if the runaway had not been there to catch her. Laurence—she knew now—would not have noticed even then. He would have let her tumble from the ice castle while he gazed triumphantly out to the frozen water and recited some poetry he had composed on the spot for how beautiful it was, the two of them, standing on the rim of that emptiness together.

"Miss Lindsey?" said a deep voice. Bel saw the broken boots, the ragged gray trousers she knew so well, and took the hand that Johnny

Mulcane offered her. The cold scent of the snow washed his own fetid odor from the air and she breathed easily as he pulled her up, his hand releasing hers as soon as she was righted.

"Thank you," she murmured, looking no higher than his slack waist. The hired man hovered for a moment, his breath loud, rattling. It had been over a year since her father had let him go. When Bel asked why, her mother had lied. They couldn't afford to keep him, she said, as if Bel had not heard the man lurch from the toolshed every afternoon, wiping his mouth. Whatever the reason, Johnny had dutifully vanished that September like the warm weather, leaving dead leaves unraked across the garden.

Bel took a test step with her hip. It felt solid but sore. "How are you, Johnny?" she asked finally, raising her chin to meet the hired man's eyes.

There was no reply. Johnny Mulcane had already shambled away down the hill, his hatless head bowed, a small bald patch reflecting the muted sun.

"Bel," Laurence called from a block's distance. With arms folded and knees splayed back, he had the same impatient posture as the boy who long ago had told her not to run from the lost slave, as if he had lived through nothing since that moment, nothing at all. "Are you coming?"

Nodding, Bel looked back down the hill after Johnny Mulcane, but the hired man was gone; only his footprints remained, marring hers and Laurence's, aiming in the opposite direction, each one holding a lake of shadow that would grow as the light faded.

When they finally entered the hardware store on Church Street, a ring of hardened slush had attached itself to the hem of Bel's dress. In the remaining quarter mile to the store, she had magnanimously forgiven her cousin his oversight, and then proceeded to become annoyed with him again as her hip began to ache. She gave a loud sigh as they ducked into a shop filled with hammers, saws, nails, and paint. A yellow dust had settled over everything, and their entrance seemed to cause a disturbance in the back of the room. After an expressive clatter, a tall, lean man emerged, brushing his hands against a leather apron.

"Yes, sir," he said to Laurence. His droopy eyes slid over them both. Everything about the man pointed downward—his long onion-colored nose, his sagging lips, the slope of his shoulders—and yet his voice was friendly and resonant. "Can I help you with something?"

Laurence looked suddenly baffled and picked up a saw, testing the blade against his palm. The teeth made small white marks where they pressed the skin.

"In the market for a saw, are you?" said the man. "I've got some better ones in the back."

Her cousin set the tool down. "I'm actually calling to ask about a friend of mine. A friend of a friend," he said with a trace of irony. The man showed no reaction to the password, although Bel studied him hard. Were they going to rescue another slave? "I mean," Laurence continued, "I'm home on furlough from Virginia, and I had a friend who was treated very kindly by a man who might be a relative of yours."

"Oh no," said the proprietor. He backed up a few steps and held up his hands before letting them be dragged earthward like the rest of him. "You must mean Walt."

"Walt Whitman," Laurence said thoughtfully. "I think that was his name."

"What do you want to know about him?" the man asked. His mouth screwed into a small red knob. "Did he borrow money from you?"

"No." Laurence shook his head. "My friend knew Mr. Whitman's sister lived in Allenton, so when he found out I was coming here, he asked me to be his messenger."

The man appeared relieved. He leaned against one of his wooden shelves, letting his hand dangle in a box of nails. They made a small chinking sound as he stirred them with his fingers.

"My friend wanted someone to tell Mr. Whitman that he saved his life," Laurence added softly.

"He ain't still pretending to be a doctor at them hospitals, is he?" Alarm flooded the man's gray eyes.

"No. With his words, I mean," Laurence said. "He helped him to understand some things."

The man righted himself, swaying in the dimness of the aisle. His motion stirred up another cloud of dust, and Bel sneezed. She was disappointed about the "friend of a friend" business and she allowed herself a small sniff. The noise seemed to waken the two men from their disjointed conversation.

"As I said," the owner began. "I've got some better saws in back. If the lady will wait."

"No." Laurence glanced at Bel. "The lady is cold. I'll come back some other time. Does Mr. Whitman ever visit you?"

The man's lips tightened again before he replied. "Unannounced," he said. "Without so much as a by-your-leave. But my wife will tell him what you said. She has a soft spot for him, you know." He shrugged. "What women will put up with."

Bel stared at the pool of slush and dust on the floor, her body quaking with a fresh shiver. "Laurence," she said, aware suddenly that this conversation might drag on forever, prolonged by the man's reticence and Laurence's curiosity. She was exhausted, less by the exercise than by Laurence's needy and difficult presence. She wanted to be alone. "I'd like to go home."

"Of course. We need to go home." Laurence reached out and shook hands with the man. "Thank you, sir," he said, his starved cheeks folding back as he grinned.

"Don't mention it," said the man, with a shrug that settled his shoulders even lower than before.

Bel took Laurence's arm and let him lead her out past the files and hammers, which suddenly reminded her of weapons—swords, axes—dulled beyond their original purpose by years and years of war.

Chapter Thirty-six

The remaining weeks in January passed at a furious pace. Two deep snowfalls drifted up the sides of trees and whitened the roads. Although he spoke little of his years at soldiering, Laurence came to Greenwood often, entering the house unannounced to steal Bel away for some long tramp through town. Her parents, eager to see their nephew come alive again, did not protest until Bel ruined several dresses and earned the great irritation of Mary, who was responsible for rescuing the damaged hems. After listening to the servant's shrill keening over the laundry for the fifth day in a row, Faustina insisted the two cousins take some form of transportation when they went out. Consequently, on the last week of Laurence's visit, Bel finally got escorted sleighing like the other wealthy girls with brothers or sweethearts back from the war.

The mild winter sun shone down as Laurence bundled Bel in the sled and plunked down beside her. Today, he had a hard and angry energy, like a penned horse waiting to be let out of his stall. Everything about him had grown since he arrived in Allenton: His hair and beard were longer, his cheeks full and pink. Even his narrow hips took up more of the seat than she expected, and she edged away to give him more room.

"Are we ready?" Laurence asked without looking at her.

"Ready," echoed Bel.

For three weeks, they had confessed nothing about themselves, although they talked long about their parents and servants and the other young people of the neighborhood. That day, Bel was determined to tell Laurence of her distant, tremulous romance with the French tutor. As the seasons passed, her memory of Louis had faded, much as she tried to revive it by recalling their conversations in the library, by scouring the kind, remote letters he sent to the family for any hint of emotion. Bel no longer thought about him every day, although she wanted to. Surely Laurence, who once wrote that he had met and liked Louis, would be the one to encourage the affair to bloom.

As the sleigh coasted down the lane, Bel let the buffalo robe swallow her up to the chin. Ahead of them, the bay mare kicked up small white coins.

"Where shall we go?" asked Laurence.

"I don't know," Bel said, hoping they would end up at Battery Park, where the other sleighs gathered. "Not far. It's supposed to snow later."

"I could take you to meet one of my pards, a bully fellow named John Addison. He's staying with his aunt on the south end of town," Laurence offered, needlessly slapping the reins on the horse's back. The sleigh skimmed faster down the street, and they passed a lost red scarf trailing in the snow. The shadows of the elms crossed over them.

"That's far," Bel said.

"You're right. Besides, he's such a hero, you might fall in love with him," Laurence paused, and then added with a note of ownership, "And I couldn't allow that."

"Why not?" Bel demanded.

"Oh, I don't know." He forced a laugh. "You shouldn't fall in love with a soldier. We're a sorry, dishonest, murderous lot."

"You don't believe that." Bel brushed a strand of hair back from her face and settled deeper in the buffalo robe. This new conveyance was much more pleasant than walking.

"You're right," Laurence said, peering behind them as if he suspected they were being followed. "I've met the best and the worst in men since I enlisted."

The horse plodded steadily up the steep hill. Past the crest, farms stretched along the Winooski Valley, barns and rail fences stranded in snow-covered pastures. The city would be behind them in another mile, and the sharp air of the country would make their voices loud and consonant. Bel had not thought Laurence would take her in this direction, because the other young people always gathered at Battery Park in the winter. A track had been worn hard and slick there, and the men raced one another until their female companions lost their hats and emitted laughing shrieks of protest.

"Do you want to go back to Virginia?" Bel asked, hesitant.

"I have to go back," Laurence replied quickly. "I reenlisted."

"That's not what I asked."

"But I would give you the same answer, no matter how many times or ways you asked me," he promised with weighty dolor. "Duty leaves little room for personal opinion."

This statement seemed to close the argument. Bel knotted her hands beneath the buffalo robe and sighed. How could she bring up Louis Pacquette when Laurence was behaving like this? And yet she yearned to invoke the tutor's name, to see him again in her mind's eye, bending over a book, or standing on the ladder to the hayloft, holding a candle.

"Don't worry," Laurence said softly, almost as if he expected her not to listen. "I'll never leave you."

As they mounted the crest, the horse's head sagged, making her mane spill forward. At the top, Laurence halted the sleigh. "Look back," he commanded, pointing to the jagged rows of lumber buildings and houses winding up the flank of the hill. The few evergreens in Allenton shone like green banners in the colorless ruins of winter. Smoke bulged from a hundred chimneys, stalled by the cold. Bel glimpsed the other sleighs circling in the park.

"What do you see?" Laurence asked, his arm tightening around her. She squirmed a little.

"I think Mary Ruth's brother is winning," she said. "They're the ones with the big blue sleigh. What do you see?"

A cloud of breath masked his mouth as he answered. "I see you as a young girl, standing on the rim of that very lake, and me watching another man catch you from falling."

Bel stared at her lap. "I guess I didn't understand what you were asking."

"You used to understand me."

"I used to worship you," Bel said, her cheeks hot. "I'm not sure that's the same thing."

Suddenly, Laurence's arm flexed again and his face was close to hers, faintly stubbled and rimmed by the omnipresent Union cap. She felt the cold pressure of his lips, the warm air that seeped through and touched her tongue, before she realized he was kissing her.

"Bel," he whispered. His mouth tasted like lemon peel. "I know it's wrong to fall in love with you, but—"

"Don't!" she cried and fisted her hands against his neck, pushing him away. Laurence slid back, his eyebrows knitting together. He brushed his chest and sleeves as if dust had fallen on him.

"I'm sorry," Bel said miserably, staring at the horse's immobile tail. It seemed as if they had crested the hill hours, even years, before, and she couldn't remember a word they had said on their way to the windy summit above Allenton. "I don't feel that way about you. I couldn't."

"Is it because of him?" Laurence demanded. "That ugly tutor of yours?"

"No." Suddenly, she saw Louis more clearly than she had for months, his brown eyes raised toward the winter light streaming through the library window.

"Because we're cousins?" He turned to her. "Of course, I've thought about that, too, but I'm not asking—"

"Laurence," said Bel, interrupting him. "It's because of you."

They sat there for another long moment—Bel facing forward into the rolling valley, the chalked blue rim of peaks beyond, Laurence's spine twisted to allow him to look down over the city. She could feel the heat of his body beneath the buffalo robe, but he did not try to touch her again.

"I'm sorry," she offered again.

"For what?" he asked in a low voice, his face in profile. The dark circles beneath his eyes made him look much older than twenty-one. He directed the horse in a full circle so that they aimed toward the lake. "Shall we go to the races?"

Before Bel had time to answer, he slapped the reins again, making the horse trot and then canter down the white lane. The sleigh began to gain momentum, barreling past the snow-drowned trees, the few houses like outposts on the hill, past rail fences leaning, heaved up by frost, past buried gardens and the rickety sprays that in spring would fill out to yellow forsythia.

"Stop," she called out when she could find her voice. The sleigh was dangerously close on the heels of the running horse. Laurence's expression did not change, although she saw him try to pull back on the reins. This had little effect. The mare had no desire to be run over by her passengers, and she careened sharply to the left, kicking into the hard snow that clung to the street's edge. The sleigh wobbled and spun and Bel fell against her cousin. His bony elbow bruised her ribs.

As the horse continued her mad sprint, Laurence let the reins go with a little toss. Beyond the city, the lake shone a tawny gold, like the back of a deer, and Bel had the feeling she was riding straight into the center of its spine. There was a crunching sound as one of the sled's runners swerved up the bank, tilting their conveyance to the opposite side. This time, Bel's cousin fell on top of her and she punched wildly, not caring if she hurt him. Her knuckles skidded against the wool of his coat.

With a last lunge, the horse's maneuvering wrenched the sleigh at a right angle to the street, where it stopped and began to tip, spilling its passengers with comedic slowness. Skidding to a halt, the horse turned her head to watch the damage she had caused. Laurence's shoulder ground against Bel's scalp as they crashed into the shadow cast by the sleigh and scrambled apart. She shoved a small pile of snow from her lap while Laurence cursed and thrashed around for his lost cap. He did not ask her if she was all right.

As she gripped the sleigh's edge and stood slowly, Bel had the feeling they had lapsed into strangers again, like two people thrown together on a railroad car, partners of circumstance, not of blood. She saw the cap half-buried beside Laurence but did not point it out, watching him with pity as he groped in the snow. She could not imagine being him—always searching for something he could not find—and she wondered with sorrow how he had come to be that way, and what woman would love him truly if she didn't.

A few spectators emerged from nearby houses, holding their heads low against the wind.

"Took a spill, did you?" a black-haired matron said with some satisfaction as Laurence restored his cap to its usual jaunty angle. "I sar it coming." She nodded to another approaching onlooker, a man Bel recognized as the one who delivered their eggs every Wednesday. His appearance was highly suited to his profession, for he had a bald and oblong pate that shone in the summer as if it were glazed.

"Need some help, Mr. Lindsey?" the man said to Laurence. "Any bones broke?"

"We're all right, sir," Laurence said stiffly. "We just took a turn too fast."

"I'll say you did." The black-haired matron, first to the scene, spoke with some authority to the other arrivals. She was standing in a pool of slush, but it did not seem to bother her.

"Let's get this tipped back again," the deliveryman advised. "Let's get you back in the lane."

Bel edged away as Laurence, the egg man, and a towheaded young boy gripped the sides of the sleigh and dragged it, creaking, from the snowbank, setting it back to its rightful position. The boy watched Laurence with undisguised awe.

"Faster than the railcar," he said appreciatively, slapping the flank of the sleigh.

"Don't you even think of trying that again, young man," the matron cautioned, looking to the clouds for reassurance. She had fleshy, immobile lips that moved out of time with her words.

"We won't," Bel assured her, irritated by the warning. More people were coming now, stamping down the lane to gawk at them. "It was an accident. He let go by accident."

"Soldiers," the egg man grunted in a friendly way. "You only got three weeks to impress the ladies and you try to squeeze it all in at once. Ain't no use a'tall to try and stop him, Martha." He nodded to the matron. "He's going back to war soon."

"I'm going to war, too," said the boy, thrusting out his small chest. "As soon as I'm able."

Laurence, who had been staring at the ground, now wheeled on the boy. "I hope to God it's over before you're able," he said fervently. His feet squeaked as they spun in the snow. "I hope to God the war won't wait for you."

The boy's mouth opened and shut, but he did not speak again. Laurence checked the traces on the horse and took the reins in his fist before climbing back in the sleigh. He offered his free hand to Bel. "Thank you," she said to the onlookers, taking in their squinting, well-meaning faces and understanding for a moment Laurence's dislike of other people's kindness, for it came so close to pity. "We're fine now."

The sleigh lurched forward and a cold wind rose up, separating them from the others. As the distance grew, the onlookers' faces went blank and featureless as a far-off hill. Only the young boy, smaller than the rest, was easy to pick out. His body was so still, he could have been a stone. Loneliness flooded her. The buffalo robe, stiff and snow-filled, lay across her ribs like something that had never been alive. They coursed down the street without speaking, and the sounds of the city overcame them: the ringing of the blacksmith's hammer, a man skidding down icy steps, the thump of a maid beating dust from a rug with a paddle.

"I'd rather not go to the park anymore," Bel said finally to the bitter air. She fixed her eyes on the approaching walls of the brick church, as if reading something there.

"No?" said Laurence. "Can you imagine what my father will say when he finds out?" he asked in the old conspiratorial tone.

"You might be gone by then." Bel shrank to a tiny ball beneath the buffalo robe, suddenly cold. "I won't tell."

Without answering, Laurence steered them toward Greenwood, letting the sleigh skim across the lost red scarf, snowy and crushed. Bel turned around to watch it after they passed. At first, she thought

267

the sleigh's blade had severed the wool, because a snowy gap bloomed where they had run over it. Only later did she tell herself that the weight of their passing had merely shoved the scarf's center deep beneath the snow, that it was still one piece, and its owner would come back for it and take it home.

Chapter Thirty-seven

M y dear, your Miss Bottum just raves about you, your mother thinks you need some experience in the world, and all we have to do now is convince your father," concluded Aunt Pattie, who had spirited Bel away to the drawing room to talk her niece into accompanying her on the Sanitary Commission's spring tour of the hospitals in Washington. The idea thrilled Bel, and she was already drafting plans for her boastful call at Mary Ruth Cross's house when her aunt continued. "I need a quiet, useful girl like you. My own daughters would be far too busy making beaus of the soldiers to do me any good."

While Bel didn't appreciate such immediate dismissal of her own beau-making prowess, she nodded obediently and tore out the five or six stitches she had just made in a new white shirt for Louis, who continued to write polite letters to the whole family. Bel's sketching was far more advanced than her stitching, as Miss Bottum, the drawing tutor, had attested, and Aunt Pattie had convinced herself that the only way she could outdo Mrs. M.J.'s hundred-page report from the year before was to hand in an *illustrated* version of the medical care the brave boys received.

"Of course," continued Aunt Pattie, who needed very little reciprocal conversation to keep her going, "it will be a hard thing for a girl like you to see men suffer like this. Mrs. M.J. and her daughter were absolutely scandalized by some of the places."

"I don't mind," Bel said in a small voice. "I could stand it for Laurence's sake." Her cousin had left just days after their sleigh ride, their old camaraderie replaced by a stiff formality. After three weeks with no word from the soldier, she blamed herself for the deadness in his eyes as he said good-bye. He was so sensitive, she scolded herself. She could have pretended to love him.

"My dear son, I hope he learns to be among us again once this war is over," Aunt Pattie was saying. "He was so happy to be here, especially to see you. And he ate well," she affirmed. "But he wasn't the same."

"No," Bel said, thinking of the upset sleigh and Laurence thrashing in the snow for his lost cap when it was right beside him. "He wasn't the same."

"Mrs. Van Sicklin said that someone in Laurence's regiment was shot for desertion right before they came home on furlough. Laurence never spoke of it, did he?"

Interested as she was in the gossip, Bel resented this prying, for she realized Aunt Pattie had not garnered any real news from her son and was hoping Bel had succeeded where she had failed. Why couldn't they leave him alone? "No," she said shortly. "We didn't talk about the war. You know he didn't want to talk about it."

"I see." Aunt Pattie reared back with a creak of whalebone. "Well, I'm sorry I asked."

"He was so tired," Bel added softly. "He wanted home to be home."

They sat in silence for a moment, watching the fire.

"I hope you can bear seeing what war does to all those brave young men," Aunt Pattie said.

"I can stand it." Bel swallowed hard. Hadn't she stood it already?

"So many of them are suffering from terrible wounds, far worse than what we saw in Brattleboro," Aunt Pattie cautioned her. "They reach out to any womanly figure they see, you know. I couldn't let you visit the wards unchaperoned."

The thought of being paraded about for weeks by her loquacious aunt was singularly unappealing to Bel. Balancing it, however, was the notion of seeing the capital and getting closer to Laurence and Louis. She wanted desperately to escape Greenwood, which had grown stagnant and cold after her cousin's departure, with Daniel often away on business and Faustina involved in her remote life of books and letter writing. The only excitement was Uncle George and Aunt Pattie's Wednesday visit. This particular night, George and Faustina had stayed in the parlor, listening to Mary play Irish songs, while Bel and her aunt crept off to talk about Washington. Aunt Pattie had become positively conspiratorial as the plan took shape, and Bel found a new appreciation for her fashionable aunt. She treated Bel more like an adult than her parents did, and seemed eager to show her niece the world beyond Greenwood.

"I declare the war will be quite over by the time you finish that shirt," said Aunt Pattie, watching Bel restitch the seam.

"I've been making two," Bel confessed. While he was home, Laurence had claimed his old shirt was worn-out and had commissioned a new one.

"Two," Aunt Pattie repeated in a considering voice. "One for Laurence, and one for . . ."

"A friend," Bel said, and blushed. She didn't want to say the name of her tutor, afraid the news would leak back to her mother.

"Well . . ." Aunt Pattie released a long, oniony breath. Her blue eyes fluttered over Bel's face. "Does your friend know you are making this shirt for him?"

"No. It's a surprise. And I'm going to send it that way, too. So he doesn't know whom it's from," Bel said, the idea suddenly coming to her.

Just then, her mother and uncle entered the drawing room, their faces flushed. "Did you have a good round?" Aunt Pattie asked.

"Their Mary has a lovely voice," said George to his wife. "There ought to be another beatitude blessing those who can sing, for they truly bring paradise a little closer."

Aunt Pattie gave a strained smile, as if she thought he had enjoyed the singing a little more than he ought. Her own puritan heaven would have a respectable amount of toil in it.

"Mary doesn't need a beatitude to bolster her claim on paradise," retorted Faustina. "With all her righteousness, she's already staked a large plot up there."

"And sown it with good Irish crops." George laughed in his sister-in-law's direction.

"I was just convincing Bel to leave your nest for a while," said Aunt Pattie, her expression difficult to read. "Can you bear letting her go under another woman's wing, Faustina?"

"If you wish it." Faustina turned to look out the dark window. "I can't speak for Washington, but I know you'll be a fine influence on her. You must convince her father first, however."

Her uncle settled on a chair with a gusty sigh and regarded his niece.

"Papa won't think it safe," muttered Bel. Daniel Lindsey was more conservative than his brother and often lectured about "influences" on his young daughter, the word suggesting an evil, amorphous wind that could seep through the cracks of the tightest door. Despite his fear of influences particular to the male variety, he had not guessed Bel's attraction to her tutor and simply assumed that his daughter's good sense wouldn't allow for any such romance. But Washington?

How many temptations could trip a young, rich, and compassionate girl into making the wrong decisions? Bel finished the last stitch on the long side seam of the shirt and let it fall to her lap. The motion made the concealed swan necklace slip toward the groove between her breasts. She had kept it hidden for an entire year.

"He should let her go. Shouldn't he, Faustina?" said George defiantly. Strained by his full stomach, his buttonholes tightened like eyes in the sun.

"It's not our choice," Pattie gently reprimanded him. "Besides, our girls have always stayed in Allenton."

"Can't you see that Isabel is nothing like them?" George demanded, making Bel duck her head and redden without knowing why.

"Whatever do you mean?" Aunt Pattie straightened her spine. "She's slow at stitching, but she can sketch beautifully, and she's a passable singer—in a group."

"But she wants more in her life than to decorate drawing rooms, Pattie." George did not see that his criticism made his wife wither in her chair, or he would have stopped. Instead, he had turned on his niece, the slope of his body like a stone that sits for centuries on the brink of a cliff, poised to fall but not falling. "Her mother fed her ideas and she wants ideas; Laurence fed her faraway places and she wants to travel there. You can't raise a girl like this and not expect her to want something different, to go somewhere. And you want to go, don't you, Bel?" His commanding voice filled the room. Bel fiercely tied a thread and did not answer, her cheeks hot. "Don't you?"

Instead of facing him, she looked up at her mother, at her slightly bent shoulders and graceful waist, at hips so narrow, they should not have been able to have borne a child, but if so, then only one. She saw Faustina's lips press to a thin line, and the tears in the corners of her eyes yellowed by lamplight. Then, behind her mother, Daniel appeared, striding down the hall, his expression distant, half-shuttered with daydreams of new buildings, fountains, and statues to grace still nonexistent parks. And behind him, the walls of Greenwood, cold and mellow in the winter night, keeping them all from the whine of the wind and the bitter, glittering streets.

"No," she shouted, lying. "I don't want to go." Her father entered the room, winding his pocket watch. "Don't make me go."

Her volume made Daniel flinch. He stared at the timepiece as if it and not his daughter had spoken so loudly, and he shook it hard in his good right hand.

Chapter Thirty-eight

It was the second week in March when the letter came. February had departed with a sudden thaw, leaving snow in dirty piles across the garden, the raw yellow-green grass running like scars beneath. Ground not fully unfrozen held the rain above it and leaves drifted in the shallow pools around tree roots. The early warmth, though pleasant, felt strange to Bel as she sloshed into the garden. It was like a joke that goes wrong and leaves the company regretful instead of pleased.

Cold water seeped through her boots, making rude spongy noises when she stepped. The world was open again and she its first trespasser. Wilderness Spring. She had gone out bonnetless just to feel wind that would not cause her scalp to tingle with pain, but after a few minutes, she hurried back inside, hoping her mother would overlook her allowing the sun to touch her face. Entering the dim foyer, Bel saw the errand boy had left the single letter that arrived that day, along with the new *Frank Leslie's Fashion Gazette*. She stared at the envelope. "Miss Isabel Lindsey." It was postmarked Washington, D.C. The serious, economic cursive of her tutor contrasted sharply with Laurence's looping hand, and Bel knew the former instantly. She pushed the door softly shut behind her before snatching up the letter and scurrying to her hiding place in the bay window.

As she squirmed deep into the window seat, she slowly tore the government-issue envelope. There was a single soft sheet of paper folded inside. Already blushing, Bel pulled up her knees and spread the letter across them. A gray-white air blew through the bare tree branches, making them knock the windows of Greenwood. Pressing the swan locket to her lips, she forgot the quiet house around her and began to read.

Dear Isabel,

It seems improper for your humble tutor to begin with such familiarity, but I have spent a great deal of time writing letters to you in my mind, and over the course of such missives began to admit the great affection I feel for you. These are not the words of the teacher who left you, however, but those of a soldier on the brink of dying for a cause you were so right to believe was worth dying for.

I fear we head into grave battle, Isabel. I have no misgivings about the cause in which I am engaged, and I am willing to lay down all the joy in my life—even the thought that I may see you again—that all men might be free.

The recollection of those few hours I spent in your company comes back to me daily. How briefly I knew you, and how strong is my will to remember every detail of our conversations of slavery and consequence, the awful verbs of my native tongue, your delicate frown over your stitching, and the way you would not look at me when we danced, shy bird.

I do not know if you want to hear such memories from a workingman like me. But the soldier's life has made me reckless, and on the chance I will never see you again, I will say to you, Isabel, that if death takes me, I will return to you always in the lifting

*wind through the maples, in the fathomless deep of the lake, in
every season and on every stranger's face.*

*Dear Isabel, remember me, and that one man loved the up-
right soul in you.*

Louis Pierre Pacquette

Bel shuddered as she finished the letter. The very earth seemed to
have shifted around her, the balance of trees in the yard somehow
lifted beyond their roots. She relished imagining the disappointed
face of Mary Ruth Cross, the eyebrows slamming down from the
blond hairline as Bel whispered to her of the letter—and surely Louis
would win his own medals for bravery; surely he would come back
from the war so decorated that one day her parents could not refuse
him. Mary Ruth's brother had already ascended from private to sergeant. Surely the worthy Canadian might at least make colonel.

The steps of someone approaching interrupted Bel's reverie. It was
her father going to get his mail. She shoved the paper back in its envelope, stowing it in the folds of her dress. Making herself very small and
very quiet, she listened to the gazette rustle as he picked it up and
walked back across the room.

His shadow stopped outside the blue curtain.

"Hidden like a fairy queen in her flower. How's my brave Titania
this morning?" he greeted her, peeking through the split in the fabric.
In the clean, gauzy light between the curtain and the window, his face
looked animal-like and large. Bel shrank back.

"Oh, she doesn't want to be disturbed, does she?" He laughed,
showing his teeth.

"I was just thinking of spring," Bel said.

"Don't believe this mad wind." He looked out the glass. "We'll be
buried under six inches of snow by the end of the week."

Bel forced herself to smile. "Of course, you're right, Papa. I was just wondering what spring might be like in Washington. I hear they have marvelous gardens there."

He let the curtains fall back and spoke to her from beyond the blue waterfall of cloth. "Gardens and Lee's army on the verge of invading. Not the spring I want my daughter to see," he concluded, and strode off, slapping the rolled gazette against his hand.

Bel leaned back with a sigh. The quickest way to get rid of her father was to talk of Washington. How she truly wished to go to that city, but she could wait. Louis's words told her she could wait, and he would not forget her. She hid the letter in her dress, deciding to sneak it to her bedroom, where she could read it again without disruption.

Walking across the sunny drawing room to the oak staircase, Bel was stirred to a grandeur she had never before experienced, a princess on the verge of becoming queen. Her tender ray of affection for her cousin was suddenly eclipsed by a larger light she didn't dare to say was love. Step by step, up the circling stair, she let her inner eye run over the memorized features of Louis, his proud, intent nose and black hair, his straight shoulders, and those rough hands that touched book pages as if they were the finest silk.

So absorbed was Bel in this pleasant exercise that she didn't see her mother coming down the flight. A dreamy procession of the letter's promises ran through her mind, and it was not until she recognized her mother's slippered feet on the stair in front of her that she looked up.

"Who gave that to you?" Faustina's voice rang out, harsh and aggrieved. Bel's hands closed around the hidden letter.

"Gave what?" she asked. Her mother loomed like a storm cloud, her creamy shirtwaist blocking Bel's way up the stair.

"This," Faustina said, reaching forward to grip the swan locket Bel had forgotten to stow back beneath her dress. Faustina's face had frozen into a mask, her features perfect but her eyes like a stranger's behind them.

"I found it," Bel said, stepping aside as the hands stretched toward her neck.

It was a motion she blamed afterward on the mute disobedience of her body, its unwillingness to be crushed. Later, when Bel replayed the moment, she imagined herself still instead of swaying, the pain of her own skin and bones taking the blows. Yet in that one betraying instant, her mother lost her balance and tumbled forward down the stairs. She fell with the stiffness of a trunk pushed down the rapids of a creek, both ends jarred and broken but the center slow, weighted with its own fixity. Faustina's hands battered against the banister as Bel ran after her, the bird locket banging against her breastbone, her hair falling across her shoulders, still cool from the garden.

"Mother," she cried, unbelieving. Faustina's legs splayed on the floor like the feet of the chickens Grete brought from the butcher. Bel crouched down to rearrange the upthrust knees to a ladylike position, smoothing the gray skirt over them. Her mother groaned.

"I'm sorry." Bel looked into Faustina's face. A jagged cut crossed her right cheek, and bruises were swelling along the corner of her mouth. Faustina's eyes fluttered rapidly and she fainted.

"Mother," Bel screamed, thinking worse. She heard the quick step of her father on the landing.

"What happened here?"

Bel turned her head with the slowness of years to see Daniel coming down the stairs, his stiff pant legs bent at the knees, polished shoes shining. His voice was heavy with fear and anticipation, as if every time he descended the spiraling heart of Greenwood, he expected such a scene: Bel leaning over her fallen mother, Faustina's body deflated like a bellows, the clatter of his own arrival, too late to save them. *It wasn't me,* she wanted to shout, but nothing emerged from her open mouth. The front door, not fully latched after she came in from the garden, blew open with a bang. A warm, muddy wind entered the house, and she could hear the slushy clop of horses passing on the street outside, a coachman slapping the reins across their broad backs.

"It was an accident," Bel finally managed to say, and turned back to her mother. She used her cuff to dab at the blood on Faustina's cheek.

"Let the doctor do that," ordered her father. "Mary!" he shouted, going down on his knees beside his wife. "Mary!"

The red-haired servant appeared, panting, with a feather duster raised like an ax. Her freckles darkened to rust when she saw her fallen mistress. She stepped forward and then halted, unwilling to enter the scene. "Send for the doctor," Daniel commanded. "Now."

Mary ran out the open door, still wielding the duster. The ugly thaw blew over them the scent of frozen things finally turning to rot. Faustina stirred, her mouth slackening to take in air.

"Why did you let me fall?" she murmured, and opened her eyes, not looking at Bel, but at her husband. He arched over her, and Bel noticed how his skin had aged in the years since the war started, loose at the wrist and chin, and growing the film of brown spots that marked the hands of the old.

"I wasn't there," he said, as if this were an answer. "I was upstairs."

Bel thrust herself into their gaze. "I didn't mean to, Mother. Please. I didn't mean to." The silver chain dangled the swan in the air above her mother. Resting her eyes on the bird, Faustina fainted again with a soft wheeze. The air grew empty and cold.

"You shouldn't stay," Daniel whispered to his daughter as she drew back. His eyes flickered over the locket without recognition. "You're clearly upsetting her."

"But I didn't do anything," Bel said loudly, hoping it would wake her mother. Faustina stirred briefly, and then her face fell to the side, away from the open door.

"Let her be, Isabel." Her father's voice was still gentle, but he shouldered in closer, pushing Bel aside and blocking her view of her mother. "I'll take care of her now. It's *my* duty," he said.

"It isn't your duty. You love her." Bel stared at the chord of muscles in the back of his neck, willing him to answer. He didn't.

"She fell, Papa. Why don't you believe me?" she asked.

Sighing, he straightened her mother's collar and hair, as if arranging her for a display.

"Ask her, then. I'm sure she'll tell you everything," Bel added bitterly, her hand closing around the swan that he was incapable of noticing, that had made her perfect mother fall.

When I was sixteen, my mother fell down the stairs, a voice narrated for Bel as she rose and stumbled out, past her father haloed in the light of the impossible spring. She went into the garden and sat on the bench by the lilac tree, remaining there even after the doctor came and then left, calling to her that her mother was fine. Inside her mind, she retreated to tell Laurence the story over and over when they were old and finally together again.

The world would be different then, the war finished and the two of them alive long past their spouses. They would find their childhood hiding places, and curl deep in the moss to confess to each other the lives they dreamed they lived. *My mother fell down the stairs when I was sixteen*. With distance, it was easier to believe the accident she had just seen: the flare of her mother's white legs exposed above her stockings, so vulnerable, like a paper boat set on the sea—and why Daniel Lindsey could not understand that the fall happened as a consequence of motion and gravity. *My father blamed me.*

Chapter Thirty-nine

It was Grete who finally rescued Bel from the garden, after the girl's body had gone stiff and achy from exposure to the damp, chill air. For hours, she had sat with the chewed remains of a bread crust in her palm, the way her grandmother had once taught her and Laurence to feed the birds. The steaming bread went cold and hard, but nothing came except Grete, who made scolding noises as she knocked Bel's hand clean. Then she ushered the girl back to the kitchen, seating her on a stool by the hot black stove.

"She wants to see you after you dry out," Grete said, and added her familiar warning, pointing at the stove. "Beware." Ever since Bel was little, Grete had issued the same edicts for the kitchen. No touching, no picking, no tasting, unless a sample was offered by the cook herself. Today, Grete had many samples, her broad face gone red with worry and exertion as she fed Bel a spoonful of beef stew, the crumbs of a broken cookie, the heel of a just-baked loaf slathered in butter. After several minutes of eating and thawing, Bel finally spoke.

"I didn't do anything, Grete. She just fell," she said, and Grete peered at her like an old turtle who has all the time it wants to measure the world before deciding on its virtue. Finally, she nodded, but it was a curious nod, transfixed suddenly by the silver locket that hung from Bel's neck.

"It's mine," Bel said defiantly. "I found it in the coach barn last year."

"So," said Grete. "I think you should put it away once more."

"Why?" Bel's heart quickened at the thought of learning the swan's secret.

"When I was a little girl," Grete began evasively, stirring the soup with her heavy arm, "I asked my mother all the questions I could think of. 'Why was the sky blue?' 'Why does water make that sound when it falls?' 'Why can birds fly and not people?' And she said to me, 'Someday the things you have no answer for will be the ones that make you happy.'"

"Are you happy?" Bel asked, disappointed by the cook's answer.

Grete grunted. "When I haf my own house, I will be happy."

"I'm not happy," Bel said. Her skin felt baked and cracked by the kitchen's heat.

"You will be," Grete predicted, offering Bel another taste of stew. She needlessly scraped the sides of Bel's mouth with the spoon to catch the spill, as she had done when Bel was a child.

"My stockings are dry," Bel said through a mouthful of warm potato. "Can I go see my mother now?"

Instead of answering the girl, Grete handed her a glass of melted snow. It tasted earthy and cool, and Bel drank it all down, letting Grete gently tuck the bird back beneath the safe cover of her dress.

"Please," said the cook. Bel had never heard her say the word before, even in exasperation. "It came from another sweetheart, one your mother had before your father. Someone your Papa never knew about." Grete turned and began to dust flour across the table in soft white constellations. "That's all I can tell you," she added, spreading the piles smooth.

When Bel ascended the stairs for the second time that day, it was her father who stood at the top, waiting for her, his left hand gripping the rail as if he, too, might fall. In his right, he held something white and thin, and Bel's stomach sank when she saw it, remembering the letter she had received that afternoon and thought was still carefully stowed in her dress. She felt the place where the envelope had rested, but the letter must have slipped out in the flurry after her mother fell.

"Is Mother ready to see me?" she asked in a shaking voice, her anger with him suddenly replaced by fear.

"She's sleeping again. She asked for you," he added. "And once we discuss a small matter"—he wagged the letter—"we can visit her together."

Bel followed her father to the dim fire-lit library and sat down opposite him in the same chair she took for her tutoring lessons. He tapped the table with the crease of the paper before beginning.

"Bel, you have some of the finest prospects for marriage in Allenton. You're a bright, pretty girl from a wealthy family, and there are hundreds of appropriate young men who—" He stopped abruptly and rubbed at his forehead. "I just never thought you would take an interest in men so early. Lucia and Anne, yes, but my studious young daughter, who would just as soon play in the mud as go to a ball? And all for that mincing tutor of yours?"

"He's not mincing," Bel shot back.

"What did you promise him?" Her father rubbed his forehead again, looking suddenly weary.

"Nothing." Bel's color rose. She stared at the white ash falling beneath the grate. What had her mother promised *her* secret sweetheart?

"And from that nothing, he presumed to write you"—he made a noise in his throat—"a letter that speaks of a certain intimacy." The grandfather clock gave five low chimes. Bel's mouth tasted of salt and emptiness.

"Father, I haven't changed from the daughter you just spoke of." At this, her voice cracked, for she *had* changed. Even the word *father* sounded strange, like an exotic name that would not obey the tongue. "I just finally found a friend—and a kindred spirit. I didn't know he would write that letter," Bel insisted. And if I hadn't found it on my own, she thought with anger, I never would have known.

"Then why did you hide it?" He turned the paper over and over in his hands, as if repeatedly bringing it to light.

"Because it's mine." Bel met his eyes with all the coolness she could muster. "Because he might die and he wanted me to know that he cared for me, even if nothing comes of it." She paused. "You said yourself that our generation is different from yours."

Her father laid the letter down, his clean, pared fingernails just touching the wood. He did not say anything for a long time, and Bel began to shiver. Her dress, soaking wet at the hem, dragged against her ankles. But Daniel Lindsey was thinking. He was the type of man who could wait on decisions for indeterminate periods of time. Once made, however, they were irreversible. Bel knew enough not to interrupt him—it would only make the consequences worse.

"I see that my Greenwood has become not a house of your happy childhood, but the cage of the foolish dreams of a girl eager to fall in love. I'm afraid if you stay here much longer, this inappropriate romance will grow, augmented by the lack of any other suitors," he began. When he made up his mind, her father spoke in paragraphs, charting his argument like a theorem. "In addition, I fear your childish resentment of your mother has somehow led to her fall, and I cannot leave the two of you alone when I go away on business."

"I told you it was an accident, Papa!" Bel exclaimed, but he banged the table with his right fist, a judge whose courtroom had become unruly. The left lay on the table like a wilted flower.

"So I am sending you to Washington with your Aunt Pattie," he said. "And I will instruct your aunt to have you assist the good nurses so you can see what it is like to be the wife of a workingman, or worse, a spinster."

This granting of her innermost wish shocked Bel. Now it seemed more like a punishment than an escape to leave her mother and Greenwood. "If you bid me to, Father," she said, trying to imagine Washington, like a giant Allenton, rising before her. "When do I leave?"

"Next Thursday," he said.

"May I go see Mother now? I want to see her." She stood up awkwardly, her thighs banging on the table. Her body was a loose door, almost disconnected from her mind. *Washington.* He nodded and led the way out of the library, still holding the letter and smelling of pipe smoke. Bel looked back at the empty table where she and Louis had once sat, and pictured herself meeting him somewhere on the busy streets of the capital. She would run to him—she didn't care—he would be her family. She would let him crush her against the blue wall of his uniform, closer than the waltz—

"The doctor has pronounced her shaken but not seriously hurt," her father said, repeating what Grete had told Bel out in the garden. "She needs unbroken rest for a day or two, so please don't tell her about your departure yet. I don't want her to worry."

He opened the door to the cold, dim bedroom where Faustina lay.

Bel saw herself pass across the room in the cherry vanity mirror that hung on one wall. Because her mother had set it at her own perfect height, Bel's reflection was visible only from the shoulders down. Staring at her headless self, Bel realized it must have been months since she had last entered her mother's chamber, because she remembered being short enough to see her image if she ducked a little. The room itself was gloomier now, as if the shadows Faustina cast in it had lingered, layering over one another until the air was grainy with darkness.

The bruises had twisted the right side of Faustina's face into a clownish grin, and Bel smiled back before she realized this was her mother's fixed expression. Her green eyes swept over her daughter, looking for the swan and not finding it. She gave a milky sigh.

"Good evening, dear," said her father.

"I'm sorry," Bel whispered at the same moment, her voice tight.

"For what, sweet girl?" Faustina winced. "I tripped." She reached up slowly and touched her daughter's cheek. "Don't cry," she added, and brushed away tears Bel didn't know were there.

And from that minute on, it was true. The fall had nothing to do with Bel. She watched her father's face soften and allowed him to squeeze her shoulder in apology.

Around them, the room had the wet, papery smell of illness, and Bel tried not to breathe it in, longing at once both to depart Greenwood that instant and never to leave her parents again, because their complicated hearts both fascinated and disappointed her. For so long she had thought love was just like the swan story, waiting for a message and receiving it, and then sending your own reply, back and forth for years. Watching her father tenderly kiss her mother on an unbruised section of her cheek, now she wasn't sure.

"My dear wife," he said with uncharacteristic emotion. His pink scalp shone through his thinning hair.

Faustina's eyes met her daughter's as he kissed her, and Bel thought she could see in them a deep and unremitting sadness. She touched the hard locket beneath the cloth across her breastbone and saw her mother nod imperceptibly, as if approving of the fact that it was hidden.

Bel did not let the silver bird emerge again until she had safely bidden her parents a tearful good-bye, laden with valises of plain, sensible clothes for her trip to Washington, and she and her aunt had changed cars in Albany, leaving the most opulent Pullman of the Lindsey line for a humble first-class car to the capital. Bel could not stop missing her mother, who had improved enough over the last day to get up from her bed and walk stiffly to the window, where she told her daughter in a low voice to be careful about what she dreamed of, and to fight all kinds of slavery, especially that of the heart. It was the kind of statement that suggested no reply but silence, and at that very instant, Bel finished her second soldier's shirt, the last stitch tied into a knot. In answer to her mother, she held it up, white, billowing, and let it drift back to her lap.

As she and her aunt left Vermont on the rocking Pullman, the land changed, the steep, tumbled green hills replaced by the river basins of New York. Lake Champlain stayed behind them, a flat scarf of silver-blue. The trees and the people, too, looked less hardy and defiant. Quiet-faced strangers had gathered like a stalled parade at Troy's tidy wooden station when Bel finally pulled out the locket again and examined the silver bird, its bent neck curled like the start of a letter.

"Let me see," said her aunt, pale and blond in the switching panels of sunlight, shade, sunlight, shade. The train screeched to a stop. A hairy, frog-eyed man got on, heaping at least twenty carefully wrapped packages and crates into the aisle before taking the seat opposite. His worn attire didn't look quite good enough to ride first-class, and he lounged with an uneasy air on the stiff cushions, occasionally parting the red curtain to peer out on the platform.

"Sutler." Aunt Pattie nodded in his direction as she scrutinized the locket. "Your mother used to wear that." She opened the clasp in her officious way, her stare widening as if she were surprised at the emptiness inside.

The man rearranged his nest of crates, touching their contents gently. "Thirty pies," he announced to the dimness of the train. "A crate of lemons, good soap, and some cologne water for the soldiers who want to remember what it was to smell sweet for the ladies."

"Sir, I caution you against the disreputable elements of the railway," Aunt Pattie said with a hungry glance toward his pies. "My husband, who happens to own a line, says that all sorts of thievery goes on."

"I ain't about to lose nothing." He smiled with genuine friendliness, revealing a blackened tooth. Affronted by his grammar, Aunt Pattie shifted again toward Bel, still holding her niece by the chain. Bel squirmed as the sutler's wet eyes lingered on her hair and shoulders. He would not be included in the range of people Faustina called "polite company." Aunt Pattie tugged on the pendant, and the chain bit into Bel's neck. Leaning forward reluctantly, she resolved not to wear the swan in the open anymore. The train shuddered into motion again, making the crates clack together, and the sutler bounded up from his studied slouch to protect his wares. Aunt Pattie pulled her even closer.

"You ought to get the hinge fixed by a jeweler, dear. One day, it will just fall apart in your hands," she said, wagging the loose halves of the silver bird to prove it.

May–June 1864

Chapter Forty

The place was called Chancellorsville, another meaningless appellation, except that a battle had been fought there the year before, and some of the skeletons remained, dredged up by spring rains. A spongy, starless sky hung over the soldiers. Although it had been dark for hours, no one could sleep, and they clustered around the fire, needlessly toasting their already-warm hands.

Digging with his bayonet beyond the light was blue-eyed Addison, silent even when his body shifted. A wet winter had rusted the weapon's blade, pocking the tiny reflected version of his handsome features. He did not appear to notice it as he carved channels around the edges of what looked like a mushroom-colored stone, clumps of clay sticking to his pants. He stabbed down hard and his reflected face blinked out.

Everybody in his company ignored this strange bout of energy. Only Laurence flicked periodic glances beyond the fire to measure the sergeant's progress, as if he knew he were alone in his curiosity and wished to hide it. Stretching out his long legs, he yawned and let his blond hair fall into his eyes, half-listening to the rest of the men, who were talking about their general. They had all seen him riding the day before in the old patched coat of a private, his hat askew and beard uncombed. *Grant,* one said, *was not a gentleman, and that's why he was the best kind of soldier.*

If Grant was in charge all this time, we wouldn't be fighting on the same battlefield as last year, said a veteran who wanted to scare the new recruits into understanding they knew nothing about war. *I don't know anymore if I'm sleeping on roots or bones.*

Addison kept digging, stopping occasionally to wipe his forehead with his sleeve.

As their talk slowed, Loomis pulled out the locket his wife had given him long ago and kissed her image inside. Another fellow flapped his bedroll three times before lying down. The newer men, just down from their small towns in Vermont, began to form their own superstitions that very night, touching a letter in a breast pocket, whispering a name.

The sergeant's stone finally loosened, and he pried it up with his bayonet so that it rolled toward the flames. It bounced awkwardly, hollow and scratched across its yellow-white face.

This is what we all are coming to, said Addison, rising unsteadily. *And some of you will start toward it tomorrow.*

The skull bumped against a stick blackened by the fire. Bending forward, the sergeant pulled it back from the blaze and let it rest with the sockets aimed upward at a cream of night clouds, the toothy jaw slack and swallowing.

When the companies entered the thicket, the captains drove them to the intersection of two roads. The dusty lanes ran through an endless forest of thorn trees, chinquapin, and dwarf chestnut, burred across the land like the hair of a newborn, thick and tangled with its own shadow.

Gunfire shattered the stillness. Songbirds made sharp cries before they vanished, diving into hollows and caves. Addison looked instantly lonely, as he always did in battle, the rest of the world receding as he focused forward, his nose thrusting horselike into the wind. Behind him, too tall for this skirmish, Alfred Loomis stooped to save himself, his back bowed to an invisible ceiling.

Light blared through the stunted trees, peeling cool morning from the air and replacing it with the heat of a windowless room. The branches cracked like glass beneath their feet, and Laurence remembered suddenly the taste of blackberries, their laden sweetness filling his mouth.

When the firing began, their close formation was torn apart, the sergeant in the middle, Loomis looping left through a stand of new birch, his paddle-sized feet slipping on the mossy stones. The three friends knew one another so well that when Loomis drifted out, the others glanced to where he headed, the lone dead tree, jutting like a finger from a fisted hand.

Ahead of them, the soldiers on the front line fell slowly, with grand and ridiculous gestures, their arms flopping out to conduct a wild orchestra, or swimming slowly down through the leaves. Addison's line would be next. A bullet sailed into the hollow of the dead tree behind Loomis's head, just missing him. He gave a sigh of relief. He did not see the angry swarm of bees that hurtled out of the hollow by the hundreds and aimed like an arrow of rain against the back of his neck.

At the first stings, he spun around, batting their bodies away with his cap until his hands swelled. Soon the insects covered his ears and the slick crown where his hair was falling out. Howling with pain, he straightened from his safe crouch and began to sprint in the direction of the enemy. The others called out in warning, but he did not hear.

He ran with his arms open, embracing the bushes as they whipped his chest. A shot in his stomach, then another, broke his stride and he dove forward until the branches swallowed him. Following their quarry, the bees sang a hymn of exhausted anger that, against the crack and whine of bullets, sounded like praise.

It would be nightfall before the two remaining soldiers began looking for their friend. By then, his face had swollen tight as an egg, the features nearly erased. He could have been anyone, husband and father to a thousand orphaned sons perched on a flour barrel in the general store, baking their shins against a winter fire, running to answer the knock on the door.

The signal rose through the forest, a low three-note whistle of the dove. It meant *found.* As night fell, rebels had started to fire at the searchers, their own men among them, making branches glow in sharp relief, then vanish.

Bats lost their patterns of flight and slammed into tree trunks with hollow, popping sounds. One fell on Laurence's neck, and he swiped it away, hissing through his teeth. He had found his friend by his socks, where the brogan split and peeled aside and an irregular net of black thread shone through. There was no face left.

He sat back on his haunches, balancing his rifle across his thighs. The air weighed hot across the dead leaves and, far off, he could hear a narrow creek trickling over root and stone. Earlier, Captain Davey had ordered them to fill their canteens there. They'd held the silver lips down in the gravel bed and waited as the slow, silty current entered them. Laurence had stayed longer than the others, hovering over the cool vein, searching for the reflection of his face. He whistled again, three low notes.

When Addison staggered in, he stepped on the body's flung right hand and skidded to a halt. He stared into the hole below the ribs, where ants were marching over the intestines in a relentless line. Every time the wounded man breathed in, the ants would waver and lose their footholds, only to regain them again. The earth around the torso had darkened to mud and the corpses of bees lay scattered across it, like drops of rain that would not sink.

Loomis, the sergeant said, although he knew the man could not hear him. Then he unhitched his revolver and aimed straight into the body's half-shut mouth. Laurence watched him dully, holding a narrow chain, the hinge of its locket split open by a minié. One half had fallen somewhere into the field of dead bees and the other bulged like a cheek between his finger and thumb, the woman's face inside cracked across the eyes.

Addison fired. It was louder than the whole war, that sound. The line of ants faltered, but only for a moment, less time than it took for him to turn away.

When the minié hit Laurence in the shin, he thought he could walk anyway and was surprised to have his leg collapse beneath him. He rose again and fell again, swaggering like a drunk through the brush. It was the second day. The regiment had moved on, past the intersection, through an open field, and into more unyielding thickets. Addison had left him behind because Davey was wounded, shot in the thigh.

Laurence.

The name burst into light above the chestnut tree. It was not to be believed. His leg was absent beneath him, his right hand split across the palm.

Later that day, the regiment swept back past him in retreat, and he thought he saw Addison running, his cap lost, his bronze hair streaming like a banner. He could not be sure. The woods were the bleached color of locusts, of a manic season.

Laurence.

It was not to be believed. Addison injured beside him, holding his bloody cheek. Yesterday's face scarred to a mask by bees.

Toward evening, the fires came. They were lovely at first, a tingle in the bushes, a flicker of candles in a darkened church.

At first, Laurence tried to drag himself backward to the ragged Union line, but the burning blocked him with a shimmering wall. Mottled with holes, the underbrush took the smoke and raised it skyward. The light followed. He dug a channel of earth around him with his one good hand and waited. Addison must be looking for him, riding through the fire on a borrowed horse.

Laurence.

Screams pitched from the men who were burning alive. His hand throbbed. The leg was still absent, a weight he dragged behind him on a chain. He dug deeper, watching a soldier scramble up a tree, the flames licking after him. Somewhere the corpses of bees turned to ashes above a fresh-dug grave.

The whistle, the signal for *found*, never came. He stamped at the fire with his one good foot. Smoke seared his eyes, dry and stinging. He breathed it in, let it enter him, while his good hand spread a caked mud of dirt and spit across his skin.

Dipping and waiting, the shapes of buzzards loomed high above the fire. He remembered a boy saying it was bad luck to look away from a buzzard before it flapped. The birds made high circles on the night. The yellow flames went white, roaring in his ears. He heard the trees yield and break, their branches swinging down to be consumed.

Laurence, I'm here.

It was not to be believed. The air was like day. He stared skyward as the fire crossed his circle of earth, felt the heat in his boots as it touched his feet, playing over them.

The buzzards spun higher, riding an invisible current, wings stretched, motionless. His nails cracked as his toes began to burn.

Flap.

. . .

It was not a ghost standing above him, but the shape of a man, the very breadth of darkness in the bright rings of fire. His bare skin wore the sheen of coal before it burns. Ridged across his naked body were scars of chains, of lashes up the back. The fishhook mark of his lost tribe curled beneath his left eye.

Without saying a word, he kicked at the soldier with his good foot, motioning for him to rise. After awhile, the sharp pain woke Laurence and he got to his feet, stumbling into the forest, his eyes shielded by one sooty arm. Burning leaves coasted to the ground around him. He turned. The man had vanished. His knees gave way and he would have caved in, but a falling limb knocked him between the shoulder blades, the blow like a heavy fist beating him onward. He kept walking.

When he reached the narrow run of water that ran through the woods, he tripped on a root and tumbled with a hiss into the stream. The red haze of the sky went loose above him, like a bandage wearing off a wound. It unraveled slowly, peeling back layer by layer until the screams returned, the heat of the fire around him, the bright stars of sparks lighting the moss. He could feel one half of his face lifted away.

He burrowed deep in the muddy bank. A damp, crumbling hair of roots cascaded over his eyes. He waited, listening to the screams belly through the woods and vanish, the crash of charred trees. His mouth tasted of soot and blood. Slow water dragged his scorched clothes away from him, his skin tightening where it was touched by flames.

When he reached for his face, the side that rested on the earth was familiar, the curve of cheek, the bristle of lashes. But the side exposed to the sky sifted like char, the eye sewn shut by fire.

He struggled to remember the name of his rescuer, but the name meant nothing, two syllables that drowned in the stream. As a minnow swam against his one good hand, he could feel the cold, intricate lace of its fins, its mouth opening and closing against his thumb, trying, failing to swallow him whole.

Morning played over the dying fire, sweet-songed. He was lying on the forest floor with a hundred other bodies, gathered for burial. The sound of the shovel chinking in the earth reminded him of an old guilt, a hole in his life that would never be filled.

He could go now. The men still alive murmured of a distant train. But he was ready to go without the rails his father had laid for him.

Laurence.

Then his body was taken from the others, stabbed by a thousand knives of sunlight.

The Canadian had come to carry him, a man he had hated for his narrow, hawkish face, for the way he would not be defeated by anything. And he hated the man again for saving his life. He tried to fall, but the man would not fall. The forest vanished, replaced by fields, and they were still running, the Canadian's steps ragged and jolting. Let me go, he tried to say, his voice overcome by the approach of the train, a metal cloud, a storm bringing wind but no rain.

The train ride was a separate dream, one where he could not move or speak except through the humming clack of the wheels over the tracks. The country outside the window streamed into a single swath of green. The man on his right was dead and his hand kept hitting Laurence's side, as if he were trying to remind him of something.

The ceiling of the train was a scratched pine color. When the car moved around the curve, the wooden floorboards joined the moaning of the men. The hot air smelled of smoke. Watching over him was the

Canadian who had saved him from being buried alive, holding his red-soaked arm. *Live,* he urged again and again, his strange accent shortening the word.

For a long while, he thought that he was already dead. But when the train stopped at its final station with a resounding hiss of steam, he felt his guardian's hand on his chest, fumbling in the breast pocket. *Live,* he said as he inspected the cool metal of half a locket, the portrait inside.

Solemn as a priest, the Canadian tossed the woman's broken face to the floor. It got stuck in a crack, someone's mother and wife staring up at them all until the conductor opened the doors to the car and the bright light blinded them.

Laurence.

Only much later, when the train shuddered to a halt and he was carried to a still place where birds crossed the square of sky behind his bed, only when he knew for certain he was not still in the ring of flames, did he recognize who was calling him.

For a long time, her name remained a kind of forgiveness he could not utter.

When he finally answered her, a door flew open to an empty house, moss on the windowsill and dead bees lying in the hearth. A staircase led to the second floor, each step breaking as he took it. Heat filled the attic room, its single window wearing a flap of oilcloth, yellow and ancient.

Isabel, and the boards made hollow sounds as he crossed them, the spiderwebs softening the corners where beams reached like dark arms. When he pushed the oilcloth aside, the yard unfolded below him, green and rippled by wind. Sunflowers bloomed in the garden, and the welt of sky above bore clouds the color of milk that spilled not rain, but snow, drifting gently down over the warm air, white flakes sinking everywhere and his hand reaching out to hold them as they melted.

Chapter Forty-one

Y es," she said, kneeling beside him. The room was filled with the bass murmur of men. Her smile wavered as she stared steadily onto the half of his face that looked back at her.

"You . . . calling . . . me?" His voice stayed underwater, the bubble breath of the fish.

"Yes," she said again, turning her honey-colored head to glance over the sea of beds. Soldiers were strewn like shipwrecked sailors across them. A filtered sun shone into the room, the yellow of melted butter. "I should tell your mother and father."

"I don re . . . memger—" he began, and she placed a finger on the half of his lips not covered by bandage. After a few hours, the damp linen would go lucid and she could see the hole where his eye had been burned away. The socket fixed a stare on the ceiling, while the healthy eye shifted restlessly about the room, unable to focus.

The soldier did not yet comprehend he was missing his right leg and the fingers of his right hand. Only the thumb remained, poking like root from its bandage. For hours, the girl had watched the thumb twitch, the stump of the lost leg rear up, making a wave in the sheets, while the good limbs slept peacefully, unmoving. The patient still smelled faintly of the ash that the cooks swept from the stove.

The balding, moonfaced surgeon was fond of relating the story of this soldier to the other surgeons and nurses. He had lost so many to ordinary deaths from infection and disease that when a fellow survived like this, he had to tell it to the world to believe it. He called the soldier "Shadrach," after one of the survivors of Nebuchadnezzar's furnace. A man who could die and live for his convictions, the surgeon claimed.

So few had lived through the fires in the Wilderness, a thick woods outside Chancellorsville. Most had perished that night, and the rest in the remaining days, when they lay on the forest floor, waiting for the ambulance to reach them. Shadrach had lived through every horror the battlefield could offer and then the train ride to Washington, largely due to the ministrations of another casualty, who had stayed with him all the way from Chancellorsville.

The guardian angel was a Canadian who had taken a bullet in the arm on the first day of the battle, and then disobeyed orders by staying and searching for Shadrach, bringing him personally to the hospital. He now worked as one of the invalid nurses in the ward and was due to return to his regiment as soon as his arm was fully healed. "Jean d'Arc," the surgeon called him in his joking way, for the Canadian had also come from the fire. The brusque Irishman could never remember anyone's name unless he issued it himself. His appellations were not particularly clever, but because every soldier feared and respected the man with the ether and cases of sharp metal tools, they were all accepted without protest.

Once Shadrach was safely in the ward, Jean d'Arc wrote to the patient's family in Allenton and discovered that his mother and cousin were already in the capital. The Canadian found them at the Willard

Hotel, one of the most illustrious of the temporary residences of Washington, run by two Vermonters. Pattie Lindsey and her young charge would breakfast at an enormous buffet of fried oysters, steak and onions, and steamed fish, gliding past the important personages of Washington on the way to their polished table in the corner.

The Willard's lavishness had made Bel simultaneously nervous and excited, for she had never seen such poise or finery in small-town Allenton. Aunt Pattie was of the mind that one must be *quite* fortified for one's duties, and she fixed herself plates so gargantuan, Bel heard a southern woman whisper to her friend about the insatiable appetite of the Yankees. In the afternoon, they would visit hospitals, breezing through the Patent Office and other improvised wards where the wounded lay in postures of suffering and quiet acceptance, their naked flesh sometimes exposed to Isabel, who would blush and look away.

The girl would blush at little now, after three weeks in the heart of the busy hospital off Ninth Street. The opulent velvet room at the Willard was sacrificed for a hard cot in the basement, where the female nurses were discreetly placed far away from the wounded. The girl's aunt had fallen ill with fever almost immediately after seeing her son, but she refused to leave the building while Laurence was in such a delicate condition. Consequently, Isabel and her uncle George traded shifts between another basement room of the hospital and the ward upstairs. Below, Aunt Pattie alternately coughed and dreamed and wept, while on the top floor, Shadrach had lain silent until now.

It brought tears to the surgeon's eyes to see the three of them gathered around Shadrach's crippled form. He was certain the boy would never wake again, and he looked disbelieving when the girl told him that her cousin Laurence had spoken to her.

"Shadrach, I mean," she said softly as she led the surgeon to the bed. The soldier had drifted off again, his burned lashes making a sooty curve above his cheek.

"Are you sure now, Miss Lindsey?" asked the surgeon, bending over him like a robin reaching for a worm.

"He said my name," she answered simply. She resumed her perch on the stool beside the bed. "He said Isabel."

Chapter Forty-two

Every day, the vigil changed over Shadrach's body. Isabel and her uncle switched at noon, crossing each other on the stairs, their bodies swollen with lack of sleep, eyes meeting, locking, looking away. In the anxiety over his wife and son, Uncle George no longer paid much attention to his niece. He spoke to Bel only of deliberate things, asking her how well the hospital was supplied with bandages, how many wounded had come in that day, how long her aunt had stayed awake. He bowed his head like a penitent as soon as he passed her.

Upon reaching the ward, George would raise his chin, stride in, and shut the window behind his son, scaring the sparrows that gathered on the sill. The once-handsome man insisted on watching Louis, the invalid nurse, change the dressing. He did not flinch at the sight of Shadrach, but peered with tender interest at where the fire had melted his son's skin against his ribs and shoulders. He lightly touched the white dust that bloomed over it and the flecks of soot that were buried in the soldier's cheek. Shadrach's empty eye socket shone back at them, a yellowed cave of pus. The boy was beyond the ugliness of the maimed, who peopled the ward like a new race, the slow shufflers and awkward lifters, their skin knit back together by the amateur hand of man. He was just a shell for the little spirit left in him, hollow and cool to the touch.

On the morning that Shadrach woke and spoke to his cousin, the Canadian's rough hands finally stopped trembling. He understood that Isabel's uncle tolerated his presence because he had saved his son. He understood that his place had been carved by his rescuing, that as long as he continued to save the boy, this slot remained for him. Consequently, he had quailed at the daily changing of the dressing as a student who dreads a test he knows he'll fail. Shadrach's father was a firm believer in work's ability to elevate the worker, however, and he observed Louis with grudging praise, day after day. For a while, they both believed in Shadrach's recovery, cracked jokes, and spoke to the sleeping soldier about his imminent return to Allenton. But on that afternoon, the invalid nurse knew the patient would never see his home again. When he lifted the bandages, he noticed immediately that the skin that had once tightened to a raw pink sheen was loose, giving way to dark patches of gangrene.

"Tell me again how you saved him," the father said in a hoarse whisper as Louis heaped the used bandages in an old chamber pot. This was their other conversation, repeated over and over. The man knew the story so well, he would interrupt like a child who guesses what is coming on the next page but must hear it all anyway, this tale he knows the end to.

"He was lying in the creek bed with his face down—"

"Before that—"

"The fires?"

"Yes, the fires."

"The captains left alive thought no one could survive the fires that swept through the trees. The flame was high and bright and we heard the men screaming as they died."

"But my son—"

"But your son was lying in a creek bed with another body beside him—"

"And the body—"

"And the other body was burned beyond recognition. I thought it was his sergeant, but they found him a mile away, shot through the head. I don't know who it was. Some say a contraband, others—"

"Someone saved my son."

"Someone saved him," Louis repeated bitterly, changing the story because he was tired of the father's wish for the savior to remain unknown and therefore grander in gesture. "I saved him. He was half-buried when I found him. I carried him from the forest, and when no ambulances came, I carried him farther, until I could find a train to take us—"

He laid the fresh bandages across the seamed skin of Shadrach's ribs.

"Someone saved my son," continued the father. "A man who respected him. And you will stay as long as he stays." This was a command not to remain. The nurse met the father's eyes across the deflated body.

"As long as we both shall live," he said.

"Do you love her? Then go when this—" He gestured to the body but did not finish. Shadrach slept peacefully on the cheek that was not burned. Louis refused to answer.

"A man like me can reward you in many ways," the father said, threatening, his voice the low growl of a dog that knows it will be beaten but fights anyway. "What do you need?"

"A chance," said Louis, starting in on the face. He gently peeled off the bandages, revealing the featureless gap between the patient's eye and mouth, the nose sunk to a black coil. The father sucked in his breath.

"What else?" he said. The smell of the body was terrifying and rich.

"Another," said Louis.

Chapter Forty-three

Because many of the wounded men could not walk, much less bear their own plates, Louis, two other recovering soldiers, the homely spinster nurse, and Isabel carried trays of coffee, soup, and sandwiches around the room to the hungry. Mealtime was a chaotic affair, because the large dumpling of a German soldier always wanted twice his share, while the duck-faced New Jerseyan had to be cajoled into taking a single bite of bread. The stomach cases were the worst. They looked on, their mouths watering, strictly forbidden to consume anything but broth and coffee. Bel made a big to-do of fixing their coffee just how they liked it, black, or with milk or sugar, so they would not feel left out.

On the day after her cousin first spoke to her, she reluctantly left him sleeping after mealtime and descended through the floors of the hospital to the basement. She passed her uncle on the way up. They nodded to each other. No change. She knew he would watch Louis lay on fresh bandages, and then Louis would leave father and son and meet her in the alcove behind the stairs.

It was their secret place, discovered one day when they hid together from the spinster nurse, who had become enamored of Louis and followed him everywhere. They laughed in helpless silence as she stomped up and down the steps, her skirt tightening around her ankles, petticoat unraveled at the hem. Then, somewhere in the dark, their hands had found each other, and then their mouths. Bel never guessed a man's lips could be as soft as butter forgotten on the table in summer. Blind, and in hushed whispers, they arranged to meet there the next day, and the next, until the rendezvous became fixed in their schedules. Bel dreamed all morning of holding the knobs of Louis's spine, feeling her shoulders made small by the pressure of his cupping hands.

But first she had to attend to her aunt. First, the day had to reach its midpoint in the chilly basement. Aunt Pattie claimed one damp gray room below, and Bel's uncle kept a fire perpetually going in the narrow grate. It was a dismal place, its white paint peeling, the rats scratching through the cabinets, and the kind of insects that live in the dark underground always crawling up the walls. Today, Aunt Pattie was a mound of cheese-colored sheets and a cold, sweaty face that brightened when she saw her niece.

"Dear girl," said Aunt Pattie, the motor inside her voice diminished to a slow hum. "How is my son?"

"He's sleeping," Bel said, and lowered herself to the stool by her aunt's bed. "As if he were pricked with a needle that would make him sleep a thousand years."

"Goodness," said Aunt Pattie with a chuckle that broke into a cough. Her fever had caused her to lose weight, and the old lines of her face were visible again. She looked like an aged doll. "I don't know if I'll last that long."

"Oh, Aunt. You could last forever." Bel's back ached from sitting so many days by her cousin's bed. She shifted to find a more comfortable position on the stool, and her eyes fell to the Bible on the table. "Would you like me to read to you?" she asked.

"In a minute, dear," said Aunt Pattie with a wave of her bare hand.

The rings she always wore were gone. "I want to tell you something."

Bel shifted again, lifting her skirts. She could smell the sourness of her aunt's body, and remembered how perfumed Aunt Pattie used to be, always drifting into the house drenched in lilac cologne. "Yes?" she asked.

"I've been watching that spiderweb up there." She nodded to the corner above the doorway, where an elaborate gossamer web held the bodies of several dead insects.

"I can get it down," Bel offered, but her aunt shook her head.

"I always thought that it was accident—that the flies flew into it out of stupidity or poor eyesight. But I've been watching them, Bel. You should see how fast they fly into that beautiful thing." She paused. "As if they're trying to break it, or, at the very least, scar those perfect, perfect strands."

Sensing an oncoming lecture, Bel stared stubbornly at the floor. Her aunt was going to say that she didn't approve of the way Bel was working, that her rough hands were unbecoming of a young lady of her station.

"They can't bear it," Aunt Pattie concluded finally. "It's too lovely. So they die because of their jealousy. And after awhile, all the rips and scars do their work, and the web is ugly, just like they wanted."

"Are you hungry, Aunt Pattie?" Bel asked, hoping to change the subject. "I could see if there's anything left in the kitchen."

Aunt Pattie continued as if she had not heard her. "The first time I saw your mother, I realized I had never understood what human beauty was. It wasn't an accumulation of pretty, external things, but some interior difference between people—like the way Greenwood is lovelier than our house, because I wanted something from Paris, and your father built something for Allenton." She sighed. "And as many suitors as I had in our little town, the whole world could have fallen in love with Faustina Gale."

Bel saw her mother dancing with Louis at the Twelfth Night party, her beautiful head tilted back to laugh.

"I'm sorry now that I was so jealous of her." Aunt Pattie's voice was rusty-sounding and thin. "That we didn't become better friends."

"You still can," Bel said, a sadness welling in her. She didn't want to understand her parents' lives like this.

"I'm glad you're still young enough to believe that," said Aunt Pattie. "I worry how this war is aging you, dear Bel. When I was young, I had only to worry if my husband was in love with his brother's wife." She smiled. "Hardly a concern worth noting in these times."

Bel felt as if her heart might stop. The swan locket lay cold against her collarbone. "I think you need some sleep, Aunt Pattie," she said as she struggled to stand. A leg of the stool pinned one of her petticoats.

"Sit down, girl. You didn't know, did you?" Her aunt turned her face to the wall. "Of course not. Everything changed once you were born and they had a child of their own. But when your father first went away to school, it left George and Faustina alone for the first time on their family farms outside Allenton. They roamed everywhere together. George hadn't met me yet—so how he could not fall in love with her?" Aunt Pattie grunted. "It didn't matter. After they spent a winter pretending it wasn't true, your father came home and married her, as the Gales and the Lindseys had always planned, in the spring of Faustina's eighteenth year."

Bel sat down again, remembering her mother and uncle arguing behind the Chinese screen at Twelfth Night, remembering all the times she had seen them together fighting or laughing, the energy in both their eyes when they were in the same room. Her aunt went on, her voice hard, as if she were delivering a punishment.

313

"When George started courting me a year later, I fell foolishly in love with him. I thought he would get over her, and he did, eventually. But it took years—years I could have spent with that Canadian fur trader who doted on me, or that sickly young man from Boston who would have died and left me a fortune. I could have had anyone in town except a Lindsey boy, but that's whom I wanted."

"Why are you telling me this?" Bel demanded.

Aunt Pattie's eyes fluttered shut. "I only meant to apologize, my dear. I only meant to say I was sorry we weren't kinder to each other. Now that my son is dying, I don't want any anger in our family."

A silence fell over the room as Bel registered the last statement, wondering if the fever had overtaken her aunt, if nothing she said were true. She watched a stillness pass over her aunt's features and knew that the older woman had drifted into sleep.

"He's not dying," she protested dully, but Aunt Pattie did not answer except to snore slightly.

Just then, a knock on the door startled Bel, and George Lindsey bustled in behind a tower of logs. He set them down with a clatter, then turned toward his niece.

"Well, was she awake? She said she had something to tell you." His gray beard had whitened, rounding his jaw like a snowdrift. Grape-colored shadows gathered beneath his eyes. Uncle George always smelled of cigars, and lately of stale sweat, an odor that made Bel think of Johnny Mulcane.

"Not really." Bel tried to smile. How long had her uncle been in love with her mother, and when had it ended? Since their days in the hospital, she had seen him display such tenderness to his wife, he could not still be pining for Faustina. Every time she came downstairs, he was bending over Aunt Pattie, whispering to her and smoothing back her hair, or reading her stories in a fond voice.

"Is something wrong?" He looked genuinely worried. They stared at each other across the gray light of the basement, each searching the other's face. Bel wondered then if the swan locket had been given to her mother not by some unknown suitor but by Uncle George—if it was their secret that had drifted from it the night she and Louis sat in the hayloft together. She could show it to him right now and know for sure.

As she hesitated, a fly careened lazily into the spiderweb above the door. The threads held fast as the black insect struggled to break free. It wasn't beautiful, that silver trap, when something was dying inside it.

"She was telling me about how she fell in love with you," Bel answered finally. "I think she misses you when you're gone." She did not touch the necklace that hung beneath her clothes. Before living at the hospital, she would have done it, would have insisted on laying bare the truth, but now the world of Greenwood hardly mattered. It was a memory she had set aside with her own girlhood, to be revisited later, if only she could remember how to go back.

George leaned over the bed where his wife rested. Aunt Pattie's damp eyelids quivered slightly but did not open. "I'm here now, Patricia," he said, and kissed her.

Bel stood up from the stool and swayed toward the threshold, her body weary. Her wrists ached from drawing pictures of the wounded and carrying trays and helping the nurses make the beds for the incoming men. Her hands were chapped and scraped, but she didn't care anymore. She wanted Louis to be proud of her, to know she was as capable as any man's wife.

"Good-bye, Uncle," she said softly, closing the door. He was busy heaping wood in the grate and did not hear her above the chink of logs.

Bel hurried up the stairs to meet Louis in their hiding place, the dim alcove that smelled of plaster and left a film of dust on both their clothes. The tutor was already in the shadows, holding his wounded arm, which bothered him daily. The rebel bullet had hit him just above the elbow, and carrying Isabel's cousin the fifteen miles to the nearest train had worsened the injury.

Bel entered the gloom and stood inches away from him, raising her eyes to his. There was a single crack of light in their universe, where the back of one stair had loosened. Looking through it, Bel glimpsed the sturdy heels of the spinster nurse descending, heard the limp of a soldier climbing to his ward. Louis's lips met hers, lightly at first, then pressing hard, until their teeth clashed together, until she could feel the rough hairs of his unshaven face. He groaned and let his injured arm fall on her shoulder. The minutes burned around them.

She could never tell him what her aunt had said, for what would he think of her family then? Besides, it was one of their rules never to talk during this time. Conversation wasted the precious minutes in its polite rounds, and all the news of the hospital was apparent anyway: Weevils had gotten into the flour, Bel's aunt was finally healing to the painful cure of calomel, the fat German was buying food from the New Jerseyan with bribes of tobacco, and Shadrach was dying.

In her mind, Bel hardly called him Laurence anymore. Her cousin had become the child of all the ward—and hers and Louis's in partic-ular—mute and always in need. If she did not listen for his breath, he might leave her, and so her trysts with the tutor always ended with her pushing away from him and running up the stairs, smoothing her hair as she went. Usually, she was greeted by the changeless silence of Shadrach's face, but today it might be different—today he might say her name again. The cool air of the alcove still on her skin, she entered the ward and tiptoed to her cousin's bed, trembling. He was just wak-ing, as if it were finally morning in his mind, his good eye fluttering open to find her having never left his side.

Chapter Forty-four

At the same time Bel rushed up the stairs, Louis descended to the busy street to smoke and watch the coaches of Washington pass in an endless procession. Situated down an alley off Ninth Street, the three-story inn had been converted a year into the war to accommodate the casualties streaming into the capital. The traffic surging past the hospital had the same cheerful speed as in all big cities, as if everyone had somewhere to get to soon. Louis was surprised by the distances in Washington, for he had expected tight, packed streets and found instead that the capital designers had planned for a future not yet realized, when more residences and offices would fill in the gaps between the Grecian government buildings. Undeterred by their expanding city, the residents of the capital bumped past in their many conveyances—wagons and coaches and even peddlers' carts, pushed by barefoot boys whose voices were hoarse from shouting.

That afternoon, Louis unrolled the brown plug of tobacco a hemorrhaging soldier had given him before he died. His pard, the soldier explained, was a North Carolinian who had fought with the Yanks because his father and mother had both come from Massachusetts and he didn't want to make war on his own blood. The finest tobacco in the world grew in the fields outside the North Carolinian's house.

The precious plug had been taken from the body of the fallen Southerner at Spotsylvania, had traveled to Cold Harbor, where its new owner was wounded, and then ridden back to the Washington hospital in his coat. When he died, he thrust it into the nurse's hand, saying in a trembling voice that a fine smoke could keep a man alive in a bad time. The plug had two deep red blotches on it, the blood of the two friends held apart by a short, ropy distance. Louis tore the tobacco carefully around these marks, each day getting closer and closer.

He had seen so much blood since his enlistment, this was not squeamishness, but respect for those who had passed on. The dead were a strange lot, always coming back to a man when he thought he'd left them behind. If Louis had not heard that Laurence Lindsey was missing in the burning Wilderness, if he had not abandoned his own regiment to find the soldier's body blistered in the shallow run, he might have joined the dead, for their way seemed easier than that of the living. They never had to fight again. They never had to hear a young man cry for mercy when a surgeon sawed off his leg.

Old Sawbones told Louis he was the best assistant he'd ever had, steady and quiet, but also gifted with an ability to make men want to live. He protected Louis from his captain, who had ordered him back, by saying that the injured arm was infected and needed more time to heal. He also taught Louis the names of the instruments: finger knife, scalpel, bistoury, and sharp-pointed tenotomb, the metal of each glistening in a small wooden case. The surgeon even let Louis help with the joint resections, a complicated surgery performed on soldiers who might heal without an amputation. *You're a quick study, Jean,* Sawbones had said in his brisk way after they'd made an excision in a soldier's knee. The soldier was weeping silently, staring away from their work. Louis had gripped his own healing arm and didn't answer.

His lungs burned around the sweet smoke. An ebony carriage skimmed by, skirting a hog that had wandered into the street. People always emptied their slops into the gutters in Washington, and a whole community of swine supplied itself daily from the refuse. No one seemed to mind. The pair of girls in the carriage looked at him and giggled expectantly. Louis gave them a taut smile. He loved Isabel with the simplicity of a man who knows there is only one profession he is good at and cannot imagine a reason to steer away from that path. It was her imperfections that drew him to her—the red mark above her lip where the pigment extended like the paint dribble of a careless artist, her gawky feet, the weight of her wide jaw when he cupped her face in his hands. Even her grief drove him to a senseless passion, for in it he saw the woman she would become, the steady, intelligent wife and mother.

In contrast, the frivolity of the passersby irritated him. He didn't understand how there could be people in this city, in any city of the world, not mourning for what he had seen. During three days of fighting outside Chancellorsville, he had nearly forgotten his own name, stumbling along with his company until his arm was nearly shot off and he joined the casualties in a bloodied clearing, waiting for the overtaxed ambulances to come. Only when he heard that Isabel's cousin was missing did he feel like his life had a purpose again. The sergeant had been shot through the head, and his captain, sick with grief, lay against a pine tree, waiting for his wounded leg to be bandaged, telling the stories of his lost men over and over to anyone who would listen.

Leaving him, Louis had charged into the scorched wasteland, searching through men burned past recognition, rolling them back from the sooty earth. The tall, straight Laurence he had known for a brief half year was no longer alive, but in his place, a nearly lifeless figure with half a face curled in the ashy stream. Shadrach, survivor of the fire. On the bank just beyond him had lain another human form, so badly burned, it could have been a stone or a tree trunk softened by flame. Had someone saved Laurence Lindsey? Had someone died for him? Maybe. Or maybe it was just a story a father wanted to tell about his lost son, so he could keep believing that death was an injustice, especially for the young.

Louis tamped out his pipe on the brick wall of the hospital and turned to go back inside. He could hear the shouts of men upstairs clamoring for mealtime, their loud voices reaching the street. In one of the open windows, sparrows jostled for a place on the sill. It was Shadrach's window. He was awake and asking his cousin for a mirror. He wanted to see himself.

She pretended she didn't know what he was saying. "Your mother is fine," she said. "Getting better every day."

"Mirror," he repeated.

"Are you hungry? I can get you some bread."

"No." He beat the sheet with his stumpy thumb.

"The window, then," she said, and pulled it down, scaring the sparrows away. She rubbed the dirty streaks with her sleeve. "You can see your reflection there."

She helped him twist his face toward the glass. It was late afternoon, clouds crossing the summer sun, intermittent and gray. His face shone ghostlike, a man on a passing train, the features blurred by shadow and speed. He leaned back, satisfied.

"Open again," he commanded. The train lifted him through the gap between beds, rearing like an insect over a stone, but with a motion all its own, mechanical, clicking. The girl obeyed, struggling as the pane stuck. After a minute, a few sparrows returned, pecking at the sill.

As she bent back over him, a locket fell out from beneath her dress. The bird shape jogged an old memory, vague and incomplete. He recalled stealing it from deep in his father's bureau as a young man, trying to give it to a runaway slave, a man wearing the face of fear and bravery. How many times had he seen that expression since? With the ignorance of boyhood, he taken out the note inside the locket, which said in his father's script simply *my heart* and replaced it with one that said *freedom*. Something valuable to sell, he had thought then. Now it seemed cheap and ordinary.

Chapter Forty-five

Later that day, his cousin tried to feed him, bread, potatoes, a thin soup with carrots floating in it. He let three spoonfuls of the warm liquid fill his mouth before swallowing, and refused the rest silently. She perched a crust of bread on his chest and carried the tray away. When she came back, it was gone, and she smiled with secret triumph, for the soldier was asleep again, his bandaged head toward the open window.

At dusk, she retired to her shared basement bedroom, down the hall from her aunt's, where she sketched every evening until she fell asleep. The surgeon had seen the sketchbook and encouraged Bel to continue, claiming her pictures might have medical merit, if nothing else. Her aunt's Sanitary Commission report abandoned, the idea of real usefulness thrilled Bel, and she diligently drew the puffy, healing limbs that had been resected, excised, and amputated in the ward. The surgeon collected the pictures for a book he was writing on war medicine, and he promised to credit Bel when he found a publisher. His encouragement pleased Bel so much, she grew fearless in asking the soldiers to expose their thighs and stomachs so that she might see them properly. When a fellow would tease her for her unladylike interest, she simply sighed and stamped her foot until he obligingly peeled back the sheet.

At night, Bel drew for pleasure, learning from her own mistakes how to suggest perspective with shadows, how to start a face with the shape of the head first. The spinster nurse, who took the other bed, stayed up late gossiping with the cooks, and evening remained Bel's precious piece of solitude, interrupted only by the visits of one intrepid Lucy, the little colored girl whose mother worked at the hospital. Bel would draw everything, mostly the soldiers in the ward, and the small dramas she saw from the window above the street: a free Negro tacking up a picture of Abraham Lincoln above his blacksmith shop, the sutlers loading their carts, the prostitutes with their painted faces. Washington was much richer and messier than Allenton, with thugs everywhere and a big smelly canal in the middle of the city, where people threw their sewage and anything else they wanted to get rid of. Once, on the way to a hospital with her aunt, Bel had seen a dead dog floating in the water, its white hair peeling off in clumps.

She placed her sketchbook across her lap and began to move the charcoal, this time making a portrait of the Negro girl who came to take the chamber pots. Lucy would sometimes stop to watch her draw, twisting her head from side to side as the charcoal moved across the page, and Bel decided to surprise her that evening with a portrait of herself. She sketched the girl's splayed legs first, the pink crescent scar on the back of her bare ankle, and then her faded cotton dress, her straight shoulders and frowzy hair. She wrote *Lucy* in the bottom corner, and drew a doorway to the invisible room where the girl stood, as if waiting for someone to come in.

"Ma'am . . ."

Bel looked up and saw Lucy in the threshold. She nodded approvingly at her sketch, for the posture was just right, the expectant gaze.

"Come here, Lucy," Bel said. Her own Yankee accent sounded grating compared to the soft, sighing voice of the little girl. "I have something for you."

Lucy bounded in, her mouth half-open in anticipation of the sweets Bel sometimes handed her when her mother, Ruth, was not looking. Ruth was a cool, indifferent woman who did not seem to trust or talk to anyone, allowing Lucy to be her interface with the world. "Ma'am?" she asked, the sigh lengthening.

"It's you." Bel showed her the white paper. Lucy stopped in mid-bound, letting her arms clap to her sides. Her eyes went big. "See," Bel said, pleased. "I wrote your name in the corner. L-U-C-Y."

The girl began to shake her head, slowly at first and then with a wild, whipping frenzy. She slapped her hands against her thighs, driving the head faster on its axis.

"What's the matter? Did I spell it wrong?" Bel turned back to the sketch, frowning. Rats started scratching in the wardrobe where Bel kept her dresses. Their torturous scraping would go on for hours.

"It ain't me. *It ain't me,*" Lucy shrieked, and ran from the room, her thick legs suddenly clumsy, unable to keep up with the speed of the rest of her body.

Bel stared, stunned, at the sketch, wondering what about it could elicit such an adverse reaction. There was Lucy, outlined with her back to the viewer, her curly head twisted toward the door. Bel had used discreet shadows to reveal the color of her skin, leaving the rest to the imagination. Her eyes smarted from the rejection. She already missed the girl's fuzzy hair tickling her arm as she leaned on it. The rats scratched again. Vaulting from her bed to the wardrobe, she pounded on the loose pine door to scare the rodents away. "Damn rats," she said under her breath, relishing the curse because it made her feel better about Lucy. "Goddamn dirty rats."

The wardrobe sank into insolent silence. Bel marched back to the bed and stared dully at it. "Goddamn scourge of the earth," she uttered with victorious baseness, and hunched over her sketchbook, unable to draw. After a few minutes, Ruth appeared in the doorway, dragging the girl behind her. In Ruth, Lucy's sturdy build had already realized itself in trunklike legs and a generous belly. "Ma'am," she said in her flat way. "I don't suppose you knowed what made my Lucy bust up cryin'."

"I was trying to give her a gift," Bel stuttered. "A portrait."

"A potrate," repeated Ruth, coming no farther into the room. Her right hand wagged as the captive Lucy squirmed at the end of it, the girl's face still streaming with tears. "Let me see."

Bel stood up and showed her the sketch. Ruth narrowed her eyes, her wide head growing even wider. "I'm sorry, ma'am," she said softly. "I know you tried to make something pretty for her." She paused and leaned in, refusing to unplant her feet. Lucy now hung like a limp coat from Ruth's hand, curiosity halting her tears in midstream. "But my baby scared you trying to make her look that way and she don't want to look that way."

"But—" Bel began.

"I speck if you don't know why, you ain't never gonna know," Ruth said with an air of finality, and ushered her daughter back into the hall. Bel heard their feet scrape into the distance as she stared down at her neat little sketch. It isn't fair, she said to herself, tears squeezing through her eyes. It wasn't fair that they make her feel like that for trying to be nice. She let the tears fall onto the sketchbook, blurring it, and sobbed for herself and Laurence and her mother and everyone who could not change his fate or the fate of others.

What did she know about drawing people? The only things she could get right were grass blades, frost on the windowsill, a maple surrendering its bright red leaves. One inch of Ruth was more complicated than all the hills around Allenton. How dare she try to encompass any of these dark strangers she wanted so desperately to be free? The rats began scratching again, and she threw the sketchbook at the wardrobe before running from the dingy room. On the way out, her foot knocked the chamber pot that Lucy had forgotten or refused to collect. The pot swayed from side to side, sloshing its unpleasant contents, but did not spill. "Goddamn Lucy," Bel said, and left it there, where the spinster nurse might trip over it.

Exhausted beyond sleep, she went back upstairs to watch Louis move among the wounded, drifting over their prostrate bodies like a restless ghost. He slept only in the brief hours before dawn, sprawling in a corner of the ward and folding his head in his hands. Tonight, he exchanged a glance with her and went back to his ministrations. Irritated that he did not notice her reddened face, Bel stomped over to the corner where her cousin lay. She was starting to feel the tears well up again when Shadrach woke.

"'My soul is among lions,'" he began, speaking to her slowly and softly by the window's moonlight, "'and I lie even among them that are set on fire, even the sons of men.'" And then he was telling the stories of the fellows in his regiment, most of whom, she guessed, were dead. Some of what he said frightened Bel more than the sight of his missing limbs and the scarred face that curled beneath the bandages. She sat slowly down on the floor, crossing her arms over her knees the way she had in girlhood.

The soldier did not look at her when he spoke, but stared at the ceiling stains, dark and curved at their rims, as though some god had invented clouds to cross this interior and then abandoned them there without the wind to push them. Bel watched the ceiling, too. She propped her head on the cool plaster wall behind her and listened fiercely, every word sinking into her memory. The stories of his comrades, John Addison and Lyman Woodard, Pike and Gilbert and Loomis, appeared across the ceiling above. She could see them all, and cried when one died, grieving as his image vanished like a reflection shattered by flung stones.

She did not know if the other men heard the soldier they called Shadrach, for none believed he would ever wake again. Laurence's voice was soft as water through the hands, and the dense white moon coming through the window enveloped the two of them, separating them from the rest of the ward. She listened to the hours passing outside the web of silver light, Louis on his incessant rounds, and, dimly, the sounds of the sleeping soldiers, their sighs and anxious breaths, the restless turning as they fought the enemy in their dreams and sometimes won, sometimes lost. Meanwhile, John Addison was rescuing the horses at Bull Run; the orchard at Antietam rained down its cannonballs; Lyman Woodard was mincing on a makeshift stage in a dress stolen from a girl her age. Listening, Bel began to consider if the depth of feeling she always measured in herself was only the depth of her emptiness waiting to be filled with stories like this. She reached up to touch her cousin's arm. It was cool and stiff, like candle wax. She let her fingers slip from it and fall to her lap again.

When dawn began to crack through the wall of night, Shadrach's voice slowed to a trickle and ceased. He had not told of the battle where he had lost his limbs and burned, but still, the story appeared to be over. He turned his face from her and slept, the good side facing the ceiling, sprouting a dark stubble of hair. The growth surprised her, and she resolved to ask Louis to shave it away. He was coming toward her with a tray of dressings, his expression neutral. Except in the alcove, they never betrayed their emotions. How she longed to tell him the stories she had heard, but Louis did not look at her as he set the tray down next to Shadrach to work his gentle miracle. It was time to leave him and greet her aunt.

She descended to the damp room in the basement, nodding coolly to Ruth, who was polishing the banister on the way down. Uncle

George must have left for more firewood, she realized. Her aunt was sleeping, her single window opaque with light. A moth had died against it in the night, and Bel swept it to the floor with her hand. Would Aunt Pattie remember what she had told her the day before?

The blue dimness made the older woman look like a fish trying to hide, its body immobile against the current. Her once-rosebud lips had grown flabby and showed the effort of breath, puffing and sinking back. The rats must have come without Uncle George knowing, because the plate of food Bel had brought down the night before held a constellation of black droppings.

"Have you come to dine?" asked Bel's aunt, waking and seeing Bel hovering above her, the plate in hand. Her face was open and expectant. Clearly, she did not remember her confession.

"No, I fear you've already had some other guests." Bel set the plate on the table beside the bed. "I came to tell you that I persuaded Laurence to eat three spoonfuls of soup, and a crust of bread, I think." About the stories, she would say nothing, for they were hers to hear and hers to own, for staying with him while the others could not bear it.

"You think?" Aunt Pattie shifted her head sideways. The dose of calomel had thinned her hair, and Bel could see her aunt's pink scalp.

"Well, I'm certain about the soup," she said, suddenly uncertain. "The bread, I left for him, and when I came back, it was gone. I thought he was being stubborn. You know how he can be stubborn."

"You've come to tell me you think he's getting better," said Aunt Pattie. "That soon he'll be able to walk down here and see me, and then we can all go home."

"Yes," said Bel, her voice trembling. Her aunt had spoken with a strange bitterness.

"Well," said her aunt in a gentler tone, turning her face away from

Bel. "I would like to see him tomorrow. George is enlisting some boys to help me up the stairs. I am tired of this room, and I won't be kept away from my son," she said with an air of defiance. "I'll go to him if he will not return to me."

When Bel repeated her aunt's command to Louis, breaching their contract not to speak to each other in the alcove, he nodded and said, "She knows."

"Knows what?" Bel asked. The dark air smelled like chalk. She pressed closer to Louis.

"That he is about to leave us," Louis said simply. Bel could feel his shoulders rise into an apologetic shrug.

"How can you say that?" she demanded, shoving her face into his shirt, feeling the buttons bruise her cheek. "You saved him."

"I can't save him."

"You already did."

"It was selfishness. I knew that way, I would see you again." He took her elbows and pushed her gently away from his body. "And I don't deserve any sort of praise."

Bel felt the tilted end of the days they had balanced between them, the fulcrum their few stolen minutes in the alcove and the hope that Laurence might live.

"You say you hate slavery, Isabel. The worst kind of slavery is to keep a man alive, suffering, when he cannot ever walk again, or look at his reflection without weeping," continued Louis, his voice a soft rasp. She strained to see his face and couldn't, only the measure of darkness between them. "Don't make me do it much longer."

"But he woke yesterday. He spoke to me." She was pleading now, pushing against the current of his threat.

"If you insist, I'll leave tomorrow. My arm is almost healed, and my company needs me," he said, his face unseen, his accent suddenly thick and foreign. Bel shoved the stranger's hands from her and began backing out of the alcove.

"He told me about all his friends," she said. Her skirt swept the damp, crumbling plaster. She heard a cricket sawing its leg in the false night behind her. "Why would he do that if he didn't want to live?"

Louis did not answer, but when he came out into the light, he was cupping the cricket in his hands. It sang through the cage of his fingers as if it did not know it was trapped. Frowning, Bel turned away and began walking up the stairs, her steps steady as a drum tap. When Louis opened his hands, the insect sprang back toward the dark, where it became a voice again, bodiless and grating. He listened for a moment, letting his head tip against the cold wall, knowing she would not wait for him.

Chapter Forty-six

Later, Isabel would remember the single day she did not meet Louis behind the stairs as the end of one part of her life—the part where the future was intertwined with a desperate hope that everything might be the same again, one day, restored like a shelled house to its former grandeur. Louis came to change the dressing alone, quickly, as his strength was needed in the raising of Aunt Pattie. Their eyes met above the shallow breaths of the body between them. The nurse was wearing the shirt Bel had sewn for him, and she saw for the first time the mole high in his black hairline, the thickening of the beard across his face. His not-quite handsomeness seemed distant now, an abstraction of the man she loved and not the man himself. How young I must look to him, she thought suddenly, and stared down at her soft, unveined hands. And yet, although only seventeen, she felt like an old woman. A breeze from the window blew over her, and a sparrow landed on the sill, bright-faced and timid.

"Stay," she said quietly to Shadrach's half a face, although she meant it for Louis. The other men of the ward were playing cards or reading, their knees jutting up in their sheets. Laurence had spoken only a few times, moved only in slight shifts of his amputated limbs, and only when she was watching over him. Had she dreamed it all?

The other soldiers never turned their heads, even the Illinoisan in the sling right next to him. What's the use? she thought. What could possibly be the use of keeping him this way when they had their memories of a brave, thoughtful boy who never got in trouble for anything, even for trying to save a runaway slave? Somewhere, that man might be free now, one of the emancipated hundreds who streamed into Washington, carrying his small bundle of possessions. If he were, did that mean their part in the war was over?

Since their failure in childhood to rescue the runaway, Bel had thought of abolition as the one thing that continued to unite herself and her cousin, beyond his misplaced passion for her, beyond her sisterly refusal. Slavery was their last wilderness, the place they had to rename together. And yet now she saw in the faces of Ruth and Lucy, in the pained waiting of the whole city for the war to be over, that slavery would go on long past emancipation. Even the noblest soldier could not overturn the consequences of that institution. The endless suffering terrified her. Staring down at the masked body of her cousin, she felt as if she were balanced on the edge of a cliff, considering how long the leap would take.

Shadrach shifted, sketching a loose arc with his one good hand. The sheet creased beneath his thumbnail. The motion made Bel notice how his wrist resembled her own, the bones on either side jutting out as if there weren't enough flesh to hold them. They were not princely wrists, but the ugly, functional appendages of soldier and nurse. And they were the same ones she had seen moving across her father's drafting desk as he drew his plans. The same for the good hand, the same for the crushed. She'd always known that blood tied their families together, but what about the deep, unrelenting structures of bone? Did it matter which man her mother had loved long ago? She could never feel alone again.

Louis began to change the dressing, letting her watch for the first time as he peeled away the onion-colored bandages to the husk of skin beneath. Shadrach's chest was a pattern of blood black rivers. Bel gagged and turned away from her cousin's ragged breathing. "I'm sorry," she whispered, running from the decision Louis was asking her to make.

She did not stop until she reached the basement, where her uncle was orchestrating the raising of his wife. Like all the endeavors of a group of men, the procedure had to be copiously plotted and calculated before it could begin. George, the surgeon, and the other two invalid nurses were estimating the number of steps it would take to lift the woman, the radius of their turns on the landing, the amount of space they would have left in the doorways. It seemed like hours before Louis joined them and the collected men began to ease Aunt Pattie from the bed.

Isabel followed the caravan lifting her aunt up three flights to the high ward. Illness had softened the large hull of the woman's body and made her flabby, difficult to hold. Even her husband wore the strained face of a man who wished he might be anywhere else but upon that narrow stair, lifting his wife higher, step by grunting step. She rode in their arms, imperturbable and silent. That morning, Bel had helped her into a dress the pine color of the Green Mountain Boys, and Aunt Pattie bore a resemblance to a snowcapped hill in springtime, her wisps of white-blond hair drifting skyward, a green cascade of cloth sweeping the floor. The men began to adopt the rhythm of the Irishmen who laid the Lindsey rails: swing, step, lift, swing, step, lift, up one flight, past the alcove where Bel had hidden daily with Louis in a brief, trapped eternity of touch. He did not meet her gaze.

At the next landing, Bel slipped ahead of them and ran up the steps to the high ward. She could not walk fast enough past the bed of the German, past the new boy with the stomach wound, the Maine soldier ill with dysentery, past the one-eyed man, to the bed where her cousin lay.

Shadrach's good arm stretched toward the window, his palm open. Two mud-colored sparrows dipped over the hand, feeding on the chewed lump of the crust she had left him the day before. So ordinary, these messengers. Their beaks stabbed into his palm, stabbed again. He was watching them, his head swept toward the window. The bandage had slipped, revealing the ash where hair had once covered his temple, the featureless stretch of his cheek and chin, melted to one. The two halves of the face were separate, like a broken plate that will no longer fit together, some piece flung so far, it will be missing forever. So ordinary, the afternoon absorbed the birds as they flew away. His good eye was fixed on a distant place.

She heard the commotion of her aunt arriving, the sound of the men's boots scraping the floor. Their strained faces appeared at the threshold. She hovered in front of the body, protecting it from the awkward ship approaching, her aunt's forehead slick with sweat, blue gaze wide as the blind's. The ward fell into a deep silence. Even the hiss of cards stopped. Even the man who moaned in his sleep, and slept constantly, paused to breathe. Bel touched the dry ridge of skin where her cousin's ear had melted against his head. It fell away like a leaf. The procession neared, jostling the iron ends of the beds. She met the eyes of her uncle, stunned, like someone had driven a nail through them, and then those of Louis, steady, as if he already understood how it could be that the one time they weren't listening, the answer came. Her aunt's mouth was just opening, her son's name rising like a keen over the waiting sea of stranded men.

Isabel waited to refuse them all, to say it was too late.

Chapter Forty-seven

He was on the train again, his father's house, only this one was filled with bodies, the wounded and dying, their arms bandaged by corn husks and the strips of a neighbor's uniform. In the next car, he could see the hospital where his cousin waited, her long hair pinned beneath her cap, the way she stood with her knees arched back. There was so much light in there.

But now there was someone calling him from his own car, swaying in the square open door where the fields blurred a yellow-green. Tall and big-eared, he had the long black beard of a sage waiting to go gray. He was climbing a ladder, his grasshopper body springing toward the top of the train, where one could ride in the open wind. There were others above; he could hear them beating their heels on the wooden roof and singing. He could hear the high sawing sound of an accordion. Dust fell through the car, and he went to the opening to take hold of the rungs. The rusty metal flaked away in his hands. He hesitated.

The fields yielded to mountains, parting for the train like the frozen blue crests of a wave. He could smell snow somewhere deep in them, in a mossy cave, or a cleft of boulders pitched against each other for a hundred thousand years. As he started to climb, he saw the grinning faces of his friends above, and a cloud behind them, heavy and winged, like a white bird coming to meet him.

Chapter Forty-eight

It was nearly nightfall when the young man emerged from the hospital for his daily pipe. The building had been quiet all day with the death of one of its well-known inhabitants, the son of a railroad magnate from Allenton, Vermont, who survived the fires at the Wilderness, only to die a few weeks later in a clean white bed. A liveryman across the street paused in his repair of an old saddle to watch. From the stories of his wife, a hospital cook, he recognized the young man as the nurse who never stopped working in the wards, whose gift with the sick had become legend. According to the gossip, he was also in love with the cousin of the burned soldier, and he had long kept the boy alive for her.

About an hour before, the young woman in question had stood under the same blue wooden sign for the hospital, hardly old enough to be allowed out unchaperoned, but dressed in the severe garments of a spinster. Her face, though lovely, was marked by the strain of so much loss. She would be the kind of woman to cede her beauty quickly to age if she didn't escape the daily sight of suffering, yet she stood by her uncle with the air of a prisoner about to be locked away for years.

Two hacks halted in front of them. One would take the girl and her invalid aunt, one her uncle and the coffin that held the soldier's corpse. They would ride the train north again, through the flat terrain of the coast to the high, rolling state from which they came, and bury him. The aunt was stuffed like deflated dough into a hack, and the girl followed, staring up at a window on the third floor that was mobbed daily by sparrows. At the same moment her head wrenched back with the momentum of the hack's exit, the window opened, scattering the birds, and the nurse stood there, looking down at her. Around his neck he wore something small and silver.

The liveryman's old busybody of a wife came trotting across the street after the hacks pulled away. She claimed that Old Sawbones had been trying for weeks to convince the commanding officer of the Canadian's regiment to allow him to stay on at the hospital as a surgeon-in-training and not to fight again. The officer refused. But just that afternoon, the dead soldier's father had gone to the U.S. Army office and paid the three hundred dollars that released the sons of rich men from the draft. He said if he couldn't save his own boy from this foul war, then he might as well save someone else's, and he named the Canadian as the beneficiary.

The commanding officer agreed to the following terms for Louis Pacquette: As long as the war lasted, the Canadian had to work at the hospital, but the day the sides made peace, he could be mustered out honorably with the rest of the regiment, continue his studies, and one day return to Allenton a surgeon. *What a dream for a poor tutor, what an American dream,* the liveryman's wife had said proudly. She lowered her soft, sagging cheek to be kissed and bustled back across the street.

Now it was evening, the day drained to shallow pools of light that lingered on rooftops and in windowpanes. The Vermonters were gone, and the nurse stood with his legs splayed slightly, his weight on his heels, and prepared his pipe. Carriages shuttled past, creaking on strained springs.

If the liveryman had not returned to his work just then, he might have seen the curious reddish color of the tobacco the nurse loaded in the bowl and lighted. It had the consistency of paper that had been splashed by rain and dried again, and it burned without leaving an ash.

Discussion Questions for Reading Groups

1. In the beginning of the novel, Bel and Laurence each choose to rescue the runaway slave for different reasons. What are these reasons and how do they play out in the rest of the book?

2. Bel's mother Faustina reads the cousins a story about two lovers who communicate for years via a white swan. Over the course of the book, what does the swan mean to Faustina? to Bel? to Laurence?

3. The novel contains many bloody battle scenes. How does Laurence's attitude toward battle and mass killing change from his first battle to his last?

4. Laurence has to make a terrible choice in the river at Bull Run. If you were in the same circumstance, what would you do? How would you face your comrades afterward? Does Gilbert ever forgive Laurence for Pike's death?

5. Descriptions of winter appear often in the novel. What role does the season play in the story? How does the experience of winter differ for Bel and Laurence?

6. How does music influence the lives of the soldiers?

7. Laurence carries Walt Whitman's *Leaves of Grass* into war. How does his relationship to Whitman's poetry change over time?

8. Like many Union soldiers, Laurence's comrades first went to battle to save the Union, not necessarily to end slavery. How and why did these attitudes change over time?

9. In the early war scenes, Addison is a strong if unofficial leader in his company. What happens when he is promoted and given official responsibility for his friends' lives?

10. When Bel's mother falls down the stairs, Bel thinks her father blames her for the accident. Does he? Why or why not?

11. During wartime, desertion is a crime punishable by death. If you were in Laurence's position and had to choose between obeying martial law and saving the lives of your friends, what would you do?

12. How does the novel's language change in the section that describes the Battle of the Wilderness? Does this affect how you perceive that final battle?

About the author

A native of Vermont, Maria Hummel has won several awards for her poetry and fiction, including a Bread Loaf Fellowship, Randall Jarrell Fellowship, and Academy of American Poets Prize. She has published work in *The Georgia Review, Crab Orchard Review, Manoa,* and *Los Angeles Magazine,* among others, and a selection of her poetry is collected in *City of the Moon* (Harperprints, 1999). She currently works as a writer and editor at The Museum of Contemporary Art, Los Angeles.

Author Statement

"The Vermont forests are filled with old stone walls, cellar holes, and mossy wells, the remainders of people who farmed the land in the nineteenth century. Growing up in these woods, I was fascinated by the untold stories of such remains, and my first novel drew its inspiration from the years before and during the Civil War, when the state was covered in sheep farms, the lumber barons pitched their castles above Lake Champlain, and thousands of young men were called to fight on distant battlefields.

One day I had a vision of two children sitting on the cliffs of a frozen lake and hearing a voice below them, the voice of a runaway slave. Their decision to help him would change the rest of their lives, setting off a chain of events that would lead to one enlisting to fight and the other falling in love. So I began with ice and a winter sky and journeyed all the way to the fiery Battle of the Wilderness, for which the book is named."